DOCTOR WHO – THE NEW ADVENTURES

Also available:

THE NEW
DOCTOR WHO
ADVENTURES

LEGACY

Gary Russell

First published in Great Britain in 1994 by
Doctor Who Books
an imprint of Virgin Publishing Ltd
332 Ladbroke Grove
London W10 5AH

ISBN 0 426 20412 3

Cover illustration by Peter Elson

Phototypeset by Intype, London

Printed and bound in Great Britain by Cox & Wyman
Ltd, Reading, Berks

To the best Mother in the world – for getting me to read at such an early age and cultivating my interest in *all* things readable. Thanks.

Introduction

To crib liberally from American writer Peter David, if you don't like introductions just go straight to the start of the book; you won't miss anything important. I'd like to think you might miss something interesting, though.

The Ice Warriors were created by Brian Hayles, a writer who tragically is no longer with us. One of my earliest and clearest memories of *Doctor Who* was *The Seeds of Death*, Hayles' second outing for the wily Martians, in 1969. From then on they were always my favourite monsters and their appearances in the first two instalments of the Peladon saga (*The Curse of Peladon*, 1972 and *The Monster of Peladon*, 1974) further imbued them with a believability and background lacking in the majority of the other 'rubber suits' that paraded *ad nauseum* across the screens of the world.

Whether it was Ice Lord Izlyr's attempts to assure an understandably disbelieving Doctor that the Martians had turned their back on militaristic conquest, or Eckersley's admission that Ice Lord Azaxyr desired a return to the 'death or glory days' of their empire, the Ice Warriors oozed sophistication and intelligence. The mark of a good writer (Robert Holmes and Malcolm Hulke being the other *Doctor Who* writers that immediately leap to mind) is the ability to make every character exist in varying degrees of grey rather than as whiter-than-white good guy and evil black-hatted baddy. No one in the two Peladon stories is perfect, certainly none of them are simply evil; they all exist and do what they do. By creating the medieval society of Peladon, Hayles took the rules of *Doctor*

Who and subtly twisted them – turning *The Curse of Peladon* from being just a superb story into a masterpiece of social commentary.

I only met Brian Hayles once, at an open-air science fair in Windsor, in the mid-seventies. When I realized who he was I shoved my copy of his *The Curse of Peladon* novel under his nose and asked him when there was going to be a return visit. 'Ah,' he said. 'Tom Baker's the Doctor now, so they wouldn't recognize him.' Ever the eager (pushy?) teenager, I asked him what he would do next on Peladon and, like any clever person faced with the enthusiasm of youth, he turned the question back on me, What would *I* like to see done? So I suggested a long, convoluted and frankly ridiculous adventure, but he smiled and nodded, saying that he liked the ideas (I imagine he was being not entirely truthful) and so they have stayed with me ever since. None of those ideas are in this book, however, except the ending: an ending I considered logical and even if I did catch him surprised, I'd like to think Brian Hayles really would like it too.

No book exists without the help of a lot of other people and *Legacy* is certainly no exception. In no order whatsoever, I am indebted to: Paul Cornell for 'being really cool' about my use of characters from all his excellent books; Kate Orman for coming to England and just being a fiery Pakhar; Terrance Dicks and Malcolm Hulke for making me want to write *Doctor Who* in the first place; Adrian Rigelsford for allowing me to plagiarize aspects of his excellent *Doctor Who – The Monsters* book, specifically the events surrounding the Sword of Tuburr; Jamie Woolley for being 'serpentine' (that didn't come out right!); David Saunders and Chris Dunk for getting me into this *Doctor Who* world; Alan McKenzie for the initial big break and John Freeman for the bigger one; Peter Darvill-Evans and Rebecca Levene for being damn fine and honest (with much-needed criticism, I might add) editors – and for listening when I had panic attacks and a blank screen.

Neil C, Paul C, Nick P, Barnaby E, Simon S, Paul V,

Simon 'Scibus' M, Nick B, Warwick G, Mark G, Ian M and especially Gareth Roberts for the support, friendship and Jackie impros.

Justin, Andy, Craig and Jim for wanting to help and accepting my (probably erroneous) refusals.

Marc Platt and Nigel Robinson, two of the greatest guys in the world, who read and critiqued my original 1991 submission.

And of course *special* thanks to John Ainsworth, for just putting up with bad moods, frayed tempers, late nights and exceptionally loud music.

GPR 12/93

PART ONE
THE PAST

1:

My Shadow in Vain

The storm ripped its way through the almost never-ending darkness that encircled Peladon. Flashes of lightning reflected off the planet's tri-satellite-dominated heavens and flared back against the dark side of Mount Megeshra; highest, widest and most deadly of Peladon's mountains. The terrible winds roared loudly enough to deafen anyone foolhardy enough to venture out, if they were not smashed to the rocky ground first.

At the foot of the mountain were the sturdy granite settlements where the Pel miners and soldiers lived with their families. Each day, in their respective groups they would enter the network of tunnels that had been carved into the mountain, digging and building for the planet's future.

One day, it was said, a vast citadel would sit atop the mountain, a defiance to the angry gods who sentenced Peladon to its stormy fate.

One day.

Half-way up and inside the mountain, a large habitation had already been constructed. Linked by many tunnels, a huge circular building occupied about three hundred square feet of the blackness. Flambeau torches illuminated, badly, the walkways within the structure, and heavy burgundy drapes acted as walls between the rooms.

Sat in the very centre room, surrounded by the largest and brightest torches, was a man. Long, untidy brown curls hung to his waist and a streak of burgundy ran through the centre of this hair from forehead to tips. His face was scarred and pitted – physical medals gained in

3

countless battles against countless now-dead foes. A torn burgundy toga hung from one shoulder, looped under his loins and back up again. Fur boots kept his feet from the chills and a massive barbed spear was slung over his back, held there by leathery knotted thongs. At his side hung a massive double-bladed serrated sword, its metal dulled by the mixed blood of its many victims.

The warrior shivered. In spite of the torches. In spite of his massive, perfectly toned physique. In spite of the fur boots.

'By the gods of Peladon, it is bitter today, Chamberlain.'

'Aye, Lord,' agreed the seedy old man hovering behind him. 'The gods appear most displeased – ' The moment he had spoken, the aged chamberlain knew he had made a grave mistake. His lord pulled himself out of his wooden chair, kicking aside one of the flambeaus.

'Dare you suggest that the gods are angry because of *my* actions?' bellowed the warrior. 'Have I not slaughtered my foes, their families and villages single-handedly? Have I not wiped out all unbelievers and desecraters? Have I not destroyed deviants of colour and love? Do you tell me that I have done all this only to anger them? Well?'

The old chamberlain smiled weakly. 'Of course not, my Lord, I merely said – ' He got no further because his head was silently and swiftly detached from his shoulders by the double-bladed sword. It bounced twice and came to rest at the foot of the drapes.

'Captain!' roared the warrior.

An instant swish of an opposite drape and a younger warrior appeared, a single-bladed sword drawn in anticipation of attack.

'Put aside your weapon, loyal Gart. I am in need of a new advisor and chamberlain. Get me someone. *Now*!'

Gart sheathed his sword, bowed and vanished as swiftly as he had come.

The warrior knelt beside the corpse. Blood was pouring out of the severed neck like water from an overturned goblet. He sat the corpse upright, assuming this would stop the flow. Instead it just spurted more. With an angry shove, the body was pushed back floorwards again. The warrior snarled, looked around and saw the head to one side. The eyes were wide open, staring accusingly. 'Bah!' He gave the head a savage kick, noting with relish the sound of the nose bones crunching, and it vanished under the drapes.

Gart reappeared, two old men hovering meekly behind him, bowing and scraping as if their lives depended upon it, which they did.

The warrior looked them over. 'Hmm. Look.' He pointed at the corpse, whose blood-flow was stemming slightly now. 'Disappoint me and that is your fate. Understand?'

The two old men understood.

Totally.

Absolutely.

Without any doubt at all.

The warrior nodded. 'Right. Names?'

'Voss,' said one.

'Uthron,' said the other.

'Voss,' said the warrior, 'I don't like your name.'

'It was the one I was born with, my Lord.' Voss shrugged.

'It is the one you have died with as well!' Voss didn't have time to draw breath as the double-bladed sword tore into his side, slicing him neatly, if not bloodlessly, in two.

Uthron's already parchment-like skin went a shade whiter.

The warrior laughed. 'His response should have been to change his name, eh Uthron?'

Uthron realized that his volatile Lord was not likely to like whatever response he gave to that question, so he swallowed hard and said, 'Indeed, my Lord,' and nothing else.

'Chamberlain Uthron, I wish you to record in the palace records that I, the greatest warrior ever born on Peladon, have been appointed by the gods to become king of Peladon. From now on, the name Erak will be known throughout history as the first and greatest absolute monarch of this planet.' Uthron bowed a little bit lower than before. Erak nodded. 'You may go, Chamberlain Uthron.'

'My Lord . . . *Your Majesty*,' he corrected quickly. 'Where do I locate the palace records to mark this momentous occasion in?'

Erak stared at Uthron. He cocked his head first to one side then the other. Then he grinned. 'By the gods, Uthron, you are a wit! I shall enjoy you being my chamberlain. There *are* no palace records, yet. You will have to start them from this moment. Off you go!'

Uthron had moved to the drapes when Erak beckoned again, this time in a rather bored tone. 'Oh, Uthron. Get someone in here to clean this lot up, will you?' He lazily reached out with his sword and skewered Voss's head neatly through the eyes.

'Yes, Your Majesty.' Uthron left swiftly.

Two hours later, after three wenches had carried, mopped and dried, Erak sat back in his throne, closed his eyes and remembered glorious battles.

It was raining. Hard. The battlefield was pure mud, and he was almost forced to jump every time he wished to move. Faithful Gart was at his side as they slashed and hacked their way through the menfolk of Narral's village. Narral – pretender to Peladon's throne. Ha!

Before long every able-bodied man in Narral's village lay dead in the mud. Erak had lost none. Narral himself stood in front of a large stone hut, sword brandished.

'Erak!' he yelled. 'You have no right to take rule of the planet. We have survived generations with each village appointing a headman to be on the joint council. You are an evil butcher, not a king!'

Erak had smiled and rocked back on his heels with laughter. 'And you, Narral, are the last of those weak-willed councillors. They all lie dead, their villagers with them.'

'Then you will have no one to lord over, you monster!' Narral shouted back.

Erak strode towards his foe, as much as the mud would allow. Narral waved his sword in front of him but Erak grasped the end, ignoring the cutting edge. He squeezed and the blade shattered. With his other hand he reached out and grasped Narral's right shoulder, crushing the bones to dust. He grinned at his agonized foe, palmed his right hand, drew it back and then pushed forward, ripping directly into Narral's stomach. As his hand went in, he grabbed Narral's backbone and pulled down sharply. Narral died instantly as his neck was broken, and Erak withdrew his hand. Tossing the body aside, he marched into the hut. An old woman, three boys and six girls aged, Erak guessed, at between nine and fourteen, cowered at the back.

Gart entered. 'My Lord?'

Erak threw a bloody arm around his friend's shoulder. 'Gart – our warriors need amusement. The girls are theirs – when they have finished with each one, they may of course dispose of them.'

The old woman gasped in horror. Erak's blade flashed briefly and she fell dead. 'The boys?' asked Gart.

'Our brave warriors must be hungry, Gart. There's little meat upon them, but these wars are hard for all of us. It is a long while since we have tasted meat!'

The three boys instinctively gripped each other as this time Gart's sword sung its lethal song.

Erak was awakened suddenly by a noise. He sat up in his chair, furious that his memories of past glories had been disturbed.

Of course, there had been a fair bit of dramatic license in his dream – Narral had been an old man who died of a seizure early on in the battle; Erak had lost fifteen men and although the young girls had been raped and slaughtered so as not to breed inferior or tainted stock, there had been no little boys to eat. That part had come out of necessity months later when needing a threat to ensure his own children went to bed on time. 'Go now, or your father will eat you as he did Narral's sons!' was a frequent bellow in his chambers.

The drapes were drawn back and Uthron cowered there.

'Well?'

'Your Majesty – there is a young warrior to see you. He . . . he . . .'

'Out with it, Chamberlain! You need not be afraid of your king!'

Uthron, of course, was completely terrified of his king and being told that he ought not to be only made things worse. 'Your Majesty, he says – and I only report what he says – that he challenges your right to be Peladon's monarch. He says . . .'

'Yes, yes, I get the idea, Uthron. Send this new pretender in – I'll soon kill him and be done with it. Off you go.'

Moments later, Erak confronted his would-be usurper.

He was a young man – probably in his late teens. A shock of blond hair hung to his neck, the traditional burgundy stripe not yet stretching to the tips of his hair. Like Erak, he wore a simple toga, his of white. It barely covered a lithe but taut frame, muscle and sinew evident but not exaggerated. The boy had not seen a great deal of combat but was clearly fit and healthy. He carried only a short training sword but something about him sent an unaccustomed chill through Erak.

It was his eyes. Piercing blue eyes, of the sort normally associated with scholars and artists. Yet they possessed an inner fire that left Erak in no doubt he faced a mature, intelligent and capable fighter.

Determined not to let it be seen that he was slightly surprised by the newcomer, Erak reverted to his brazen, gruff act. 'Well, well, well,' he laughed. 'A boy. A child whose loins have barely felt gravity. Who would send such an innocent against me, King Erak of Peladon?'

'My Lord,' the boy said in a soft but strong tone. 'My Lord, you cannot be king until you are publicly enthroned.

8

You must let the people see this event, so that they may truly know it has occurred.'

'Of course!' Erak nodded quickly. In fact he had no intention of being crowned in public. *He* knew he was king, and besides some foe might take the opportunity to assassinate him. However, he could not say this in front of the child. No. 'My coronation will be a spectacle for all to behold. Lavish and glorious, it will mark a new age for Peladon.'

'Indeed it will, Your Majesty. An age of death, doom and destruction. An age when a man who slays young girls out of fear will rule. An age when a man who cuts down old women in case they spit at him will rule. An age when a man who fears his own shadow and murders old men because their names do not sound right will rule. In short, *Your Majesty*, an age in which Peladon will succumb to, and never escape from, sheer terror. No age of greatness but an age of stagnation, deceit and lies. You are not fit to be king of a cesspit, let alone an entire planet. I shall stop you.'

Erak looked at the boy, and laughed. 'You have guts, I'll grant you. I suspect that they shall be set before me on a dish before this night is out however, boy. What do they call you?'

'I am Sherak.'

'The name is familiar, boy, but I cannot place it right now.'

'No, Your Majesty, I did not expect you to. I am too lowly, too far beneath you. Yet I shall be First King of Peladon. A benevolent and just king who will bring his people together in unity, trust and –'

Erak had drawn his double-bladed sword and lunged at Sherak before the boy had finished his sentence. Sherak's own blade parried expertly and held the blow. Erak reached behind him and drew his barbed spear. He lashed out towards Sherak's head, but the younger man ducked, letting his sword take more pressure from Erak's. At the last second, he spun on the balls of his feet, whipping his sword away and Erak unbalanced, his double-bladed tool crashing into the ground. 'You are a cold warrior, boy,' acknowledged Erak. 'But your inexperience shows – sadly there will not be time for you to profit by my teachings.'

Sherak leapt towards the drapes and tugged at them. They fell with ease, crashing into the flambeau torches and igniting in seconds.

For a fleeting second, it crossed Erak's mind that Uthron, Gart and the others in his upper echelons ought to have been alerted to the battle and arrived to cut the boy into sixteen equal parts. Maybe this one he really would eat. Now that *would* be a story for his sons . . .

His reverie was broken as Sherak flicked a blazing drape towards him. Using his barbed spear, he scooped it away, but the barbs got entangled in it and he let go.

He only had his sword left.

It was all he needed.

The boy had got cocky; he was walking backwards, towards a flambeau that he hadn't overturned. Any second now and Erak would have his chance.

Sherak moved back – he could feel the heat behind him and guessed what Erak was hoping for. But Sherak could turn that to his advantage. Just as he neared the torch, he feinted and yelled as if burned. Predictably, Erak lunged, but Sherak was still a good three paces from the torch. He ducked to one side, kicking out and knocking the torch forward. Erak brought his blade down savagely – straight into the flames. With a screech of pure rage and pain, Erak dropped his sword as the flesh on his hand bubbled and blistered.

Sherak took the advantage, kicking Erak's smouldering sword away from its owner.

'I don't need weapons – I have myself!' yelled Erak, thinking of his fictitious murder of Narral. He lashed out with his good hand and Sherak ducked. Not quickly enough, and a glancing but powerful blow sent him crashing into the wooden throne which shattered under the impact.

With a roar of triumph Erak scooped up his barbed

spear from the burnt remains of the drape. A slight tug and it was free.

Sherak realized his mistake and tried to scrabble back, but the broken throne slowed him and he looked up into the mad eyes of Erak – the man he'd come to kill, who looked instead like destroying him!

With a final bellow Erak grasped the hot spear in both hands, relishing the pain from his burnt skin.

'Die, pretender. Peladon is mine – ' Erak stopped; he suddenly felt very hot. He looked down as his own double-bladed sword erupted through his chest, sending chunks of hairy flesh and shattered bone to the floor. As his ruptured lungs deflated, he staggered round, the last of his strength fading. He dropped the spear as he saw Gart standing there, having just released his grip on the sword.

'Why?' Erak wanted to yell. To scream. 'Why have *you* betrayed me?'

Instead, globules of blood spat from his mouth. An airless gurgle rattled in his throat and he fell to the floor.

'Because,' Gart said in reply to the unspoken question that, after seven years of campaigning with Erak, he knew would have been in his lord's mind, 'I hate you. You are the most evil, inhuman monster that ever set foot on this planet. I have been training my son for this day since the moment he could walk. For sixteen years he has trained. He has dreamt. He has planned for the day when he would wipe the blight that was Erak from the face of our planet and the records of our history. And he has done so.' Gart knelt to his former lord and master for the last time. 'May the gods make a plaything of your body and torment you for eternity to somehow atone for the evil you have done in your ill-begotten lifetime.'

Gart felt a hand on his shoulder. 'He is dead, father. Do not waste your energy on the defeated – use it to shape the living.'

The soldier looked up at Sherak and smiled. 'You will make a good king and leader for our people.'

'And you, father,' Sherak said, 'you shall be my first warrior – the king's champion.'

11

'And I?' croaked a voice from the other side of the room.

Sherak crossed the room and gripped Uthron's hand. 'Your part in today's events shall be rewarded, Chamberlain. Only you could have kept Erak's maidens and staff away during our battle. The position of chamberlain is still sorely needed. You are known and respected by the miners and the villagers. Will you remain in your post under a different king?'

Uthron coughed and pointed at Erak. 'He would never have been a real king. But you? You make me proud to be a Pel.' Uthron dropped to one knee and crossed his chest with his right arm. 'May I have permission to address the king?'

Sherak turned to his father, who immediately adopted the same position.

'May I have permission to address the king?' he echoed.

The son looked at the father and the friend, and laughed. 'I haven't actually been crowned yet!'

Five summers passed. King Sherak, the first appointed monarch of the planet Peladon, matured into a wise, loved and successful king. He reunited the scattered people of Peladon, made the Pels feel at one with themselves and their home. The more superstitious amongst them noted that more and more mornings gave way to bright, rainless afternoons and evenings. It was as if with Erak's death, the ancient gods were appeased and content to allow Peladon to forge its own destiny.

Nevertheless, it was on a very stormy, dark afternoon that Sherak decided to explore the dark side of Mount Megeshra.

He greeted Uthron, now getting quite unsteady on his feet, at luncheon, asking him to find a strong equinna that he could use as a mount. Uthron warned his liege against the action.

'My Lord, the dark side of the mountain is not named thus due to some poetic conceit. It truly is a dangerous, unexplored part of our land!'

'Then how does everyone know it is so awful?'

Uthron sighed. 'Because those that have set out to explore it, either on foot or on beast, never ever return. Only one riderless equinna has ever returned, badly mauled and assaulted. The poor animal died very soon after. At least take some of your stoutest guards with you.'

'And they would volunteer to join their king on such an apparently foolhardy escapade?'

'Your Majesty knows the bravery of his palace guard.'

'His Majesty also knows,' countered Sherak, 'that his guards are not stupid. They would come if I ordered – which I would not – and some would come through loyalty. But none would innocently volunteer for such a journey. Besides, loyal Chamberlain,' he said, resting a hand on the older man's drooping shoulders, 'I *have* to go alone. Call it madness, call it suicide or call it a compulsion. All I know is that I must do this. To appease the gods and, more importantly, to appease my own soul.'

Uthron seemed to sag a little more. 'And your fath . . . your champion? What does he say to this recklessness?'

'Which recklessness is this, wise Uthron?' said a concerned voice from behind them.

Sherak rose out of his small but ornate throne and stepped down the raised dais it sat upon. His father stood by the double doors, the light from the nearest flambeau flickering over him, casting dark shadows around his eyes and mouth.

'Oh father, I knew you would argue. I intended to go without your knowing.'

'To the dark side of Megeshra? Is that your plan, my Lord?'

'It is.'

'I forbid it!' Gart stepped forward, a flash of fury crossing his face. 'And I speak as your father. A father who has never forbade anything of his child until now.'

Sherak looked at his father. It was true that Gart had never raised his voice, let alone a hand, against his son. Instead he and Uthron had guided him, wisely and pleasantly, into becoming a popular man of the people. But this was the time to be defiant. To be strong.

'I hear what both of you say. I love you both and respect your fears. But despite that, my mind is made up. I will go, this very afternoon. And nothing you can say will stop me.'

Deadlock. The three men stared at each other. After what seemed like hours but was less than a moment, Uthron bowed and stepped back. He knew that his king would brook no further argument from one such as he – this was a matter for father and son. 'I shall return later, my Lords.'

'Stay,' hissed a furious Gart. 'Your king needs guidance from you.'

Sherak frowned. '*Your* king?' he repeated. 'What do you mean by –'

Gart proudly drew himself erect. 'Whilst you insist on this madness, I neither serve nor acknowledge Sherak of Peladon. Your king, Uthron, no longer has a champion. Or a father.'

A second later Gart was gone.

Slowly Sherak turned and sat again on his throne.

Uthron was at a loss. 'My Lord?'

When Sherak again looked up at the old man, Uthron noted a new gleam in his king's eyes. The blue eyes seem to have almost turned steel-grey. There was no laughter, no joy, no life reflected in that face.

'Find me a mount, Chamberlain,' he said. 'Find me the strongest, best-trained equinna in my court. I ride in one hour. No one is to know where. No one is to know why. And anyone who follows me will die, at my hand, in seconds. Understand that, old man, and nothing else.'

Sherak almost jumped off his throne and turned to the back of the chamber, where a single door was concealed behind a burgundy drape, interwoven with gold. The king went through the door and Uthron heard the bolt being slid back on the other side. There would be no following him.

Unknowingly echoing the thoughts of a bestial warrior

14

five years before, Uthron realized that for the first time he had seen how cold a man his well-loved liege really could be.

As the equinna bounded away from the underground stable, carrying its master on its strong back, Sherak allowed himself a last look back at the Citadel.

The miners and builders had spent three summers and winters struggling against Peladon's elements to haul the vast slabs of granite up through the network of tunnels. Much of the main facade of the building had been carved out of the rock itself. Many a builder had fallen to a horrible death during construction, a victim of loose rocks or the savage winds.

Eventually it had been built – a home for the royal courtiers and soldiers, while the miners and other craftsmen had remained in their villages at the foot of the mountain. A magnificent building, reaching up and proving to the gods that Pels could survive on this harshest of worlds.

Sherak turned away from it. If he survived the task before him, he would finally know he was fit to lead the Peladon people. Uthron and his father could not understand. Yes, he had defeated Erak – but in reality it had been Gart who had delivered the death-blow. In fact Sherak might well have died if not for his father's intervention. But the people believed that it had been he, not his father, who had the victory. And although Gart never, ever mentioned it, Sherak knew. Sherak had not proved himself to be a king that day; merely a figurehead – someone to rally the people around. He wasn't embarking on this quest for the Pels. He was doing it for selfish reasons.

He wanted to prove himself to himself.

Ignoring the howling winds and heavy rain, he rode on, his familiar burgundy cape flying behind him.

Four hours later he knew he was in unchartered lands.

The terrain was rocky and lethal. His equinna was limping slightly and his own bare legs were scratched and bleeding from the shrubbery that littered the tops and bottoms of the hillocks they rode over.

He tugged the reins and with a snort, the equinna turned left. They rounded a set of boulders and Sherak pulled them to a stop.

They had halted at a sheer drop. Hundreds of feet below was a flat plain, lush with green grass and fruit-bearing trees. In the distance, the more familiar rocks and lifeless terrain. He again stared at the eden below. How could such a beautiful area exist in such a tiny and remote section?

He could see no way down for the equinna, but hunger and thirst plus a large helping of curiosity made Sherak want to explore. He tethered his mount to a rock and opened the satchel slung over its back, behind his saddle. Three items: Erak's double-bladed sword, Erak's barbed spear, and a sack of food for the equinna. Setting the last at the beast's feet, whereupon it greedily started munching, he strapped both weapons to his back.

He looked as far as he could see left and right, but there was no obvious path down. It would be a steep and potentially lethal climb. But something told him that this was the task he had been searching for – his own personal demon to be conquered.

There was nothing for it but to start to climb down. And no place better than where he stood.

The first few yards were easy, footholds and hand-grips were easy to come by. It was almost as if someone had deliberately dug out body-length holes in preparation for his quest. Memories of Uthron's comments about people going but never returning from the dark side flooded back. Had those lost warriors and adventurers created these convenient holes?

If so, what became of them?

Suddenly he realized he was simply hanging there. He had reached the side of a smooth square of rock. No handholds. No footholds. Just flat rock. He couldn't move any lower. His feet scrambled for even the slightest ridge but there was nothing. Slowly he looked up – the top

16

seemed far away and for a moment he felt dizzy. Was this it? The end? Where all those that had preceded him had faltered, dropped and died?

Carefully, he moved one hand out of its hole, gripping tighter with the other. He felt around him, but to no avail. With all his strength he took the whole weight of his body, ignoring the natural pull of gravity, with his one hand and swung around so that he no longer faced the rock but the horizon. He allowed himself a look down. Another hundred feet at least, and a crop of lethal-looking rocks directly below him.

He noted that the rain had stopped, and the rock face kept the wind off him. The fruit trees below swayed in only the slightest breeze. That was the secret – this rock wall protected the paradise below, blocking it in and keeping the harsher elements out.

Sherak was not the greatest scholar but even he realized that the grass was short, the trees not unkempt. Something looked after this paradise. What? A nomadic tribe of undiscovered Pels? The gods?

A bestial roar answered his question instantly and uncomfortably.

He looked down again. An equinna-sized monster was staring up at him. Crouched on all fours, its black/brown fur stood on end. Even at this great height, Sherak could sense eyes boring into him. He took a look at its head – a blunt snout ridged with bone and a lethal pointed horn, ready to gouge any foe. Long, sharp claws at each foot probably ripped its prey apart and as it snarled at him he saw the rows of incisor teeth, again long and sharp.

'By the gods, I think this *was* the mistake Uthron and my father claimed.'

With that he lost his grip and fell.

Sherak never actually saw the branches that hung outwards from tiny crevices in the rock but subconsciously he must have been aware of them. He reached out as he fell and grabbed one. The jolt as he stopped not only ripped all the ligaments in his left arm but caused him to swing around and slam into the rock face. He knew from

17

the sharp reports that more than a couple of ribs had broken and he gasped loudly. He was sure that he hadn't damaged any internal organs – he could breathe and his heart was pumping fast but not excessively.

He looked down. He had broken his fall ten feet above the creature and the rocks. Scattered round the rocks were bones and at least two human-looking skulls, although one had clearly had its owner's head caved in at some point. His forefathers had been this creature's lunch and he looked very likely to be next on the menu.

The pain in his wrecked arm reminded him of his injuries but before he let go, he wrestled the barbed spear off his back.

Peladon's distant sun glinted briefly off the shaft and distracted the monster below for a second or two.

Sherak relaxed his grip on the cliff face and dropped.

He expected his last seconds to be a breaking of his bones as he hit the rocks, followed by shredding at the claws of the monster. Instead he landed squarely on its back, knocking it to the ground and winding it. As this realization dawned, Sherak rolled away, wincing as his damaged body complained at the treatment he was giving it. 'Give in and die,' his ribs seemed to say. 'Let the beast eat,' pleaded his arm. 'No,' Sherak's inner strength replied, 'not without a fight.'

He looked over at the beast and grabbed at the spear. Slowly shaking its head, it moved towards him. It nudged at the ground with its tusked nose. Smelling Sherak out.

Of course, he realized, it must live inside the rock face, that's why I didn't spot it. It can't see out here very well, so it's using smell.

There was a terrible roar.

It wasn't the creature in front of him. Sherak looked beyond it and coming out of a crevice were four identical monsters, shaking their heads at the sudden light. Sherak brought the spear up, ready for a fight. The first creature suddenly turned its back on him and roared at its associates. They roared back and Sherak winced as his head ached at the terrible noises. Suddenly one of the newcomers stood up on its hind legs, waving its paws towards Sherak and popping its claws. Sherak was convinced that what happened next was in slow motion but that just had to be his memory playing tricks. The upright monster leapt forward but the first one, 'his' one, jumped up, raking its claws through the other one's belly in mid-air. With a screech of anguish, the new one dropped short of Sherak and swung round on the first.

Sherak had no idea whether 'his' one had done this because it wanted him for its own food or because, as he hoped, it realized he posed no danger. Either way, it had helped him and was now engaged in battle. His instinct told him to run away but his heart told him to help.

He leapt forward, waving the barbed spear. It slashed through the mêlée of fur but, Sherak realized in horror, it missed his foe and sliced into 'his' monster. Nevertheless, it carried on fighting. Sherak took a step too near and was caught on the side of the head by a claw, gouging three scratches into his cheek. He yelled at the pain and salty taste of blood in his mouth, then wiped at his cheek, to keep the blood from splashing into his eye and drew Erak's double-bladed sword. He brought it down on the attacker's neck, severing whatever muscles were there. It didn't even moan as it dropped dead to the ground, eyes staring wide.

Sherak's original foe grunted at him and turned towards the assembled group by the crevice. It roared, louder than before and they slowly turned and went back in.

'You saved me, monster. You protected me. Why?'

As if in answer, the creature stepped towards him, staring at the double-bladed sword. Sherak noted that the sunlight glinted off it every time he moved, almost rhythmically.

The creature seemed fascinated by the light. Sherak kept twitching the sword, making sure that the light reflected back into the creature's small eyes. Instead of roaring, it seemed to almost purr and settle down in front of him. Gingerly, Sherak reached out with his blood-soaked hand and touched the creature's accidental injury from the spear. As his blood touched the creature's, Sherak felt a thrill go through his body.

And he realized his quest was over.

He had tamed the savage beast. They had protected each other and were now some kind of simplistic blood-brothers.

After a few moments, the beast stirred. It looked up at Sherak and he momentarily wondered if he had been wrong. Had it let him lower his guard only to strike him down?

No. The creature lurched away, licking at its wound. Just as it re-entered the crevice it turned back and roared. After it vanished, Sherak settled back on his haunches, looking at his two weapons.

A rustle behind him made him swing round. He winced as his ribs reminded him of his injuries. Munching at the grass was his equinna, saddle intact.

'You found a route down? There is no doubt that Peladon animals are more intelligent than their masters.'

Slowly he remounted, strapped his blood-tainted weapons to his back and let the equinna return him to the Citadel.

Sherak's return had been magnificent. Crowds had flocked to see him, cheer him and praise him. Two medical men had attended his wounds and once he was comfortable, he returned to his throne room to rest – one place where he could determine who could and could not disturb him.

He snatched a piece of parchment and quill and began to sketch out an image of the monster's face. His protector. No – the Royal Protector. He glanced at the drapes adorning the plain throne room. Yes, the face would be savage but a reminder of his humbling but exciting victory over legend.

He called for Uthron.

Moments later the old man hobbled in.

'My Chamberlain – I succeeded. And I have brought back a new love for the people. Something for them to revere as I do. The Royal Protector and Sacred Beast of Peladon.' He held the sketch up to Uthron.

The old man took the picture. 'Aggedor! You have seen the legendary beast?'

'We are blood-brothers, Uthron,' said Sherak and retold his adventure.

At the end he clasped Uthron's shoulder. 'I want that put everywhere. On doors, on sculptures, within our garments and drapes. It will be a symbol of the unified Peladon.'

'It will be done, my King.'

Sherak sat back, wincing slightly at his wounds. 'So, where is my father? Where is the king's champion? Why is he not here to help celebrate his son's victory over legend and the gods?'

Uthron swallowed and straightened himself up. 'He is gone, Your Majesty. Shamed at his outburst, he packed his belongings and left the Citadel shortly after you rode away.'

'We must find him!'

'Your father is a great warrior and a proud man, my liege. He has left the mountain altogether and no one knows where he is. He does not wish to be found. Or shamed any further.' Uthron paused, waiting for a response. Instead, Sherak stared at the floor, mute and ... sad? Angry? Uthron could not tell. After a moment, the king looked back at Uthron, the blue eyes again having turned cold as steel. 'So be it, old man. Take that parchment and do as I requested ... ordered.'

Uthron bowed low and left the throne room. As he stood outside the double doors to catch his breath, he thought he could hear laboured sobs from within. Clutching the parchment tightly, he sighed and went to see the palace sculptors and painters.

Sherak, First King of Peladon, died aged sixty-five – a good age. He married a beautiful maiden, a distant relation of Uthron's, and bore five children, including two boys. The eldest died in his teenage years after an accident

21

in the caverns and so the younger boy adopted his father's crown. The new king never met Gart, his grandfather, but was filled with tales of the champion's bravery by his father. All records of Erak's pretence to the throne were wiped from history – he was just remembered as an evil baron defeated by the young King Sherak.

Aggedor went on to become a legendary beast and protector. To invoke his name was the ultimate praise and to blaspheme it was punishable by death. A high priest of Aggedor was appointed to all subsequent royal courts. These could also trace their lineage back to Uthron, making a vaguely incestuous but compact royal bloodline.

Many generations later, a new young king sat on Peladon's throne. He was Kellian and his throne room was forever occupied by two older men. Both brown-haired, in long flowing capes of burgundy and silver, their burgundy hair stripes were also picked out in their beards. Cousins; Torbis was the king's chancellor whilst Hepesh was the high priest of Aggedor. Kellian valued both men's friendship above all else, although he had been heard to comment that Hepesh's interest in Aggedor verged more on the obsessive.

When the strange lights in the sky came, Hepesh said it was a portent of doom – Aggedor would one day rise to smite his enemies and these lights were that enemy. Torbis was more rational and offered to take a party out to see where these lights had landed.

Kellian agreed and Torbis set off. It was rumoured that pots of iron could be found where stars crashed, but no one had yet proven this. Maybe Torbis would be the lucky one.

The prize Torbis returned with was not a pot of iron but something far more precious to the young king. She had short blonde hair, large watery blue eyes and a broad, ingratiating smile. Her robes were tattered and blood-soaked, but she still carried herself with an air of nobility.

'My name is Ellua, Princess of Europa. I am from a planet called Earth, many light-years from here.' The words meant little to Kellian – perhaps she was what she said, an alien. Perhaps she was an emissary from the gods. Either way, her beauty and charm were worth far more to him than pots of iron.

It transpired that her ship and two escorts had been caught in an ion storm and lost their way. They were heading for the Galactic Federation base on Analyas VII when they were caught in Peladon's forceful orbit. 'Your three moons are a very strong deterrent for low-level shuttle flying, my liege,' she said at one point. One of her escort ships had gone too low and the other two had come in to try and mount a rescue. All three had ultimately plummeted to the ground and although the ships were wrecked, no lives had been lost, but one pilot was severely injured.

'If we don't get him to Analyas VII urgently, he will die.' Kellian had been struck by her pain and anguish over the man's well-being.

'But surely he is only a servant. A courtier? Is his life really worth that much to one such as you?'

It was the only time Kellian ever remembered Ellua getting angry. 'His position is irrelevant! He is a man like you. A living person. Of course his life matters. All life is sacred – it's not to be decided on royal favour!'

Using their communicators, Ellua's entourage contacted a Federation support ship and so received help. They took away the wounded man, who was later reported to have made a full recovery. Kellian and Ellua, however, never strayed from one another. She told him of the many worlds in the heavens, of the evil and the good. Of the Federation and what it could do to help his planet.

She married him a year later – Torbis acting as regent although Hepesh refused to bless the couple; another less xenophobic priest married them. Within six months Kellian had applied for Federation aid and membership.

A diplomatic team arrived to assess the planet and quickly departed, suggesting that Peladon was still needing to establish its own social structure before the Federation would interfere. They assured the king and queen that they would return in about twenty years to reassess. Ellua alone was made aware of one other thing about Peladon – the Federation were very interested in the natural trisilicate that lined its caverns. Peladon would have a great economic future if the Federation could one day mine that trisilicate. Only as the twenty-year deadline neared would Ellua tell her husband that. To announce that now would encourage him to risk Federation involvement too early. She knew that the Federation were right – Peladon needed further social development and, as queen, she could help foster that.

Another year later, a son was born. Kellian wanted to use a traditional royal name, passed through the generations. 'It would be appropriate as he will be king when we join the Federation. The name Sherak has long been beloved of our people and a symbol of change for the better.'

Ellua disagreed. 'I think the best name would be the one that would announce him on other worlds with great flair and flourish. A memorable name. He should be Peladon of Peladon!'

Over the next few years Kellian and his wife, aided by Torbis and, to a small extent, by Hepesh, educated the boy.

The old men would place Peladon on his father's knee and tell him of Aggedor. Of his planet's history. Of the Federation and of all the great things each could bring to the other.

One day Hepesh and Torbis quietly placed him upon the actual throne. He was twelve years old.

'I cannot sit here, my friends. Rightfully, it can only be my father's place!'

Hepesh cleared his throat and with a brief glance of disdain at Ellua, stared straight at Peladon. 'Though the blood that flows in your veins is mingled with that of strangers, yet you shall be Peladon of Peladon. Greater than your father. Greater than any past or future king.'

Ellua knelt down beside him. 'My son, your father has

been taken from us. A hunting accident. You are now the Prince Regent. Torbis and Hepesh will teach you and guide you. They shall do this until you are of age, whereupon you will be anointed as king.' Ellua took Peladon's right hand and placed it in Torbis's. She then took his left and placed that in Hepesh's hand.

Ellua then went to the front of the throne where her bewildered son sat. She sank onto one knee and placed her right arm across her chest. 'May I have permission to address the king?'

Peladon of Peladon burst into tears. He was only a boy.

But he was a prince. And he would grow into a wise king and lead his planet into a new future . . .

It was a graveyard in space.

But unlike traditional graveyards, it was not full of people buried beneath the ground, but a sector of deep space, dotted with spaceships. Hundreds of ships, scattered aimlessly around as if put there and forgotten over aeons. Ships from a hundred different planets and civilizations from thousands of years of their respective space travelling. It was like a vast butterfly collection, a ship from every race and of every design imaginable. Placed there by beings of immense power.

A short way beyond these wrecked hulls was something completely different, something in full working condition. A vast, dark space station, so massive it could almost be mistaken for an entire city hovering in space. Ovoid in shape, its centre was dominated by a huge communications tower, tapering upwards, tiny lights blinking on and off around the spire. Smaller towers and pyramids dotted the rest of the surface, jutting outwards in every possible direction, more flickering lights sparkling on each protuberance. Every so often, raised circular platforms were spaced out, so dark that despite the nearby lights they could hardly be seen. It was as if the platforms sucked the light in, replacing it with an eerie total blackness, like a series of black holes. Suddenly one of the platforms split into four even triangular parts which rose up and outwards. Instantly a fierce, bright column of light shot into the blackness of space, sending light reflecting off all the nearby wrecks. The column of light was almost like a living thing, searching out a victim like a cobra seeking prey. It latched onto something: a plain white rectangular box, totally uninteresting and bland to look at. It pulled the box downwards, the column of light shrinking as the box neared the gaping hole. As the box went through the platform, the light vanished and the four triangular sections snapped closed, restoring total darkness to the surface of the station.

Inside the station, two men stood watching the arrival of the white box. On a station big enough for hundreds of thousands, they were the only occupants. Neither of them knew the history of the station; whoever had built it had long since faded into obscurity. Its original purpose was lost in the annals of history. But these two men were regular visitors to it – a fact kept completely secret to their peers, superiors and lessers. Their reasons for being there were even more secret.

A third man walked out of the box. The door slid shut behind him, a seamless join.

'My apologies, gentlemen. My TARDIS is in need of an overhaul.' He ran a hand through his blond hair. Blue eyes glistened with remarkable intelligence.

'Perhaps you should start to use the new Time Rings. I am informed that they are now working most effectively.' The eldest of the three nodded his balding head to the newcomer. He, like the other two, was dressed in a white tabard with black piping along the sleeves and round the shoulders. It was not his normal clothing – as the Chancellor of the High Council of the Time Lords upon the distant planet of Gallifrey, he would normally wear long heavy brown robes and a high collar. Here, however, he and his fellows were equals.

'Well,' said the newcomer, 'what happens now?'

'My Lord Goth,' replied the shorter, dark-haired one. 'I have examined the possible time lines. Each of them shows Peladon having a part in the future of galactic harmony via this Federation. However, I would bring your attention to one very important event. In seventeen years, King Peladon of Peladon requests representatives from the Galactic Federation to see if his planet can enter the alliance.'

'As we hoped it would,' said the chancellor.

Goth nodded. 'Indeed, Chancellor, but let us hear what our learned colleague has to say on the subject. Please proceed.'

The younger-looking man nodded. 'One of the delegates is from the Arcturan system. As you know, the most probable outcome is that Arcturus will at this point become intertwined with the fledgling terrorist force known grandly as Galaxy Five. Arcturus sees an opportunity to stir dissension within the Federation and orders its delegate to sabotage the proceedings. As events transpire, the Alpha Centaurian delegate is killed by Arcturus's naive Pel agents and the Martian delegation is blamed. War breaks out and the Galactic Federation falls into disarray and galactic peace is thwarted forever. Needless to say, the Daleks, currently hatching plans revolving around a time destructor and their army on the non-affiliated world of Kembel arise and take dominance over this entire galaxy. One of the ironies is that the primary Arcturan homeworld is totally vaporized in the first minute of hostilities.'

'Not an encouraging picture,' Goth commented.

'Indeed not,' agreed the chancellor.

'We do have a solution,' the darker Time Lord offered. The other two looked interested. 'As you know the renegade, the Doctor, was found guilty of crimes and sentenced to exile on Earth. Recently some of our esteemed . . . associates sent him to the planet Exarius to defeat the Master and his use of the fabled doomsday weapon.'

'So?' said a cautious Goth.

'Well, it would not be difficult to manipulate the Doctor once again, this time ensuring Peladon has the future we require for it.'

The chancellor held up a hand. 'I don't think we could allow this abuse again. There were severe ramifications after the Exarius business. It blatantly contravened our policy of non-intervention. We are supposed to observe. And that is all.'

'I agree,' said Goth smoothly. 'However, we also know rules are there to be broken. And who better to break them than us?'

The dark Time Lord smiled. 'Indeed. By being here, on this station, we are not *officially* recording this action. Therefore we have not *officially* acted.'

The chancellor thought about this. 'I neither like nor approve of the Doctor. Nor do I like using him in this way. However, if you are convinced it is necessary, Goth . . .?'

'I think that is the case, Chancellor.'

The chancellor shrugged. 'This conversation has not taken place, gentlemen.'

'Of course not, Chancellor,' said the other.

The chancellor rearranged his tabard, as if shrugging away the station's existence. 'The Time Lords have high morals and we cannot be seen to disregard them on a whim.'

'No one ever doubts the wisdom and morality of our Time Lord associates,' said the dark Time Lord slowly.

Goth held his hands up. 'I think this discussion is over, gentlemen. Shall we return to Gallifrey?'

'Immediately,' said the other Time Lord. He walked to a box similar to Goth's and pushed on its side. A fierce yellow light blazed out of a newly formed gap, elongating his shadow, and he stepped through. With a loud wheezing and groaning sound, the box faded away. Goth and the chancellor went to their respective boxes. Goth waited as the chancellor's TARDIS vanished and then activated his own. Unlike his comrades, Goth's TARDIS was surrounded by the column of fierce light and he left the station the same way he had arrived.

The station hung in space, its lights now off. Around it the wrecked spaceships hovered, silent observers to one of a select few Time Lords' darkest secrets. A space station

28

where their grimiest, nastiest plots and subterfuges were created, away from Gallifrey and a long way out of the High Council's jurisdiction. Or interest.

Interlude 1

Pakha: 8394.774 (old calendar)
'Power! Victory! It's all mine!'

Vor'r'na, chief gatherer and elder forager of the Pakhars, stood defiantly in front of the tall, bedraggled form of the alien interloper. Proudly pulling himself up to his full one-metre height, he scooped up a handful of pebbles in his paw. Carefully he took a step back towards the Wavis Ravine. Momentarily it flashed through his rodent mind that legend claimed it was bottomless. Just as quickly he dismissed the thought – a recollection as inconsequential and petty as the form his mind was housed in. He deserved better!

As if daring the alien to crawl closer he drew back his lips, revealing a snout packed with vicious-looking incisor teeth, saliva drooling between them, long gobs of it splattering to the rocky ground.

The alien knelt up, about five metres away from Vor'r'na. He slid his hand through his shock of white hair and wiped dust from his beaky nose.

'Vor'r'na. This is so unnecessary. Just take the Diadem off and pass it to me. It's affecting your mind. You don't really want to kill – '

The alien's words were drowned out by a screech of pure loathing. Another recollection – Vor'r'na realized it was a typical noise emitted by his people when angry. Mentally he chastized himself. He was now above such ridiculous subconscious reactions. He hurled the pebbles at the alien.

As the alien twisted sideways to avoid them, Vor'r'na

saw a party of torch-bearing Pakhars heading up the narrow tunnel in front of him. He heard himself screech again, this time adding a few choice obscenities that the alien would barely understand.

The distraction was enough and the alien was suddenly scrabbling towards the Pakhar. Desperately he reached out to try and grasp the Diadem from Vor'r'na's furry head, but Vor'r'na saw the move and darted back.

Too far.

The Doctor swore as he saw Vor'r'na topple backwards. As the Diadem slipped from his head and into the ravine, Vor'r'na's face took on its familiar peaceful look for a split second, followed by sheer terror. His shrill scream echoed around the caverns for some moments after he followed the Diadem down to certain death.

By the time Legislator Gar'ah'd and his fellow Pakhars had scampered into the cavern, the battle was all over. All they saw was the Doctor looking forlornly over the precipice.

'Legislator, you have offered us a great reward. Many would say it is a reward we do not deserve. We came upon you somewhat . . .' The Doctor paused, stroking the back of his neck as if to hide his slight embarrassment. 'Well, let us say, somewhat deceptively.'

Jo Grant was smiling up at him. He nodded in acknowledgement and looked back at Legislator Gar'ah'd. Jo tightened her grip on the Doctor's hand in encouragement as Gar'ah'd spoke.

'Doctor . . . my friend . . . that is all behind us. I, my courtiers, indeed the whole of Pakha owes you a great debt. A little deception to win our confidence is hardly a crime.' The legislator raised his hands high and spread his arms wide, his cloak billowing out behind him like a grey sail caught in a sudden wind.

'My People,' he bellowed. 'My People, two days ago we witnessed great salvation for Pakha. Let us use the wisdom, the honour and the knowledge that our new friends have given us. Let us cast aside the shadows of our dark past. Tomorrow a new age begins for us – literally. A new calendar, a new era and a new challenge.' He paused, and looked the Doctor straight in the eye. The Doctor shook his head, a little sadly, and after a few seconds Legislator Gar'ah'd continued his proclamation, his face and voice never betraying the disappointment he felt.

'Our friends, the Doctor and Jo Grant, are leaving us. They shall, however, be forever remembered. I have failed to convince them to stay and help us further, but that is their right. They have shown us how to be an equal People; a People who must put aside the wrongs of war, bitterness, resentment and envy. The Pakha of yesterday is dead. The Pakha of tomorrow is upon us. Tonight, we celebrate! We cannot allow our guests to leave without showing them our hospitality.' Gar'ah'd lowered his voice slightly, almost as if embarrassed by his admission. 'We showed little on their arrival and that nearly cost us our civilization. Now is the time to make amends!'

As Gar'ah'd finished, there was a second's pause, followed by an ear-shattering roar of approval from the attending Pakhars: warriors and pacifists alike.

Turning toward them, Jo glowed with pride as amongst the throng she saw old, cynical Ho'gah'th the warrior grasp hands with and then hug Nu'b'ld, the young peace-seeking rebel Jo had felt such kinship with. If those two could become comrades, then she knew that she and the Doctor had truly succeeded in enlightening the planet and its people. She smiled as Nu'b'ld looked up at her and grinned, his whiskers twitching excitedly. Jo couldn't quite rid herself of the thought that the Pakhars reminded her of four-foot-tall guinea-pigs, but she had so far managed to curb her instinct to tickle them behind their little ears or stroke them under the chin.

The Doctor bent down and whispered in her ear: 'Jo, do you want to stay for the feast? We don't have to if you'd rather go. I know that Nu'b'ld has been . . .'

Jo laughed. 'A pest? I think I can cope with him.

Anyway, I think Ho'gah'th will keep him occupied most of the evening as they swap stories of gallantry!'

The Doctor looked at Jo, dressed in the long white dress which Gar'ah'd had made her a present of. 'Should you choose to leave us,' he had said a few days earlier, 'you will always have something to remember your great deeds by. Take it with the love and thanks of the Pakhars,' he had finished. Jo had curtsied in the proper Pakhar manner and thanked the legislator.

As the Doctor stared at his young companion he realized for the first time that the young girl who had literally blundered into his life, wrecking months of solid-state micro-welding, had grown up. Josephine Grant was rapidly becoming a confident, well-adjusted young woman.

'Hey, c'mon Doctor. We don't want to miss a groovy party now, do we?' Jo's face was alight with enthusiasm and the Doctor found himself smiling at the encouragement.

'All right then, but we mustn't get away too late tomorrow.'

'Deal!' Jo shook the Doctor's hand in mock solemnity and started pulling him towards the vast banqueting hall within the fortress.

Gar'ah'd scurried forward. 'I am saddened by your decision, Doctor, but I respect your reasons. In case my duties prevent me from doing so later, I truly thank you for your help.'

The Doctor freed himself from Jo's grasp and she skipped away, having already spotted Nu'b'ld and Ho'gah'th and decided it was time to join in with their chatter.

The Time Lord gazed at Gar'ah'd in admiration. 'You have great leadership qualities, my friend. You don't need me here.'

'With the Diadem removed, our planet will never be at war again. The gratitude I offer you cannot be measured.' Gar'ah'd shrugged. 'But I must apologize. I am embarrassing you.'

'No. No, not embarrassment. I was just thinking. Hoping that no one ever tries to find it.'

'The ravine was many hundreds of spans deep, Doctor. The legends say it is bottomless. Some, like Ho'gah'th, believe it leads directly to the Heart of Pakha, where the fabled Dæmon Mianik'ha lives. If he indeed now has the Diadem, he is most welcome to wear it!'

The Doctor held up a warning finger. 'Don't make light of it so easily, Legislator. The power contained within the object's gems is enormous. Vor'r'na was just another victim of its power. He might have tried to enslave you all through the Diadem's ability to amplify his will, but ultimately, it was the Diadem's doing.'

Gar'ah'd's whiskers twitched in the way that the Doctor had come to recognize as concern. 'You still believe it was a living lifeform itself?'

The Doctor nodded slowly, again rubbing his neck as he thought about the headpiece. 'I'm not sure. And hopefully neither I nor anyone else ever will be. Jo and I encountered something similar once before and it took a concentrated explosion of nerve gases to destroy it. Whatever secrets the Diadem has, it now shares them with the ravine, and I hope it stays that way.'

The two friends looked at each other, then Gar'ah'd clasped the Doctor's hands in his tiny paws and shook them vigorously. 'May both our futures be bright, fruitful and above all, Diadem-less!' Laughing, they followed Jo's lead and headed into the festival.

Hundreds of spans beneath the surface of Pakha, the Diadem lay, battered and dented, and lost to sight. But the power within the multicoloured gem stones that adorned it was not dead.

Merely recuperating . . .

PART TWO
CONTEMPORARY

1:

Unknown and Hostile

Pakha: 384.759 (new calendar)

> *'The world of Pakha is a peaceful blue/green planet,
> roughly the size of Earth's moon. Many hundreds of
> years of tranquillity have established a new order – a
> peaceful trading planet, loved by interplanetary rovers
> and scholars alike. A planet rich in tradition and
> heritage. The Galactic Federation took Pakha under
> its benign ever-enveloping wing some fifty years ago,
> creating new opportunities for the planet's limp econ-
> omy and, without exploitation, turned it into some-
> thing of a tourist's dream. Because so many other
> worlds sent their researchers there, the planet is rich
> in museums and libraries, colleges and galleries. Art
> and entertainment from a hundred other worlds are
> frequently exhibited there, and between every Pakhar
> trader or citizen, you can find ten offworlders come
> to see a show, examine some paintings or hear read-
> ings of new and ancient literature. Of course, these
> offworlders are accepted with customary grace and
> cheer by the Pakhars, not because they feel they have
> to, but because they want to. Pakha and its people
> really are, in every sense of the word, nice.'*

Extract from 'Planetary Surveys'
by Pol Kohnel
©AD 3948 Bowketts Universal Publications

' . . . however, behind every bright facade, every garish

*exhibition and every apparent charm, there lurks
something dark and evil. Nowhere in the universe is
exempt. Least of all, Pakha.'*
Extract from 'A Rough Guide to Federation Tourist
Traps'
by Krymson LePlante
©AD 3948 Hearn Pamphlets Inc.

Safety. Damajina had to find safety.

Behind her she knew her pursuers grew closer. They
were human – their biology was more adept than hers at
continual chase.

As Damajina ran, she instinctively checked that the
laser disc was still secure in her pouch. It was, and next to
it, the clip blaster she had 'borrowed' from the Cantryan
Embassy. Her mind raced to keep up with her body:
should she stop and fight, or keep going until she found
sanctuary? Would they slaughter her or hold her for tor-
ture? Most importantly, would it hurt?

Almost tripping over her ankle-length dress – had she
known someone was going to try and kill her, she'd have
worn something less formal – she threw herself around a
corner and forced herself to stop. She was right in the
heart of the market area – lots of cover and lots of people.
They wouldn't dare shoot here. Then again, the Pakhars
would be surprised enough at a Cantryan official running
in the heat of day; she rather doubted a few trigger-happy
humans would be a much bigger surprise.

Ignoring the astonished stares and outraged gasps of
the locals, Jina dashed straight toward the middle of the
market. Instinctively she knew that the men behind had
spotted her and so, cursing loudly to make the Pakhars
move, she weaved in and out of the colourful stands,
occasionally sending innocent shoppers sprawling, drawing in all probability far more attention than she could
afford. Damn it, Jina thought, she wasn't employed for
this. A librarian, a Cantryan noble here to study ancient
Pakha history, not a spy. Why was she letting herself be
chased? Why not just give them what they wanted? Of

course, if she didn't know the answer to those questions, why was she carrying a gun?

Her thoughts were interrupted by the sight of an archaic tram-bus silently gliding along the road. Yes, if she could reach that, she'd get back to the Library faster – mind you, a flyer and they'd never catch her up. Pakhar public transport was not famous for its speed or reliability. However if they did follow her, they wouldn't dare start a scene in such a respected building as the Library. No, she was being naive. Or was it desperation? She was already aware that the three humans had no regard for Pakhar procedure or heritage. No, her only real hope was to get there first and get her information home quickly.

A shout distracted her. One of the humans, a somewhat bulky specimen she knew was called Pegg, was accusing her of theft. Yes, a damn shrewd move on his part. The moralistic Pakhars would immediately try to stop her. Sure enough, seconds later a pair of paws reached out for her but they weren't prepared for her smooth orange skin, oily through unfamiliar exertion, and so she easily slipped free. The second human, the small, gaunt O'Brien, was now running parallel with her, on the other side of the stalls. The third man whom she didn't know – her only glimpse of him earlier had been of an obviously masculine body, his face shielded from the sunlight by a small peaked cap – was nowhere to be seen.

The tram was nearer. If she ran as fast as she could, she might just leap upon it. Not much further . . .

Beside her a woman browser let out a shrill scream. Ignoring the intense pain in her eardrums, the Cantryan turned. Pegg, his blaster aimed and presumably primed, was facing her now in a straight line between the stalls. Her head darted from side to side, but she saw no immediate escape. If she wasn't careful, O'Brien would cut her off at the other end. She gambled, adrenaline taking over her motive responses where upbringing, logic and tradition had ceased.

She stopped dead. 'Yes?' she called sweetly.

Pegg looked as if he'd expected anything but submission. He faltered and that gave her inspiration. Hand darting into her pouch, she brought out the clip blaster, firing immediately. Pegg's face took on an expression of total disbelief as a majority of his lower abdomen showered over nearby screaming shoppers. Without even waiting for the body to hit the ground, she hurled herself into the centre of a stall, sending jewels and bric-a-brac everywhere.

Alerted by the blaster fire, O'Brien swung into the narrow walkway between the stalls. He expected to see Pegg triumphantly celebrating a victory. What he actually saw was a group of people around a body. It certainly wasn't the Cantryan's, and sure enough the crash of a nearby stall's contents spilling over took his attention towards his quarry. Snarling he followed. His leader was standing with the crowd, making a subtle gesture agreeing to continue the chase.

O'Brien smiled – the Cantryan would be exhausted by now. Her thin blood ought to be boiling with the excessive activity. He became aware of an approaching tram-bus and he saw the distinctive shape of the Cantryan board it. He went for his gun but a firm hand grabbed his wrist, keeping it low.

'Not here – too open.' The leader indicated with his head – a police patrol were arriving to take care of Pegg's corpse. 'There'll be no questions asked,' he added quietly, 'I've seen to that.'

'And her?'

The leader took off his cap and smiled, his eyes glinting in the sun. 'Don't you worry about the young duenna. She's mine.'

O'Brien watched as the leader strode purposefully off in the direction the tram-bus had taken. He shrugged and turned back towards the market. The Pakha police and a medical unit were taking away the body and a few blood-splattered and hysterical Pakhars. One of the police officers turned to make his way toward O'Brien but was stopped by another. O'Brien saw an exchange of words and both rodents wandered off. It seemed his leader was as good as his word.

Duenna Damajina disembarked from the tram-bus outside Pakha's Central Library.

Quietly and with as much dignity as possible she wandered in, just as she did on any other day. The diminutive Pakhar commissionaire discreetly ignored her sweat-stained dress and mumbled his traditionally respectful greeting. Ignoring the entrance to her own office, Jina instead went straight into the public area.

She glanced around. The Library was as old and crumbling as Pakha itself – yet another thing that had not moved with the times. The place was actually full of paper books! Seated at various desks and flat-screen computer consoles was a largely Pakhar collection of scholars and interested parties. A few Federation archaeologists and historians representing other worlds were present, but all thankfully ignored her and got on with their work. Jina headed for a public booth and took the laser disc from her leather pouch.

Carefully weighing the tiny 75mm disc, she looked around and then furtively punched up her Federation Emergency code. How she wished for a Federation Standard system – she could run her adapted finger-net over the microfield on her temple and using the instant access that afforded just tell the net to do what she wanted instead of having to type things onto an archaic keyboard.

The screen in front of her glowed green and a line of words appeared across it, welcoming her to IFEM. At the <WELCOME> prompt she typed her Federation password and seconds later the screen informed her she was <ON LINE>.

Jina looked towards the door. There was no sign of O'Brien or the other man. She slipped the disc into the humming drive and a second later it was registered as accepted. Although the process only took seconds, it seemed forever. Back home it would have been a Neyscrape, and she could have just got on with it; placed

41

her finger onto the DNA scan and mentally beamed her thoughts back. All this was taking up valuable time but no matter how much progress the Pakhars took on board from the Federation, they moved at a pace which suited them rather than her! Jina knew that her pursuers couldn't be too far behind. Nor was it very likely that they wouldn't work out where she was. Even humans weren't that stupid. In fact, she knew some quite nice humans ...

Jina was aware that she was breathing heavily, most un-Cantryan nobility-like. Her stubby fingers scrabbled inexpertly over the keypad, sending the relevant codes across millions of miles of the galaxy, back to the Galactic Federation Headquarters on Io.

Her access channel finally registered as <OPEN> and she pressed the <ENTER> key, sending the details of her discoveries stored upon the disc back all the way home. As it started to go, she allowed herself to relax. O'Brien hadn't found her. All she had to do now was collect her things and get off Pakha. But what of Alec? No, she would have to send him an explanation and apology later. When she was safe. Her father would sort out these troubles.

'Duenna!' hissed an urgent voice from across the way. She almost squealed with joy – it was Alec.

'You're here. My darling, something dreadful has happened!'

Alec looked immediately concerned. 'What?'

Jina steadied her nerves and told him about her flight through the market, her need to send the disc and her subsequent necessary departure. Alec suggested going with her, but Jina shook her head.

'You can't – it might be dangerous. I won't allow you to be endangered. I love you too much.'

Alec smiled and knelt in front of her. 'What would Daddy say if he heard you say that?'

'He'll know.' Jina paused and then continued, 'I've told him all about you as well. Everything's on the disc. So it won't matter.'

Alec stood up suddenly. 'You've told him what about me, exactly?' His tone was noticeably sharper and louder.

Jina was momentarily flustered. 'About *us*. Everything.' She shrugged. 'It's my responsibility.'

Alec leant across her, to cut off the transmission. 'Good thing that even Inter-Federation electronic mail can be intercepted!' She pulled his hand away.

'No, it has to go. If Father doesn't learn about those men and their plans, Pakhar culture will be totally destroyed. I can't let that happen.'

Alec stood behind her. 'All this ... excitement and danger, just for a few ancient cups and a couple of swords.' His hands rested on her shoulders, caressing them slowly. 'And, of course, the Ancient Diadem.' He felt Jina tense under his massage – and he smiled.

Jina watched his reflection in the clear computer screen. Her eyes dropped down to his waist – there, tucked roughly into his belt was a small, black peaked cap. She saw Alec's eyes follow her direction. As his hands stiffened upon her shoulders, sudden, sickening realization dawned upon her.

'Oh no ... no ... Alec ...'

' "Oh no Alec",' he mimicked. ' "Alec" isn't my real name, Damajina.' He lowered his head until it was very close to the Cantryan's sensitive ear. Only a harsh whisper, yet everything he said was painful to Duenna. 'You are a fool. A pretty, dynamic and occasionally very perverse fool. But still a fool.'

'I love ... loved you!' she hissed, still not wanting to disturb the other scholars. 'With my mind, soul and body. You ... you have betrayed that trust.' Her indignation took precedence over all her other feelings. Except one. Rationality. Her hand dropped into her pouch, gripping the blaster.

'Yes, mind, soul and certainly your body. Now, I'll have that disc out please, before any real damage is done.'

As he reached for the eject button, he felt Jina squirm to one side. Before he could register what was happening, the console exploded into flames, sending him flying back-

43

wards, his face searing in pain. He looked through watery eyes back at the console. The whole area was a mass of twisted metal and plastic.

Scholars were scrabbling to their feet in alarm as he drew his own blaster and started firing wildly. A Pakhar and a Thorosian dropped instantly, the latter collapsing into its water tank, sending glass and liquid everywhere. 'Alec' fired at the high ceiling, bringing chunks of it crashing down, rubble, books and computers going everywhere.

Instantly sirens sounded. In the confusion he had created, 'Alec' hauled himself up, pausing briefly to look at the body of Damajina, trapped beneath a lump of ceiling. An involuntary sneer on his face, he kicked out at her. On making contact, he realized her suicidal blaster shot had already succeeded. 'Bitch!'

A glance at the smouldering remnants of her console told him that the disc was irretrievable, indeed it was probably vaporized, and there was no way of knowing how much of her findings had got back to the Galactic Federation. Or the exact whereabouts of his prize, the Ancient Diadem!

Three days later O'Brien and his leader, 'Alec', whose face was swathed in medicated lint, were smuggled away from Pakha, never to return. With them, a chest containing various planetary relics. One important item was missing, however. The Diadem. 'Alec' had not had time to locate it precisely, but nevertheless he could sell what he had got for a high enough price. High enough in fact for a decent surgeon to mend his face and still make huge profits for himself and O'Brien.

Then there was the Federation to deal with. He needed to know the organization totally to achieve his ends. But alone. People like Pegg and O'Brien were commonplace, hired mercenaries he could rid himself of at any given moment, or utilize when the time was right.

He looked across at O'Brien – a good fighter. With a criminal record as long as a Denebian slime worm.

44

Keeping him would not only cut into the profits, but narrow his chances of easy entry into Federation space.

'Alec' smiled to himself. O'Brien was just another obstacle that was easily removed . . .

To the unprepared, the modern planet Peladon could be a death trap. Occasionally, during the brief daylight hours, the distant sun shone brightly and long enough to encourage a few shoots of grass and wheat to grow, but unless cultivated and harvested quickly, any hope of food being utilized soon died. More often than not, terrifying electric storms sheared through Peladon's ebon sky. Sheets of lightning illuminated jagged mountainous regions and rocky lifeless plains. The planet's three moons reflected faint light down upon humble dwellings, built into the sides and feet of the mountains where villages survived through generations of experience and acceptance of the planet's harsh and unyielding atmosphere. Terrible winds howled through the plains. Canyons and valleys almost seemed to shudder under such violent onslaughts. Wild animals scurried back to their homes before being bodily plucked up by hurricanes and dashed to death on the rocks that inevitably lay scattered around.

Despite all of this, the Pels were deeply proud of their planet and although many opportunities had arisen over the past century, only a handful of inhabitants had left their homes to seek fortunes on less violent worlds. Peladon instilled in its people a profound love and respect toward itself. A rare occurrence in the galaxy. The traditions and beliefs of the Pels were mostly unshakeable and passionate.

Over the last one hundred and fifty years, Peladon had seen many changes. As it had emerged from its apparent medieval state, industries like mining and clothing had sprung up on the advice of the Galactic Federation, to which Peladon had allied itself. King Peladon of Peladon had been the ruler who oversaw the alliance and it had been furthered by his daughter, the late Queen Thalira. Peladon's current monarch, Tarrol, surrounded himself with advisors and historians, politicians and Federation representatives, in an effort to keep his planet and people in wealth and prosperity.

However, to even the most inexperienced eye, it was painfully obvious that Tarrol was slowly but surely failing in his task, and whilst the storms lashed the holy Mount Megeshra, upon which the royal Citadel was built, Tarrol was being lashed equally violently by the tongue of his historian and high priestess Atissa.

'Never, never ever have we faced times as dark as those that approach, Your Majesty! Our history is littered with misdeeds and mistakes and each time the spirit of our sacred planet has reared up and smitten evil! This time will be no exception!' Atissa knelt before the young king, her body in the position of humility but her face, hidden from Tarrol's view, twisted in anger at her liege.

On the other side of the throne, also kneeling but observing Tarrol closely was his chancellor, Geban, son of Gebek. Thalira had offered the post, previously held only by one of noble blood, to Gebek shortly after the Federation's altercation with the terrorist organization known as Galaxy Five. Geban and Atissa's opposition was absolute – Atissa's mother was a noblewoman, former handmaiden to Thalira, now the king's lady-of-the-court. Geban's family were commoners, underground workers who three generations ago would have been put to the sword for requesting permission to enter the Citadel. Times and feelings had changed due to Peladon's involvement with the Federation, and now all classes of Pel had freedom to go wherever they chose on the planet. Only the Palace itself was still sacrosanct – nobles and commoners alike had to request permission to enter its hallowed halls. All around, the atmosphere reeked of history and heritage, and to be appointed as a guard to the Palace was still felt to be the greatest honour possible to a common Pel.

To Atissa, the liberalism was an accepted step, and one she would never dream of retracting. Indeed, all around her were examples of this liberalism. The flambeau torches did not burn with real roak, but carefully regulated gas flames. The aroma of incense came not from traditional heated herbs, but from Federation devices that could simulate any known smell. The clothes they wore, the materials their frequently repaired dwellings required, even the food they ate were all replicated and supplied from off Peladon by the Federation. Nevertheless, Atissa was still the latest in a long line of fervent traditionalists and firmly believed that the new ways had to respect and uphold the past.

Geban was more informal and relaxed, a proud and patriotic lover of his planet, but more open to change and opportunities than the high priestess. He found that his role demanded he act as a balance between the overt liberalism of King Tarrol and Atissa's frequently exaggerated traditionalism. Geban shifted the weight of his powerful body onto his other leg and waited for Atissa to end her rather repetitive tirade.

Every time a storm brewed, crops failed or someone spilt a goblet of wine, the priestess claimed the spirit of Aggedor, royal beast and protector of Peladon, had arisen with warnings of impending doom. Geban frequently wondered why Atissa maintained her stance, it had little effect on the king or himself. However, he admired her convictions and determination. In the event of tragedy, he knew perfectly well that whatever her personal feelings might be as to fault or blame, she would join Geban in fierce protection of the throne and Peladon.

The latest battle of wills between himself and the high priestess stemmed from King Tarrol's invitation to the Federation to send special representatives to the royal celebrations. It was the biennial restatement of King Tarrol's vows to the throne of Peladon, and His Majesty had made it abundantly clear that he thought a good party was in order, if for no other reason than to boost the morale of the Pels. Whatever else he might be, Tarrol was no political innocent and was aware of how precarious his planet's industrial future was.

'Your Majesty, in light of the Federation's recent termination of Peladon's mining contract, perhaps the words of Nic Reece should be noted and considered.' Immediately, Geban knew he'd said the wrong thing – he could almost feel the anger in Atissa swell up. She lifted her head imperiously and spat out her words like sparks from a disturbed fire.

'Your Majesty, it is *because* of Reece and his kind that our once-prosperous planet is in decline. Instead of entertaining his insulting, degrading suggestions, we should cut off ties with the Federation and rebuild our own economy.'

'Atissa, you know very well how highly I value your opinions and statements, but to sever links with the Galactic Federation would surely be foolhardy. We have little or no industry to support our people. We need those links with the rest of the galaxy to survive. That is why my grandfather sought their help many years ago.' King Tarrol sighed and relaxed, expecting a sharp rebuttal as always from his high priestess.

Instead both he and Atissa were surprised when Geban said, 'Your Majesty, perhaps we should also examine that route. I do not suggest we decide here and now on a policy for the future of Peladon, but both the noble Atissa and Reece have potentially valid plans. I believe we would be best served by examining all our options and exploring the merits of each.' Geban looked around him and pointed at a carved bust of Aggedor by the double doors. 'No one loves our planet more than myself, Your Majesty, and no one wants us to set ourselves on the proper path, more. But I do believe we must make the correct choice and it will take much time, effort and discussion to find that choice.'

King Tarrol looked towards Atissa, a questioning look on his face. With a cursory glance at Geban, she lowered her gaze once more. 'Geban counsels well, Your Majesty. I cannot pretend that Reece's suggestion does not fill me with loathing just to think upon it, but nevertheless I too believe time is needed to find the right and proper future for our planet.' She again looked towards Geban, who nodded at her, a ghost of a smile on his lips. Atissa did not return the smile.

The king leant forward wearily in his high-backed throne. 'My advisors are, as always, loyal and trustworthy. Chancellor, seek an audience with Mister Reece and suggest a meeting between us. High Priestess Atissa, as always, I value your wisdom. I seek an inventory of the relics to offer Reece so that we can examine his suggestions with solid evidence to support it.'

Scooping up her robes, Atissa stood, bowed low and left the throne room. Geban watched her go. 'She has much fire, Your Majesty. She will fight you and Reece with every breath in her body.'

'And do you think she is right, Geban?'

'As yet, I have not decided. As I said, I believe strongly in having all available information. But my instinct is to follow the Federation representative's advice. The Federation has done much to improve the standard of living on our planet, I would not see that casually discarded.'

Tarrol reached out and touched Geban's shoulder. 'You have given me much wisdom and advice, as always, Chancellor. I will remember it. Please leave me now, I need to prepare for the other Federation visitors' arrival.' Geban bowed and followed Atissa's route out.

Alone, King Tarrol leant back in his throne, coughed sharply and remembered.

He remembered his childhood, running amok through the caverns and tunnels of Mount Megeshra, the half-hearted angry shouts of his nurse as she chased him.

He remembered his mother scolding him, telling him that one day he would be old and wise and rule the planet in her place.

He remembered meeting Atissa, a few years older than him, and not ever willing to play in the tunnels, always telling him that they were sacred.

He remembered meeting Geban when both men were in their teens. Tarrol immediately decided that once he was king, should Gebek the miner pass away, he would have no hesitation in appointing his son as his replacement.

Finally, he remembered his mother's handmaiden, Lianna, Atissa's mother, breaking the news that Queen Thalira, Chancellor Gebek and six courtiers had died in a space shuttle accident in space, sending their bodies, entombed forever, spinning somewhere millions of miles away to drift for eternity. An empty coffin lay in the royal tomb, the only reminder of his mother.

Now he ruled. Atissa and Geban stood beside him. Yet everything his mother and grandfather had believed in was beginning to turn sour. He did not know what to do next.

'Mother, what would you do?' he coughed, a tear rolling down one cheek. 'I need your help!'

'The Galactic Federation. The last bastion of democracy.' The Doctor twirled his fedora hat on the end of his umbrella point, subconsciously making sure it never stopped moving, without paying it the slightest attention.

Bernice wasn't sure which impressed her most – the Doctor's endless ability to absent-mindedly perform conjuring tricks whilst piloting the TARDIS, or the vast sprawling empire on the surface of the moon of Jupiter below.

'Io. One of the seven hundred wonders of the universe, Benny,' the Doctor continued. He slipped on his old and rather worn sweater with the bright red question marks sequenced across it, unaware of his companion's disinterest. 'It took seventy years of hard terraforming and many millions of Federation credits, but on the whole it was probably worth it.'

'I wonder how much it'd take to get you to stop making me giddy,' Bernice muttered. 'Besides, I've seen just as impressive terraformed worlds all over the place. Hardly special enough to be a wonder of any universe, I'd have thought.'

The Time Lord turned to look at Bernice, his deep-set eyes almost glowing with anticipation, enthusiasm etched in each of the many laughter lines that were engraved into his face. Desperately trying to ignore the hat, now suspended at ninety degrees along with the umbrella but still spinning round, she immediately returned his gaze and put on an innocent and wholly insincere grin.

'Sorry? Did you say something?' The Doctor casually flicked his umbrella, dislodging the cream-coloured hat which spun towards the hat stand by the corridor door. Bernice tried not to look too impressed as the little hat not only landed safely on a hook, but continued spinning, albeit slightly slower. She returned her gaze to the Doctor, who was beaming rather childishly.

'I learned that trick from a friend in the Moscow State Circus. Impressive, isn't it?'

'Not really,' returned Bernice. 'So what's so special about this Galactic Federation of yours?'

The Doctor lazily pointed at the image on the TARDIS scanner. It showed vast gleaming spires that rose from various points around the many buildings on the moon below. Huge skyscrapers vied for the record of tallest building, whilst below, long metallic buildings connected them all like strands of a huge spider's web. Despite their distance from the system's sun, the buildings reflected back what light they caught, making the whole place iridescent, frequently changing hue as if it were actually breathing. Around the spires and skyscrapers, tiny flyers darted in and out like insects, whilst around the base, transparent covered walkways were peppered with tiny moving dots, the people of the Galactic Federation going about their business.

'Ten million living beings, Professor Summerfield. Representatives of every civilized race, and a few less so, brought together under the common banner of peace, prosperity and universal harmony. It's taken many decades of work on the part of a few founder members, but it is really quite wonderful. And,' he grinned broadly at her, his Puckish, lined face almost turning entirely upwards, 'we're about to land.' With that, the Doctor flicked a couple of switches and the TARDIS, released from her 'pause' mode, reactivated her time rotor and with the familiar swell of resonance, the ship materialized.

'And once we're there? What next? A quick spin around the offices to amuse myself and Attila the Hun in there?'

Bernice nodded her head towards the door from the TARDIS console room. Somewhere down the corridor, in her room, the Doctor's other companion Ace was probably sitting in her room, testing her twenty-fifth century weaponry whilst simultaneously charging up her patented cans of Nitro–9. 'Come on then, Doctor. Let's see what's out there!'

'In a moment. First I have to tell Ace something.' The Doctor scurried into the depths of the TARDIS before Bernice could reply. With a shrug she leaned over to the TARDIS databank, built into the console. She punched up references to the Galactic Federation. 'Might as well get a bit of homework done,' she grunted to herself.

The Doctor didn't venture into Ace's bedroom too often. He was almost frightened of what he might find there. Discarded cans of Nitro–9; half eaten McDonalds; he'd once seen her knock the stuffing out of a large teddy bear with her old baseball bat, swearing at it and accusing it of betraying her. A short while later he had sneaked in whilst she was having a bath and found the wrecked toy. On its shabby back was the name Mike Smith in permanent black ink. That was when he'd realized how much he misjudged Ace. How he'd never really noticed how much she kept bottled up.

Now the room looked quite different, stark and uncluttered. There was no evidence that the occupier was a young lady from 1980s Earth. Instead, it gave off the impression of a hotel room, somewhere that no one allows themselves to get comfortable in. Like an army barracks. Part of the reason for this was the recent loss of the TARDIS. Now, the travellers occupied the less-than-reliable Type 40 TT capsule that had belonged to an earlier incarnation of the Doctor, an incarnation from an alternate timeline. Despite the cosmetic changes the

Doctor had wrought, he was also aware that neither Ace's nor Bernice's room contained any of the mementoes that they had previously possessed.

Her familiar black bomber jacket, 'Ace' emblazoned in loud, proud silver letters across the back, was lying in a crumpled heap in a corner. On top of it, a trooper's blaster, a reminder of her military training. Discarded but always in sight, the two objects seemed strategically placed as if to underline her two different lives.

The Doctor took all this in in a moment. That, and the fact that Ace was nowhere to be seen. He paused for a moment as he closed the door and looked down the corridor.

'Of course . . .' he muttered after a few seconds.

'Ace?'

She didn't move. She didn't blink. Perhaps she hadn't heard him. In front of her, ten video screens were rapidly flashing schematics. It took the Doctor only a moment to realize that Ace was examining some very lethal-looking weaponry.

'Again!' she barked at the screens. Then: 'Two up.' The second screen seemed to grow larger, its image becoming clearer. 'Okay TARDIS – this one'll do. 3-D plus complete history. Text, not verbal.' She sat back in her chair and swung her legs up onto the desk top. The ten screens melted into thin air and the image she had requested became a semi-solid schematic, turning in front of her. Part of it was encased, revealing it to be a blaster of sorts. Other portions were sectioned so she could see inside it and admire the sophisticated structure.

She reached out with her hands, as if stroking the gun, although it wasn't really there – just an image created holographically by the TARDIS.

The Doctor was impressed. Only a handful of his companions had ever managed to get the TARDIS to work for them like this – and Ace had actually reprogrammed a lot of it. She had convinced the machine to reconfigure itself so that the computer-based parts resembled the twenty-fifth century hardware Ace'd been used to. Voice commands, holographic representations... she'd even replaced the old food machine with a more sophisticated replicator that dished up real edibles rather than nutrient bars. All things he'd intended to do but never actually got around to.

'I'm impressed,' he said.

The images all dissolved, the darkened room brightened and the black militarian walls once again became cream-coloured roundels.

Then, as if she was moving in slow motion, she turned her head.

She was wearing a pair of personal stereo headphones. The player itself lay between her legs. The Doctor smiled: this was the Ace he'd known before – before the distrust, the arguments and the bitterness. Recently, after their struggles in Earth's alternate timelines and more recently on Olleril, she, Bernice and the Time Lord himself had found themselves on a more even keel. And he couldn't be happier.

'Not interrupting, am I?' he asked with a smile.

Ace tugged an earphone away. 'Suede,' she said.

'Goat skin. Rubbed to a nap and worn in cold weather by selfish humans who think it looks better on them than it did on the goats.' He smiled broadly. 'Somehow I don't think that's what you meant, is it?'

Ace shook her head. 'Indie band. Circa 1994. Picked this tape up when we stopped off in Liverpool last week.'

'Ah. After Professor Summerfield's field trip to "Ancient Mersey" as she called it. Wanted to see the birthplace of the Beatles, I think she said.'

Ace nodded. 'Yeah. She bought a tape of *Sgt Pepper*. Then claimed it was classical music. Some people!'

The Doctor squatted down. 'Another friend of mine from Bernice's era said something similar.'

Ace removed the other earphone and switched the Walkman off. After a second's pause, she smiled up at the Doctor. 'Hey, Professor...'

'It's been a long time since you said that.'

'I know. Still, it's a long time since you've worn that awful jumper. Going somewhere cold?'

The Doctor just smiled and pointed at the space where the schematic had been on view.

'What d'you think?' asked Ace.

'As I said, impressive. Only Susan and Romana ever accurately got the TARDIS to reconfigure things. Adric tried but his mathematics wasn't quite up to it. He should've asked K9.'

'I wanted to check up on the thirty-ninth century. You said you had something for me to do.'

The Doctor nodded. 'And I imagine that large gun you were looking at may come in handy.'

'That? Bog-standard really. Obviously things haven't changed much in the armour-stakes over the last thousand years. Anyway, what'll I need a new gun for on Io?'

'Ah,' said the Doctor. 'Now, there's the rub. Benny and I are going to Io. You're not. Well, not for long.'

'Meaning?'

'Meaning that I've been invited somewhere, but with a few built-in conditions. Here's what I need you to do . . .'

Lianna rarely questioned anything that her rulers did. She was conditioned that way, a product of her upbringing. When she had been a young girl, King Peladon had invited the Galactic Federation to become involved in the planet's progress.

As Lianna grew older, she became a handmaiden, lady-in-waiting and general confidante to Peladon's daughter, Thalira. When the Galaxy Five organization tried to make Peladon their outpost to launch their attack on the Federation, Lianna was amongst those who, in however small a way, helped save Peladon's honour by defeating the aggressors.

She both cursed and praised the day that Queen Thalira had announced she was to visit the headquarters of the Galactic Federation, at the invitation of the Draconian Chairman. Thalira had taken Lianna aside, saying that she was determined to prove to the Federation that Peladon could stand on its own two feet, and that the lessons of the Galaxy Five event had been learned. Thalira was to go alone, with just two bodyguards to form her retinue.

Lianna had wanted to object, to say that her mistress would need ministrations and company. Thalira had laughed – the Federation were sending a deep space cruiser to collect her; all that she could need was on board. It would be a long journey and Lianna would not enjoy it. This Lianna could not argue with; she hated space travel. Her couple of short sojourns to diplomatic meetings always resulted in a terrible sickness. The trip to Io would take nearly a week and a half. Too long for Lianna to cope with.

So she had remained, looking after the young king-designate. In a break with tradition, Thalira had remained monarch even after her male heir had been born. The few raised eyebrows this caused were nothing compared to the self-confidence it gave the queen. She knew that Tarrol would be king one day, but she still had a long life ahead of her. The boy should enjoy his boyhood before assuming such an all-consuming role as Peladon's ruler.

Chancellor Gebek had made sufficient over-protective noises and it was agreed that he and some other courtiers would accompany Her Majesty to add state presence to the voyage. Lianna remembered Thalira's laughing face as she bode Lianna farewell, commenting on her loyal lady-of-the-court's stomach upsets as they set off. Lianna remembered Gebek's promise to look after their mistress. Lianna remembered her own husband, Lofan, proudly accepting the posting as one of Gebek's courtiers and wishing his wife and daughter a sad farewell.

Above all, Lianna remembered turning to the young Atissa and saying that the queen and chancellor would return safely soon. The Federation would protect them. Atissa had asked about her father and Lianna had promised that Lofan would bring her a present from Io. Atissa hadn't wanted a present. She wanted information. How the Federation kept records on planetary ancestry. How they respected the traditions of the planets under their care and protection.

Now Lianna breathed deeply, preparing herself, and pulled back the heavy, ornately decorated drape that covered the entrance to her daughter's quarters. The finely woven gold stitching that outlined the face of Aggedor, the royal beast of Peladon and the symbol of their heritage, resumed its almost serene look as she pulled the drape back into place behind her.

She went through a stone doorway into the Sacred Temple. There, a huge graven statue of Aggedor took pride of place. Its face, chiselled out of the best Pel granite, seemed to stare down at her, its one horn pointing lethally upwards, tusks and fangs lining the jaw. However savage Aggedor looked, Lianna knew of the sheer beauty and docility of the real, long-extinct beast. The last victim of Peladon's battle against Galaxy Five, it had fought and given its life to defend Queen Thalira.

Incense hung heavily in the air, itching Lianna's nostrils. She rubbed her nose and looked down at the cloaked figure kneeling before the statue.

'If only you could have seen the real Aggedor,' she said, her voice wistful at the memory.

Atissa looked up. 'We must be thankful that we still have these images to remember him by. If the Federation have their way, that will no longer be so.'

Lianna sighed. It was an old argument. Indeed, she thought wryly, most arguments anyone ever had with Atissa were old. 'That is not true, daughter, and you know it. Reece merely thinks they are – ' her mind searched for the relevant word. It was one Reece used a lot. 'Marketable,' she said at last.

Atissa got up and looked her mother directly in the face. 'One day, when the Nic Reeces and Federations of this universe have plundered and destroyed our heritage in the name of progress, you will remember these words and regret them.' Pulling her long cloak around her, Atissa stormed back into her private chambers. Lianna went to follow, but the heavy wooden door swung closed in front of her.

Ten years ago, Atissa would have been put across her mother's knee and soundly spanked for such wilful rudeness.

Ten years ago Thalira would have told her off as well.

Four years ago, Thalira suggested that Atissa should pursue a course of study – Peladon needed a high priest and royal historian. Atissa's instinctive interest in such things made her an ideal prospect.

Four years ago, Thalira had laughed and bade her loyal handmaiden farewell.

Four years ago, the news had come through about the shuttle accident two days into their return journey. A systems malfunction, the official Federation representatives had said, presenting the Federation's official commiserations to the suddenly enthroned King Tarrol. The occupants would never have known, their atmosphere would have gone in half a second and they would have died instantly.

Now it was the biennial restatement of King Tarrol's vows to ascendancy. Twenty-six Pel years old and king of an entire planet. It was not a responsibility Lianna envied. Atissa was two years older than her liege and Geban a year younger. Three young heads upon whom the fate of an entire planet and its people rested.

Lianna was suddenly very tired. The message she wanted to pass to her daughter lost its importance and she left the chamber via the rock-hewn doorway to the right of Aggedor. She moved the flambeau holder that opened the door, and did the same to another on the other side to close it. Feeling suddenly despondent, she headed back down the gloomy tunnel to her quarters. Empty since the loss of Lofan. Empty since Atissa moved into the Sacred Temple. Empty since Lianna had realized, with the knowledge that only a mother can have about her offspring, that the gap between them was insurmountable. And above all, empty since her life ceased to have any real meaning. Until now. Now, she was involved with something that might have, to some extent at least, healed the breach with Atissa. Lianna sighed as she entered.

Somehow, deep, deep down, she doubted it.

Townsend cursed loudly.

Lambert and Sadler had managed to get into the Federation shuttle-field on Japetus without being spotted, but the moment he and Cooper had tried to follow, the alarms had gone off.

'So much for subtlety!' Cooper snapped, shooting Townsend a look of desperation. He indicated for her to go left, while he went right. Federation forces were not renowned for their intelligence and Townsend hoped the old jokes had a vein of truth in them. Seconds later, Cooper's capture proved the jokes wrong.

Without hesitation, Cooper had surrendered. Townsend nodded to himself – she was keeping to regulations. If only Sadler and Lambert stayed low, the operation might be salvageable. So might their reputations. And their fee.

As Cooper was being led towards the nearest hut, two Federation troopers hung back. They're expecting more of us, Townsend decided. Oh, what the hell – there's only ten or eleven of them at most.

Trooper Edwards' attention was caught by Trooper Wyman, who was staring intently towards the undergrowth near the shuttle-field entrance. Their infra-red scanners had shown four life forms in total. Two already inside the field, two elsewhere. They'd got one, three more to go. He hoped that the commander's plan, to make the intruders think they'd given up, would work. Edwards thought was how unlikely that was – these were probably highly trained mercenaries; certainly the woman's weaponry indicated they were no casual joyriders looking for a fix. He turned to pass his comments on to Trooper Wyman when his companion's head vanished in a red blur.

Without a second's hesitation Edwards was on his belly, rolling and firing into the bushes. He was aware of the other troopers dashing out of the hut, firing behind him. Edwards caught sight of a movement behind the shuttle-field entrance and fired towards that. In reply, blaster shots came back, making plate-sized holes in the dry ground around him.

Commander Rudzka shouted her orders out and the troopers spread, making themselves hard-to-hit targets. Edwards took a second out to mentally thank Rudzka for her strenuous training – no one had ever believed they'd needed the training, now they were wrong. Seconds later Rudzka and her adjutant Lieutenant Payne were on the ground, a few metres either side of Edwards. He pointed to the bushes, he knew at least one mercenary was there. Payne nodded and started to roll right, towards Wyman's headless corpse. Rolling over behind the body, using it as a sort of shield, Payne began strafing the shrubbery. There was a yell and the firing from the bushes stopped. Rudzka immediately turned her attention towards the shuttle-field entrance where three troopers were edging their way along the mesh fence, expertly dodging the blaster fire from within.

Edwards glanced around him. Four of his comrades seemed to have joined Wyman, and Payne was rolling towards each body in turn, checking for pulses. Evidently he found none and he got up on his haunches. Edwards grimaced, Payne was an easy target like that, but it implied he trusted his troops to keep the blaster fire away.

Less than two seconds later, Payne's dead body was hurled forwards. Edwards spun round, firing wildly, and saw the girl they'd captured earlier. She had been under the guard of Trooper Kyte. Damn, Kyte was probably in pieces inside the hut. Damn – Edwards had been planning to ask Kyte out the next weekend. Damn! Damn! The girl flung herself sideways, and Edwards' fire raked through the hut. In his peripheral vision, he saw Rudzka running left, dropping and rolling to avoid being an easy target. Edwards did the same, but in the opposite direction. The girl couldn't fire at two people at once.

Evidently the girl considered Rudzka a more dangerous

target, concentrating her fire in the commander's direction. Rudzka fired a volley in the hut's direction, but the girl was a faster roller. She came up, firing wildly and Rudzka dropped, her last shots going erratically upwards.

Edwards had the girl in his sights. As he squeezed his blaster trigger, his thoughts turned to sheer hatred. 'This is for Samantha Kyte,' he spat. As he fired, he shuddered. Everything had suddenly gone cold. Freezing. His hand shook, the blast smacking into the ground in front of him. He felt the whole world tip – he seemed to be falling, down to a dark pit . . .

Townsend lowered his blaster. The trooper ahead of him fell face-down, Townsend's blast having shredded open his back. Cooper looked up and ran towards him.

Lambert and Sadler were pulling open the shuttle-field gates, kicking aside the corpses of the troopers they had killed.

'Well, that's what I call one hell of a cock-up,' said Cooper, veering towards the gates.

Townsend slowly wandered over, staring at the bodies around him, trying to detect any signs of life. Satisfied that there were no survivors, he joined the others.

'Well, that's what I call fun,' laughed Lambert.

Sadler looked in mock horror at her partner. 'I bet you were a real bully at school,' she said.

'School? What school?' Lambert turned to Townsend, awaiting orders.

'No time for fun, people.' Townsend pointed to the shuttle bay. 'Lambert, your technical skills are needed. And be quick – I expect another delivery of troopers soon.'

Lambert nodded and headed off towards the nearest of three parked shuttles. Sadler following.

Cooper looked ready to follow, but Townsend tapped her arm.

'Yes?'

Townsend tried a smile. Not very successfully. 'How about "thank you"?'

'Why? I knew you were playing possum. One of your oldest tricks.' She jerked her arm away and headed off after the others. Townsend stood and shook his head. Some people . . .

Seven minutes later, three convoys of troopers, along with four laser cannons, roared towards the shuttle-field. Troopers rushed around like excited ants, covering the perimeter fence from every conceivable angle and waiting.

Two minutes went by, a shuttle took off and as it attained five hundred feet, the laser cannons opened fire. The troopers ducked as molten metal and plastic rained down around them.

After clearing up the bodies of their massacred comrades, the contingent left, leaving just a skeleton staff to administrate the area.

Half an hour on and a second shuttle took off, ignoring the futile hand-blaster shots that accompanied it from the troopers. Seconds later the craft zoomed out of sight and away from Japetus.

'All right, take the main feed from number three, then. What the hell's your problem?' Tugging on a loose thread from her thick woollen jumper in frustration, and noting with some distaste that the hole in the cuff got bigger, Ker'a'nol stomped angrily away from one of the holo-camera technicians. 'Cretin,' she spat angrily.

'Problems?'

Ker'a'nol looked up. 'Yeah. And you're the biggest right now. What are you doing here, anyway? Think I can't run my own news crew without you holding my tail, yeah?' Underlining her anger, the short grey tail that poked out of the back of her slacks flicked.

The human her annoyance was aimed at placed a hand on his chest, a false look of total innocence and hurt crossing his middle-aged face. 'My dearest Keri, I wouldn't dare suggest such a thing. I'd like to return home with all my bodily extremities still in place.'

Keri rubbed her face and snout with both hands and

then threw her immediate superior a withering look. 'Listen, Neal, I've been all over this galaxy. I've covered atrocities on the Nematodian Border, I've lived with Orion android warriors on Bala and spent ten months of my life pretending to be a Rigellon's bond-slave, all to get the best stories for GFTV–3. Rest assured, I don't need your ... somewhat large bulk, getting in the way of me covering a blasted feudal monarchy event. Now sod off and let me do my job!'

Neal Corry smiled and shook his head as the fiery Pakhar stomped off, swearing at any of the camera or sound technicians that got in her way. He turned to Jav, the Pakhar operator of holocamera two. 'How long's she been in such a charming mood?'

Jav shrugged. 'Forever? My first time working with her. Can't say I'm impressed.'

Corry paused. 'I thought you covered Operation "Galactic Storm" with her?'

Jav looked at Corry for a moment before replying. 'Err ... no. Wasn't me.' He wandered away before Corry could say anything else.

'Problems?'

A familiar question from a familiar voice. Corry found himself smiling even before he turned around.

'Reece? Nic Reece?' Corry grabbed the newcomer's hand and shook it somewhat over-enthusiastically.

Reece nodded and extracted his left hand, flexing the fingers subconsciously to try and get the blood running again. The Federation's Earth representative to Peladon smiled at the GFTV–3 producer. 'It must have been a long time, Neal. Good to see you.'

Neal Corry waved his hands dramatically around him, almost beheading a passing sound technician. 'Wonderful place you've got here, Nicholas. Any good bars?'

'On Peladon? Do me a favour. There's a mad woman here, the king's high priestess who, given half a chance, would disembowel us and offer our entrails as a sacrifice just for suggesting alcohol was on the planet.'

'Good thing I brought a crate of bourbon, eh!' Corry laughed, and slapped Reece on the back.

Reece looked around furtively. 'Let's go and discuss this in private, old man,' and he led Corry away.

Their retreating forms were watched by the GFTV–3 technicians. Holocameraman Jav gave Reece an extra long, hard look before returning to work.

Geban watched as Keri approached him. He still couldn't quite get used to the idea of what to him seemed like a giant plain-rat running a Federation communications system. Still, she'd requested an audience, and it was his job to greet her.

'Well, do I get to see the king?'

She went straight to the point. Geban smiled to himself. Thankfully Atissa wasn't present – such ignorance of protocol would have caused her to go screeching to Aggedor's spirit for days. Then again, that *did* have its advantages . . .

'Good evening, Ms Keri. His Majesty, King Tarrol of Peladon has agreed to see you. Before we enter, may I ask if I can get you any refreshment?'

Keri looked Geban straight in the eye, her whiskers twitching furiously and her snout slightly wrinkled. 'Yeah. A good sonic shower to get your blasted trisilicate dust out of my fur and clothes. And some heating and light down in those tunnels. Yeah.'

Geban nodded at each complaint. 'The trisilicate I can do nothing about, I'm afraid. It is part of this planet's structure and although most of it has long since been mined out, trace elements are still within the atmosphere. Our king is looking into ways of increasing the heating within the tunnels. When the Federation removed their mining operations, they also removed their humidity controls. The lighting cannot be improved – our generators cannot run much more or the dwelling areas will be deprived. We did have more but – '

'Yeah, I know. When the Federation miners moved out, they took the phosphoric lighting controls. Blasted miners.

Blasted Federation. How about you kick my boss off planet – that'll do for now!'

Geban took a moment to realize who she meant. Then he smiled. 'Ah, the . . . extrovert Mister Corry. With the alcohol on his skimmer.'

'He's got alcohol? On Peladon? Oh, wonderful, how to get us all kicked off. What is the IQ rating of a holostation boss, eh Geban? Minus ten million by the look of it. Yeah.'

'Not to worry. So long as it stays on his skimmer and our high priestess doesn't find out, I think we're safe.'

Keri looked up at the chancellor eagerly. 'No, please, tell her! It'll get that git off your planet and my back. And sacked with any luck.'

'I thought he owned GFTV–3?'

Keri nodded. 'He does. It was just wishful thinking, yeah. Now, where's the king?'

Unconsciously echoing Corry's sentiments, Geban found he liked the fiery little Pakhar. She was a refreshing change to the formal Federation visitors Peladon usually had.

Slowly the chancellor opened the throne room doors and King Tarrol looked up from his throne. As Keri entered her whole demeanour changed, and Geban noted another positive attribute to the Pakhar. She curtsied and deferred to the king most properly.

'May I have permission to address the king?'

Tarrol nodded and waved her forward.

'My most gracious thanks to Your Majesty, King Tarrol of Peladon, for granting me an audience at this most busy time,' she continued. 'I hope I will not take up more than a few moments of your valuable time.'

Geban listened for a trace of sarcasm or insincerity in her voice, but there didn't appear to be any. He caught his king's eye. Tarrol had also heard of Keri's reputation, and he too was clearly impressed by her. The king motioned her forward.

'My Lady Ker'a'nol, you are a welcome visitor to my throne room. Your reputation of bravery and – ' he quickly tried to think of the correct phrase, 'your *investig-*

ative journalism has reached even Peladon. It is our honour to have you as a guest.'

Geban noticed the Pakhar visibly relax. Things were going to be all right for all parties concerned. Geban had not been chancellor all his life, but he could recognize diplomacy when he saw it. And this Keri exuded it with total professionalism.

'Tell me more about this hologram system you have brought to Peladon for the festivities. It is not a technology we possess yet. I would like to understand it better.' The king indicated for Keri to sit on a stool beside him. She sat. Geban turned to leave, but Tarrol requested that he stayed.

Keri outlined her business. She evidently enjoyed her work for all her moans and bluster, and seemed immensely pleased at her successes.

'. . . and so you see, Your Majesty, it converts the images to electrical impulses and beams them back on a subspace carrier wave to Io. There they are re-sent and spread amongst the Federation worlds. Your whole restatement vows can be witnessed by anyone who wants to see them.'

'But if they don't want to see? I should hate the Federation to feel that they had to watch something that they did not *want* to watch.' The king still seemed perplexed.

Keri smiled. 'Please do not take offence, Your Majesty. Should they not want to watch, they simply turn their image of you off.'

There was a pause as the king digested this information. Then he smiled. 'You are indeed fortunate. I only wish certain people on Peladon could be 'turned off' when I do not wish to see or hear them.'

Geban nodded.

Ker'a'nol looked at the two men and smiled. 'Ah,' she understood. 'You don't mean High Priestess Atissa by any chance?'

None of them saw Atissa standing at the back of the throne room. She had entered by the right-hand passage, that led directly to the living quarters – a route only she

66

and Geban were allowed to use. As she stood and listened to herself being ridiculed, she felt anger welling up inside. And a deep shame. Her king considered her a joke. The Pakhar, Ker'a'nol had encouraged this, she had placed the idea in Tarrol's mind.

Atissa swept out as silently as she had entered. Keri did not realize it, but she had just made herself a very, very bad enemy.

2:

In a Glasshouse

*'Space. Vast, dark and cold. Tiny pinpricks of light
reveal planets and stars. Across the interminable dis-
tances between each pinprick, minute specks float.
These specks are spacecraft. From many different
worlds, many different races, but all with one
common aim: to be somewhere else.*

*The foremost craft of the Galactic Federation, the
Deep Space Cruiser* Bruk, *owned and piloted by
the Martian Star Fleet, is one of the largest and sleek-
est vessels ever constructed. To those fascinated by
interstellar travel, it is the sort of ship that they will
go anywhere just to catch a glimpse of.*

*Ship spotters queue for hours on end at space ports
to see it arrive or depart. To admire its craftsmanship,
wallow in its splendour, note its registration number
and discuss for hours the many trips it might have
made, the things it might have witnessed and the
miracles it might have performed.*

*For some, however, it is just a mode of conveyance,
something to take you from A to B and, hopefully,
back again.*

*Ship spotters call such people soulless – less pas-
sionate people call them passengers.'*

The Ship Spotters' Almanac (53rd Edition)
Ed. J. V. Way.
AD 3908 Bowketts Universal Publications

The first thing Bernice noticed as she followed the Doctor

out of the TARDIS was the smell, like fresh, slightly damp roses. Sniffing at the overwhelming scent, she followed the Doctor down a long Perspex corridor, deserted apart from an automated service robot which appeared to be washing the walls. Outside, the unlikely combination of bright green grass, palm trees and a few multicoloured shrubs which she knew instinctively were not from Earth bathed in the light reflected from the spires.

'You've missed a bit.' The Doctor patted the service robot and pointed to a smear on the perspex wall with his umbrella.

'Apologies,' squeaked the robot and hurriedly set about resquirting, rewashing and repolishing the offending mark.

Nodding to himself, the Doctor continued his amble, leaving Bernice to commend the robot on its speedy rectification.

'Doctor,' she called, 'far be it from me to pry, but where exactly are we headed?'

The Doctor said nothing but pointed forward with his umbrella.

'Thanks. That's a great help,' Bernice muttered and decided to keep up with the Time Lord. Familiarity, in her case, bred further familiarity and she knew from experience that if she lost sight of the Doctor, she might spend years on Io without finding him. Somehow, that didn't really appeal.

They continued their walk for the most part in silence. Occasionally the Doctor would point out a particular bush, fruit or animal outside and reel off its origin, but apart from this small talk, Bernice realized she would get no answers to her questions just yet.

After about a twenty-minute walk, by which time the TARDIS was a speck on the horizon behind them, Bernice could hear the soft burble of voices. As they continued it got louder and she realized that their route was going to meet at a T-junction with another, an apparently busy, noisy one. A few minutes later they stopped at the end of their corridor and Bernice was impressed.

In front of her, for the most part ignoring her, what

69

seemed like hundreds of people walked or ran along the connecting corridor. She stared hard: very few humans, she thought, but many humanoids, although some were of colours she'd never seen. Come to think of it, they were colours she couldn't have even imagined! As they mingled amongst them, the lights far above seemed to reflect on the faces of some of them, although she noted that it tended to be on the more exotic species rather than what she could only think of as bog-standard humans.

After another ten minutes of walking the Doctor stopped and looked around and above them. Then he looked left, right and back the way they had come.

'You don't know where we are, d'you?' Bernice tapped her foot against the pavement.

He touched her foot with the tip of his umbrella to stop the tapping and looked up at her with a sheepish smile. 'I wouldn't say that.'

'Well, what would you say, then?'

The Doctor coughed slightly, swung his umbrella up and started counting sections off along it. He then slung it over his shoulder and started counting and pointing in various directions. While all this was going on, Bernice raised her eyes heavenwards. She smiled politely at the passers-by who looked intrigued or bemused by the strange-looking man who muttered and pointed to himself. She shrugged her shoulders at one tall blue woman who looked as if she were about to ask whether the Doctor required some kind of medical attention but then seemed to change her mind at the last moment.

After a few minutes, a dark-clad militaristic human wandered over. 'Can I help you?' he asked, his soft voice a startling contrast to his severe uniform.

'I hope so,' muttered Bernice. 'Where's the nearest bar, I need – '

'Directions as we're rather lost,' finished the Doctor, dropping the point of his umbrella to the metallic floor rather heavily to attract Bernice's attention.

'As usual,' she added, determined to be right for a change, and giving the Doctor an 'I told you so' look.

The security guard smiled warmly. 'Don't worry, Doctor, you're not too far off the right track.' Both he and the Doctor ignored Bernice's astonished gape and the guard started giving directions. When he'd finished, he gave the fuming Bernice a winning smile and sauntered off.

'Do I get an explanation, or do I assume the entire universe will recognize you wherever we go?' In reply the Doctor placed his arm around Bernice's waist and said, 'I knew I was on the right track. This way.'

Bernice was pleased to see that Federation hospitality was exactly as she had expected it to be. Lots of drinks on offer, lots of friendly faces and a majority of their hosts had two arms, two legs, one head and smiled a lot. Of course, a smile to them could be the equivalent of a snarl to her, but as neither of her ankles had been bitten off, she assumed they were friendly aliens.

On arriving at what appeared to be their main destination they had been whisked up seventy-seven floors to the suite of the Cantryan commissioner, whom it now appeared was not only the current chair of the Federation Council but also an old friend of the Doctor's. Then again, she thought, so was everybody she ever met. Christmas cards must be a nightmare!

Although in her time there had been much co-operation between the various species that inhabited the galaxy, wars and bickering were still constant thorns, pricking away at the good relations. Bernice was glad to see that things had apparently changed for the better. From what she could see and had briefly noted from the TARDIS databank, the Galactic Federation was a massively successful inter-species exchange programme. As new planets applied for – and usually received – membership, so a cultural cross-pollination occurred as each new planet brought something new to the Federation while receiving the combined wisdom and services of every other planet.

The Cantryan commissioner was overwhelmingly charming, and his suite of offices positively radiated welcome, the decor, furniture and plants all serving to reinforce a relaxed atmosphere.

The only change to this occurred at the point the Doctor asked the commissioner about his family. As far as Bernice could gather from listening in, the commissioner's eldest daughter had died recently in an accident on a distant frontier world. Once the Doctor had offered the relevant condolences, the topics of conversation grew more pleasant and cheerful.

After a while, Bernice was left in a small room adjoining the one where the Doctor and the commissioner sat talking. It was cool and well shaded; the Doctor had said something about the Cantryans not liking too much heat or light. Few plants, but lots of paintings were dotted around, and Bernice flopped down on a large soft chair, sighing in comfort after the long walk.

After her eighth sigh (she was getting bored by now), Benny was pleased to hear a door behind swish open. She looked up expectantly, but it wasn't the Doctor. Instead, a Cantryan youth stood awkwardly, holding a try of drinks and trying not to look pissed off.

'You look pissed off.' Bernice swivelled her chair round to face him properly.

The boy stared back at her for a moment and then strode into the room with all the manner of someone desperately trying to give the impression that he owned the place. Benny decided that tact on her part was necessary and so stood up in greeting.

'Nice place you've got here, I have to say. Nice plants. Nice pictures, too.' Evidently she wasn't getting anywhere. 'Nice wallpaper,' she added without thinking.

The boy sighed. 'What wallpaper? It's painted granite. Even a human can see that!' He pronounced 'human' as 'hooman', and made no attempt to hide his sneer at the word.

Be pleasant. Be nice. It's his home. Benny tried to smile but his rudeness had clearly offended her jaw muscles. All she could manage was an exaggerated rictus grin. Gritting

72

her teeth, she resisted the urge to knock his down his throat and took a glass from the tray. 'Thank you.'

The boy, like most Cantryans Bernice had seen in the tower was astonishingly slim. Orange skin that resembled bad sun-tan lotion was about the only thing that immediately struck her as vaguely alien. On closer inspection, Bernice noted that Cantryans only had three thick fingers on each hand and also noted the lack of fingernails. Her mind sped through her mental catalogue of aliens, but nothing came to mind to indicate anything similar about any other race she'd studied or encountered. Except Sontarans, she suddenly remembered. They only had three fingers. They'd also have shot her and the Doctor by now, so it seemed fairly safe to assume there was no relation.

The boy looked about fifteen and had bright eyes that somehow promised a far warmer soul than was being presented. However, it was his face that caught Bernice's attention. Etched into the skin to the side of his right eye, just on his temple was a rectangular image. At first she thought it was a tattoo or some such decoration but as she stared she realized it was slightly metallic; filaments embedded into a few centimetres of his face. It reminded her of a very complicated micro-electronic chip board, like those in the personal microfaxes of her time. As he passed her a beaker she noticed that the first finger of his hand had a similar set of filaments embedded in it. She realized that it must have been these tiny implants that had been reflecting the light on the faces of the crowds she had spotted earlier. Clearly this was some kind of custom that she had yet to properly encounter.

Apparently aware that she was staring, the boy withdrew his hand quickly as she took the drink.

'It's only a Neyscrape,' he said.

'Oh. Right,' replied Bernice.

He shrugged indifferently. 'I s'pose you're one of those Gaia humans. Don't like the cyperspace net and refuse the implants.'

Bernice thought quickly. 'Oh, it's not that. It's just that we travel so much, neither the Doctor nor I have had time to – ' The boy had already turned away, presumably bored of her explanation. 'Oh well,' she thought and sipped the drink. Instantly she began coughing. The boy looked immediately amused.

'My apologies, Professor Summerfield,' he said without any trace of regret in his voice. 'The Doctor suggested you would prefer what he called "the heavy stuff".'

Bernice shook her head, and tried to speak. Her voice came out as no more than a pained whisper. 'It . . . it's no problem. Just a bit stronger than I'm used to.' She cleared her throat and took another sip. 'Not having one yourself?'

The boy shook his head. 'Liquidized Guntha guano is not a delicacy on Cantrya. I don't think I would like it.'

As what he had said sunk in, Bernice stared at her host, then at her glass and then back at the boy. Clearing her throat again, she gingerly placed the glass on the table in front of her. 'Very nice,' she lied.

'I'm glad it pleases you.' He was also lying.

'So. D'you work here all the time?' Bernice wasn't sure what 'work' entailed, but this youngster was the only company she'd had for a while. And however hostile, a bit of mental one-upmanship would pass the time so she decided she wanted to make the most of it.

'Yes. The man your friend is with is my father.'

'So it was your . . .' Bernice stopped herself, but not in time.

'Yes, my sister Damajina. We have grieved, so please do not be embarrassed.' There was a pause before the Cantryan boy continued. 'We do not see many Tellurians these days. What is Earth like?'

'Haven't been there for a few . . . years,' she said evasively, thinking that such a straightforward question had to have a suspicious meaning to it.

'Have you been on other planets or in space?'

God, this was desperate conversation! Bernice tried a smile. 'Oh, a bit of both really. I'm an archaeologist.'

'Oh, how fascinating. I've been to the Horun ruins on Phaester Osiris. It was boring.'

74

Bernice nearly gagged. The Horun ruins – but they were just legend! 'They found them! When?'

'Well, over three months ago, I think. It's been on all the newscasts . . .' The boy trailed off and Bernice realized her expression must have been pure astonishment.

'After all these years . . .' Suddenly she thought that she was probably scaring the boy. Poor sod, thinks he's in a room with a madwoman. Still, it wasn't her fault that the Doctor hadn't told her exactly what century they were in. 'Well, I'd like to visit them sometime. For once, the Doctor can take me where I want to go.'

'You'll be very bored. The place is just full of stupid people from the stupid Braxiatel Collection with stupid trowels taking three days to uncover half a stupid metre. A drilltech would be far quicker . . .'

'You heathen! The reason they're taking their time is to preserve what's there!' Benny was suddenly furious. Furious with this boy for his dismissive attitude towards the Horun ruins; furious with the Doctor for not telling her what century they were in and furious with herself for not being there. She swigged down more of her awful drink.

The boy suddenly laughed. 'So it's true. You humans really don't have a sense of humour!'

Bernice looked in astonishment at the boy as he flopped into one of the chairs. 'Hey, relax, human. I was only joking. Well, about the drilltech – the ruins *were* boring. I only went as a diplomatic courtesy. My father was still investigating . . . my sister's death.' His smile had gone.

'Were you two close?' she offered.

The boy nodded. 'We were friends more than anything else. Jina was far older than me. She was a sort of archaeologist, too. Like you. I miss her.'

'You seem to know a lot about me. I'm afraid I can't say the same of you.'

'My name's Damakort. They call me Kort. And researching my father's guests is second nature to me by now. I've been doing it ever since I could read.'

'You like it here on Io? With your father?'

75

Kort shook his head, suddenly sullen again. 'I want to go home. I'd even agree to see my mother. My father wouldn't let me. Said it was important for me to follow a diplomatic life.'

Benny shrugged. 'Seems a bit harsh. Isn't there anyone else here of your age to talk to?' Again Kort shook his head. 'There was . . . My father doesn't understand me,' he said after a pause.

'How many youngsters have said that over the centuries?'

Kort suddenly went into another sulk. Benny wasn't sure if this was genuine or another sham. 'Oh look, if you can't take a bit of a joke, then there's no point in talking,' she said, as reasonably as she could. 'After all, you started this.'

Kort looked up and a smile spread across his face. 'I like you. I'm going to enjoy travelling with you in the TARDIS.'

Benny gaped. 'Now wait a minute – '

There was a shout from the next room. It was the Doctor's voice.

'We'll continue this conversation later,' she said, getting up.

As Bernice went through the door Kort nodded slowly. And smiled. Things were going well.

As Bernice entered the room, she guessed immediately that the mood did not match the surroundings. Soft armchairs, plush, thick carpets and the soft pastel watercolours on the wall could not disguise the atmosphere. She looked at the Cantryan commissioner. Immediately she saw the familial resemblance with Damakort. The same burnt orange skin, the thin face and hands with stubby fingers that looked as if they'd punched on one data-pad too many. She looked across at the Doctor, pacing up and down in front of the window. Bernice prided herself on her ability to gauge people by their body language, but the Doctor had always been her one blind spot. However, the last few months of exposure to his foibles and

76

mannerisms still gave her the message that he was upset. No quick wit and flash attitude was the instinctive message she was getting from his subliminal posturing.

The Doctor pointed at a seat, a serious look on his face, and Bernice sunk into the billowing cushions, waiting to hear whatever it was she had been summoned for.

As he looked at her, unspeaking for a moment, Bernice decided that the conversation she had missed had not been the happy reminiscences she had assumed. The Time Lord's face had a far-away look, as if he was not entirely in the room with them. When he spoke, she thought it was more as if he were talking to himself than to her or the Cantryan commissioner.

'A long time ago I visited a planet where the inhabitants only knew war. They fought for many years, each side never defeating the other – every time one army got the upper hand, something would cause factions of that army to change allegiance. It was as if some totally evil force were using the people as pawns in a game. War is a terrible thing, but when it goes on interminably, each new generation automatically picking up weapons and carrying on, with nothing else in their lives but to fight and die, no real knowledge of what they're fighting for, it takes on an even more horrific meaning.

'When I visited that planet I hoped I had cured it of its malaise. I found an object called the Diadem which I believed, indeed still believe, was inhabited itself by a wholly malevolent lifeform dedicated to war, thriving off the emotions that war creates. I removed the Diadem from the people and freed them. They became a vast amicable society, completely turning their backs on anything other than a philosophy of peace.' The Doctor paused for thought.

'Space hippies!' Bernice immediately wished she'd kept quiet at the look the Doctor shot in her direction.

The Doctor wandered over to a window and stared down into the heart of the Federation base. His face clouded over, a mixture of disappointment and frustration etched into every line, every pore.

'That planet was called Pakha. The commissioner's daughter died there, sending back a message that people had been stealing great Pakha art treasures and selling them on the black market. One of those treasures sought was the so-called Ancient Diadem. Damajina was unable to confirm whether it had been located by the profiteers.'

The Doctor turned to Bernice and continued earnestly, 'Benny, if the Diadem has been found, it could unleash the most terrible curse upon this galaxy. All the years of peace that the Galactic Federation has striven for will be wiped away in an instant. It only takes one man or woman insane enough to wear the Diadem, to try to harness its power, and the whole galaxy will be plunged into a potentially never-ending war.'

Bernice realized that whilst the Doctor had been talking, she had been unconsciously holding her breath. She let it out and sank further in her chair, strangely exhausted. Even the Cantryan commissioner seemed shaken by what he had heard.

'Doctor, when my daughter ... Jina, sent her message, we had no idea of the significance of the Ancient Diadem, only that these people chasing her wanted it badly. And as we now know, they were ultimately happy for her to die rather than let us know about her discoveries.' The commissioner slumped back in his chair and Bernice noticed how very old and very tired he looked. It seemed as if just listening to the Doctor's story and recounting his daughter's final part in it had aged him terribly.

The Doctor wandered slowly across the room, picking at a thread hanging loose from one of his jacket buttons. He twirled it around his index finger, tightly, making his fingertip bulge white.

'All right, my friend, I'll go,' he said finally. 'I would never forgive myself if I didn't do something to find and perhaps this time totally destroy the Diadem.'

'Thank you, Doctor.' The commissioner managed a wan smile. 'Our latest intelligence reports suggest that our suspect, a human, must be within the Rho system. The trail ran ... dry, I think you would say, a few weeks ago.

Among the information my daughter supplied, we learned that our enemy is something of a master of disguise. He . . . he formed an alliance with her, and betrayed her. One of his compatriots was killed on Pakha, the other, a mercenary named O'Brien, was found dead in a crashed shuttle on the second moon of Jahn. From there on the trail stopped. However, our projections of his possible flight path suggests that he might be hiding on the planet Peladon – '

The Doctor sat suddenly, and rested his chin upon the crook of his umbrella, a grim smile on his face.

'Peladon. Like a second home. Yes, Commissioner, definitely a good place to start our hunt.'

'You will have help, Doctor. I am sending a delegation from Mars. Officially they, and you, are going for the biennial restatement of King Tarrol's Ascendancy Vows. Peladon is steeped in such traditions but relations are not as secure as they once were. We are hoping that a Federation presence will strengthen Tarrol's convictions to remain part of our organization.'

Bernice leant forward. 'How difficult would it be to spot our man? Are the people of Peladon human-looking?'

The Doctor nodded again. 'Totally. He could fit in easily and we'd never spot him.'

'But how many travellers go to Peladon?' insisted Bernice. 'Surely the locals could spot a stranger a mile off?'

The Cantryan stood up and adjusted his flowing robe. 'Professor Summerfield, Peladon is saturated with offworlders at the moment. That is why we suspect he will have headed there. Holocrews, journalists, cultural attachés; half the Federation are showing an interest in the events. An absolute monarchy is such a rarity in these times, people will wallow in the splendour for as long as possible.' The commissioner turned away from Bernice and held his arms out in a gesture of helplessness to the Doctor. 'My friend, my old friend, I can do no more than thank you for your help and look forward to your safe return.' He looked across at Bernice again. 'Your knowledge of the Martians is, the Doctor assures me, second to none. Naturally, I hope you will feel able to go.'

As Bernice smiled at the Doctor for his trust, the commissioner spoke again. 'I have another reason for wanting you to go. My son, Damakort – have you met him?' Bernice nodded as he continued: 'Well, he has been invited as my personal representative. I do not want him to go – I know it will be dangerous, but nevertheless, my role as Federation Chair requires me to put aside my personal feelings.'

Bernice frowned. 'Excuse me for suggesting this, but if you are aware of the danger, can't you send someone else? Protocol or not, he is your son.'

The commissioner shrugged and the Doctor intervened quickly.

'Commissioner, we will be delighted to take Damakort with us. Bernice will make an excellent nanny.'

As Bernice politely smiled at the joke, her eyes were sending the Doctor vats of acidic looks, but he didn't appear to notice. She got up, straightening her vinyl jacket.

The Doctor bowed slightly to his old friend.

The commissioner then took the Doctor's hand in his and, despite his great age, knelt before the Doctor. 'My life is yours.'

Clearly shaken by the ancient regal honour bestowed upon him but nevertheless extremely flattered, the Doctor remained where he was as the Cantryan rose once more. As he slid his hand away, he spoke softly.

'For our friendship and for the memory of your daughter, I shall not let you down, my friend.'

Leaving the commissioner staring out of his seventy-eighth storey window, the Doctor and Bernice left the suite.

After a moment the door slid open. Damakort entered and put his hand upon his father's shoulder. Without looking at him, he placed his hand upon Kort's and clasped it tightly.

'Take care, my son,' he said. Kort nodded and walked back out.

The commissioner sighed deeply, thinking of his wife; angry, bitter and estranged. Of his daughter; young, beautiful, a scholar and now dead. And his young son; facing dangers and evils on Peladon. A single tear trickled down his aged face, one of many he had shed recently. He hoped it would be the last.

'Well! Martians!' As they left the tower and emerged back onto the covered walkway Bernice found herself running slightly to keep up with the Doctor. 'Hey, where's the fire?'

'Probably all around us, "Professor Summerfield".' The Doctor stopped suddenly, and Bernice overshot him. As she turned back, she noticed his face had what Ace called his Donald Duck look – lips pursed, eyebrows down and a wrinkly frown on his forehead. 'I don't like them.'

'What, the Martians?' Bernice paused and looked hard at the Doctor.

'Yes, the Martians. Fierce, militaristic, loyal, dependable, honourable – and yet I wouldn't trust one further than I could throw him.'

'How far's that?'

The Doctor smiled slightly. 'I couldn't lift him half an inch.' He resumed walking and with a resigned sigh Bernice followed, knowing she was not going to get to the bottom of this one in a while. Instead she asked, 'Where are we going now?'

'To the spaceport. We've a ship to catch.'

'You mean, we're not going in the TARDIS? We're leaving it and Ace here?'

The Doctor nodded.

'All this must be pretty serious then. After all, it's bad enough letting the TARDIS out of your sight, but her as well? What's going on?'

'She has a mission of her own.'

'How much of this Diadem and Peladon stuff did you know about before we landed?'

The Doctor smiled. 'Bits. This and that. Some of the other. I knew enough about stolen art treasures to send Ace off to Pakha. I suspected the Diadem's involvement, but the commissioner confirmed it. Peladon is an added bonus.'

'And Kort?'

'The son? Well, that didn't exactly surprise me. Noble blood, you see. Diplomatic courtesy. Nice boy, is he?'

'Not really. Teenage angst. Where are we meeting him?'

'At the spaceport.'

'What a shame. He was looking forward to travelling in the TARDIS.'

'His father, I expect. Filling the child's mind with nonsense and romantic tales of derring do.'

Bernice caught the Doctor's sleeve. 'So, how do we get to the spaceport?'

The Doctor pointed his umbrella towards the crowded walkway and seconds later, Bernice heard the hum of a flyer above her.

'Citizens. Where to?'

'Spaceport Two, if you please.' replied the Doctor. The flyer landed beside them and they crammed themselves in. The synthetic voice suggested that they hold tight and seconds later they found themselves flying just above the walkways and crowds. Bernice looked out of the window – other flyers skimmed about, and she could see into huge office blocks where multicoloured humans and aliens went about their daily business. She gasped momentarily as another flyer skimmed towards them but at the last minute it veered off to the right and swung around the corner of a tower block. Ahead of them, the walkway seemed to stretch to infinity, but just as Bernice started to wonder if they'd taken the wrong direction, their flyer turned left and the voice announced that they would be at the spaceport in four minutes. She looked across at the Doctor, but he had relaxed in his seat, his crumpled fedora hat tilted forward, covering his eyes. He certainly wasn't asleep, but experience told Bernice that it was best to let him think

82

when he did that, it was like a sort of personalized Do Not Disturb sign.

Finally the flyer started its descent and smoothly stopped outside a vast open area, secured by wire fencing. Large double gates bore the notice that this was indeed Spaceport Two and a large rectangular slab of stone stood just inside the gate.

The Doctor tipped his hat back and beamed widely at his companion.

'Here starteth the adventure, "Professor Summerfield",' and he thanked the flyer as the door opened.

'Do we leave a tip?' she asked but before the Doctor could answer, the flyer's voice replied 'Your contentment and safe arrival is enough. Thank you,' and it took off.

The Doctor traced around the notice on the gate with his umbrella point and then walked purposefully towards the slab of rock.

'Good morning. I'm the Doctor, this is my associate. We are expected, I think.'

Bernice looked on with bemusement as the Doctor talked to the stone. Just as she was about to make some biting comment, the stone's centre glowed slightly orange and the gates swung silently open. The Doctor sauntered through, doffing his hat at the stone. Bernice slowly followed and then stopped and stared at the stone. It glowed again and the gates closed. Suddenly Bernice was aware of the Doctor's umbrella crook on her arm, giving a slight tug.

'It's rude to stare,' he admonished.

'Bu ... but it's just a rock ...' Bernice looked, bewildered towards the Doctor and back at the stone.

'It's an augmented Ogri. I'll explain one day. Right now we're in a hurry.'

With a final look back at the now plain-looking stone, Bernice shrugged and mentally noted the name Ogri. 'Of course, should have known,' she thought sarcastically. 'Where I come from, everyone's got one.' That spurred on her next question.

'By the way, Oh Great and Wise Know-All, what year

are we in? Just so that I don't make any *faux pas*. I know how you hate to be embarrassed by such things.'

The Doctor shrugged. 'Mid-thirty-ninth century, give or take a decade. I'll know more when we get to Peladon.'

'Mid . . . frag, that's the furthest we've been. No wonder I don't know what an Ogri is! And by the way, why didn't you tell me about the Horun ruins?'

No reply.

She followed the Doctor towards a metal hut, the word 'Reception' emblazoned across its door.

The door slid silently open as they approached, and a uniformed male Lurman, his silver hair decorated with an astonishing array of baubles, oozed charm at them.

'You must be the Doctor and Bernice. The Chair of the Federation informed us of your arrival. High Lord Savaar is awaiting you in the hospitality suite aboard the *Bruk*.' The receptionist smiled at Bernice, his eyes hinting at . . . she didn't know what exactly but, she thought, he was the first person she'd met recently who might have been worth her discovering what made him tick. He looked well built, late twenties or early thirties, and those silvery eyes . . . She smiled back.

'Fancy a trip to Peladon?' She tried her best to look coy.

The receptionist suddenly looked alarmed. 'I . . . I don't think my mother . . .'

The Doctor once again came to the rescue, sliding his umbrella around Bernice's wrist and yanking her towards the exit.

'Come along, Professor,' he said loudly. 'We've got to find Damakort.'

Outside, the Doctor looked vaguely disapprovingly towards her.

'His mother?' Bernice tried to take another look back through the glass door but the Doctor gently pulled her along.

'Lurmans age mentally a great deal slower than humans

do. He's the human equivalent of twelve years old, I should think.'

Bernice shook her head. 'Shouldn't be working then, should he?'

'All Lurmans work hardest during their youth. It's when they mature you've got to worry about them.'

'Why?'

'Because they tend to go into show business. Come on!'

Shaking his head in resignation, the Doctor led her around the back of the reception hut and stopped. There in front of them was the Deep Space Izlyr-class cruiser *Bruk*.

Sleek seemed too dull a word for it. It was, in a functional way, Bernice thought, quite majestic. She'd seen a lot of ships in her time but this was certainly one of the more impressive. It was, she guessed, about a quarter of a mile long and about three decks high. Brilliant white metal, with pinpricks of green-tinted Perspex windows and two vast nacelles at the back, obviously the *Bruk*'s drive system. She couldn't see the front properly, it was too far away, but the slightly raised blur she could see suggested the bridge to her. Not too far away, a set of steps led to an open hatchway. Something vaguely green stood waiting there.

'Our invitation,' muttered the Doctor and wandered off towards the steps.

Bernice nodded. 'I'll go first,' she said, brushing past him. 'After all, I'm the appointed Martian expert. And you'll only be rude to them.'

The Doctor stopped. 'I beg your pardon?'

'Oh, speak ancient Martian do you? Know how to address a High Lord correctly, without insulting him? I might not know Ogri and Lurmans, Doctor, but Martians are my speciality, remember?'

The Doctor gave a little bow. 'You are right of course,' he said and Bernice desperately tried to hear a trace of sarcasm, but failed.

As she reached the steps, she felt her heart begin to beat fast. She had indeed studied Martian history. Back in the twenty-sixth century, the Martians were known as a warrior race, mostly extinct. She knew that there had been an attempted invasion of Earth back in the late twenty-first century. That had been repelled, and had led to a new era for the Ice Warriors. Realizing that to survive they needed friends, not enemies, they had resettled themselves on a new planet which, naturally, they named New Mars. It had taken many decades, but it was known that gradually a less aggressive Martian hierarchy had succeeded the militaristic one and New Mars ceased being a threat to other worlds. For a second the derogatory term 'Greenies' flashed through her mind. A memory she couldn't place. She'd never actually been to the original Mars, but suddenly she had a vision of skimming across its plains and hills, chased by ... the Doctor? No, not exactly her memory, someone else's ... Fred ...? Who was Fred? She'd have to ask the Doctor about that one.

Bernice had studied the Martians because it was this regression from warring that fascinated her. In such a short space of time a proud, quite vicious race of warriors had become a reclusive species who rarely allowed visitors to New Mars. Much of what was known, by her time at least, was based on supposition and archaeology on the real Mars, a planet easily colonized by mankind.

The chance to solve some of those mysteries herself – well, that was a challenge worth putting up with the Doctor for!

She dashed up the stairs as quickly as possible and ran straight into the green something she had seen earlier.

'Please. Take care.'

The creature in front of her was at least eight feet tall, humanoid and, from what she could see of its skin, came in varying shades of green. A hard material, however, covered most of the creature, like some kind of armour. Only its arms and legs seemed bare; sparkling, obviously reptilian skin rippled as it moved to stop her. As her eyes went up the knobbly body she managed to stop an involuntary shudder as she looked up at the face. Most of the creature's head was encased in some kind of knobbled helmet, its eyes concealed behind two protective red glass coverings. Only the mouth and chin were visible, thin green lips hissing the warning at her. Bernice had seen many pictures and drawings of a Martian ranking warrior, but none of those had quite prepared her for the real thing. She looked down at the hands – encased in massive clamp-like gloves, made of the same material as the armour. Tufts of fur poked out of the wrist ends, as they did at various other joints in the armour. Nestled on the right wrist was a slender white tube which came to a solid bulbous head just below the fur. From her studies, she knew this was a Martian sonic disrupter. One of the most lethal weapons ever.

The Martian moved its head as it looked down at her in a vaguely snake-like way, but slower, almost comical, as if it was going to fall off at any moment.

If Bernice had any thoughts about laughing, however, they vanished again as it spoke. The voice hissed at her, as if coming from deep within the huge frame, and yet it was quiet but clear, like air escaping from a punctured tyre.

'I said, please take care.'

'Don't worry, I can take care of myself, thank you.'

The Martian's voice hissed again, barely audible over the sound of its breath.

'I apologize. I was concerned that you had not seen the slight drop behind me.'

Bernice looked into the corridor of the *Bruk*. There was indeed quite a drop to the first inner step, clearly no problem to someone as tall as the Martian, but for her . . . She looked up again at the figure.

'Thank you. The Professor here can be a little enthusiastic!' The Doctor had caught up with her and was also noting the drop.

'I am Sskeet. I am High Lord Savaar's adjutant. He is currently in discussion with Marshal Hissel, the *Bruk*'s commander. He says he will join you in the hospitality suite as soon as we are ready for take-off. If you will follow me.' Sskeet breathed in, and Bernice listened to the strange sucking sound – Sskeet was clearly not used to making such long speeches, but seemed pleasant enough.

'Marvellous vessel you have here, Lieutenant Sskeet. The pride of the Federation, I suspect.' The Doctor indicated for Sskeet to lead on.

Sskeet nodded slowly as he plodded ahead of them, leading them along a plush corridor that, Bernice decided, made the Federation headquarters building look dowdy in comparison. 'It has an honourable history. We are proud that it has been selected for such an important Federation duty.'

'And an even more honourable class name. Izlyr. I met him once.' The Doctor ran his fingers along one of the picture frames that dotted the walls. 'Is there a picture of him aboard?'

Sskeet nodded again. 'It is in the command area. Perhaps you would like to see it sometime?'

'It would be an honour. Is he alive still? It was over a hundred years ago that we met.'

'Supreme Lord Izlyr retired to the planet Bennion about twenty years ago. I believe he is still there.' Sskeet suddenly stopped and indicated a plate on the wall. On it something was written on a plaque in Martian scripture. Bernice scrutinized it and realized that it said 'Hospitality' or something similar.

'Open,' hissed Sskeet. Bernice allowed an eyebrow to raise as part of the wall in front of her, along with the plate, momentarily shimmered. A rectangular space appeared and she could see into a room, although minuscule flickers of white dotted her vision now and again. The Doctor nodded at Sskeet and wandered through the space, so Bernice followed. As he came through, Sskeet again spoke into the air with a firm command of 'Close,' and the wall solidified behind them. 'The computer has evidently not been serviced adequately. I apologize. The engineer for this section will be admonished,' the Martian hissed.

'Not on our behalf, please,' said the Doctor. 'A few

stray molecules never hurt anyone.' He brushed some imaginary door particles off his white jacket. 'There,' he smiled. 'No problems at all.'

Bernice turned three hundred and sixty degrees, looking around the walls of the room and up. It was massive, a high ceiling beautifully decorated in pastel greens and quiet reds. Around the warm-looking walls were various decorations and artefacts and directly opposite was a smoked-glass-lined square recess with touch-sensitive controls above it.

Sskeet pointed towards the controls. 'The servicer will dispense any refreshment you require. It is programmed for Tellurian cuisine as well as one hundred and seventy other Federation delicacies.'

The Doctor sat heavily in one of the lounge chairs, soft cushions billowing slightly beneath him. 'Sskeet. You have been charming. We will sit here and await High Lord Savaar's presence in comfort. Thank you.'

With a nod Sskeet shuffled out, the door appearing and disappearing around him.

The Doctor pointed to a nearby *chaise longue* and Bernice sat herself down. 'Nice doors.'

'Holograms?'

The Doctor shook his head. 'No, just a computer-controlled refractive molecular arranger. Touch it and you'll find it solid. Keeps the warmth in and others out.' He looked across at it. 'Open,' he called softly. Sure enough, the space shimmered into existence and they could see the corridor outside. 'Close,' he said and it vanished. He turned back to Bernice. 'Just checking.'

'So, Doctor,' said Bernice, nodding her head at the wall where the door wasn't any more. 'So that's a Martian is it? Seems perfectly harmless to me.'

'Indeed, Benny. But I've had experience of the Ice Warriors before. I know what they're capable of.'

'Ice Warriors?'

'A name coined about, oh six hundred years ago – after your time. At one point, human archaeologists discovered

89

a long-lost Martian warship buried deep within a glacier in England.'

'A glacier? In England? You're joking! Aren't you?'

'I did say it was after your time. A result of some nasty solar flares.' The Doctor smiled at Bernice's bewilderment. 'Anyway,' he continued, 'they dug it up and named it an Ice Warrior. Looked just like Sskeet, in fact. Of course, most Martians of that era were like this lot – peaceful, but not Varga's ones.'

'Varga?'

'Leader of this crew. They had crashed on Earth millions of years ago, in the height of their death or glory days. Naturally, he wanted to claim Earth as part of the Martian empire. He never believed us that Mars was an Earth colony and little trace existed there of his people.'

'You told him, I suppose, about New Mars, and the changes?' Bernice realized she didn't need an answer to that. 'Okay, so you didn't. What happened?'

'Well, there was little reasoning with him, and eventually the humans destroyed him and his ship.'

'You of course, had no part in this murder.'

'Bernice, when you're stuck in a dangerous situation, the decisions you and others around you make don't always bear up under scrutiny, but at the time they seem logical and acceptable.'

Bernice nodded, not entirely convinced. 'And this one encounter turned you off all of them?'

'Oh no, no. I met them on Peladon the first time I went there and, you'll be pleased to know, had my nose put severely out of joint. Lord Izlyr – '

'Oh, the one you name-dropped earlier?'

'Yes, that's right, stop interrupting, thank you. Anyway, he was a good sort and we teamed up. The next time I went to Peladon – '

'So how many times have you been there?'

'Two. *Anyway,*' he said pointedly, 'the next time, a group of them were up to their old tricks. And I've seen a couple of other groups who bend the rules a little to favour a military solution. I mean, on Magnus – ' Bernice realized the Doctor could go on forever if she didn't interrupt him again.

'Okay Doctor, history lesson over, I think. Now, tell me about this place, Peladon. Why are we going, the commissioner's plea aside?'

The Doctor delved deep into a jacket pocket. Bernice had long suspected that, like the TARDIS's interior, the Doctor's clothes also existed in different dimensions. Most of them, she mentally added a little unkindly, dimensions where fashion was not a word that had ever been used. He always produced the most unlikely things from within them, and this time looked like being no exception.

'Ah ha!' The Doctor showed her a tiny sculpture. It was an animal of some sort, carved out of stone. It stood upright with clawed paws raised, as if ready to strike. Massive canine teeth jutted out of the snout, and a lethal-looking horn protruded from the top of its head. Shaggy fur was carved into the image and, all in all, Bernice decided it wasn't something she was in a hurry to meet. She said so.

'Not a problem,' the Doctor said, rather sadly. 'Aggedor is long dead. The planet Peladon is steeped in, to use your terms, a kind of medieval co-existence with technology. When I first visited, the planet was just entering the Federation, although the Pel traditionalists were against it, as were certain Federation members. Izlyr and I helped sort that out and the planet eventually became part of the Federation. I next went back around fifty years later, when Queen Thalira was enthroned. Pels don't have particularly long life spans, and their turn-over of monarchs is quite high. Thalira had to cope with an attack from an organization, helped by Ice Warriors, who wanted to overthrow the Federation. Peladon is a planet rich in trisilicate and the Federation mined it there. The terrorists set out to scupper the mining but again the evil was overthrown and I left. I haven't been back since. I gather this new King, Tarrol, has been ruler for two years, hence this prestigious occasion. Next question?'

Bernice shook her head. The Doctor wandered over to the servicer.

'Drink?'

'Just water please.'

'Coming up'. There was a short buzz and two large handleless crystal mugs materialized, a transparent liquid fizzing slightly inside. As the Doctor returned, he passed one to Bernice.

'Not exactly easy to hold, are they?' She indicated the mugs. The Doctor made a motion with his hands, imitating an Ice Warrior's clamp-like hands. Bernice nodded in understanding and sipped quietly on her drink.

It looked as if it was going to be an interesting voyage.

At around the same time that the Doctor and Bernice were boarding the *Bruk*, another, smaller ship was gaining a VIP passenger as well. The freighter *Arrow* was headed for the Rho system. There, it would deposit the majority of its cargo. Unknown to most of its crew apart from the captain and her first mate, the *Arrow* would then detour via Pakha where its VIP would disembark secretly. The captain was being well paid to do this irregular drop-off and keep her mouth firmly closed.

Currently squatting in the cargo hold was the VIP. Clad in a figure-hugging midnight black one-piece combat suit, she was a small but slender young woman. Her dark, creaseless clothing was only illuminated by the word 'ACE' emblazoned across the back in silver glitter. At her side, a wrist computer, a throat mike and a customized helmet made from the remains of a Dalek dome. She was clipping the computer onto her wrist when the cargo hold door opened far slower than it was designed to. She stroked a nearby blaster until she heard an already familiar curse and the door was given a swift kick. Although it didn't hurry the door up particularly, it evidently satisfied the aggressor's temper.

'Crukkin' doors! Never work.' As the door crawled the final few inches Ace smiled up at First Mate Bill Cook. 'Why can't we have RMAs I'll never know. Anyway,

Captain Riddler asked me to check on you.' He smiled through grease-stained face. His unfashionable stubble only endeared him to Ace; he was as much a rebel as she.

'Yeah, I'll bet she did.' Ace stood up, tucking the blaster into its slim holster down her right thigh.

'Didn't know we had a trained commando aboard,' muttered Cook.

Ace shook her head. 'Long time ago. Bit like riding a bike though, you never forget.'

'You want to eat with us, the crew or by yourself?'

'I ought to stay away from the crew but I could use some company.' Ace checked her chronometer.

'I'll come for you in about an hour, okay?' Cook turned to go.

'Cheers, Bill. And thanks to both you and the captain. I know you weren't given much choice, but both I and the Doctor appreciate this anyway.'

Bill Cook smiled again and nodded. 'Yeah. Well, we both owe him something and it adds a bit of spice to life. See you later.' The door slid closed far behind him far quicker than it had opened. Ace looked at her wrist computer into which the Doctor had programmed his instructions. She checked them for the fourth time. He was relying on her to get this done. 'Pakha, here I come,' she muttered.

'I'm bored.' Two words guaranteed to turn the Doctor's familiar hangdog expression further towards an imitation of a bloodhound. 'I'm bored, because I can't see anything.' Kort sulkily wrapped his arms around his small body, knees hugged up tight to chin, determinedly not catching the Doctor's eye. 'I'm also cold.'

'They're Martians, they need the cold.' Bernice had quite liked Kort back on Io. He was playful and innocent and clever. He was also on Io. Now, on board the *Bruk*, he was miserable, spoilt and incapable of doing anything except moaning. The initial play-acting on Io had developed into the real thing. It reminded Bernice of Ace in one of her moods. 'You get shot of one, only to get

93

another,' she muttered to herself, hoping the Doctor hadn't heard.

Kort had joined them a few moments before the *Bruk* took off from Io. He had waltzed in, head held high, dressed in full Cantryan regalia, claiming that 'Father' had given him what amounted to, in Bernice's eyes, *carte blanche* to be rude, snooty and demanding to everyone and everything.

Even Sskeet, normally hidden so well under his armour, was clearly flustered by the young orange humanoid. Bernice decided it didn't take an expert in human body posture and behaviour to know how close Sskeet had come to clumping Damakort round the back of the head when he'd complained the first time about the temperature. Bernice wasn't convinced she had the Martian's resolve and could foresee an occasion, probably within thirty seconds, when she would put the boy over her knee and smack some manners into him.

The Doctor, however, took the passive approach. He attempted to divert Kort's attention from the cold and bring a smile to his new young companion's normally cherubic features by 'discovering' a large coin in his left ear.

Kort looked at him as if he'd just been sick all over the floor and yelled far too loudly, 'Window! I want to see outside!'

Bernice groaned. She wanted to point out that the computer could hear him at normal volume, and it didn't need a Plasticine-level sound-check. Instead she sighed and watched as the Doctor patiently pointed out through the newly formed window.

'What exactly do you want to see?' he asked.

'Space. Stars. Something better than this room,' Kort over-dramatically gestured around them.

The Doctor unfurled himself and jauntily swung his umbrella around his wrist like a bad imitation of Charlie Chaplin. 'All right. Let's go and ask the marshal if he'll let you up onto his bridge. From there you'll see all the stars you'll ever want, twinkling, flashing and shooting past. You can be the Luke Skywalker of the Martian Fleet.'

Kort wrinkled his orange button nose. 'Luke who?' With a little sigh the Doctor took him by the arm and headed for where the door ought to be, telling Bernice that they'd be back shortly. As Bernice watched them disappear, she looked up above the assigned space and shook her head. She stared in awe. Above the door area was something that simply couldn't be there. Surely it wasn't . . .

She walked over to get a better look. It was a sword. But not just any sword, if she knew her Martian history. It was slightly curved, not quite as much as an eighteenth-century cutlass, but enough of a curve to make it a formidable slicing weapon. Down one side it was lethally thin and sharp, but on the underside it was peppered with ferocious barbs, with tiny and almost imperceptible twists on each point. Just one look told Bernice that she could never carry it, it clearly weighed too much. Indeed, she doubted many humans could carry it. It was a Martian weapon from their very ancient past.

It was the legendary sacred sword of Tuburr. The stories went that in their warrior past, the young Martians would take an endurance test of survival. It had often crossed Bernice's mind that before the Earth terraformers arrived, just living for five seconds on the surface of Mars would have been a sufficient endurance test. Mars was nowhere near as cold as, say, Pluto but even so, Earth's harshest arctic ice storms would be a doddle compared to a Martian storm. That's why she admired the race so much – they 'weathered' things so well. Maybe the name Ice Warrior wasn't such a bad one after all.

The young Martians, if they survived their time outside on the tundra, armourless and weaponless (some reports said it was a week, others put it at a far more unreasonable month), then took the oath of Tuburr – apparently the first great warrior, who had made the Martians what they are. Or rather, were. This oath involved them plucking the shaft of Tuburr's sword from the heart of a red-hot brazier with their bare hands. Many archaeologists theorized that this was the reason Martians wore huge clamp-like gloves, because originally the young warriors' fingers would have been fused together permanently. Personally, Bernice had always doubted that. It seemed more likely that it was merely a convenient glove shape. One day she'd ask to see a Martian's bare hand and count the fingers.

Bernice pulled herself away from this fascinating aspect of history and wandered over to the drinks dispenser. She was really quite intrigued by the splendour of the ship they were on; a Deep Space Izlyr-class cruiser, normally used for carrying parties of diplomats to and from different parts of Federation space for crucial meetings or highly regarded social functions. Sometimes, the Doctor had told her, the ship itself hosted conferences, especially where delegations demanded neutral ground for discussion.

All around her were trappings of varying cultures; token reflections of the various races and delegations that frequented the lounge. She ran her hand over an ornate tapestry which showed a picture of women drinking by a stream. As her hand glided over the surface, the picture shimmered and changed, the women had moved, the drink was gone and someone was playing what Bernice assumed was a musical instrument. Intrigued, she touched it a second time and the picture changed once more – now displaying the same women riding horse-like animals, playing a polo-like game. The musician was still there, but he'd been joined by two fellows.

On the furthest wall, hanging next to the refreshments servicer, were a collection of differing lengths of solid Perspex-looking piping. Near to the drink dispenser the Doctor had used were an array of objects in a glass case. Bernice recognized an ancient stethoscope and a scalpel but the rest appeared totally alien to her. She wandered over and looked at a tiny placard, written in four languages, one of which was Earth Standard, another High Martian. She opted for the latter, deciding to test her knowledge of the language. It stated that the items were medical implements from through the ages, donated to the ship by the famous Calfedorian hospital and science base, Cal-Med One. As Bernice approached the drink servicer, another door in the suite appeared behind her with the tiniest of air-hisses and she turned slightly.

'They were donated by our previous Federation Chair after his final tour of duty as a Draconian ambassador. His last major investigation took place in the Calfedorian system and he was given the cabinet as a parting gift. On succession to the leadership, he generously allowed this craft to display them.'

Bernice swallowed. No matter how many times she had met the person who had just spoken, she could never stop being in total awe and – if she were honest – complete fear of him.

High Lord Savaar strode towards her, his small booted feet markedly slimmer and more obviously regal than Sskeet's clumsy, heavy shoebox-like soles. Savaar casually waved his arm towards the drink dispenser. 'Refreshment?' he asked.

Bernice just nodded her throat suddenly drier than ever.

The Ice Lord looked at her impassively and then pressed a few buttons with his stubby fingers. Fingers! She was right! Bernice realized that this was the first time she had seen Savaar, indeed any Martian, without their armoured uniform or helmet on.

She remembered her first sight of Savaar, a few hours earlier, before luncheon. Having finally got used to Sskeet hovering around, she had been further surprised when shortly after Damakort's arrival, High Lord Savaar had entered the lounge, his body encased in a much sleeker and smoother body armour, a flowing green cape flecked with silver, a smooth domed helmet and less bulky glove-clamps.

'Aha,' the Doctor had whispered. 'An Ice Lord.'

Now, as he stood in the VIP lounge of the DSIC *Bruk*, she could see the man behind the mask, to coin a phrase. She luckily stopped an involuntary shudder at Savaar's green reptilian features, heavily knobbled and lined, his black serpentine eyes staring directly at her, two eyelids nictitating sideways over each eye with alarming frequency.

He still wore his long flowing cape, but the armour had been replaced by black leathery trousers and a tight-fitting cotton-looking jerkin, a red sash from shoulder to waist down his left side which denoted his very high rank. One thing that had not changed was his imposing stature – he towered above Bernice, almost bending at the knees as he offered her a tall glass of brown liquid. Condensation had gathered around the rim of it, a faint wisp of steam flickering upwards.

'I believe this is a particular delicacy of your excellent planet,' he rasped, taking a sip of a similar drink he had ordered for himself.

Bernice remembered what the Doctor had said on Io. She was, after all, the Martian expert and mentally shook herself. She bowed slightly. '*Dass hunnur, ssli hoos-urr Savaar.*'

Savaar cocked his head slightly, his tongue moistening his lips. '*Ssperr hunnur urr tass, Shsurr.*' He stood up straight. 'I am frankly honoured by your greeting, Professor. I had not realized that our most ancient customs were that well known outside Martian inner society.'

'Oh, I get around, my Lord. Besides, I am deeply flattered by your reply. I understood that I would have to have been married into your family for such an honourable statement.'

Savaar waved his hand theatrically. 'I have not been home for many years, Professor. The opportunity to . . . to demonstrate my familial greetings is most welcome.'

Bernice grinned. 'I hope we shall have more such opportunities, my Lord. Now, here's one of my familial greetings.' She raised her glass in a toast. 'Chin-chin!'

She took the glass to her lips, then drank. Her throat nearly exploded and she managed to turn a yelp into a slight cough. 'What . . . what exactly is it?' she gasped.

Savaar looked concerned, inquiring whether he had

chosen the wrong drink. Bernice shook her head, saying it was very nice, just far stronger than she had expected.

'Irish cream, I believe it is called. I thought it best to warm it for you. I am aware how much of a discomfort the temperature aboard the *Bruk* must be for you. Unfortunately, to raise it further would impair the function of the marshal and his crew.'

Ignoring the fact that the drink was nothing like any Irish cream she'd ever tasted, she nodded again, finally finding her voice and mettle again. 'Anyway, Nice ship you've got, my Lord,' she said.

Savaar regarded his Tellurian guest with quiet interest, keeping his attention on her eyes which seemed to burn with an almost obsessive curiosity. Her body was slightly taller than her humanoid companion, the Doctor. She wore her dark hair short, one strand drooping uselessly towards her left eye. Savaar was no expert on Tellurian fashion, but he suspected that this was a deliberate affectation to enhance whatever attraction she had to the male Tellurians. She was slender, but not thin – her tight-fitting red top showed her feminine curves and a degree of muscle unusual in a female. She had clearly worked hard – her academic appellation was probably earned rather than just bestowed. Savaar admired that: Martian hierarchy was built upon achievement rather than linear privilege. Her trousers, chinos he had heard her refer to them, were loose-fitting, a complete contrast to her top garment. He could see the pockets contained many items, but Sskeet's subtle scans as she had boarded the *Bruk* revealed no hidden weapons.

He noticed that she had a satchel slung over her shoulder and attached to her belt was a flask – clearly containing liquid refreshment of some sort. He wondered if the dispenser on board the *Bruk* was not to her satisfaction. He was quite surprised when she touched it.

'It's all right. I actually prefer the stuff you've got here, my Lord. I only carry this out of habit.'

He nodded, intrigued. There was more to this Professor

Summerfield than he had assumed. Apart from a quite astounding knowledge of protocol, she was clearly capable of reading physical language. Something rare in Tellurians, towards Martians at least. In many ways an advantage for a warrior, but in this case, a distinct disadvantage for him. He would keep a careful eye on this development. He was not entirely sure of her motivations. Was she there simply because she was the Doctor's associate? As an archaeologist, what exactly would her role on Peladon be? Something to ponder later, perhaps. He smiled and waved the title away, 'Please, in this room, all Federation representatives are equal in rank and status.'

Bernice thanked him politely and then, desperate for something else to say, pointed at the Perspex piping and asked what they were.

Savaar strode over, and she noted how well he carried himself, his eight-foot, slender but muscular body held with shoulders back, military-style. 'These are wind chimes from the planet designated S14.' He ran his hand along them very delicately, much to Bernice's surprise. The most beautiful and soothing musical notes floated out of the chimes and she found herself smiling at the sound. 'Beautiful. From Deva Loka, eh?'

'I am glad that you appreciate the music. And the planet's own heritage rather than its Federation installed classification,' Savaar said.

Bernice grinned, warming to the imposing warrior. 'I wonder what Danny Pain would have made of those,' she quipped.

Although the reference was totally lost on Savaar, he graciously smiled at what he rightly assumed was her humour. He sipped his own drink and bowed his head slightly in her direction. 'I regret I must take my leave of you now, *Shsurr*. My work absorbs a great deal of my time.'

Bernice paused and looked Savaar straight in the eye.

He had twice used the phrase *Shsurr*, a phrase from the High Martian dialect. 'May I ask one last question?'

'With pleasure.' He bowed slightly again.

Bernice pointed to the sword above the door. 'Is that what I think it is? The sacred sword of Tuburr? Here, on this ship?'

'You have studied our history?'

'Well, a little. I'm an archaeologist by trade. High Martian history is a favourite subject of mine.'

'Mine as well, *Shsurr*.' Again, that word. Savaar indicated the sword and nodded. 'It is a replica. The original is, alas, no more. Like all great objects from history, one day it is there, the next the books make no further references to it.'

'It's a very good replica. Do you think the original was stolen?'

Bernice was convinced that a look of consternation crossed Savaar's leathery face, and his black eyes flicked from side to side a little too quickly. If he was put out, however, his voice betrayed nothing.

'It has been suggested that when my people . . . changed their attitudes many centuries ago, the sacred sword was deliberately lost, hidden on Olympus Mons, as it represented a darker time. As an explorer of the past, you must be aware that while the people of one era consider an item of custom a worthless embarrassment, future generations regret its loss.'

'And recreate it?'

Savaar smiled. 'The image or the ideals?'

Bernice wondered if this was all a game to him. 'Maybe both?'

They were interrupted by the far door reappearing, revealing the Doctor and a still very bored-looking Damakort.

Without taking his eyes off Bernice, Savaar lowered his head again.

'As you say, *Shsurr*, maybe both.' A brief polite nod in Damakort's direction and he created a doorway in the same place that he had entered through.

101

Bernice finished her drink and looked over at the Doctor and his charge. Kort immediately began discovering the joys of the wind chimes, but clearly had no grasp of harmony or melody. Bernice metaphorically gritted her teeth.

'I'm so glad you're enjoying yourself, Benny. I thought you might get bored as well. So, how's your new friend?'

'Charming. Very charming. Which is more than I can say for some around here.' That last remark was clearly aimed at Kort who, having given up proving that tone-deafness was not just a peculiarity of humans, was now making the polo-playing people in the picture move at an alarming rate.

The Doctor sat on a huge padded seat, so large that his feet came off the ground, and rested his chin on the crook of his umbrella, one of his favourite positions when pondering a puzzle. 'What did he want?'

'We talked about this room. And the sacred sword. He was pleased that I knew my Martian history.' Bernice flopped into a cross-legged position on the floor in front of him. It occurred to her that she probably looked like a puppy trying to please its master. Oh well.

'Yes. I'm sure he was.' The Doctor nodded to himself. 'Showed a lot of interest, did you?'

'Well, I know enough about Martian culture to know when to be polite.'

The Doctor heaved himself out of the chair and wandered over to the Deva Lokan wind chimes. 'Indeed, you do. That's why I wanted you here, not Ace. That and the fact that you're not likely to start chucking bon-bon bombs at courtiers.' He picked up a nearby mask from some apparently primitive culture and placed it over his face. As he spoke through it, his voice became distorted, changing octaves regularly. 'What a nice Ice Lord. I mean, here he is, in charge of a diplomatic mission to Peladon, and yet he still finds time to come and chat to you.' The Doctor put down the mask and continued: 'And he even used the phrase *Shsurr* on you. The Martians equivalent

102

to M'Lady, and a very complimentary phrase in Martian society.'

'Yes, I know that.'

'Ah, but he expected you to know it. You've been showing off your Martian diplomacy. But I also knew it. And he knew I did. And I knew he knew I did. And . . . and I also let slip to Sskeet that I'd known Izlyr.'

'So?'

'So, if they named an entire class of spaceship after him, Izlyr must have gone on to be pretty high-ranking after I met him. Supreme Lord Izlyr! Either they are genuinely impressed with my meandering through Martian hierarchy, or Savaar is bluffing me, trying to take me down a peg or two.'

'I know how he feels sometimes,' said Bernice.

'But why? What are the Ice Warriors up to that I have to be put in my place? My connections and your knowledge of Martian history and culture mixed with your inquisitiveness seem to upset them somehow. I wonder why?'

High Lord Savaar, now redressed in his full military clothing, strode angrily into the command area. Hissel, his own similarly domed helmet glittering with the jewels that designated his rank, turned to greet him, but only managed to half-raise his arm in salute before Savaar angrily waved the gesture away.

'The Doctor suspects me of treachery.'

Hissel looked up in surprise. 'How can you tell, Excellency?'

Savaar produced a tiny black box from within his robe. 'Run: previous four.' A recording of the Doctor's reasoning played.

'He is clever,' stated Hissel, 'but not clever enough. Everything he says now, we will hear.'

Savaar looked at Hissel in resigned annoyance, thinking not for the first time that Hissel must have more class on his side than brains. There was no other way he could have become a marshal. 'Of course the Doctor suspects we're listening to him, why else go to such an elaborate charade? He's testing me as much as I'm testing him.'

Stung by the reprimand, Hissel returned to his controls and merely commented that they were approaching Peladon.

For the first time Savaar smiled, and then hissed gleefully. 'A worthy opponent, this Doctor. Or an indispensable associate. I wonder which he will prove to be?'

On the planet below, preparations were being made.

In the Citadel, decorations were being set up, Pel guards doing their best to make King Tarrol's restatement day as auspicious and spectacular as possible. Lianna, the lady-of-the-court, oversaw everything, just as she had when she had been lady-in-waiting to Queen Thalira.

In his royal quarters, King Tarrol and Chancellor Geban were discussing how to receive the Federation visitors. Atissa stood quietly by the doorway, listening but aware that her input would be unwise and unwelcome at this stage.

In the Federation Representatives' quarters, Nic Reece and Alpha Centauri, the two incumbent Federation representatives, were examining recently transmitted details of Savaar and his crew, and were somewhat surprised to discover that three non-Martians were among them.

'Surely, it cannot be . . . *the* Doctor?' squeaked one of them in delight.

The holocrews bustled around, getting in everyone's way, but Keri didn't care. As far as she was concerned, the Pels were in *her* way. Yeah!

Below, deep within the catacombs of Mount Megeshra, in what had once been the Federation refinery but what was now a forgotten area, dark, foreboding shapes moved around in the gloom. They monitored everything that occurred in the castle hundreds of feet above them, listening in to innocent conversations with hidden surveillance equipment, illegal under Pel law but well concealed from all prying eyes.

And amongst all that, one person out of the thousands that populated Peladon plotted and schemed. Stealthily integrated into Pel society, he waited. Waiting for his chance to strike out and claim his prize, regardless of the cost to life and tradition, to culture and to peace. Patiently he observed everything. Before too long, Peladon would witness turmoil of the variety it had never known before and, like a spider at the heart of its web, he would be there to ensnare his prize, and laugh at his victims. The same way he had laughed as Jina died in front of him. The same way he laughed as he had casually shot O'Brien in the back after feigning a job for him.

However, the man who had once been known as Alec on the planet Pakha had not foreseen everything. He had not predicted the arrival of the Doctor.

3:

Machine and Soul

The hanger had been carved out of rock nearly one hundred years previously. Once Peladon had been accepted into the Federation upon the recommendation of Delegate Izlyr and Senior Delegate Amazonia, the first change that the planet's new benefactors insisted upon was the creation of an area where Federation shuttles could land and be protected. As Peladon didn't possess the right atmospheric conditions to enable the temperamental matter transporters to be installed, a vast cavern was hewn near the top of Mount Megeshra, although on the far side of the Citadel's placement, once known as the dark side. A network of tunnels was mined by Geban's forefathers to enable swift and secure transit between the hanger and the delegates' conference rooms.

Geban stood just outside the suite of rooms, trying not to feel impatient. The alien delegate from Alpha Centauri was a pleasant if visually alarming person but had a tendency to take three hours to do something that would take Geban three minutes. Preparing to meet the *Bruk*'s shuttle had been in Centauri's schedule of events for some days now but the news that it was almost landed had sent the fussy hexapod into hysterics.

'I must make sure everything is all right for such dignitaries,' he had trilled in his ridiculously high-pitched voice. At least, Geban always thought of Centauri as a 'he' although strictly speaking 'he' was neither he nor she but an 'it'. A hermaphrodite: all of Centauri's people apparently looked identical. A green helmet-shaped head with one cyclopean watery eye dead centre, looking out and blinking at an alarming rate. Six arms waved around over-dramatically every time Centauri gesticulated to underline whatever exaggerated point he was making, and whenever he walked (Geban had never seen whatever passed for feet under Centauri's yellow wrap-around robe), his whole figure bobbed up and down as if in perpetual deferential respect. Quite a useful attribute in such a hierarchical society, but nevertheless an attribute that quickly induced dizziness if you tried to count how many times Centauri bobbed per minute.

Despite those potentially aggravating characteristics, Alpha Centauri was immensely popular with both the Federation and the Pels. He had lived on the planet ever since King Peladon of Peladon oversaw his planet's enrolment, Centauri claiming that he never really missed his home planet because Peladon offered a rich vein of intelligent and diverse people and personalities. This suited the Federation, who needed a permanent representative situated there, and suited Peladon because Centauri was about as inoffensive as it was possible to imagine without being nauseating.

Geban smiled as Centauri finally wobbled towards him. 'My apologies, Chancellor, for keeping you waiting. Mister Reece and I wanted to ensure that the Cantryan would feel comfortable with the temperature of his quarters. Although Peladon is such a frightfully cold planet he may –'

Geban held up a hand in understanding. 'Of course, Ambassador. But I really think we ought to be on our way.'

Centauri's normally olive-green head and arms glowed a peculiar jaundiced yellow for a second. 'You don't think they will be angered at waiting, do you? Only, I respect your thoughts on this for as a chancellor you have to be such a diplomat and you must feel free to chastise me if I am causing –'

Again, Geban waved his protestations aside. 'Ambassador, really, there are no problems. Let us go, *now.*'

Geban emphasized the last work, thus brooking no further delays from the small monocranial figure beside him.

For a second Centauri stared up at Geban, and slowly blinked his one very watery eye. 'You are correct, Chancellor. I am just a silly – '

Geban could see where this was leading and started walking, knowing Centauri would keep up. He decided to lead the conversation. 'Mister Reece is not joining us, I assume?'

Centauri coughed lightly – which reminded Geban of the pitch necessary to shatter glass goblets – and waved three or four arms aimlessly. 'I did try to persuade him but as you know he's not really a man of – ' Centauri paused, searching for a polite word.

'Protocol?' ventured Geban.

'Indeed,' confirmed Centauri, much to Geban's relief. Ploughing through Centauri's mental thesaurus to find the right word to describe Nic Reece wasn't something he relished. However, Geban had to admit that words to describe Reece weren't the easiest and most traditional to come up with. Tall, muscular, with boyish looks that belied his age, he could pass for a human in his mid-twenties but, although his contact with humans was reasonably limited, Geban guessed he was nearer his mid-thirties. A good age for Pels but still young for a human. How lucky humans were to live to such spans as one hundred and twenty plus. Medical science had not really enabled the average Pel to live much over sixty-five, although that was a direct benefit from the Federation. Prior to their arrival, the average Pel only lived until their early fifties. For miners it was usually ten less, due to the thin atmosphere in the mines.

Reece had been on Peladon for about two years now, baring the odd extended vacation on Earth with his family. He was a happy man who apparently enjoyed his work, but never let it dominate. The moment he had arrived on the planet, he had gone out of his way to meet everyone and be friendly. He had a passionate interest in the planet's heritage which, Geban suspected, accounted for his notion of opening the planet up as a museum and gallery. However, Geban also suspected that it pained him almost as much as it pained the Pels to suggest this.

Geban liked Reece and knew that the feeling was mutual. He hadn't spoken to him much recently – since returning from his last break Reece had hidden himself away or been dodging Atissa. Geban didn't blame him. He'd also noted that Reece clearly knew Neal Corry from the video station. Another friend from afar. Still, once the restatement celebrations were over, he knew Reece would be back in circulation.

A squeak from Centauri alerted him to the fact that the shuttle was arriving – the roar could be heard this far into the caverns – and together they hurried along.

Having got used to the smooth, almost imperceptible movement of the TARDIS, Bernice sat rigid beside Sskeet as they juddered into the cavern, the steady roar of the shuttle echoing even inside the craft. As they slowed to a stop, she let out a breath she hadn't realized she'd been holding. As she turned to look behind her she saw Kort staring wildly through one of the windows, an excited glimmer in his eyes.

'Ground floor. Peladon and assorted treasures,' she quipped as the Doctor used his umbrella to point out a couple of tall guards waiting for them. Kort was nodding. Savaar marched over, also indicating out of the window with a clamp. 'I see that, as I suspected, the Federation representative is late.'

'Look,' said Bernice. 'Here comes someone ... or thing ...' She caught a waspish look from the Doctor. So, she thought, it was all right for him to dislike Ice Warriors because they were reptilian, but she wasn't allowed to be put off by a green lollipop wearing a yellow smock. Typical of the man. Savaar, meanwhile, was hissing satisfactorily. 'Ah. At last. Ambassador Alpha Centauri arrives. I wonder who that is with him.'

'One of the miners, judging by his hair.'

'You are familiar with Pel ... fashions, then, Doctor?'

inquired Savaar, putting his helmeted head at a slight angle.

The Doctor ignored the sarcasm and simply replied, 'No. You just have to know their customs. Most Pels wear their hair long and slicked back, the traditional mauve stripe therefore highlighted. The miners, however, dye theirs black with white flecks and wear it wide and bushy. It keeps the roak dust out of the eyes and ears.'

Bernice leaned over the back of her chair. 'Excuse me for asking, but if this is such a feudal state, why is a miner greeting what must, in effect, be like visiting royalty?'

The Doctor swung round, jabbing his umbrella at her. 'And you, Professor Summerfield, ought to know better than to rely on textbook descriptions and evaluations.'

Kort snorted in derision. 'Instead of arguing, why don't we get out of this shuttle and go and say hello?' All eyes turned to look at him. 'Well, it seems the polite thing to do.'

As Sskeet operated the door controls, Bernice muttered something about the word 'polite' not being in Kort's normal dictionary, to which the Doctor mumbled back something about leopards changing their spots when it suits them. Unable to work out whether he meant Kort, the Martians or herself, Bernice picked up her orange woolly sweater and followed the Doctor out into the cool Peladon cavern.

King Tarrol sat on his throne. Around him, courtiers and requisitioned guards were decorating the room with brightly coloured banners and pendants. Near the door Neal Corry was telling a smartly dressed Pakha holocam operator where exactly to aim the lenses. All that could be done to make the restatement vows as important, resplendent and fun as possible was being done, but something was gnawing at the king's heart. Something Atissa had said a few days before. Something about Aggedor feeling mocked and seeking retribution. Tarrol was not a superstitious man deep down, yet something made him wonder whether what he and Geban usually dismissed as hokum from Atissa's over-active imagination might have a grain of truth in it. Could he, Tarrol, be the first royal victim of Aggedor's many prophesies and curses? Did he have the right to so easily dismiss his ancestry? He had two days before the vows to make up his mind. Would he accept Nic Reece's proposals or would Atissa's fanaticism win him over? Either way, his restatement speech would reflect his ideals and drive for Peladon's future development under his reign.

Surely no king or queen in history had to make such difficult decisions.

'It's bloody dark down here! Where's the frobbin' flashlight?' Fehler stumbled forward swearing and cursing his way towards the supplies box. Behind him Professor Sharrod was wrapping up their abseiling gear.

'For heaven's sake, Fehler, do stop whining. Your eyes will get adjusted to the dark in no time at all. Just do what I did – as we entered the darkness, close one eye. Your brain then adjusts quicker and you can see instantly in the dark.'

Fehler muttered something incoherent about mohrrübe, but Professor Sharrod was now engaged in ceremoniously unclipping his flashlight from his beltpack. He liked to make every move a dramatic one, flourishing his tools of the trade with outrageous flair, as if thirty thousand people were watching him. Fehler tutted to himself as his own flashlight illuminated the cave system in front of them. He'd been the professor's assistant ever since they'd met at university, drawn by the middle-aged don's complete devotion to archaeology and single-minded determination not to let political or personal sniping affect his decisions about where or what he worked upon. Fehler was totally devoted to Sharrod, but of course would never let it show.

'Fehler! Fehler! Get back here, m'boy! Look at this!'

With a sigh, Fehler turned back and saw the professor crouching by a pile of pebbles.

'What is it, Professor? Fossilized Pakha droppings?'

'Don't be ungracious, Fehler. It's their planet we're on, remember?'

'They're not likely to hear me down here, are they?' Fehler shook his head and crouched down.

'Under ... here ...' The professor was tugging at the pebbles. Fehler frowned. They didn't look heavy enough to cause that much exertion.

'It's as if ... they're magnetic ... attracted to whatever they're burying!' the professor wheezed. Fehler added his younger strength to the struggle and moments later the pebbles were all pulled away.

Revealed was a small circular object. Although grimy and battered, Fehler could see a brass – or was it golden? ... colouration. Dowdy gems adorned what Fehler could only assume was the front.

'It's a circlet or crown of some sort.'

Sharrod was nodding enthusiastically. 'You know what it is, of course! You know what we've found!'

Fehler suddenly felt a chill go through his body. As if someone had walked over his grave ... He shuddered and looked at Professor Sharrod. For a second he could have sworn that the professor's face was illuminated from below, as if the circlet had been brand new and shiny, not old, battered and covered in Pakha's carbon dust. Sharrod looked up and Fehler stepped back in alarm at the professor's intensity. His eyes seemed to be ... 'possessed' was the only thought that entered Fehler's brain.

'Professor Sharrod, I think we should tell someone about this.'

Sharrod turned back to the circlet, sharply. 'No! No, this is mine ...' He breathed in slowly. 'After thousands of years, we ... *I* ... have found what others had sought. The rumours, the legends and the mysteries are solved. I have the Pakha Ancient Diadem. Never again will anyone mock me. No one will scorn my theories or discoveries ...'

Fehler tugged at the professor's sleeve. 'No one ever did, Professor ...'

'Oh, yes, they did. Everyone mocked me. Sharrod the Fruitcake, isn't that what you students called me? You all thought I didn't know, didn't see the smirks! But I did, Fehler! You're just as guilty!'

Fehler was getting worried. Sharrod's normally mild, almost submissive and absent-minded demeanour had vanished. Fehler didn't care for the aggressive, paranoiac professor now facing him.

'Professor, let's take your discovery back up top. Let Vega Lexus examine it –'

Sharrod lunged towards Fehler, an unnaturally strong palm slapping into the student's chest, sending him sprawling on his back. 'That . . . that shrew thing!' Sharrod was spitting as he spoke, his face twisted in unreasoning fury. 'That alien creature! I wouldn't give it the time of day!' He lunged forward and scooped up the Diadem, wrapping it in the folds of his safari jacket. He unravelled the coiled abseiling plastic rope from his tool pack.

'Up!' he snapped. Like an artificial snake, the hooked end of the rope flicked forward and then darted up into the darkness. After a few seconds, while Sharrod just stared at the bundle under his jacket, an electronic beeping told him the rope had tethered itself to the next available ledge. Clipping the bottom of the rope into his belt-hooks, Sharrod grabbed it and, without a glance at the dazed Fehler, shouted, 'Pull!' He started to rise as the plastic rope tugged him upwards.

Fehler stared at the professor's form departing into almost pitch darkness. He thought he could see the professor illuminated faintly by his flashlight. As he stepped forward, his foot kicked something. He shone his light on it – it was the professor's torch. He looked up again and then realized: the professor's illumination was from the Diadem as it glowed with renewed energy.

Bill Cook lay back and smiled. Lazily he reached out and wrapped an arm around his sleeping partner. Her soft but regular breathing amused him – such fire and drive when awake, such stillness and innocence when asleep. He stroked her pony-tailed brown hair, rubbing a couple of strands between his fingers. He wondered what her mis-

113

sion was – she hadn't been one for pillow talk – straight into action, no playful coyishness or flirtation. She was trained military: even a civilian servicer like him could tell that. She was obviously used to deep-space missions on her own, she travelled lightly, anything she needed was attached securely to her body suit. Her conversation whenever he brought her food always neatly steered away from any details about what she was actually up to. Apart from her name being Ace, he'd actually learned very little about her. He shrugged mentally. Did it really matter?

He heard a click outside his door and turned his head slightly.

Before he could register anything else, he was aware of a sudden blur of movement across his field of vision as the door slid open. Framed in the doorway, bright corridor lights silhouetting the figure, was Captain Riddler. He knew it was her by the sudden exclamation of 'Cruk!' she gave. It took him a second to say, 'Lights' and another second to see the cause of Riddler's consternation.

Ace was totally naked, but evidently that didn't concern her. She had her blaster jammed tight into Riddler's cheek, her left hand patting Riddler's waist, obviously looking for a weapon.

Cook waited until she'd finished the frisk before he spoke.

'Er . . . Ace, meet Captain Riddler.' He tried to smile. He failed to convince either of them he meant it. 'Ace . . . meet Captain Riddler . . .' he tailed off helplessly.

Without taking her eyes off Riddler and keeping her blaster levelled, Ace walked back towards the side of the bed she'd slept on. With professional ease she scooped up her discarded body suit, tossed her blaster into her left hand and began pulling it on. The blaster never wavered, even as it was returned to her right hand as she completed her dressing. As she finished Ace lowered the gun, sliding it into the holster on her thigh. She shook her head as if clearing it of cobwebs and without a glance back at Cook marched through the door. At the last second she looked back and stared at Riddler.

'Sorry, Captain.'

Riddler stared back, then spoke. 'For sticking a gun in my cheek or for being in my cabin?'

'Take your pick. Probably both.' Ace turned and walked away, aware that Riddler's gaze was following her. She looked back momentarily. 'Yeah. Definitely both.' She watched Riddler go into the room, and the door slid closed. A second later and she heard Cook scream in pain. Ace smiled slightly. She knew exactly what Riddler must have kicked to get that level of pain out of a man.

Ace managed to get back to her cargo hold via the same rarely used back routes and service areas that Cook had used to get her to his – and as it turned out, Riddler's – room. She kept in the shadows just in case one of the night-shift crew saw her. But that was unlikely. She was too good at her job for that.

Ten minutes later she was curled up in a foetal ball. Asleep but, as always, subconsciously aware, ready for action. Hugged tightly in her hands, as a child hugs a teddy bear, was her blaster. The one she'd been examining in the TARDIS computer room.

Hyn't'n always prided himself on his work. In fact he was so proud, he would go in the tavernas at night, lean on the bar and surreptitiously tell the barman and anyone else in earshot exactly what top-secret job he was doing. Ironically, it was only because most Pakhars thought he was a consummate liar that he managed to successfully carry on his business. Someone feeling generous could claim that Hyn't'n was a master of the double bluff. Someone being practical could far more accurately claim that however good Hyn't'n was at his job, he was a great security risk and one day someone would have to shut him up.

Sadler looked down at Hyn't'n. 'I never liked snits and pimps. Especially big-mouthed ones who sit in bars and tell everyone what their employers are looking for!'

Hyn't'n glanced behind her. Cooper and Townsend were sitting on a table, wryly watching Sadler. Lambert was ignoring them all; he was staring out of Hyn't'n's hutch window. The little Pakhar desperately wanted to swallow but Sadler's tight grip prevented him from even breathing properly. He tried to squeak but all that happened was his whiskers twitched more frantically.

'Nothing to say, Sadler. What a shame.' Cooper started to stand up and immediately bumped her head on the low ceiling. 'Cruk! Stupid little rodents. Stupid little houses!' She sat again, rubbing her crown. Townsend smiled slightly, but Hyn't'n was not sure whether this was at Cooper's discomfort, her abuse of Pakhars in general or Hyn't'n's own situation.

'So,' Sadler continued, squeezing just a bit tighter. 'Just how much did you blab in your drunken binge last night?'

Hyn't'n's reply was a strangled squeak of panic.

Sadler seemed to relax her grip slightly. But only slightly. 'Sorry, didn't quite hear that?'

'Nothing . . . I said nothing . . .' Hyn't'n stammered. 'I wouldn't say anything that would jeopardize our deal! Believe me!'

It had all gone horribly wrong, the Pakhar decided. He had a reputation, he knew, with offworlders. Although many Federation citizens believed Pakha to be the perfect tourist spot, a great deal of crime, petty and large, took place in the Rho system, and Pakha was as good a laundering spot for people and smuggled goods as ever. The more people believed in its integrity, the easier it was to hide its squalor.

These four Tellurian mercenaries had contacted Hyn't'n five days before, after their shuttle (apparently the third they'd used since leaving Japetus) had arrived at Space Dock Seven. They had wanted maps, information and currency to get them to the Wavis Ravine. Hyn't'n of course knew how to help them, just as he always knew how to help such groups. His fame obviously spread far and wide by word of mouth; he never needed to advertise – everyone just came to him. And never had anything

gone wrong. Until now. Somehow, the mercenaries suspected they were being followed. For some reason, they
blamed Hyn't'n. He couldn't understand why. Unless the
man from the *Arrow* had betrayed him. But he'd seemed
so reliable . . .

'Please . . . let me go . . .' he choked.

'All right,' said Townsend. 'We're finished here. Let's
get to the caves before our shadow finds us. With any luck
we'll be off Pakha before she even arrives.'

For a second Hyn't'n relaxed – they were going to leave.
Then he knew, with the same realization that anything
doomed suddenly becomes supernaturally aware of, that
he was in danger. The last thing Hyn't'n had time to think
of was that he wasn't going to get to the bar tonight.

Sadler smiled at the satisfying crunch mixed with a
sound like fabric tearing. Then she relaxed her grip and
reached over, pulling the dead Pakhar off her other hand.
Her fingers were soaked in blood and gore where they
had dug right into Hyn't'n's throat. Wiping the blood off
on the corpse she followed the other three out, stopping
briefly to open a small cupboard. She picked up a small
tin and as she left the hutch she tugged it open. Inside
was the credit slip they'd paid Hyn't'n with. 'No point in
letting money go to waste,' she thought as she pocketed
the slip. Casually she tossed the tin into a nearby bush
and caught up with Townsend, Lambert and Cooper.

'I enjoyed that,' she said to no one in particular.

No one replied.

Some time later, Ace stood over the dead Pakhar. On her
computer, a transcript of the mission details the Doctor
had beamed across to the TARDIS from the Federation
Headquarters on Io before he and Benny had left.

Ace wasn't disappointed to be missing the events on
Peladon. She guessed that the Doctor knew she wouldn't
fit in too well. Being polite and courteous to kings and
queens when people were dying wasn't really her.
Benny was far better at that. She smiled slightly. Bet

117

she was missing out on some young stud, though. Lucky Benny.

She nudged Hyn't'n's body with her foot and then knelt down. Waving the flies from the creature's shredded throat, she touched his fur. Cold but not rigid. For a brief second, a memory flashed through her mind. A memory of school. Of being Hamster Monitor in Miss Marshall's class. Of coming in at eight one morning to find both hamsters dead. Of touching them. Cold but not rigid. Dead about three hours, Miss Marshall had guessed. Any longer and the bodies would have been immobile. Ace had suspected that Boyle creep of sneaking into the school at night and suffocating them – it was the sort of thing he'd do just to get at her. To get at 'Dotty'.

Now it had happened again. Someone had beaten her to this hamster. And killed it. Her contact, the person to show her where Damajina had been working when she made her discoveries about the Ancient Diadem; the piece of hardware the Doctor had told her about. The Doctor had warned her that there might be other parties searching for it and obviously they were prepared to kill to keep their trail cold. Ace wasn't averse to killing in self-defence, but this wanton murder of the rodent-like Pakhar who she'd never seen before upset her more than she thought possible.

She crossed the room, slightly bowed due to the low ceiling level, and went into a back room. A straw bed was in a corner, a few personal odds and ends and a large brush. On the straw bed was a simple sheet, lightweight to cope with Pakha's warm climate. She scooped up the sheet and went back to Hyn't'n's body and carefully covered him.

She looked back at her information pad which Cook had given her. The only other place to try was the taverna where she was told she would probably find Hyn't'n if he'd not been at his hutch. Swinging her backpack onto her shoulder, she left the hutch for the first and last time.

In the bushes nearby, a set of whiskers twitched. Beady eyes followed her retreating form and when she was out of sight, a black-furred Pakhar scampered towards Hyn't'n's home.

The Doctor ran his hand across a pillar, feeling the familiar rippled stonework and admiring the cream and lilac paintwork. The familiar duo-tone design of the Citadel had not changed in the passing years. Atop every pillar was a flambeau, the proud but savage face of Aggedor carved into every one. 'Home from home.'

Bernice nodded. 'Nice holiday cottage you've got here, Doctor. Needs a spot of brightening up and the spooky sculptures could do with going, but yeah – it's got potential.'

'Don't let any of the Pels hear you say that, Benny. Aggedor is a sacred beast on the planet. And more so in the Royal Citadel than anywhere else. Nice chap, I remember, very partial to Venusian lullabies.' The Doctor began to warble slightly out of key under his breath:

'Klokeda, partha, mennin klatch,
  Ablark, araan, aroon.
Klokeeda shunna teerenatch,
  Aroon, araan, aroon, araan . . .

'Yes, thank you Frank Sinatra, that'll do,' whispered Bernice. 'The locals are giving you funny looks.'

The Doctor looked back over his shoulder. Kort was chatting amiably to Geban and the Time Lord was impressed. The arrogant child had briefly been replaced by the experienced diplomat. Admittedly the Doctor overheard phrases straight out of the Galactic Federation *How To Be A Diplomat* handbook, but delivered with a panache and enthusiasm that made the Doctor smile. And Geban was obviously good enough at his job not to say anything either.

Someone cleared their throat noisily beside him. By the pitch he knew without looking that Alpha Centauri was there.

'My dear old friend, how are you?' the Doctor ventured. Centauri simply stared back and after a few seconds the huge leathery green eyelid flapped down and up.

119

Centauri's pupil had dilated significantly and the green hue of his flesh had darkened considerably.

The Ambassador bobbed a couple of times, as if looking this strange figure up and down. The last time that the Doctor had visited Peladon, Centauri recalled that the man had been nearly thirty centimetres taller. He'd had a wash of snow-white hair and worn expensive velvet suits and a cloak or two. Facing him now was a short, slightly younger man with a deeply lined face, sad eyes and a dowdy, crumpled cream suit on. Whereas the other Doctor had been a picture of sartorial elegance, this Doctor looked like he'd been dragged through a hedge backwards.

'I confess . . . Doctor,' he squeaked hesitantly, 'you don't look quite the same as you did all those years ago.'

Benny had joined them by now. She could appreciate Centauri's problem. Although she hadn't ever seen the Doctor regenerate, she had glimpsed the odd sight of his former selves during tense moments inside the TARDIS for various reasons, and she found it disconcerting that one person could have seven bodies, all of which created different personalities, and yet always be the same. She was no theologian but had once said to herself that while the outside changed, it had to be the Doctor's soul that crossed from body to body. That unique something that made the Doctor so totally different to everyone else she'd ever met. 'That's nothing, Ambassador,' she interrupted. 'From what I can gather the faces and personalities he's had since you last saw him confuse everyone he's ever known.'

'Nevertheless,' shrilled Centauri, 'bearing in mind the . . . um . . . difficulties you faced here last time, plus the fact that in the fifty years between your previous two visits you had barely aged a year, I can only accept that you are who you say you are.'

'Thank you, Centauri,' smiled the Doctor. 'I am genuinely pleased to be here with you again. I am only sorry that friends such as Queen Thalira and Gebek are not here to share this reunion.'

'Their deaths were most unfortunate and inopportune,

it must be said. I felt I had to stay on and help the new king, Tarrol, with his responsibilities. He clearly required someone of experience and diplomacy to help him.'

'Of course.'

There was a pause as Centauri's green returned to its more traditional olive colouring. He bobbed again and waved three of his arms at the Doctor and Bernice. 'And I, too, am glad to have such a valued old friend back amongst us. And with such charming company as well.'

Benny smiled. 'Thank you, Ambassador. I'm grateful to see that Federation interests on Peladon are being so well looked after.'

Centauri glowed slightly plum at that, which Bernice took to be mild embarrassment, and bobbed away towards Geban.

'Oh very smooth, Professor Summerfield,' murmured the Doctor. 'Why not add some strawberry jam and be *really* sickly?'

'It'll avoid awkward questions later,' she retorted and slipped her arm around his. 'So, start the guided tour. I can't wait to meet the king! I mean, sentient computers, Silurians, punk rockers and zombies I've seen, but real honest-to-God alien royalty? Now there's a first.'

Laughing quietly, the two time travellers followed the Federation party into the caverns.

Three hours later and the Doctor heard a tap on the door of the quarters assigned to him by Centauri. He got off the well-cushioned chair he'd been dozing in and pulled the door open.

Nothing.

With a shrug he returned to his chair and settled down again. A second later, the knock was made again. Sighing to himself, once again he opened the door.

Facing him was an elderly lady, possibly the oldest Pel he'd ever seen. She wore a long purple robe with silver lining on the cuffs and neck. Her greying hair was up in a bun, but her eyes still sparkled blue. Despite her age, this woman, the Doctor thought, had once been very beautiful and that beauty had matured into a stately elegance.

'Ambassador Centauri said you had changed your appearance, Doctor. I had not realized quite how much.'

The Doctor smiled. 'You have me at a disadvantage, my Lady,' he started but the lady smiled and put her fingers to her lips to quieten him.

'May I come in?' she whispered.

The Doctor nodded and she walked past him, pulling her robe up lightly. As she turned, her profile was caught by the flickering light of a flambeau behind. The Doctor took a good look at the lady before him and finally recognized her.

'My apologies, Lady Lianna. I have been clumsy in my manners.'

'Nonsense, Doctor. You are as elegant and charming as ever. After all, when you were last here I was but a handmaiden to Queen Thalira.'

The Doctor raised a hand to quieten her this time. 'Nonsense. You do yourself a disservice. Queen Thalira talked of your friendship with the highest regard. She held your views, opinions and advice far higher than any other. And none other of her staff were prepared to accompany her to the mines when fleeing Azaxyr's wrath.'

Lianna smiled at the memory. 'And that was such a long time ago. I simply came to re-acquaint myself with you and hope you would remember a loyal servant.'

'Indeed I do, my Lady. But I also remember a loyal friend and that is far more important to me.'

'Talking of old friends, Doctor, I see you are travelling with Professor Summerfield. I just wondered what became of Miss Sarah Jane Smith. Her guidance to the queen and myself during that awful business with Galaxy Five was not only useful at the time, but the queen radically re-shaped Pel society as a result.'

The Doctor indicated for Lianna to sit but she declined. 'When I next see her,' he said, 'I shall tell her that. She will be very pleased indeed, I am sure.'

Lianna turned to go. 'Doctor. There are things I must

tell you. Things that I cannot say to the other Federation representatives. But you . . . you are an independent, despite your Federation connections. You have the trust and friendship of Peladon and I fear events will soon occur that could seriously affect our future prosperity.'

'Is that why you asked me to be quiet at the door? In case you were heard?'

Lianna smiled tightly and humourlessly. 'No, Doctor. I asked for quiet in case my daughter saw me here. She would not approve.'

'Your daughter . . .'

Lianna opened the door. 'Another time, my friend. For now, I am glad you are back. Whenever Peladon faces danger, it makes use of its guardians. Twice both you and Aggedor have saved us. Now there is no Aggedor and the full responsibility falls upon your shoulders. We will talk after dinner.' With that, Lianna was gone.

The Doctor sat on his chair to ponder the significance of her words. 'Her daughter would not approve? I wonder . . .'

His reverie was interrupted by another knock. Lianna again? He crossed and opened it, to face a chest. At least he guessed it was a chest. It was hairy, bits of it were wrapped in leather and it was wider than the doorway. He looked up slowly. Looking down on him was a veritable giant of a man. His black hair was streaked with its traditional mauve wave, and a scar ran down from hairline to jaw on the left side of his face. At his side he wore a massive double-bladed axe.

'Are you my escort? Is it dinner time already?' The Doctor realized his voice sounded unusually quiet and mousy. Then again, his visitor was unusually large and stocky. The giant nodded, baring some very crooked teeth in a wide grin. The Doctor nipped back and stuffed a red-spotted handkerchief in his breast pocket, did up his matching red-spotted tie and smiled back. 'Lead on, old chap. I'll just follow you.' His silent companion, not unsurprisingly, led on.

* * *

A few minutes later and the Doctor stood outside the throne room. A jumble of memories flooded back. Jo Grant, Princess of TARDIS. Sarah Jane Smith and her Women's Liberation. Izlyr and Ssorg. Azaxyr and Sskel. Eckersley and Arcturus. Hepesh and Ortron. Every fifty years he returned to Peladon and gave it a little push. Friends and enemies helped or hindered.

What of Savaar and Sskeet? Were they friend or foe? Were they the danger Lianna feared? Why was Alpha Centauri still here, years after he should have retired? Why had his old friend, now the Federation Chair, sent Damakort to Peladon when Savaar was regal enough an observer? To observe the observer?

All these questions and not enough answers.

He stared at the huge double doors, Aggedor's face carved, as ever, into them. The giant pushed them open and the Doctor took a deep breath. He looked down and saw his hand was shaking.

Bernice tried to hide the relief on her face as the Doctor finally arrived. He bounded forward, winked slyly at her and dropped to one knee in front of King Tarrol, sitting to Bernice's left.

'May I have permission to address the king?' asked the Doctor.

Tarrol nodded back in courtesy and the Time Lord arose. Tarrol then stood himself, reached across the dinner table and held his hand out. The Doctor shook it and Tarrol grinned. 'Alpha Centauri assures me that is the correct greeting on such an occasion. I'm not exactly sure, however, of its meaning.'

The Doctor still held Tarrol's hand. 'It goes back many thousands of years to Earth's rather vicious history, Your Majesty. In ancient times the warriors would drop their swords and grip each other's sword hand – therefore fighting could not continue. It marked peace. Now, it symbolizes friendship and trust.'

'Your record, Doctor, on our planet already imbues you with our friendship and trust.'

124

'I am grateful. I hope I can gain your friendship and trust personally as well as regally.'

Tarrol nodded. 'I hope so too. Now, please join our feast. Your companion, Professor Summerfield, is a most amusing guest.' The king looked at the giant who had escorted the Doctor. 'Thank you, Torg. Please join us.'

The Doctor sat to the right of Bernice and smiled warmly at her. She grinned back and spoke through gritted teeth in a manner only the Doctor could hear: 'Thank God you're here. He's very sweet but boring as hell. And chauvinistic!'

The Doctor took a spoonful of broth. 'A hundred years ago you'd have been put to death for not having royal blood in your veins if you so much as breathed in here. A lot has changed.'

Bernice tugged at her unleavened bread. 'He said they actually make this stuff by hand on occasions like this.'

'Things have changed even more than I thought. Last time I was here, it would always have been like that, not just on special occasions. The Federation influence is massive. And something is very wrong, by the way.' The Doctor casually leaned across the table and absently removed a glass of wine which was nearing Damakort's expectant hand. He swiftly placed a glass of water in the boy's hand, ignoring the venomous look he received as a result. To add insult to injury he calmly topped up Bernice's glass by pouring the procured wine into hers.

'What makes you say that?'

'An old friend told me. I'll explain later.' He casually raised his own glass and gently toasted Savaar and Sskeet sitting opposite him. As he expected, Sskeet ignored the gesture and Savaar made an even smaller toast back.

'Still some chairs empty, I see,' murmured the Doctor as he finished his broth. Bernice looked around the L-shaped table. The king was at the head of the largest bit. She sat to his right, the Doctor to hers. Dead opposite her was Damakort and next to him the giant Torg. Then Sskeet, Savaar and Alpha Centauri. Next to the Doctor was an empty seat and beside that a couple of high-ranking Pels. On the other section of the table was Geban, who she'd learned was the king's chancellor, and two other courtiers. At the far end were two people she was especially interested in. One was a tall, regal old lady in exquisite purple, and beside her was a tubby, fussy little man who picked at his food melodramatically, laughed raucously ever so often although no one else did and had an annoying habit of twiddling his fingers nervously before picking up the next bit of food. At the head of that section of the table was another empty seat.

Pretending to be pointing at a dish of jelly-like relish, the Doctor's fork aimed squarely at the older lady. 'That's Lianna, the friend I mentioned.' The Doctor dipped some meat into the relish. 'I imagine the empty seat is her daughter's. I assume they don't get on.'

'She should make the most of her mother while she's still got one,' murmured Bernice.

'Quite,' said the Doctor. His fork speared a large piece of root vegetable. 'I wonder who's supposed to be next to me.'

'Probably the guy whose just walked in. He certainly isn't the old one's daughter, anyway.'

Tarrol rose again and shook hands with the newcomer. The man bowed slightly and crossed to Savaar.

'My Lord, what a very great pleasure to see you again.'

Savaar placed his arm across his chest in Martian salute. The human copied the gesture perfectly. Savaar nodded and said, 'I trust you are well after your vacation, Mister Reece?'

Nic Reece grinned boyishly. 'Too right, old chum. I needed the break. Four years on one planet is a long time. Even a planet as charming as this,' he added quickly and apparently sincerely to the king. Tarrol merely smiled and waved towards the empty seat beside the Doctor. As Reece walked around he stopped behind Damakort's seat.

'Hiya Kort, how's things? Dad sent you out here now, has he?'

Kort nodded, any words lost in a mouthful of meat and vegetable. But his eyes flashed a smile. Bernice noted the

126

way Kort seemed to relax the moment he was spoken to. Nic Reece was obviously an old friend of everyone.

Reece turned and looked across at her and the Doctor.

'Doctor! How wonderful to see you again. New body I see, but the nose is a definite improvement.' The Doctor shook hands as Reece seated himself. 'It's been a very long time, Mister Reece. You're looking very fit and healthy.'

'Oh you know me, Doctor. I try to keep fit and healthy. Little jog around the catacombs twice a day – keeps the flab at bay.' He dropped his voice *sotto voce* as he pretended to take a swig of wine. 'And it gets me away from Centauri's flusterings for a few hours as well.'

The Doctor nodded understandingly. 'By the way, I don't think you ever met Professor Bernice Summerfield. She's an archaeologist.'

Reece shook Bernice's hand enthusiastically. 'Marvellous, quite marvellous. You'll love Peladon, it's rich in artefacts. Hmm, I notice Atissa's not here yet.'

'Lianna's daughter?' inquired the Doctor, topping up Reece's wine.

'More than that, Doctor. She's Peladon's high priestess and totally loathes me. Luckily the feeling is intensely mutual.'

Bernice leaned over. 'So who's the camp one boring the pants off Lianna?'

'Oh that,' Reece smiled. 'That's Neal Corry, top holovid bigwig for GFTV–3, here to cover the restatement vows and keep his ratings up. Do excuse me; if I don't say hello to him, he'll sulk for days.' Reece popped a chunk of meat in his mouth and stood up. 'See you, Professor. Good to touch base again, Doctor.' He sauntered over and Lianna's face lit up with pleasure at his arrival. Bernice guessed it was a mixture of delight at his presence and relief that Corry would have to simper over someone else. She grinned. She liked Reece a lot.

'You dark horse, Doctor. You didn't tell me you knew someone as horny as that!'

The Doctor finished off his drink. 'Must have slipped my mind, Professor. Funny thing, the memory.' He poured himself some more wine and offered the decanter to Bernice.

She shook her head and placed a hand over her glass. 'What d'you mean? Didn't you know he was going to be here? He seemed very pleased to see you again. We don't meet too many old friends of yours who you can say that about,' she added wryly.

'Thank you.' The Doctor again rescued some wine away from Damakort. 'Nice chap, that Nic Reece. Only one thing wrong with him.'

'I knew it,' groaned Benny. 'What now?'

'I've never set eyes on him before in my lives. Nic Reece may know me, but as far as I'm concerned, he's a complete stranger.'

Fehler reached the top of the ravine. He hauled himself up the last few centimetres and lay on the top, panting. Of Professor Sharrod, there was no sign. Picking up his kit, he wandered back to their encampment by the cave mouth.

After ten minutes walk he was suddenly aware of the quiet. Surely the others in the group couldn't have been asleep.

'Winmill? Gris? Larroq?' No response. He shivered suddenly. He could have sworn . . . no . . . it wasn't possible. And yet he felt as if he was being watched. 'Vega Lexus?' he called out to the red-headed Braxiatel burrower that the University had placed with the group. Lexus was, like all his Vegan race, perfect for cave explorations – his infra-red sight and strength made him ideal for investigating places like those on Pakha. Professor Sharrod hadn't wanted him along, but as the Braxiatel Collection was co-funding this, what they wanted was law and –

What was that?

'Professor? Gris, are you lot pissing about? I'm not in the mood for – ' Fehler stopped. His flashlight picked out a form. He knelt down and grimaced as his trousers soaked up the water he'd knelt on. He aimed his light

128

down, gasped and recoiled back. 'Lexus?' he tried to say, but it only came out as a hoarse croak. With horrified realization he touched his knee and shone his light at his hand. It wasn't water, it was blood. Vega Lexus' skull had been caved in savagely. He shivered again, and started running back to the encampment. 'Gris! Larroq! What the cruk's going on?'

Fehler tripped over Winmill's body first. Fehler didn't exactly like Winmill – he was too damn good-looking by far. All the girls fancied him. He also got to bed most of them. Nevertheless, seeing that renowned handsome face staring up at him, its neck twisted at a very severe angle, Fehler felt very sick.

And very frightened.

Slowly now he moved forward. He could see the dim light of the phosphorous fake fire at the encampment. A figure could clearly be seen hunched over it.

'Professor Sharrod?'

'Come over, m'boy,' Sharrod replied. 'I've made a fascinating discovery, Fehler. Really exciting.'

'But Professor . . . Vega Lexus, Winmill . . .'

'They couldn't see my discovery, Fehler. Couldn't understand what I now know is true!'

Fehler was at the encampment. He could see Larroq's body – her throat tightly bound by the Professor's rope, her dead eyes bulged in panic. Beside Sharrod, still moving slightly, was Gris. The Professor's trowel was embedded deeply into the back of his neck and every time Gris tried to move, another small spurt of blood would spray up. But Fehler's attention was on Sharrod. He wore the Diadem on his head and his hands were now pressed against his temples.

'I am the first, Fehler. The first non-Pakhar to wear the Ancient Diadem. I now understand its power. I understand its aims and ambitions!'

Fehler managed to find his voice, although it was a bit strained. 'Aims? Ambitions? Professor Sharrod, it's only a crown. A piece of regalia. A Pakha artefact!'

Sharrod's face twisted in fury, highlighted by the green

phosphorescence. '*Artefact!* What do you know, human scum?'

Fehler frowned. 'Professor, you're human, too. Not a Pakhar or anything else . . .'

Sharrod kicked out at Gris, causing more sprays of blood. Some of it splashed across Fehler's cheek but he gritted his teeth and ignored it.

'Professor, what have you done to our friends?'

'*Friends?*' shrieked Sharrod. 'Friends? They are alien trash. I . . . *we* are all that matter. I am – '

Sharrod was cut off as a plate-sized hole appeared in his chest. He fell dead, face-first into the fake fire, the Diadem falling off his head. Fehler looked up. Four black-clad, heavily armed figures stood at the cave mouth. A woman with long, red hair lowered her blaster.

'Thank you,' she said. 'You've saved us a long and boring search.'

A man stepped forward, his manner suggesting he was their leader. 'Okay, Lambert, Cooper. Get the vacuum-case and get the Diadem. Use the rods to pick it up – it mustn't touch anyone's body.'

Fehler watched as a woman with cropped brown hair and a blond man walked over with a large plastic container.

'Open,' said the man. With a hiss the lid slid back. The red-haired woman gave her two associates a long metal rod each and they scooped up the Diadem, dropped it in the box and the man told the container to close. With a hiss of escaping air the lid shut, vacuum-sealing the Diadem inside. 'Okay Townsend, it's ours,' said the red-haired woman.

'Right, Sadler. It's your responsibility now.' Townsend looked down at Sharrod's dead body. 'Thanks, Prof.'

Sadler carried the box while the blond man searched Sharrod's body. 'Nothing else.'

'Okay, Lambert. Let's go.'

The crop-haired woman waved her blaster in Fehler's direction. 'What about him?'

'Yes,' cried Fehler. 'Please get me away from here!'

Townsend paused. 'Cooper, it's up to you,' he said to the crop-head.

Fehler stepped forward, smiling desperately at her. 'Hi, my name's Pol Fehler and I – '

Cooper blasted his head off.

As the mercenaries walked away, the Ancient Diadem safely in their possession, Gris's trowel-embedded neck gave one final spasm and his last gush of blood erupted and splashed on the floor, mingling with that of Sharrod and Fehler.

4:

Strange Charm

'God, that wine was good,' said Benny to no one in particular as she bounced off another stippled wall. Savaar moved a fraction faster and caught her as she stumbled unsteadily from the rebound.

'Whoops!' she giggled, 'I haven't been like this since my thirtieth birthday . . . What a heavenly day that was!' she punned.

Savaar's green tongue darted out, moistening his lips.

Benny stared at him, trying to focus. 'I say,' she murmured, 'are you trying to catch a fly?' As Savaar made no response to this except to do the autonomic reaction again, Benny pointed slowly at his mouth. 'D'that again – I'll see if I can catch it!' She tried to laugh but instead belched extraordinarily loudly. Sskeet turned his head, trying to check no one was behind them.

'I'm sorry, I'm so embarrassing! Oh God,' she began to wail, 'I'm an embarrassment to the Martian hierarchy, to the Federation, to humanity, to – '

It occurred to Savaar that Bernice would probably list every person in the solar system given half a chance. He shook her slightly and she stopped, her head lolling slightly at an angle.

'Hey,' she said quietly. 'Hey, don't I know you? Aren't you my mother-in-law?' With that, she let out a large yelp of amusement and staggered into a doorway. 'Is this your place or mine? Fancy a nightcap?' Benny reached out and tugged at the silky cape hanging down Savaar's back. 'Or how about a night *cape*?'

Sskeet pushed the door ajar and gently but firmly the

two Martians eased Bernice into her room and towards the bed. She waved herself free.

'S'all right, I can put myself to bed.' She waved a finger at them, trying to look stern. 'I'm sure you shouldn't be in *Shsurr*'s bed-chamber, my good sirs!'

Savaar glanced at Sskeet and nodded. Without a word they both bowed to the unsteady figure before them and turned to leave. With a yell of excitement Bernice slumped loudly on to the bed behind them.

'Don't forget to turn out the light, boys!' she called.

Without a word Sskeet and Savaar discreetly, and with as much dignity as possible, left her room.

After a moment's pause Bernice shuffled on her bed slightly. One eye popped open and a huge grin spread across her face. She sat bolt upright and turned the almost imperceptible dial on a nearby flambeau. The flame grew noticeably brighter. She scrabbled under her bed with consummate ease, no sign of tiredness or the drunkenness she had displayed moments earlier. She yanked up her bag and extracted her diary. Over the next minutes she scribbled:

'Dear Diary.

What an extraordinary meal. Damakort behaved himself very well – I could almost get to tolerate him if he stays like this and doesn't sulk or pout any more. The Doctor has taken to this honoured guest bit like a duck to water – of course – he loves the attention. Alpha Centauri's weird but very sweet. King Tarrol's peculiar. He's very young to be a king, He looks in his early twenties but talks and acts like an old man. Atissa swanned in fashionably late and accused the entire Federation group of offending the spirit of this Aggedor thing. Going by the carvings and pictures that obsessively dominate this culture, I'd guess he'd be offended every time he looked in the mirror!

Then there's Nic Reece. Hmmm. Wonder what Ace would have made of him. Probably attempted to

*seduce him by now. Glad she's not here – I might
have a go myself.*

*Fun bit of the evening was just now. The Doctor
asked me to test the patience of old Savaar. He's not
a bad chap, bit stodgy, but could be interesting. I
played the outrageous drunk all the way back. I
insulted, belched, burped and generally acted gross.
He took it all in his stride – strikes me it'd take a lot to
rile him. Blown out the Doctor's theory that Savaar's
volatile and aggressive. I wonder why –* '

She stopped suddenly and put down her pen. Silence.

No. There it was again!

A muted shout – someone was trying to have a subtle
argument nearby.

Bernice went to her door and tried to listen through it.
The muffled sounds of the constant storm outside the
window and the thickness of the wooden door made distinct hearing impossible so she slowly tugged the door
open. Through the crack she could see Reece and someone else. Reece was trying to act the pacifist but his unseen
partner was raising her voice slowly. Atissa, Bernice
assumed, but as Reece moved slightly it was Lianna that
came into view. Bernice wasn't used to being surprised
but she had to admit this was unexpected. They'd hardly
passed a word over dinner – although Corry's theatrical
anecdotes were probably the cause of that; no one could
have hoped to get a word in edgeways.

The intensity of their argument meant that they were
oblivious to anything else. Bernice came right out of her
room and shuffled across the corridor, leaning against the
cold stone walls to listen better. She became aware that
a bit of the stippled rock was jabbing into her shoulder
but by now she was so close she dare not move – they'd
see her shadow if nothing else.

Reece was saying, 'Look, she's *your* daughter. I've tried
my best.'

'You'll never beat her, Reece.' That was Lianna. 'She's
too stubborn, too adamant in her own beliefs.'

'Yeah, well I can see where she gets that from!'

'Flattery will get you nowhere, Nicholas Reece.'

Bernice started. Lianna leant forward and kissed Reece on the lips. Not aggressively or even passionately, but tenderly. They held the soft kiss for a few seconds and she stepped back. 'Don't make me regret any of this. Please.'

Reece shook his head and took her hand in his, caressing the back of hers with his thumb. 'I won't let you down. It'll all be sorted out soon and you'll have no more problems.'

Lianna retracted her hand. 'I hope so. You are my last chance for happiness.' She turned and went.

Bernice flattened herself against the wall, pressing further into the jutting rock. As it dug in further she wanted to cry out but instead bit the inside of her mouth. Nic Reece walked straight past her, totally oblivious to her presence. Bernice watched him head back towards the Federation Representatives' quarters. After she was sure he'd gone, Bernice pulled away from the wall, finally allowing herself a gasp as the rock ceased pressurizing her shoulder. She scampered back to her room and closed the door – now *this* would certainly interest the Doctor.

As the door to her room shut, two figures stepped out of the shadows. They had had a perfectly clear view of both the argument and Bernice's spying. Neither of them had been spotted – they were both too well versed in the art of subtle shadow-hiding.

'As I suspected,' hissed Savaar. '*Shsurr* Summerfield was pretending. I wonder why.'

'Should we ask her now or in the morning?'

'Oh, I think the morning will do, Sskeet. After that little scene by Reece and the Lady Lianna, I think the morning could hold a few surprises. I think it is time we had a small talk with Lianna ourselves.'

The Doctor closed the connecting door between his room and Kort's. The Cantryan boy was fast asleep. At last. The

Doctor yawned. Still, he should be grateful – very few people stayed awake throughout the entire story of the terrible Zodin and her giant grasshoppers. Or was it Ch'tizz? He could never remember who had the grasshoppers and who had the mutant kangaroos. Still, it hardly mattered – it had taken nearly an hour to tell the story. Kort's intelligent, incisive and therefore downright annoying questions about Zodin's practical motives and the physics of the grasshoppers jumping eighteen-storey buildings had highlighted not only his inquisitive nature but also the Doctor's disposition to exaggeration.

He heard the gasp almost as if it had been right in his ear instead of outside in the corridor. Unknowingly echoing Bernice's movements fifteen minutes earlier, he pushed his ear to his door but again the storm and well-built door severely cut back his hearing. He, too, opened the door a crack and raised an eyebrow in surprise.

Lianna was talking to Savaar. Angrily.

'You had no right to come here. Not yet. Do you want to ruin everything?'

Savaar held up a clamped fist. 'I had no choice. The situation is desperate. You can tell that by the company I keep!'

The Doctor smiled. It was nice to be such a thorn in Savaar's side.

Lianna continued. 'The Doctor could help. He has in the past.'

'He is dangerous,' replied Savaar. 'Besides, how can you be sure it is the same man? Morphers are rare and his story is a little far-fetched. While I investigate the Doctor you will do as you are told or the consequences could be severe for your rather backward little planet. I will not warn you again.'

Lianna was obviously going to say more when a familiar swishing noise indicated the arrival of Alpha Centauri, his head a curious shade of crimson. The Doctor realized that in all the years he had known the mild ambassador, he had until now never seen him angry.

'What is going on here?' he chirped surprisingly quietly.

With a last look at Savaar, Lianna said, 'Nothing for the Federation to worry themselves about, it would seem,' and marched away.

'Please, Ambassador,' Savaar said before the hexapod could speak, 'go to bed. Now!' he added as Centauri bobbed, ready to protest. The crimson hue faded to a more subdued but still affronted purple and Centauri bobbed away.

The Doctor shrugged slightly and shut his door as quietly as he could.

In the corridor, the tiny click was clearly audible to Savaar's advanced helmet receivers. He turned and looked for the source of the sound.

The Doctor's quarters – of course.

Half an hour later old Fabon was wandering around what Nic Reece had termed the 'relic room' – the first stage in his plan to open Peladon for tourism. Against Atissa's better judgement but not better arguments, most of the Pel trophies and sacred weapons and artefacts were stored here. It was Fabon's current duty to check the room every night. Although it was locked securely and only he and Atissa had keys, she was quite clear in her instructions.

'You are to check it every hour on the hour. When you sleep, assign someone you trust with your life to do it.'

For five weeks now Fabon had spent his every waking moment concerned with nothing else.

He looked around, staring at the familiar artefacts. The Chalice of Blood, which every king or queen drank from on their accession day. The Crown of Sherak, Peladon's first king who had tamed the sacred beast Aggedor and appointed him Royal Protector. Most importantly, the Lance of Aggedor. A long, serrated and ceremonial spear with which, according to legend, Sherak drew blood from both Aggedor and himself, mixing it together and therefore assuring the protection every Pel held dear.

Fabon was still admiring it when five inches of tempered steel slid through his back, up into his rib-cage and severed his aorta. Silently Fabon fell on to his face, subconsciously grateful that the blade had not gone through to his front, thus ensuring that none of his blood stained the relic room floor.

His murderer reached up and grasped the Lance of Aggedor.

It was never again replaced.

Keri and holocameraman Jav were the first to find Fabon's corpse the following morning. They had arrived at around six o'clock in the morning, local time.

Neal Corry had suggested that some stock shots of the relic room would make for interesting visual wallpaper. He also muttered that they could always cut to it to cover edits if the restatement ceremony got a bit too long-winded. Ever vigilant about dropping ratings, Corry knew that although pageants and feudalism were viewer-grabbers, too much of such things were a bit of a switch-off. Quick cuts and snatches of glitz and glamour would keep the punters watching; dreary speeches and incense-waving would put them to sleep. And Corry out of a job.

Jav had moaned, as usual, about starting so early. 'Don't see Corry up and about, d'you?'

Keri shook her head. 'Rank has its privileges, Jav,' was her only reply.

Oddly enough, Corry was on the scene of the murder within moments, looking spruce and tidy; like a peacock on heat, Jav muttered. The fussy little man was mincing about, telling Jav where to point the camera, how long to stay panning up the body and generally annoying Jav to his limits.

Keri stood to one side, a false smile on her lips every time Corry nodded excitedly at her. She'd been covering death and destruction most of her professional life. One more dead body was neither here nor there. She couldn't help feeling, though, that Corry was letting enthusiasm overtake taste. One stabbed corpse hardly constituted a slot of prime-time news.

'I know what you're thinking, Keri my little fuzzbox,'

crooned Corry as he sauntered towards her. 'But think about it. Primitive backwater planet, still half uncivilized. Important local pageant, lots of Federation bigwigs and BANG!' He clapped his hands together loudly, causing Jav and the three Pel guards to briefly look toward him. Unperturbed, Corry waved his hands around. 'A murder! Who will be next? The Martian high lord? The king? The beautiful holovid reporter?' He put his chubby hands either side of Keri's snout and stroked her jaws. 'Now, that *would* be a real tragedy!'

As Corry went back to annoying the hell out of Jav, Keri wiped her jaws with her paws. Whatever his faults, Corry was on the whole a bearable human. He was clean, tidy and although excitable, never disturbed and rarely angry. She even found his obvious and frequently unsuccessful attempts to charm younger male humans rather amusing. However, going by his scent and the amount of sweat that had rubbed on to her jaws, Keri decided that the outwardly jovial Neal Corry that had just spoken to her was in fact a deeply troubled, almost frightened man. Now, *that* was newsworthy.

Savaar strode into the relic room an hour later with Sskeet, as always, one pace behind. The Martian high lord had instructed the room to be emptied of all personnel so that he could conduct his detective work. He knew Corry's reputation well enough to know that the ridiculous human would have taken great pains to disturb nothing. However much of a nuisance he and his holovid people were on Peladon, Corry and the Pakha Ker'a'nol didn't get their reputations by making silly mistakes.

Savaar was furious to see the Doctor sitting cross-legged on the floor, beside the crudely chalked outline where Fabon had fallen.

The Doctor's back was to the door but he heard Savaar's sharp intake of breath and smiled to himself.

'Good morning, my Lord,' he said without getting up or turning around.

'I gave explicit instructions that this room was to be

139

empty. I imagine you have a very good excuse for this blatant disregard for my ruling?'

The Doctor used his feet to lever himself upright, turned and walked towards Savaar. He stopped, his face about level with the Martian's neck. Slowly he looked up and grinned. 'I'm awfully sorry if I'm in your way, High Lord. I wasn't aware that you had been formally put in charge of this . . . investigation.'

'In situations like this, Doctor, the highest-ranking official always take charge.'

'Oh, indeed,' the Doctor turned away and walked back to the outline. 'My mistake. I assumed that King Tarrol outranked you. Obviously Federation egotism is as over-inflated as ever.' He dug his hand into the pocket of his white linen jacket and extracted a piece of blue chalk. He dropped to the floor again and started looking under a trophy cabinet. A quiet, controlled hiss from the doorway made him look up again. 'Please, don't let me stop you doing your investigation, my Lord.' The Doctor smiled disarmingly and returned to his burrowing under the cabinet.

'Doctor,' came Savaar's exasperated response, 'if you are trying to annoy me, be gratified. You are succeeding admirably.'

The Doctor popped up again, but all trace of humour or cheerfulness had gone from his face. Instead he fixed Savaar with a penetrating stare that dared him to say anything else.

'Rest assured, Lord Savaar, I neither intend to annoy you nor really care if I do. I too am here to do a job. Something is very wrong on Peladon. I sensed it when we arrived yesterday. I sensed it during our meal last night. I sensed it during your little chat-ette with Lianna outside my room last night. Above all, I sense it in this room where an innocent old man was rather expertly murdered. Mystery is my business, my Lord. If you don't like it, contact your Federation masters and have me removed. Meanwhile, I suggest you learn to put up with me as I realize I have to put up with you!'

Unaccustomed to making long speeches, the Doctor, now slightly ruddy-faced, tugged at his jacket lapels, ran a hand through his hair and clutched his umbrella to his chest.

Normally Savaar would have found the sight of a scruffy little human in shabby clothes, armed only with a red-handled umbrella rather pathetic; amusing at best. Confronted with the anger in the Doctor's voice and something totally alien and rather unpalatable in his brown eyes (or were they in fact black?), the Martian merely nodded at him. Rather quieter than he intended, Savaar raised his clamped hands in an open gesture. 'I suggest, Doctor, that a pooling of our resources may be in order. To determine as swiftly and concisely as possible the exact threat that this murder poses to both the Federation representatives and, of course, to His Majesty the King.'

If Martian exo-helmets allowed expression to show through, Sskeet's face would have been a picture of astonishment and incredulity at his commander's words. However, masked as it was, the only difference the Doctor noted was that Sskeet's right arm, with its deadly sonic armament built into the wrist, drooped noticeably at Savaar's words. In an instant, the Doctor's demeanour changed and he tossed his umbrella into a corner. As he slipped off his jacket and draped it over an ornate chair, he grinned at the two Martians. 'Well, let's get started, then. I'll carry on at floor level, the two of you are better suited to window-level duty, I think.'

As Bernice wandered into the Federation Representatives' dining area she was unsurprised to see Damakort already stuffing himself with a Peladon version of bacon and eggs. A steaming jug of caffeine substitute sat beside his plate. He looked up at her and grinned. A trickle of egg yolk escaped from the corner of his mouth and with unaccustomed embarrassment he wiped it away with a napkin. He pointed to the seat opposite him with his fork.

'Morning Professor,' he said, trying to speak as politely

141

as possible with a mouthful of food. 'Heard about the murder?'

Bernice nodded quietly and sat. He pushed the caffeine jug towards her. She took a pewter mug from a metallic mug-tree and poured herself some.

A couple of sips later and she felt more alive.

Kort finished his food with a final flourish of his knife and fork. He sat back in his chair and swallowed. 'I've been to a few planets where breakfast is unheard of. Glad Peladon isn't one of them. Shall I order you something?'

'No!' Benny said a little too sharply. 'I mean, no thank you. I didn't get much sleep last night, I don't think I could face food.'

'Ah, too much booze, eh?' said a gentle voice from the door. Bernice turned and smiled as Nic Reece walked over. He rested a hand on her shoulder. 'You really know how to put it away, Professor.'

Bernice shook her head. 'God, I'm not hung over. I've been drinking for too many years for that. No, I was just thinking too much and too long last night.'

'What about? Anything I can do to help?'

'Just things. Private things really. But nothing that seems important this morning.'

'Isn't that always the way?' Reece helped himself to a mug and some caffeine. He looked over at Kort who held a hand up. Bernice accepted a top-up. 'You spend hours thinking something through. Worrying or planning. Then you eventually get two hours sleep and when you wake up, it all looks totally different.'

Bernice drained her mug. 'I guess you're right.'

'We aim to please. Nic Reece: dreams explored, advice offered, art treasures priced and Pel high priestesses annoyed. A good trade if you can manage it.'

Bernice laughed for what, she suddenly realized, seemed the first time in days.

Kort noisily slurped the dregs of his drink, and the other two looked over. 'Sorry,' he lied.

'So, tell me, Professor, what brings you to fair Peladon?

I hardly imagine royal events are your forte.' Reece finished his drink and poured himself another.

Bernice looked at him. She'd met a lot of people in her rather hectic life. People she liked, lots she didn't. Nic Reece interested her more than most, but there was something almost unsettling about him. He had charm, he had very old-fashioned boyish looks, he clearly looked after himself physically and he knew how to flirt. But there was something missing. His eyes. They didn't have quite the sparkle that his body language suggested they should have. It was as if he was masking something, something he had to concentrate hard on hiding. Anger? Frustration? Pain? Yes, that was it, Bernice decided. He was terribly hurt and doing his very best to hide it. To most people, he was successful – but to a dyed-in-the-wool, experienced student of human behaviour like her, there was obviously something wrong.

Suddenly she was aware that her stare was being returned.

'Am I wrong?' Reece was saying. 'Don't tell me you do like all this glitter and glam?'

'Hmmm? Oh ... no. No. In fact I find absolute monarchies distasteful. Almost like dictatorships hiding behind respectability.'

'Oh, very good. Remind me not to use that one on young Tarrol when I'm trying to sell him my next batch of tourism ideas.'

Kort suddenly stood up, his chair scraping noisily – unnecessarily so, Bernice decided – across the floor. 'Well, I'm just going for a tidy-up,' he announced loudly. 'See you two later.' With which he marched out, pointedly pulling the double doors closed behind him. An engraving of Aggedor's face glared morosely back at them as a result.

Reece indicated the picture. 'Ugly old sod, isn't he? Aggedor, I mean, not Kort. Royal beast and protector of Peladon. Extinct. Like the economy and viability of the whole planet.'

'You mean, the Federation have got what they wanted

143

out of the planet and have now left it to rot,' Bernice snapped without realizing why.

Reece defensively put his hands up. 'Hey, me no make-a-da rules, lady. I'm just here to find a way of keeping Tarrol and the other courtiers in the mink and ermine they're used to.'

'I know. I'm sorry. I could do with a walk.'

'Company?' Reece held out a hand.

For a moment she paused and then took the hand. 'If the gallant gentleman would not object to escorting the miserable lady around uncharted waters?'

'My pleasure, ma'am.' Reece bowed. 'Follow me, I know some great catacombs.'

'Bet you say that to all the ladies,' Bernice laughed.

'Not many of them say yes, though.' The quip was jocular enough but again, just for a fleeting second, Bernice thought she heard a catch in his voice and he looked away just for a second. 'Come, lady, allow me to show you up the back passage – as the holovid producer said to the trainee tea-boy!'

With a laugh they both exited the Federation Representatives' room.

Opposite the Federation Representatives' room was a small recess, draped off by a vast yellowing tapestry with the same image of Aggedor's visage as on the interior of the double doors.

The tapestry flicked almost unnoticeably as the pair closed the doors and wandered off down the corridor.

Behind it, someone was crouched down, watching them go. As they disappeared from sight, the tapestry flicked once again. Behind it a hand reached up and tugged at an unlit flambeau. The stone wall behind the tapestry suddenly creaked and slowly swung back on a hinge. The figure nipped through the space and adjusted a corresponding flambeau, this time lit, on the rocky wall. The doorway closed and even the most inquisitive eye would have had difficulty spotting the join.

144

'How very interesting,' the inhuman figure breathed, and walked into the darkening catacomb.

Seconds earlier another person had walked quietly towards the Federation Representatives' room. He'd watched as the boy had almost jumped away from the doors as he slammed them. Shaking his head, he watched the boy slowly stomp off around the corner. Youth!

With a furtive look behind him, he hurried on. Suddenly the door ahead was flung open again and Bernice's and Nic Reece's voices could be heard, loudly and happily.

Like a cat caught in torchlight, he looked from side to side. He didn't want to be seen. Not yet. The only hiding place was a doorway beside him. His hand darted out and pulled back the wooden bar. He pushed the door open, holding his breath and hoping the hinges wouldn't squeak. Luckily there was no noise and he pushed the door to, just as Bernice and Reece wandered past, arm in arm.

He watched them through the crack by the door's hinges. 'Oh it's a jolly 'oliday wiv Mary,' he muttered quietly. He counted to ten and crept out. They were gone.

He continued toward the room. Out of the corner of his eye, he saw the tapestry opposite the door move. Of course, it must just be a breeze – the Citadel wasn't renowned for its double glazing and the ever-present storm outside was a constant reminder of how well the building was made. Especially considering Peladon's natural elemental resistance to construction.

He tugged the tapestry aside and looked at the unlit flambeau. Licking his fingers, he reached up on tiptoe and felt for the gas element inside. Cold. No element. This was a real torch, not a Federation construct or adaptation. It probably hadn't been lit for . . . oh, somewhat over fifty years.

He ran his hand over the wall behind. Sensitive finger nails scraped along the outline of a doorway with calm expertise.

'So it was someone else keeping an eye out. And I thought I knew them all . . .'

A rustling noise alerted him – someone was coming. Pulling the tapestry back across, cutting out any light, he listened.

'I'm positive everything is quite all right. Nothing can go wrong. We've both seen to that. Now, you better go or you'll be missed.'

He didn't hear any footsteps, but his keen and experienced senses told him that the silent companion had gone. Then the door to the Federation Representatives' room opened. And closed.

He put his head gingerly round the tapestry. The corridor was empty. He stared at the closed doorway opposite and grimaced. 'Now that was an unusually surreptitious, even melodramatic conversation, especially for Alpha Centauri. I wonder who he was talking to.'

Deciding not to question the ambassador just yet, he sloped off down the corridor, the way he had originally been going: following the first person who had come out of the Federation Representatives' room, the Cantryan boy, Damakort. Professor Bernice Summerfield could wait. Angry teenagers, hidden doors and conspiratorial Centaurians were far more exciting.

Damakort was bored. Very bored. He knew he was bored – it was an experience he frequently felt on Io when his father was busy on Federation business and sent Damakort to go and play on the computer net. Which was all too often.

The result of this of course was that while Damakort might not be the greatest conversationalist or diplomat, he was something of a computer genius. Unlike most of the other youngsters on Io, most of whom were just kids anyway, Damakort excelled in hacking.

It had been his skills that the encryptors on Io had called on when Jina's information came through the net. He had sorted out the corrupted files and unburied the various references to the Ancient Diadem of Pakha that Jina had neatly packaged away in suitcases with personal passwords and an anti-theft virus.

At that time he hadn't realized his sister had died passing on that information.

'Thought you got me there, Big J,' he had sent back. Of course, there'd been no reply. He had alerted his father to this fact and an investigation was immediately mounted. At the same time, Pakha was sending a diplomatic bag back with Jina's body and an apology.

The apology had come in the form of a fussy Pakha governor whose whiskers were stained with nicotine and whose fur smelt of stale straw. Damakort and his father had watched as the body bag was taken from the shuttle and straight to the crematorium. Although Cantryans were not a particularly religious race, they did have certain rituals surrounding death. A group of other Cantryans gathered at the simple ceremony and slowly waved goodbye to Jina's casket as it entered the laser furnace. Damakort remembered two things from that day – his mother, or rather, the lack of the same. And the Pakha diplomat, intruding on their grief by attending. 'It is *our* custom, Kort. He may be ignorant of our solitude,' explained his father. Somehow, Kort doubted it. The Pakha was just being nosy. It was almost as if he wanted to make sure that Jina was gone. Forever. Totally. His sister . . .

Damakort kicked out at a nearby footstool, sending it crashing against the corridor wall.

'Problem, yeah?' said a soft voice beside him.

He looked down slightly – just about level with his shoulder was a female Pakha. Ker'a'nol – the famous holovid reporter. 'No,' he replied and carried on walking.

'Oh. Just thought I'd enquire. Didn't know stool-kicking was a traditional Cantryan habit,' she called after him.

Kort spun round at her. 'Oh, very funny. I forgot, you Pakhas know bloody everything, don't you? Sticking your snouts in where they're not welcome!'

Keri's eyes widened slightly in quiet amusement. 'In my business, "sticking my snout in", as you so politely put it, tends to get it shot off. I've learned not to stick it in unless I'm sure it isn't going to get stasered.'

'Well, you haven't learned very much, then.'

'Probably not. So tell me, what's a handsome Cantryan like you doing on a scrap heap like Peladon?'

'What's it to you?'

'Only trying to make friends. What've you got against that, yeah?'

Kort tried to rationalize a reason. He failed. 'Don't know,' was the best he could come up with.

'You're the Federation Chair's son, aren't you? Damakort, if I remember my research files, yeah?'

'Yeah. I'm also a real person, not that anyone notices.'

Keri screwed up her snout in amusement. 'Don't tell me – "this is Damakort, he's my son" and "oh, what do you do, being a Federation Chair's son?" and "it must be such fun, with your father being in charge of the Galactic Federation". Need I go on?'

'No, that's pretty much it.'

'Thought so. By the way, I was sorry – very sorry in fact – to hear about your sister. She was a lovely person.'

'Thanks. Did you actually know her or is that just another example of Pakha custom?'

Keri nodded and walked over to Kort. She pushed open a nearby door – her quarters. 'Want a drink? Coffee?'

Kort's instinct was to say no and stomp off. Instead he nodded and followed her in, briefly wondering why. 'Nice room,' he said.

'It's okay – more homely than your average Galactic Crest Forte, but lacks a certain flair, yeah.'

'No teasmade.' Kort looked out of the tiny slit-window. Rain lashed down on the black rock of Mount Megeshra outside. More rocks. In the distance, rain lashing down on the plains. 'Nice view.'

'Wouldn't know. Trouble with only being just under a metre tall is that I usually can't actually see out of the hotel windows. Or castle windows.'

Kort looked around Keri's room. Mostly spartan. In one corner a bed, with bags and cases dumped on it. In the opposite corner, a pile of fresh straw. A small table with a jug of water and a goblet. On the floor next to the straw, an electronic data-pad.

'I travel light,' she explained, watching his eyes. 'So did Jina.'

Kort admitted defeat and sat on the edge of the real bed. 'So how did you know her?'

Keri cleared her throat and twitched her whiskers. She reached over to one of her bags and pulled out a plastic wallet, almost too big for her paws. She flipped it open.

'Holo six.' A hologram appeared showing Keri and Jina. They were in rough clothes, ropes slung over their shoulders, torches in their hands. 'We both went hunting for the Ancient Diadem. It took us many months but with her expertise in antiquities and my resources at GFTV-3, we were able to make some pretty accurate guesses as to its whereabouts.' She called up holo twelve. The picture fizzled away and was rebuilt as one showing Jina in the same gear. Beside her, a human male, also dressed to go cave exploring.

'Alec?' asked Kort.

Keri nodded. 'She told you about him?'

'We were very close. We kept discussing ways of telling my father. For all his high ideals about the Federation, he was very traditional when it came to inter-species romances.' Kort pushed himself back against the wall and relaxed. 'When I was very young and we first moved away from my mother and came to Io, I got very friendly with a Draconian girl. She was the daughter of some previous Federation Chair who was off visiting that Federation loony bin.'

'Calfedoria? The Cal-Med 1 base?' prompted Keri.

'That's the one. Well, as you know, female Draconians still aren't the most popular children to be had by adult Draconians and he'd abandoned her there for the duration. Both of us felt quite lost, I guess. So we became friends, swapped toys, everything. One day my father saw us playing on his lawn and read me the riot act. Kathisul was soon shipped off planet to a special school and she's now at the Z-BD University. We still keep in contact.'

'I see. I didn't know Cantryans were that fanatical.'

'I don't know whether it was a grudge because she was a different species, whether it was because she was the daughter of the man he was succeeding or because she was female – after my mother left him, he never got on very well with females again.'

'He never explained?'

'He was Federation Chair by the time I was old enough to question his actions. He rarely had time for me, let alone questions. I'm only here with the Doctor and the professor because he wants me out of the way for a while.'

Keri called up another holo, this time showing a page from an old Pakha book. 'I don't suppose you read ancient Pakha?'

Kort shook his head. 'I barely read standard Pakha.'

'We're not your favourite race, are we?'

Kort had the decency to look embarrassed. 'Before I spoke to you, the only Pakha I'd met was the diplomat that attended Jina's funeral. He smelt funny and was rather rude. I guess it put me off a bit.'

Keri started to push the hologram of the page towards him when she froze. Slowly she looked up. 'Damakort, tell me about the Pakha you met.'

'It's Kort to my friends. Why?'

Keri smiled quickly at the compliment. 'Because I want to know who it was.'

'I don't know really, he said he was with the diplomatic corps. He was rather untidy – father kept moaning about how dirty his suit was. We didn't really want him at the wake, but what could we say?'

'When Jina died,' Keri said softly, 'I gathered her possessions together. Neal Corry and I were her friends. We sorted out the return of the body and her effects. One thing I made very clear was that, in accordance with Cantryan custom, no one should go to Io, let alone the cremation. I left the planet just before she was shipped back to you.'

'In that case why did he come?'

'What was his name, your scruffy, dirty Pakha from the DC?'

'I can't remember, Ker'a'nol.'

'It's Keri – to my friends. And this is important.'

'Hyn'o'th? No ... Hyn'nn'a?' No, Hyn't'n – that was it!'

Keri stared back at the holo of the book. On it, under the ancient Pakha writings was a picture of a simple gold circlet, encrusted with bright jewels. 'I know every single member of the Pakha Government DC. There is no one with a name remotely like Hyn't'n!'

Kort took a moment to digest this. 'Are you suggesting that he was a fake? It's all a bit unlikely, isn't it?'

Keri shook her head and put her paws to her nose. 'Listen – this page is from a book about ancient Pakha. It revolves around an object of immense but horrendous power – the Diadem. It is one of the most sought-after art treasures in this galaxy. A few years back I researched a vid about it. We gave up as nothing conclusive could be traced back to a reliable source. I was contacted by your sister shortly after she arrived on Pakha. She was doing some serious work on the Diadem and asked to go through my findings. She introduced me to Alec, who she had met at a dig a few days earlier. Together she and I thought we'd finally located the Diadem. We were planning to get Alec to sort out some of his human chums to help us mount an expedition. I contacted a university professor I knew called Sharrod and his people in turn brought in a Vegan to do the initial surveys of a cave system we found. It was that afternoon, while we sorted them out, that Jina was murdered. She was going to tell Alec and beam the information back to Io, to make a hard copy in case anything went wrong. We were sure we'd found it.'

Kort was alert now, bits of Jina's last message beginning to make sense 'Go on,' he said quietly.

Keri nodded and continued. 'Right. We know that the people who chased Jina were highly "respected" art thieves – humans who would stop at nothing to get what they wanted. They could then sell it on the black market. A unique object as powerful as the Diadem – if the legends were true – would be worth, oh, incalculable millions of credits. One of the thieves died in the chase but the other two just vanished after her death. So did Alec. Shortly before I came on this assignment I did a trace on Alexander Charles Roberts – Alec. I could find no trace of him. No bank account, no ship registration, no hotel on Pakha. Nothing. He didn't exist.'

'You think Alec was behind Jina's death? But she loved him – she told me on the net loads of times' Kort frowned. 'I mean, he seemed so nice, going by what Jina said.'

'Yes, he did. Too nice in retrospect,' said Keri.

Kort sat in silence for a moment. Then he got up. 'We need to check out this Hyn't'n character.'

Keri nodded. 'But how? We need access to a Federation computer net, and there isn't one on Peladon. Believe me, I've looked.'

'Ah, but not,' Kort announced excitedly, 'on the Martian shuttle.'

'Have you got Savaar's access codes? His commands or anything, yeah?'

Kort laughed. 'We make a good team, Keri. You do the research. And I? I just hack computers. The Federation hasn't developed a system I can't slice wide open!'

Moments later they slipped out of Keri's room and towards the caverns leading to the hanger deck.

Behind them, a pair of eyes blinked. He rubbed his ears – they felt as if they were almost burning. Mind you, pressed that hard against Keri's door, he was surprised they hadn't got friction burns.

So, Holmes and Watson were off to the hanger deck. Scarlett and Rhett were off to the catacombs while someone else was hiding in secret passageways. Oh well, it was time to get back to Laurel and Hardy and see how they were doing.

Neal Corry was at a loss. Not something he was too familiar with. As the ever-present chief executive and senior producer at GFTV–3, he was accustomed to being busy and fussy. Administering this piece of advice, disciplining that error, arranging some transport. Here on Peladon, he was very much in the hands of his Pakha crew – led by the delightful and highly sought-after Keri. Three other stations had offered enormous amounts of credits to purchase her services. Enough credits in fact for Corry to disband GFTV–3 altogether and have a very lucrative retirement. Apart from the redundancies that would cause – and bad feeling – Corry knew he'd get bored. Even if he kept GFTV–3 going, without its star news anchor, they'd quickly lose out to the ever-growing Butler-Straker corporation or the ever-present CNN news networks.

Corry enjoyed his job – he liked providing entertainment to the masses and they quite liked what he provided. A perfect symbiosis. Still, he couldn't work out why he felt it entirely necessary to come to Peladon himself. He assumed it was the urge to witness at first hand the dying breed that was royal occasions. Most planets were oligarchical but Peladon still kept all those fine trappings, pomp and ceremony that Earth had once had. All that plus the fact that Pakha was getting a bit overcrowded at the moment. His surrogate home was getting a little too tourist-infested right now. The silly season was upon them and he'd decided to get away. A busman's holiday, they used to call it.

Well, here he was. Fifty-ish, balding and slightly overweight. Alone and lonely. Oh, he put a brave face on it, buried it beneath a kind of bizarre jocular bonhomie but underneath everything, Corry was sad. At his age, he was unlikely to ever find the constant companionship he sought and was resigned to that, but even the casual acquaintances, one-night stands and such all belonged in a younger period, not now. Now he was expected to carry on his life in a rather strict, presentable manner. Fifty-seven and over the hill. Bloody typical.

His reverie was interrupted when he realized he'd

wandered far too deep into the massive black-rock caverns. He'd lost his bearings.

He knew he was going downwards, but how many levels? Surely before long he'd come to some kind of sign. Maybe the entrance to one of the old trisilicate mines or something. He was just about to give up and try retracing his steps when a loud metallic clang echoed throughout the cavern ahead.

'Hello? Who's there?' No reply.

'Hi? It's only Neal Corry. From the vid company. I'm lost, I'm afraid. Can you help me?'

Still no reply.

He ventured further into the cavern. It was much darker but very soon he noticed deep scarring on the rocks. The mine workings. Where Geban's family used to work. Now, there must be some kind of sign-posting.

He wandered on for another few minutes. It reminded him of one of his earliest assignments as a fledgling journalist. He and a holovid operator named Jaim Gehässig. They'd gone to the planet Voga, a deserted asteroid that had once housed a glorious but ultimately self-destructive race of gold worshippers. It was during the famous Cyber-fad. After records proved that both Telos and New Mondas had been destroyed and the legendary Cybermen eradicated for good, a massive hysteria overtook the rich, the famous and the couch potatoes who watched the newcasts. Finding the pieces to try and build a total picture of the Cybermen and their ascendancy from humanity. Voga, it had been historically noted, was instrumental in the mid-twenty-hundreds as a force against the Cybermen, exposing their weakness toward gold. Corry and Gehässig had been sent to explore the planet and examine the ruined cities deep within its hollow interior.

There they had spent a fruitful five days, exploring, examining and recording. At one point Gehässig had got lost in one of the catacombs and Corry had trekked throughout the night to find him. Eventually they met up again – merely a hundred yards from their camp. They

154

hadn't realized that the Vogan chambers were built as concentric circles and so one always got back to one's starting point eventually. Jaim Gehässig . . .

That was then. Somehow Corry doubted that Pel mines were circular. More like a spider's web – loads of different strands. Seen as a cross-section it probably made sense. As a lonesome fly caught in the strands, Corry was beginning to panic. What had caused that noise?

He rounded a corridor and almost tripped over. He looked down at what had caused his stagger. An overturned wooden barrow, its one wheel chipped and broken. Beside it, a rusty shovel. Thick rust. It had been a long time since anyone had been down here. Yet that noise came from the direction he was walking in. Could it have just been his imagination? It got very dark in the distance but he could see clearly for another few meters or so. No harm in going on now.

He rounded another slight bend and almost yelped with joy. Facing him was a large window, bright lights behind it. The glass was frosted, but he could clearly see someone inside. A metal door was built into the rock beside it. Above it, worn away but legible, was the word REFINERY.

Of course – the door. That must have made the noise as it was closed by whoever was inside. It briefly occurred to Corry that no one ought to have been down here, certainly in a Federation structure. And if they were Federation, he would certainly have known about it.

'Hey! You in there?' he called to the shapes. The light went out. 'Oh don't be bloody stupid, it's Neal Corry. I know you're in there!'

Corry reached out and grasped the large door handle. The second he touched it his head seemed to explode. Millions of bright lights and thousands of loud screams tore into his brain. He wanted to scream. To cry out. But his brain wouldn't respond, it was busy being tortured.

In his last few seconds before a blissful final darkness swallowed him up, Corry fell to his knees. He imagined he could see that holo operator Jaim, reaching out to him.

Not as he'd been on Voga, but a few years older, as he'd been at their bitter parting, full of recriminations and arguments, professional and personal. But Jaim had a big grin on his face – that marvellous grin he'd had on Voga after they'd found each other. That marvellous grin that always told Neal Corry that everything was going to be all right.

Half a second later Neal Corry slumped to the dusty ground – sightless eyes staring up at nothing, a twisted smile on his lips.

Behind him the refinery door slowly opened and someone came out and dragged his still body inside.

It was as if he'd never been there.

The Doctor braced himself and barged through the relic room door as if he owned the place.

'You were a long time,' observed an unusually laconic Sskeet.

'I had trouble finding anywhere to get a drink from. The coffee pot in the Federation Representatives' room was cold.'

Savaar was crouching by the chalk outline of the body. 'Doctor, I have examined this marking. I have examined the floor all around it. I have played your enigmatic, if childish game. As you no doubt expected I am forced to confess I cannot find what it is you claimed was so unusual. There is nothing to be found.'

The Doctor dropped cross-legged to the floor beside him. He leant across the outline, dug a hand into a pocket of his jacket which was still draped over the chair, and produced a red apple. He offered a bite to Savaar who merely flicked his tongue in an expression of contained disdain. The Doctor shrugged. 'An apple a day keeps you-know-who away!' he said and noisily crunched into it. With mouth full of apple he spoke, gesticulating as he rolled his short sleeves up.

'You see, High Lord Savaar, this chalk outline is very important on two counts.' He produced the piece of chalk he'd had when Savaar first entered. 'First, this chalk. It's not natural to Peladon. So why was it on the floor?'

'Presumably the rather clumsy Pel guard who drew the outline dropped it.'

The Doctor held up a finger. 'Ah, normally I would agree. Except.' He rustled in another pocket and triumphantly produced a second stick of chalk. 'Except this one is the chalk used to draw the outline of the poor man's body. I got it from the "rather clumsy Pel guard" while I was refreshment-hunting.' He popped it back into his pocket and brandished the original stick at Savaar. 'So. Why is there non-Pel chalk lying on the floor?'

'Does it matter?' asked Sskeet.

The Doctor looked hurt. 'Well yes, I rather think it does'.

'Why?'

'Ah. I don't know yet, but as soon as I do, you'll be the second to know.'

'Who will be the first?' asked Sskeet, barely containing his impatience.

'Me.' The Doctor looked across at the impassive Sskeet and back to an even more impassive Savaar. 'Okay, well, let's leave Mister Chalk for the moment. Instead, let's look at the body.'

'It isn't here any longer, Doctor.' Savaar stood up.

'No, but assuming that our "clumsy Pel guard" in fact did do his job properly, it is represented by this outline. Now, gentlemen, I bring your attention to the position our poor unfortunate is in.'

The Doctor stood up and tried to mimic the position. Head turned to the left. Right arm pointing up, left folded across the chest – therefore under the body. He put one leg at an angle and placed his foot on his shin.

'Basically, that's how he fell. Now, we know from the "clumsy Pel guard" . . .'

'Yes, all right, Doctor, you have made your point about the guard. I retract my suggestion that he was anything other than professional and conscientious in the execution of his duty. Now, will you please come to the point?'

Savaar was getting more heated. The Doctor grinned slightly at this fact. He didn't know if Bernice had managed to find his breaking point the previous night, but he was certainly getting close. Perhaps dangerously close. Time to back off slightly, Doctor? Of course not.

'So, High Lord, what we have is a man stabbed through the back but not out of the front. He then fell flat on his face, dead.'

'Indeed.'

'In which case I have two questions. Firstly, most importantly in fact, is why?' The Doctor assumed a more traditional posture. He stood at the chalk outline's feet. 'He was standing here, apparently looking at . . .' The Doctor stared directly ahead. 'Assuming Mister Corry and his video team did not disturb anything at all, he was looking at the chair that my coat is now on. Hmm, quite an important motive I'd say.' He dropped into a Humphrey Bogart voice. 'Here's lookin' at chairs, kid.'

'The point, Doctor, the point?'

'The point is, Lord Savaar, that I don't think that our man was standing here when he died at all. I think the murderer placed him here afterwards to make us look in the wrong place. In which case, where should we look? This is a big room.'

Hidden behind his helmet, Savaar raised his eyes heavenwards. 'Amaze me further, Doctor. It is obvious you already know where he was standing.'

Again, the Doctor's index finger went up. 'Ah ha!' He bounded forward and went round two or three trophy cabinets in a somewhat exaggerated manner. He was enjoying making a meal of his dramatic act. He stopped in front of a shield, sword and helmet.

'Here, Lord Savaar. Here is where he was standing. Whatever he was murdered for was on that wall in front of me.'

Savaar wandered over and stared at the sword, shield and helmet. He read the placard: 'Traditional hunting equipment.' He looked at the Doctor. 'I believe the human phrase is "Big deal. So what?" '

158

'It's wrong. This gear should be in that empty trophy case over there. Up here should be something called The Lance of Aggedor. It is the Pels' most sacred relic. Their equivalent of the Crown Jewels, or the Grand Marshal's Staff.'

'If the theft of the Lance was the motive, it was fool-hardy. The murderer and thief would have known it would have been noted as soon as Atissa or Nic Reece entered this room.'

'Yes, well, I rather think that our killer was banking on neither of them being around for a while. Reece is currently engaging my associate on a guided tour of the caverns and Atissa is probably in her sacred Temple of Aggedor, praying for this unfortunate old man's soul.'

'A waste of time,' Savaar said.

'Oh, maybe. However, it is important to Atissa, and to Aggedor's many believers. I wonder if the Lance is still on Peladon?'

'No one has left the planet, have they Sskeet?'

'No, my Lord. Just a few unmanned skimmers containing the holovids that Corry's team have made.' As Sskeet spoke, he realized what he had said.

'It might have been an idea to impound them and stop anything at all taking off, Savaar,' chided the Doctor.

'Sskeet, contact Hissel. If those skimmers are still in the area, he is to blow them out of the sky.'

'I think,' said the Doctor, 'that defeats the object. Firstly, I doubt our murderer is aboard – there's still too much here worth stealing. Secondly, if you blow the Lance up, I don't think the Pels will thank you. It is used as part of the restatement vows ceremony.'

'Your suggestion, Doctor?'

The Doctor crossed back to the chair and put his jacket back on. 'Give our man enough rope and he'll hang himself. Sometime during the lead up to the ceremony, he'll use the hustle-bustle to remove a few more choice items.'

'Why? It's not as if someone can buy them and display them. They are unique and easily traceable.'

'Exactly. I once had this conversation with a detective

about a very famous but quite bad painting on Earth. Even if the collector cannot display it, just knowing they have it is enough. Greed, Lord Savaar, is the most potent motive for murder in the galaxy. It always has been and always will be.'

As they turned to leave, Sskeet stopped. 'Doctor. How did you know the body had been moved?'

The Doctor smiled. 'That was easy. As the body was moved, it splashed blood on the spot around where the murder occurred. Elementary, my dear Sskeet!'

They closed the door behind them.

As the Ice Warriors walked ahead of him, the Doctor paused for breath. That was Laurel and Hardy dealt with. What about Holmes and Watson?

Getting on to the Martian ship did not prove a problem. The pilot had left it locked and wandered off for refreshment. Keri produced her data-pad and placed its magnetic side against the comm-lock. She pressed a stud and a hologram of the comm-lock appeared. 'Handy trick I picked up on one of the frontier worlds. A master criminal showed me how to do this while I was undercover.'

'What happened to him?' breathed Kort.

'He got arrested and tried for housebreaking using this system. He never told anyone I had this, though. Honour amongst thieves and all that.' She pressed a couple of studs and a series of codes flashed across the hologram. After a few seconds it flashed and vanished. 'Did you note the numbers?' Keri asked.

'What numbers?' asked Kort.

Keri smiled and pressed a series of numbers on the comm-lock. 'Have to be quick, yeah!'

The door silently slid open and after they went in, slid closed.

They were on the flight deck.

Seconds later Kort had located the computer input. He ran the first finger of his right hand down the small rectangle of microcircuits embedded in his temple.

Keri frowned. 'Implants?'

'Sort of. My own design. Far better than the standard ones you can buy or even the ones home-made by cyberspace zapp-heads. Instant access to everyone and everything on the Fed-Net and quite a few others.' He grinned broadly. 'But don't tell my father, he thinks it's a basic plant just for me. And Jina.' He sat back in the pilot's chair, breathed deeply and quietly spoke some letters and commands.

'DMKT dash Slicer 4 dash Io dash Access stroke Access.'

The computer replied: **'Password?'**

'DMKT dash Slicer 4 dash infinite dash PSWD stroke Access.'

'Access accepted DMKT dash Slicer 4.'

Keri yelped in delight. 'Well done, yeah!'

Kort rubbed his hands. 'Okay, computer. Try this. Search. Pakha, Male. Hyn't'n. Fed Research. All parameters.' There was a pause. 'It'll take a second or two.'

'Located. More?'

'Yes please.'

'Hyn't'n. Resident of Pakha. Criminal record. Access HP only. I'm sorry.'

'What the cruk does that all mean?' asked Keri.

'Basically,' replied Kort, 'our little man has a criminal record longer than Centauri's six arms strung together. I'll have to slice into the Pakha system now. Okay, here goes. Computer: Access DMKT dash infinite dash Pakha Criminal Records dash Locate Hyn't'n.'

There was another, longer, pause as the computer found the information. Then it began reading out a long list of petty crimes in and around the Pakha homeworld and satellites. After a few moments reading the two hackers sat back.

'Wow. He's one master criminal.'

Keri shook her head. 'Not really. Mostly petty thieving by Pakha standards. Obviously a hired hand who gets dropped in the guano too often by his employers. Let's find out where he is now.'

Kort nodded and said, 'Locate subject.'

Another brief pause, then:

'Hyn't'n deceased. Body found twenty-four dash 14 dash 9-fed. Mutilated. Coroner's report suggests murder by persons unknown. Do you require more?'

Keri shook her head. 'Yesterday! He was killed yesterday! Why?'

The door behind them slid open and an angry hiss alerted them. They both swung round to be faced by the Martian pilot. Without hesitation he brought up his right arm with its sonic disrupter primed and ready.

Keri gulped. 'Oh cruk, yeah!'

Aboard the *Bruk*, Marshal Hissel regarded the information racing across his computer screens with interest. Why had the security codes on the shuttle computer been tripped? Why was information about some gutted Pakha being investigated?

He reached out for the communications console to alert High Lord Savaar when a steady bleeping alerted him. He turned to look at a small black box fitted to the sensor equipment on the comm section. The red light on top was flashing in time with the irregular bleeps.

On Peladon a similar box was flashing and bleeping.

It was secreted in the living quarters of the man who had once been Alexander Charles Roberts.

The man who had been searching for the Diadem and had sent his mercenaries to retrieve it.

The man who had pretended to love and then ruthlessly slaughtered Jina on Pakha.

The man who had murdered Fabon and stolen the Lance of Aggedor.

Holding the box in his paws and grinning was holocameraman Jav.

Down in the refinery, deep and forgotten in the abandoned trisilicate mines of Peladon, the shadowy shapes still moved about.

162

All except one.

That one sat at a console. On top was a black box with flashing red lights on top. Attached to the box was a comm-link and data-pad. This figure was sending the bleeps.

In his quarters, the Doctor sat back on his bed and grimaced. Beside him was a travelling chess set. He lazily reached out and picked up a white rook and moved it forward, taking a black pawn. He spun the set around and moved a black knight forward which not only took the white rook but placed the white king in check.

'Not quite mate, Doctor, but it's getting there,' he said to himself.

Interlude 2

'The Galactic Federation grew into existence during the first third of the thirty-second century, Earth time. After the complete failure of the old alliances and the even bigger disaster of Earth's outrageous empire, it seemed only natural that the planet should join forces with its nearest neighbours. Previous empirical races such as the Draconians and the New Martians were as quick to see the merits in such a scheme.

From those first tentative sub-space messages to each other to the final grand ceremony at the purpose-built Galactic Federation headquarters on the terra-formed moon of Jupiter, Io, lay a period of nearly three hundred years. Those who originally conceived such peaceful co-existence were long dead before fruit was borne. Nevertheless the Federation did happen. And today it still stands, a monument to the erasure of greed, malice and selfishness that had nearly doomed each of the contributing planets beforehand.'

Extract from 'Federation History'
by Grith Robtts
©AD 3698 Bowketts Universal Publications

'The trouble with the glorious idea of a Galactic Federation is that while the highbrows and top-nobs confer, consolidate and collaborate, the smaller individual gets lost and forgotten. In such cases it is far easier for the less law-abiding merchant to flourish.

The least scrupulous of these can be found almost

One of those less-than-legitimate businessmen was entering his office at the start of another business day on Japetus. Kaldor was a city on the edge of a vast sandy desert, one of three man-made cities on Saturn's second moon.

Most of Kaldor's richer businessmen made their money by sifting through the desert sands, searching for rare minerals to be shipped back to Io for distribution within the Federation. The Founding Families (as the initial terraformers called themselves) were well established now as Japetus's governing body.

Iain Martyn was neither a particularly rich businessman nor related to one of the founding families. He had arrived in Kaldor City five years ago, leaving his original colony on Earth's moon with the little money he possessed, and had set up a surgery in the city. The Founding Families would have nothing to do with him – they had their own medical practitioners, but the common or garden Federation workers used him because they could just about afford to.

Martyn also worked on the black market – it was, to be frank, the only way he could support himself in a good lifestyle. Unmarried and with no offspring, he was hit by high taxes and received no state subsidies. He also had to keep his employee, a dizzy blonde called Krau Gillatt (he assumed she had a first name, but he didn't know it – she was always Krau Gillatt to him) in work and support his

165

ever-growing holovid collection. It was said by those who visited his apartment that he probably had more discs in his living room than the GFI had in their entire archives.

'Good morning, Doktor Martyn,' chirped Krau Gillatt as he entered his office.

He nodded a greeting back and ran his micro-filamented finger down a strip on her desk. In front of him hovered pages from the appointments book. A quick flick told him that business was down this week. He shrugged and with a second slice of his finger made it vanish.

'Well?' he asked.

Krau Gillatt shook her head. 'Nothing in the other book, either I'm afraid.'

The 'other book' was a genuine paper and ink one in which Martyn kept records of his meetings, appointments and invoices for those clients who did not wish to appear on any official Federation statistics. The high-paying clients who usually requested surreptitious help. This could range from construction workers who injured themselves in bar-room brawls and didn't want their wives to know, to top Kaldor City businessmen and Founding Family men whose dalliances with the rent girlz and boyz had resulted in a case of sexually transmitted diseases and also didn't want the wife to know. Occasionally, he'd have to use laser technology to remove birthmarks or prison tattoos. Once in a while someone would come for complete physical re-creation technique, usually those on the run from Federation officials, tax men or their now-sexual-ly-transmitted-disease-infected wives.

Iain Martyn was not a specialist in any particular field of medicine or surgery, but he was a bit of a jack of all trades. He could turn his hand to most things and physical re-creation was a favourite hobby. Especially if he could slightly base the new face on a holovid star of the past. That was when work became a pleasure.

'There is one thing,' Krau Gillatt jolted him out of his reverie. 'Your last PRT client – one Alexander C Roberts? His bill hasn't been paid.'

166

'But I gave you the credit check.'

Krau Gillatt shrugged. 'I'm sorry, Doktor, but that came up blank. I ran a basic check with KalBank Inc., and they tried it through the major Federation credit systems. No luck.'

Martyn pondered for a moment. He remembered Roberts coming to him. It had been a busy week but nevertheless he could clearly remember fitting the man into his schedule. He'd had an accident of some sort. Claimed he worked in the Balos City furnaces, slagging down the non-precious minerals for the Federation troopships. A fight with a colleague had severely burnt his face and he'd been fired.

'But if you can rebuild my face, in fact give me a new one, then I can be someone else. With my experience, I'd actually get my old job back, but they'd think I was someone new.'

Martyn considered this easy enough – in fact it had been made easier because Roberts had provided a holo of the face he wanted. It wasn't in Martyn's interest to ask who the original face had belonged to: he just took the credit slip and did the job.

Normally that would be all there was to it. Bank the credits in a couple of accounts and make it untraceable – too small to interest the tax man. A bit on the side.

That was fine if the credit actually went through, but in this case it hadn't.

'Run a check on this Roberts. See if we can find out where he was before he came to Japetus.' Martyn entered his inner office and dug out the scant notes he had on his first of only three patients today.

By lunchtime, he was bored. He stuck his head out of the office door. 'Krau Gillatt, what time is the man with the hair recedence problem due in?'

Krau Gillatt was as efficient as always. Without even consulting the appointments book she said, 'Trau Briggs is due at four thirty-five, Doktor Martyn.'

It was only twelve forty-five now. Martyn smiled over to her. 'Fancy a long lunch? We could grab a bite and a drink at the spaceport bar and then you could do some shopping.'

Krau Gillatt was out of her chair in a second, brushing back her hair and adding a brighter shade of lipstick before he'd turned to get his wallet and credit card. 'I'm all yours, Doktor.'

The spaceport was a seven-minute walk and after a few morsels of smalltalk about her husband and young son (if she had a husband and son, how come she was 'Krau' Gillatt, he wondered), Martyn asked her if she'd had any luck tracing Alexander Charles Roberts.

Krau Gillatt shook her head. 'Nothing much. He certainly lied to you about working at BF. The furnace boss had never heard of him, nor had they fired or hired anyone in the last four months. I holofaxed over the image of his new face, but it meant nothing to him.' She opened the doorway of the spaceport bar and followed her boss in. 'Anyway,' she continued after Martyn had bought a couple of drinks, 'I did find out that a Alexander Charles Roberts was briefly registered with the Second Norvegica Bank, on Pakha of all places, a few months back. There's a lovely young man at Io Info-Tech who just gushed the information to me. Apparently this Roberts disappeared off Pakha without settling his rather large overdraft. The bank has issued a credit warrant.'

Iain Martyn considered this for a moment. 'Seems a bit of a coincidence. Pakha's a long way from here. Besides, if he was going to run, far better to move out to another frontier world than back to the heart of Federation space.'

Krau Gillatt had a theory on that one. 'Ah, yes, but what if it was a double-bluff? Our man defrauds the SN Bank and, like you, the Pakhars think he's going further out. Instead, he re-enters Federation Central and comes to you for a new face. By the time he leaves Kaldor and even Japetus the heat is off, the search over and he could then get out of here and on to a frontier world. If the Pakhars haven't found him in a year then their claim is void. After all, it wasn't a particularly large overdraft.' She swallowed her drink and stroked the stem of the glass.

Taking the hint, Martyn rose and went to get them both another. As he approached the bar, he was aware of a conversation between the tender and an older male customer.

'. . . no survivors, apparently. Well, I've been off work for a few days and only heard about it this morning. Of course, they made me sign lots of papers, you know, Galactic Federation secrecy an' all that. But I know *you* won't tell anyone else . . .'

The bartender gave him a look that suggested butter wouldn't melt in his mouth. Of course, he didn't need to tell anyone else, the old man was being loud enough for everyone around the bar to hear. Besides which, everyone else's conversation had died down to enable them to listen to this top-secret information. Martyn felt almost guilty for listening, but what the hell. Federation secrets weren't usually that secret.

'So,' the old man continued, 'there I was getting the floor-cleaning servicer out of its cupboard when I saw the list. It's so sad. I mean, that Commander Rudzka was such a nice woman. "Joel," she'd always say, "Joel, how's the wife? Rebekkha isn't it?" Not many troopers even know my name, let alone Bek's.'

The old man would have carried on forever if two Federation troopers hadn't come in at that moment. The bartender tried to warn Joel but the old man didn't take the hint. 'Hang on, there's more. Apparently these people nicked a shuttle and – '

Old Joel was cut off as a gauntlet clamped down on his shoulder. A man with a captain's insignia on his chest leaned over.

'I think you've been drinking, Joel. Ought to lay off it, you know. Careless, inaccurate talk and all that . . .' There was no mistaking the warning and Joel swallowed hard.

'I'm sorry, Captain Jaansen. I guess I'd best get back to work.'

Captain Jaansen nodded. 'There's a few more corridors need cleaning, Joel, before clocking-off. Coming?' It was an order, not a question really, and Joel looked as if he knew it.

Martyn watched the whole thing. Something in the back of his mind struck a chord. Alec Roberts. He'd been talking about security at the spaceport. Asking Martyn if he knew anything about their shuttles. Pretended he was into fast flyers. It hadn't sounded right back then, and in light of what Old Joel had said . . .

Krau Gillatt was quite surprised to see her boss dashing out of the bar, apparently following the troopers towards the spaceport. Something told her that Trau Briggs was going to find his four thirty-five appointment cancelled this afternoon.

'Tell me the whole story from the start, Doktor, if you please.'

Iain Martyn was sweating. He didn't like authority at the best of times – his one foot on the wrong side of the law always made him extra nervous. Now, here he was, trying for once to be a dutiful citizen (although getting the credits due to him from Alec Roberts had something to do with it) and they were treating him almost as if he was the criminal.

He told the story from the start. The five men dressed in black seated around the table listened and took notes. Copious notes, whispering to themselves and using their adapted fingers to place the information he was presenting straight into their memories via the micro-meshes on their temples, reminding the doktor of something he'd heard about monkeys, micro-meshes and the complete works of Shakespeare.

When he'd finished the eldest man, a Brigade Leader Lepav, smiled benignly – and about as convincingly as a wolf that tells a sheep that it's really vegetarian. 'Nothing to worry about, Doktor Martyn. You've done the right thing in telling us about this Alexander Charles Roberts.' Lepav leaned across the table, the vegetarian wolf looking even less plausible than before. 'And don't worry. In the military, we're not interested in your – how can I put it?

– back-street medical practices. We leave that kind of thing to the Federation Administrators, and they won't hear a word about it from me.'

A man, clearly from Io, standing at the back of the room caused Martyn to suspect that at best this was a lie and at worst he'd just sacrificed his career.

'One thing I have got,' he said meekly, 'is a copy of the holo of the face I turned him into. I could get my secretary to bring it over, if you can just connect me with her.'

'Can't we just fibre-op it up?' said Captain Jaansen, who'd been at the back of the room but was suddenly uncomfortably close to Martyn's right ear.

Martyn shook his head. 'It's on my pad – it needs my Neyscrape. It's sort of . . . confidential . . .' he ended lamely.

Lepav licked his lips. Probably wondering how Martyn would look smothered in mint jello, the doktor decided.

'Tell you what, Trau Martyn,' Lepav said. The dropping of his professional title didn't escape Martyn for a second – his career *was* finished. 'Tell you what, I'll just get Captain Jaansen there to nip over to Kaldor City and get it off her, all right?'

Martyn nodded in mute resignation.

He sat waiting for nearly half an hour, sweating enough to open a lido. Eventually Jaansen returned, a data-pad in his hand. He nodded at Lepav who took the pad and offered it to the doktor.

'Err . . . Holo Recon AR2,' Martyn said.

One second later and a three-dimensional face was rotating in front of the assembled group.

'This your Alexander Charles Roberts?' Lepav asked.

Martyn nodded. 'That's what he looks like now, Brigade Leader. I have to confess it was a very good result indeed. I don't know whose face it is . . . or was . . . though.'

Brigade Leader Lepav nodded slowly, and Martyn followed his gaze around the group. Most of them, including Jaansen, were clearly nonplussed, it was no one they knew. But the one with a Galactic Federation HQ flash on his shoulder was clearly amazed.

171

Lepav wasn't smiling any longer. 'I think I can tell you this, Trau Martyn. The face in front of us belongs to a dead man. He died about three or four weeks back in a shuttle accident. The particulars of the accident have never been satisfactorily resolved. With your information I think we're on the way to learning some new information.' He turned to the Federation official. 'Trau Secretary?'

'Oh, indeed, Brigade Leader,' confirmed the secretary. 'Now, if you'll excuse me, I must put a message through to the Federation Chair on Io. And then a call to High Lord Savaar on board the *Bruk*.' The secretary turned to Martyn and smiled. Another vegetarian wolf smile. 'You see, Trau Martyn? Your information must go to the very highest levels.' The secretary nodded to Lepav and exited.

Martyn cleared his throat to speak, but when he did, it came out almost as a whisper. 'Excuse me. What happens to me now?'

Lepav ignored him. Instead he got out of his seat. 'Time, gentlemen, for a spot of dinner. Canteen's doing a splendid roast something or other today.' He then acknowledged Martyn. 'Fancy seeing what's on the menu, Trau Martyn?'

5:

A Game Called Echo

'Are you mad?'

Atissa swung around on her mother, ignoring the astonished looks on the faces of the others gathered in the temple. 'I? Mad? Mother, it was not I who welcomed the Federation. It was not I who filled the king's head with ridiculous tales of Federation wonderment. It was not I who – '

'Enough!' Lianna waved the guards and attendants away. As they fled, she walked over to the vast granite statue that dominated the far wall of the temple. 'Look at Aggedor, Atissa. Look at him and think what he stands for in our hearts. In the very soul of the Pels.'

Atissa did not need to look at Aggedor. She knew exactly what he looked like. Exactly what he stood for. She knew all the stories, all the tales and legends. She also knew where her duty lay. 'You may be my mother but you have become a stranger to me,' she said. 'You stroke the statue but you do not believe in it. You suggest you want to invoke images of soul, passion and heritage but instead you advocate the selling-off of such things like cheap baubles in the markets. I tell you this as the servant of Peladon, as the high priestess of Aggedor and as your daughter, you, Mother, are the betrayer. You are the mad one.' She waved her hands at the incense burners, the gas flambeaus and the everlasting candles. 'Look about you and see the Federation's gifts to us. There are none! Just a few gimmicks and tricks "to keep the primitive natives amused". It is an insult and I am disgusted. Disgusted above all at you for falling for all this.'

Lianna sighed. It was a circular argument. 'I can see you are not rational at the moment, daughter. But be warned, we shall talk about this again.'

Atissa gaped in astonishment. 'Again? Again! We have done nothing but talk. You have preached Federation lies, I have preached Pel truth. We have nothing further to say, Mother. Leave my . . . Aggedor's Sacred Temple before I declare you and your allies heretics.'

'You would go that far?'

'I would go as far as I need to protect this planet.'

'Against the wishes of the king?'

'King? That weak-willed fool? Rank does not equal greatness, Mother. Remember that.'

Lianna tried one last time. She grabbed at a candlestick. 'Look at this, Atissa. Your forebears would spend weeks creating just one of these from the limited resources that Peladon offered naturally. Now we have one that never deteriorates. Never burns away. It does not insult Aggedor. It does not devalue our heritage. It benefits us in however small a way. Yet you would declare war over a matter so trivial?'

Atissa paused and stared at the other candlesticks. Then she reached out and reclaimed the one from Lianna's hand, setting it in its proper place. 'A war? Your choice of words, Mother, not mine. But yes, I would go as far as to say that it is at least a battle. And I will win that battle, because I know I am right.'

'Study the Federation histories, daughter. Examine other worlds, other places. Study them and learn just how many wars have been fought and lost, at horrendous costs too vast for us to truly comprehend, and all because someone "knew they were right".'

Atissa turned away from her mother. 'Your mind, your body, your being – all are evil.'

Lianna felt a chill drive through her body. 'You . . . you have no right to invoke the curse upon me.'

'Your mind, your body, your being – all are evil,' Atissa repeated.

Lianna turned on her heel and left the sanctum.

Ten minutes later, Atissa was still murmuring the curse but no one was there to listen.

An hour later, her life changed forever.

'Hello-o-o.'

'Over here-ere-ere,' came the reply.

Bernice grinned. Gotcha, she thought. Second cavern on the right. Which she had come down a few moments earlier, noting the side caverns. She looked across at the third cavern – about seven meters down should be a small tunnel linking the two. She could nip down that and come out behind him.

'Coming-ing-ing,' she yelled, her voice echoing around the cold walls of the Pel catacombs. As she rushed into the third cavern it occurred to her just how childish this all was. Two grown people scampering around tunnels, yelling echoes to each other like schoolchildren. It had been Nic's idea but Bernice thought it reminded her of home. One of the better memories, before the Daleks came. She shrugged the old memories off – that was then, this was now and she could see Nic hiding behind a stalagmite, ignorant of her approach.

She got as close as possible and yelled, 'Boo!' in his ear. If she was expecting a jocular reaction, she was mistaken. Instead an elbow jabbed back, catching her expertly in the solar plexus, driving all the air out of her lungs. She was floored, gasping in less than a second, tears of pain blurring her vision. As Nic bent over her, muttering astonished words of apology, Bernice was momentarily convinced that his eyes said a different story. But what . . . She couldn't concentrate on that, she just wanted to breathe properly again, and allowed Nic to gently pull her up, rubbing his hands over her back, as if pumping air back into her.

'Frag it, Benny, I'm so sorry. You caught me completely unawares and frightened the life out of me.'

Bernice managed a weak wave-away of the apology. 'Stupid . . . move,' she said. 'Someone did that to me on a dig once when . . . when I was concentrating.' She managed to stand upright, but her stomach felt as if someone had sliced it open. 'I nearly hospitalized him. I thought he'd never speak to me again.'

'And did he?'

'Clive? Yeah, became my best friend.'

'Good,' said Nic Reece. 'I hope the pattern repeats itself.' He looked at Bernice and she smiled. 'Pax?'

She laughed, glad to have the air back inside her. 'Pax? I haven't heard that in centuries.' Bernice suddenly realized that their faces were unusually close. She could see the laugh lines etched in his cheeks, around his eyes. She could almost count the stubble hairs on his chin, feel his breath . . .

She took an involuntary step backwards. He looked as if he'd been struck. 'Why?' she thought. 'Damn it, why did you do that? He's a nice guy and he likes you. Stupid!' She moved slightly forward again. As she looked closely her eyes rested upon the skin around his temples. Tiny, almost invisible scars on both sides. Most people would never have noticed, but Bernice prided herself on her instinctive and detailed examinations of everyone she met. Her frown must have caught his attention, because he slowly rubbed the right temple.

'I . . . I had one of those blasted Neyscrapes. Put it in when I was fifteen. Stupid, really. We all went out one night, had too much to drink and dared each other. Needless to say, I was the first to have one.'

'You're not a follower of Gaia then?'

Reece looked puzzled, so Bernice explained what Kort had said to her about her lack of Neyscrape.

'Oh, right,' he said. 'No, I got rid of it because . . . because . . . well, it doesn't matter.'

Bernice found herself placing a hand on his wrist. 'Nic, whatever it is, you're going to have to talk about it sooner or later. Now, tell me to bugger off if I'm interfering, but I want to help. To be a friend. And a confidante.'

'Later.' Reece reached out and stroked her face. 'Nice skin.'

Bernice suddenly squealed and backed away once more.

She ran her finger along her cheek and realized she was bleeding.

Nic looked shocked. 'I ... I'm sorry. I guess my nails are longer than I thought ... I ...'

'Hey, it's not a problem,' soothed Bernice. 'It's only a little scratch.'

Nic reached out and wiped some blood off her cheek but again Bernice instinctively flinched at the touch.

'Now I'm sorry,' she said and grinned. 'Look, let's head back, eh?' She turned and started to walk up the passage.

Behind her, Nic Reece rolled the blood between his finger and thumb and slowly licked it off. As he watched Bernice wander into the gloom his face split into a wide grin. 'Hey, Professor, wait for me!'

If he'd waited a second longer he might have become aware of the figure who had watched the whole incident. Two seconds and he would have seen the figure lumber off in the opposite direction, towards the apparently disused refinery. But he didn't and as a result missed the opportunity to drastically change his destiny.

What the hell was wrong with her? Twice in the space of half a day she'd been too late.

Too late to save the Pakhar and now too late to save the humans. She knelt over the student with the broken neck. Young. Attractive. Probably about nineteen years old. All the years of growing up; being fed and clothed, learning to walk and talk. Somewhere, some proud parents had paid for his education at the University of Pakha, and now all those years of learning, probable ambitions and plans, all wasted by a few seconds of savagery. She'd seen death many times – she'd killed more than she cared to remember, but somehow the loss of this one life seemed so ... so cruel. So totally wrong.

There was a time she wouldn't have cared. But now? Now she cared. 'You're growing up, Dorothy. 'Bout bloody time, too.'

She gritted her teeth as she stared at the pain-wracked face, eyes staring in a rigid death-mask. The body was cold but not stiff. The blood around the mouth (he'd bitten into his tongue as he died, she guessed) was sticky. He'd only been dead an hour or so. Ace thrust a hand inside his jacket and took out a data-pad. There was a small rectangle of micro-filaments in one corner. She pressed and stroked but nothing. There must be some way . . . Her eyes settled on his dead fingers. The index finger of his left hand had a similar mesh and then she saw another, slightly larger one on the side of his face. She ran the finger over the data-pad mesh, but nothing. Damn.

She sat down. 'Think, Ace. It's the thirty-ninth century. You got the TARDIS to show you how the clip-blaster worked. Think techno.' She cupped the dead boy's hand again and ran his finger down the strip on his face. The data-pad glowed faintly. 'Low batteries or low contact,' she shrugged. 'Name?'

Nothing.

She thought about what she had learned from the TARDIS. Most personal equipment was individually coded by a DNA scan, therefore stopping anyone else accessing the information or whatever. That's right! The DNA scan is connected by the two micro-filaments triggering each other and, like the gun she had, was initialled by a mental command. Therefore, it had to be not just any order but a personal one. Whatever brain activity was still fading within the young man's head had been enough to trigger the data-pad – she just had to ask the right questions.

'Who am I?' she said.

A hologram grew out of the pad – about seven centimetres high, the young man smiling happily. Probably taken in this centuries equivalent of those photo booths that used to litter stations and such like. Ace remembered herself and some friends . . . Who was there? Manisha? No, but Shreela was. And Ange. And Julian. All ducking and diving just to make silly faces four times over to use as their travelcard photocards. Julian was dead. Could he have guessed that so soon after farting around in that photo booth he'd be gone?

Nor could her unnamed new soulmate. Her dead soulmate.

'Hi, Julian Winmill here. Blood group O. I'm not telling you my age, but hell, I can remember when music was real music and not that modern guitar junk. Bring back the samplers, that's what I say. And memo to me; dupe this for Mom. I promised her a record of everything – within reason – regarding this semester.'

Julian. His name was Julian. Just like *her* Julian. 'If I ever have a son (God help us), remind me never to call him Julian,' Ace said. 'Okay. Play me back my last diary entry.'

The hologram flicked off, to be replaced by one of Winmill in the clothing he wore as a corpse. 'Well, Joolz, tomorrow's the big day. Sharrod's taking us to some cavern to find some artefact. Pol Fehler is coming – what a surprise, his tongue's so far up Sharrod's . . . oh, what the hell, who cares! Hey, Nezz Larroq's coming. I wonder . . . Oh, dream on kiddo. You know, I have this reputation of getting to lay anyone I want. How? For Christ's sake, I'm a fragging virgin! I mean, where do these stories come from? Christ, I can't believe I said that. I better wipe that in case someone ever slices this.' The hologram turned its head slightly and then back to facing front. 'Right. That was Vega Lexus calling, time to go. After this is over and I'm back tomorrow night, it's wipe-out time for you, dear diary. Seeya!' The hologram leaned forward, flickered and vanished.

Ace stared at the pad. Then down at Julian Winmill. She reached down and closed his eyes. 'I'm sorry, Joolz. I don't even know you and I'm really sorry.' Her eyes were prickling so she breathed in deeply and stood up. Instantly she knew she was being watched. Her blaster was primed and aiming in her hand faster than even she thought possible. A shrill squeak of terror told her where her observer was crouching.

'Come on out, or I'll fry you.'

A black-furred Pakhar bustled from behind a rock, one

paw in the air, the other scratching at its muzzle. Its nose visibly twitched as it got nearer.

'Are they all dead?'

Ace nodded. 'Nastily.'

'Did you kill them?'

'You know I didn't. You've been tracking me, pretty bloody badly, since I left the hutch.'

The Pakhar's snout moved from side to side. Ace had spoken to enough Pakhars earlier to recognize a sign of disappointment. 'I'm not very good at this,' it started.

Ace lowered her blaster fractionally, but kept her finger on the trigger-stud, just in case. 'Stay primed,' she willed at it. The red light on top flashed back its acknowledgment of the order. 'So,' she said aloud, 'who are you?'

'My name is Ci'm'ur. I was an . . . associate of Hyn't'n's.'

'In other words, you're also a shifty, underworld opportunist. Pleased to meet you. What happened to Hyn't'n?'

Ci'm'ur shuffled slightly. 'Wrong sort. Human mercenaries. After the Diadem.'

'And Hyn't'n told them it was here?'

'A friend of ours works at the university. Good job, too – secretary to the administrator's personal assistant. Tells us lots of things. Like about Sharrod's expedition to find it.'

'This Sharrod. Good man is he? Trustworthy? Does he know how to find the Diadem?'

The Pakhar waved towards the older man sprawled over the artificial fire, a large hole burnt right through his chest from the back. Ace sighed. 'I wonder if he found it.'

'I imagine so,' said Ci'm'ur. 'They're not here now. They've probably already got it.'

Ace moved towards him. 'I must get after them. Can I get a shuttle passage easily?'

Ci'm'ur nodded. 'I can arrange that. One hour. Port Four. Ask for me.'

'An hour! They could be hundreds of thousands of kliks away by then. Halfway across this system.'

'Not possible. I work at the ports. I give clearance for

take-offs. I arranged their exit permits. I can't stop them, but they won't be happy. I've held them up.'

'How?'

'Extended lunch break. Following you.'

Ace had to smile. 'Okay, let's go.'

The Pakhar moved forward and took her left hand, totally ignoring the blaster in her right. 'I don't know who you are,' he said. 'But I saw you look at that human boy's pad. I saw the way you reacted. You're not like them. I know you didn't know Hyn't'n any more than you knew Professor Sharrod and his students, but for me if nothing else, please find them and stop them.'

Ace nodded. 'Let's go.' She moved back to the bodies. She picked up Julian Winmill's pad. 'If I can, Joolz, I'll get this back to your folks.' Putting it in the inside pocket of her bomber jacket, she wandered after the Pakhar. She looked at her wrist computer. Just an hour to go.

Sadler stared at the vacuum pack. It was inside a transparent safe-seal, attached to the shuttle's power-systems so that it was untouchable until they landed and powered down. But inside . . . Such power. Such dreams. Such . . .

She shivered and looked away. Cruk it! The blasted thing was making her feel odd. She glanced across at Townsend's broad back, seated at the pilot's console. Lambert was on the communicator, moaning at Port Command. Something about the official in charge of telling the other officials that a bigger official had officially cleared them for take-off. About crukking time, too.

Power

Townsend relaxed. 'That took long enough.'

'Why didn't we leave anyway? They could hardly stop us.' Cooper was swigging on a bottle of something vaguely toxic.

Townsend sighed. He'd explained this earlier. 'Look, this is a stolen shuttle. We're far enough away from the major Federation space lane to avoid detection on Pakhar, but I'm not taking any unnecessary risks. Anyway, Sadler's

181

little charge,' he waved towards the vacuum box, 'is worth too much to foul up. Now, everyone ready?'

Sarcastic murmurs were his only response.

Such power

Lambert grinned laconically. 'All safety procedures intact, Captain. Passengers secured and relaxed. A servicer will soon be along with refreshments and we have thirty-nine vid channels to choose from. Thank you for flying with the Townsend Corporation.'

Townsend didn't smile back. Instead, he piloted the ship away from Pakha.

Sadler relaxed. And realized her hand was dangerously near the voice override control on the safe-seal. She whipped her hand away. What was she doing, she thought. She had to be tired.

Ambition. Domination

A smile seeped on to her lips.

Control

Her hand dropped to the controls, her eyes stared ahead.

Maximum power

Her fingers neared the override codes.

Infinite power!

'Launch confirmed, Shuttle *My'n'ad*. Good luck.'

'Thanks, Control. For everything. *My'n'ad* out.'

Ace gripped the arm rests as her new shuttle roared into the airzones of Pakha. The slight g-force held in place for a few seconds until she escaped orbit, then she settled down to relax and follow her prey. Ci'm'ur had done his bit – the mercenaries' shuttle had been delayed; hers speeded up so she was only three or four minutes behind them, running on navcom so she didn't have to do a thing. They'd programmed in the other shuttle's codes so she could trace it wherever it went. Some judicious use of the on-board computer-link and she'd essentially told her craft to 'follow that shuttle'. Good.

She kept her eyes on the hologram of her enemy.

Bernice sat in her room, alone. She had kicked her boots off and crunched her orange sweater into a pillow. She was propped against the wall, below the window, the sweater keeping the stippled rock from jabbing the back of her head. In her hands was her diary. She was staring at it, stylus in hand, but no words were being consigned to posterity. After a few moments of staring aimlessly she closed it and threw it on to the bed. She slipped the stylus into a pocket of her rather grimy chinos and pushed herself up, catching the falling sweater and stuffing it under her arm.

'Better go and see what trouble the Doctor's in by now,' she murmured and wandered out into the corridor. Her boots still lay beside her bed.

The first thing she saw was the king's champion, Torg, rushing past her. She cocked an eyebrow. Torg was a big guy and he was in a hurry. Good job she wasn't in his way. She wandered after him unhurriedly, wondering what his problem was. As she rounded yet another identical corner she heard a roar and absolute rage from ahead of her. Instinctively Bernice broke into a run and caught up with Torg.

Roughly the giant shoved her away from the doorway in which he stood.

'Hey,' she started.

Then she saw.

The room was the Lady Lianna's. She was inside. By the far wall, next to the window. In fact, she was attached to the wall via the rather lethal-looking barbed spear that had been rammed through her midriff and skewered her to the wall.

Standing and holding the shaft of the spear, his hands soaked in Lianna's blood, was the Doctor. The look of complete and utter shock and horror etched into his face made Bernice shiver. Slowly his head turned and he seemed to notice Torg and her for the first time. His eyes locked with hers and she saw something she couldn't ever remember seeing there before. She had seen anger, sadness, bitterness and hurt. She had seen joy and laughter. But never, ever had she seen total uncontrollable panic.

As Torg growled and moved towards him, he stepped back, blood dripping to the floor. He let go of the spear and it vibrated slightly as it took the full weight of Lianna's dead body.

Behind Bernice she was aware of people gathering but she didn't turn until a soft voice she recognized came from right beside her.

'I don't believe it . . .' Nic Reece stepped forward. 'Lianna! No!' he roared and tried to run to the body. With an effortless gesture, Torg held him back with his other hand until a couple of guards pushed past and took charge of the apparently listless Doctor. Then Torg escorted Reece back to the doorway, where he seemed to see Bernice. 'Benny? What's going on?'

'I . . . I don't know. I just got here and saw . . . this.' She gestured towards Lianna.

Before anything else could be said, a wail came from behind the crowd and Atissa lunged through them and into the room. This time Torg made no effort to stop the intruder. Atissa was on her knees, moaning softly.

Torg wrenched the spear free of the wall, and concealed Lianna's body as he extracted the weapon, dropping it to the floor. He laid Lianna down and another guard scooped up a blanket and laid it over the body, covering it completely.

Bernice watched Atissa for a few seconds longer until she realized the Doctor had been led away. She scanned the gathering but all she saw were the Pels' eyes, some angry, some astonished, most distraught. She pushed her way to the back in time to see the Doctor almost being dragged away, unresisting.

'Hey,' she called. No one listened so she ran after them.

Behind her, two pairs of eyes followed her. Nic Reece blinked, breathed deeply and wandered off. Neither of them saw the Pakhar holocameraman Jav watching from a nearby recess. He stuffed a paw into a pocket in his shorts and brought out the black box he had found bleeping earlier.

'Time for a little chat with your owner,' he said. Repocketing it, he wandered back to his own quarters.

Bernice caught up with the guards; they weren't particularly hurrying.

'Where are you taking him?' she demanded.

The guards exchanged looks. 'To the cells, miss,' one eventually replied.

'Oh great, can I come?'

'No . . . Benny, you mustn't.' The Doctor looked over at her, his eyes reddened.

'But . . .'

The Doctor's voice grew a fraction stronger. 'Too much danger. I need you to keep an eye out.'

The guards tugged at him. 'Come on, you. No time to talk.'

As they pulled him away, he looked back. 'My quarters. The chess set. Bring it to me later. Not yet. I've been checked!'

By this time they were alongside the relic room. Sskeet was standing by the door but he lumbered round as he heard the Doctor's voice.

'Doctor,' he started, and then took in the situation. 'What is going on?'

'That's what I want to know,' complained Bernice. 'Abbot and Costello here aren't being very helpful.'

'No . . . wrong era entirely . . .' was the Doctor's muttered response.

'And he's not much help either,' Bernice finished.

'Excuse us,' started one guard but Sskeet didn't budge an inch.

'There has been another robbery,' he hissed and waved his clamped hand towards the room.

The Doctor perked up slightly and even pulled away from one guard. He managed to get a look into the doorway. 'Of course,' he said as he was restrained once more. 'It had to be that. Only one to go.'

185

As he was dragged away, Bernice allowed herself a look into the relic room. Sskeet pointed at the far wall where the Lance of Aggedor had once been. Beneath it ought to have been the Crown of Sherak. Instead there was an empty space.

It was half an hour later that Savaar finally deigned to join the party in the cell area. Bernice looked around her. As Savaar stopped, Sskeet seemed to glide up beside him, most un-Martian like, she thought. They can be swift when they want to, then.

The Doctor was behind bars, although a quick wash had removed the blood from his hands if not his sleeves and he was looking slightly more perky. King Tarrol and Chancellor Geban stood to one side conferring, while Alpha Centauri bobbed, jittered and changed colour every four seconds. Bernice thought he was going to have a seizure if he didn't calm down. Torg stood guard by the cell door, the barbed spear in his hands.

Of Atissa and Nic Reece there was no sign.

'Let the trial begin,' announced Tarrol.

'Trial!' Bernice jumped forward. 'What bloody trial? What the frag's he supposed to have done?'

'I should have thought that was obvious, even to a human female,' shrilled Centauri unhappily. 'The Doctor is to be tried for the murder of the Lady Lianna.'

'But he didn't ... he couldn't ... I mean you can't think ...' Bernice desperately wanted to say something constructive. She suddenly realized that it simply hadn't occurred to her that the Doctor could have actually killed the woman. 'He just found her like that!' she managed eventually.

Savaar was behind her and rested a clamp on her shoulder. 'The only way you could know that for sure was if you had killed her yourself. Be very careful. Something is very wrong here.'

'Too bloody right it is mate,' snapped Bernice. 'Why aren't you helping protect him?'

'Why should I? I don't know the Doctor as you do,

186

Shsurr. I have no evidence that he is innocent, any more than you do.'

'Oh, get into the real world, Savaar.'

'Your loyalty does you credit, *Shsurr*. However, my security has already been compromised by the Cantryan boy. I can offer no reason why I should consider another of your party any more or less trustworthy.'

Bernice groaned inwardly – what had Kort done now? Still, that could wait – Savaar clearly hadn't executed him, but the Pels were quite likely to do so to the Doctor, according to Reece's descriptions of life on Peladon.

Atissa arrived.

If Bernice was expecting a grief-stricken daughter, tearful and gaunt, she was disappointed. Instead Atissa looked like the proverbial cat that had got the cream. 'By the ancient laws of Peladon, this man has committed a heinous crime. He must be punished. Aggedor demands it!'

Tarrol stood forward. 'Atissa, the Doctor will be questioned and tried. In the proper Pel way.'

Atissa turned on him, sneering. 'Pah! You think we care one jot for your Federation-tainted justice? No. Aggedor has proclaimed that he is to die.'

Tarrol attempted to speak again, furious at Atissa's words, but instead Geban walked to her. 'Atissa,' he said. 'Aggedor stands for truth and justice. He is a revered and respected guide and judge. Can Aggedor really allow an execution with no search for the truth?'

'Truth? What do you know of truth? The only truth is my mother's savage murder, and the people of Peladon demand retribution.' Atissa walked to the cell. The Doctor looked up and grinned lopsidedly at her.

Bernice sighed. Don't try your crazy charm, Doctor, for Christ's sake act normal.

'Tell me, Atissa,' he said. 'Tell me why I killed your mother. Give me a motive because I've been sitting here for an hour now and I can't think of one good reason why I would do her harm. She is . . . was a very dear friend.'

Atissa smiled and her eyes flashed. The smile vanished from the Doctor's face as if it had been switched off. He suddenly knew what she was going to say. 'You killed my mother because you are evil. You killed my mother because you are from the Federation. You killed my mother because you stole the Lance of Aggedor and then killed her with it. You killed her because you are an alien!'

She's gone, thought Bernice. She's completely and utterly insane.

'This is insane. Completely and utterly.' Keri wriggled in her seat. 'At least take these bracelets off, yeah?'

The 'bracelets' were standard Federation restraining devices: plasma fields capable of giving a nasty shock if the victim moved too much. Keri had seen them in operation many times but never expected to wear them. What made it worse was that her companion-in-crime seemed to be enjoying himself immensely.

'Can't wait to tell my father,' Kort grinned. 'I mean, how many Federation Chair's sons get done for hacking and slicing?'

'I'm so glad you're enjoying yourself, yeah. I'm rather embarrassed.'

Their current gaoler, the Martian pilot, jabbed at a button on the pad in front of him and the plasma fields flickered out of existence.

'Oh,' said a dismayed Kort. 'I was enjoying that.'

Keri suspected that the pilot had turned them off for that very reason rather than because of her pleas. Damakort clearly brought out the wearied parent in everyone, even Martian pilots.

'Thank you,' she said.

The pilot said nothing back, but instead passed over two large beakers of water. Keri gratefully swallowed hers, rubbing a few droplets off her whiskers. Kort sipped at his, still sulking at the loss of his restraints.

'What's going on, then? Lord Savaar said he'd be back shortly.'

The pilot replied without looking at her. 'There has been an . . . an incident within the Citadel. Lord Savaar is attending to it now.'

'Can you tell me what it is that I'm missing, yeah?'

'I understand that one of the king's courtiers has been murdered. The Doctor has been accused of the murder. More than that I cannot say.'

Keri looked across at Kort. The boy was suddenly looking very serious and alert. He caught her eye. 'The Doctor?' he said. 'He's a bit weird, but murder?'

'Seems unlikely, yeah,' Keri agreed. 'Frag, I've just thought of something. Neal Corry's gonna want to know why I'm not covering this, yeah!'

'The Martian pilot finally turned to look at her and she could have sworn that behind his red-plastic protected visors, she saw a smile in his eyes. 'Do not worry. Your holovids are the last thing on Neal Corry's mind.'

'What do you mean by that?' Keri demanded, but the pilot turned away. The conversation was over.

Cold.

It's so damned cold.

Why am I cold?

Teeth chattering. I can't feel my fingers or toes. How did I get here, wherever here is. I thought hell was supposed to be searing hot, not like the crukking South Pole!

The noises. The lights. Of course. There was a doorway and I . . . I touched it. Thinking of Jaim Gehässig, after all this time. They say that when you die, your life flashes before your eyes. Is that what I was seeing – the sum total of my life? One person? Frag, no. I'm *not* dead. I can't be – too much to see and do in this galaxy. Places to go, people to meet. I've spent too long at GFTV, it's become my life instead of a way of supporting it. If I ever get out of here, wherever here is, that's it. I'm giving it all up. Get in touch with Jaim and see if we could have another go. If not, well, tough luck on me. There's more to life than that.

That's assuming I do get out of here.

It's so dark. Teeth have stopped chattering, but I'm still cold. The rest of me must be waking up and adapting. Like that time on Telos – again investigating the Cyber-

189

men. Now that was cold! Christ, there was that Australian bimbo as well – whatever happened to that one, eh?

It's a blindfold! How could I be so stupid? I'm inside that abandoned refinery – whoever I saw inside must have dragged me in. But why blindfold me? My hands aren't tied, though. Maybe if I . . .

Yeeoow!

Bloody plasma cuffs. Stupid of me. Maybe if I shake my head, slowly, the blind will fall. It doesn't feel too tight, certainly not cutting any circulation off. And anyway, some movement will help warm me up and –

Someone's coming towards me. I recognize that sound but it can't be . . .

Light!

Yes of course! It all makes sense now. Now I can see.

'H**'. My voice has gone. Clear my throat. Hhhufff. 'Excuse me chaps, but what the frag is going on?'

Jav was sitting in the room. Not his room, but the room he'd sat in earlier when he'd discovered the black box. It was in his hand now. It would be worth a fortune. In front of him was a case. In it was the Crown of Sherak. Jav recognized it from his and Keri's filming in the relic room earlier. Yes, this looked like being the end of a good day.

He didn't give a damn about the Peladon treasures. Frankly, it was a primitive backwater without the basic amenities. Even the Federation equipment was a hundred years out of date. Everything broke whenever you used it. No, with the money he'd make out of this he could leave GFTV and set up on his own. Maybe a little racket on a frontier world – knocking off porn vids. A good mix of *Good Girlz* and *Joy Boyz*. A good standard of living from that.

And if he didn't get what he wanted, well then he'd just have to tell one of the Federation representatives what he'd discovered here.

He sat against the wall and thought back to his childhood on Parkha. A childhood where, as a member of one of the poorer families, he was encouraged to have a bit of a scrap, find new ways to get food and water. After that blasted tram crash, his mother was left alone apart from him. He'd fought hard to work in the holovid area – worked hard (well, cheated quite a bit, but it taught him how to get by). Yeah, it'd taken time but now he was set up for life. Maybe he'd chuck a bit his mother's way. No, frag that, why bother? He'd struck lucky, it was his call, his turn. Yeah.

'Can I help you?'

Jav smiled. 'I wondered when you'd get back. Bit of a furore upstairs, eh?'

'Nothing that can't be handled by the Federation.'

'Good. Now, look here. I have a proposition for you . . .'

'No. Let me guess. You found the stolen treasures here. And, I note, the communicator that is bringing me something – from your world in fact.'

Jav frowned. 'What's your plan then?'

'Can't you guess? I'm a dealer in fine arts and treasures. This pathetic planet is ripe for ripping off and indeed Nic Reece has talked the inhabitants into putting them together in one room for safety. Of course, that makes it even easier for me to go along and make them disappear. Might just as well hang a sign on them saying "please take one". Then I sell 'em to the highest bidder and make a fortune.'

The little Pakhar was still confused. 'So what's coming here from Pakha?'

'Ah. Literally the jewel in my crown. I spent months on Pakha trying to find it but had to leave in a bit of a hurry. Managed to find a rough location for it and sent some . . . friends to get it. When you found my little box of tricks flashing earlier it was them telling me they'd got it.'

'A black box? A homing device? That's, well, prehistoric!' said Jav.

'Not quite, but certainly a few centuries old. As technology bounds forward, it's trinkets like this, which operate on primitive but still effective carrier waves, that enable me to do business. The Federation are so busy flaunting their modern biomorphic computers and AIs

191

that a little beauty like this is ignored. It's from the twenty-fifth century, you know. Remarkably preserved.'

Jav nodded. 'Is it? Well, that's interesting but not – '

'Not what you came to see me about, eh? No, you presumably want money to stop you running upstairs and telling the Federation observers exactly what you've discovered.'

'Basically, that's it.'

'How much?'

'Enough. Enough to buy me a new, luxurious life out there.' Jav pointed towards the sky.

'Ah. An entrepreneur. I admire that.'

Jav grinned. This was going well. 'Glad you see it my way.'

'Oh, indeed I do. If I was in your position, I'd do exactly the same. However, I'm not in your position, I'm in mine.'

Jav didn't like the sound of that. 'Now hold on . . .'

'Oh do shut up, you pathetic little rat. You made a big mistake coming here. You should've held out a little longer. This time tomorrow I would be ready to leave Peladon, with its art treasures and of course the Pakhar Diadem. I could have used some help, for which I would have paid heavily. But you played your hand too early, Jav. Too early . . .'

If anyone had been listening carefully at that moment they might have heard a terrible scream as a metre-high Pakhar, by the name of Javi'ta'ko was bodily picked up and shoved through a window in the Citadel on Mount Megeshra. If they'd looked they might have seen a blur as his still screaming body was hurled hundreds of feet down the mountainside where, after four or five bounces on jagged black rock, the pulpy remains came to rest, spread over a cluster of stones.

However, with the savage murder of Lianna upmost in everybody's minds, and the ever-present storms howling and crashing around outside, looking and listening out of Citadel windows was the last thing on anyone's mind.

It was almost certainly the last thing on a desperate Jav's mind, but no one would ever know for sure.

To the person who had just thrown him out, Jav was just the latest in a long line of people murdered to keep his presence hidden on Peladon, including the Lady Lianna who, like Damajina and O'Brien before, had realized too much to be allowed to live.

But again a mistake had been made. Two people did witness Jav's unaided flight, although they were impotent to do anything about it, except store the knowledge for future use.

King Tarrol kicked out at a chair and sent it crashing across the throne room. A totally irrational and futile gesture, but it released a fraction of the pent-up anger he felt.

The doors opened and Geban entered, bowing and closing them again. As he walked towards his friend and monarch he casually righted the chair as if it was the sort of thing he did every day.

'Oh, Geban. What has gone wrong?'

Geban shook his head. 'Your Majesty, what can I say? The Lady Lianna has been killed and the Doctor looks the most likely candidate.'

'But we are supposed to be his friend. And he to us. Tell me, Geban, do you believe he did it?'

'Unfortunately, Your Majesty, what I think will have little effect. Atissa has dredged up every ancient law and unamended ruling from history to support her case for the Doctor's execution.'

Tarrol slammed his fist on his throne. 'Am I not king? Am I not this planet's highest judge and jury?'

'According to Atissa's researches, no, Your Majesty, you are not.' Geban frowned. 'I am afraid that we may have been placed entirely in the high priestess's hands on this one.'

'Why? The Doctor has not affronted Aggedor. He has not breached Atissa's shrine,' said Tarrol.

Geban nodded. 'True, Your Majesty. But by the time

we have proved that Atissa is wrong, she will have bent the will of the people and executed the Doctor. She is not well.'

'Not well?' said a voice from the doorway. Bernice jabbed her finger against her temple repeatedly. 'Is that the best you can do? Not well? She's two sandwiches short of a picnic if you ask me. Three steps short of a staircase!'

Geban rose. 'How dare you enter –'

Tarrol waved him down, wearily. 'I cannot be bothered with protocol, Geban. Let the professor speak her mind. She only says what we haven't the courage to acknowledge ourselves.'

'Thank you, Your Majesty. May I have the honour of addressing the king?' She copied the bow the Doctor had made at the meal last night. Tarrol nodded and Bernice continued: 'All three of us know that the Doctor would not murder Lianna. They were old friends. Indeed, it was Lianna who alerted the Doctor that things were not right on Peladon.'

Tarrol was immediately interested. 'Did she? Neither of them spoke of this to Us.'

'Well, I can't speak for Lianna, but I know the Doctor would not wish to alarm the king so near to such an important event as the restatement vows. I assure you that his silence was a considered judgment.' Christ, she was talking crap. Still, the king seemed to fall for it. He nodded and suggested that an audience with the Doctor was again necessary.

'I know Atissa will be angry, Geban, but bring the Doctor here. Call all the Federation representatives. We must discuss this further.'

Geban stood up, bowed and walked towards the door, swiftly and firmly grasping Bernice's arm and propelling her out with him. As they passed through the doors and closed them, he let go. 'You were very good,' he said. 'You should be a diplomat.'

'Listen, Chancellor. I don't give two hoots for your king or this planet, frankly. The Doctor is my friend and I want him off the hook. If I have to go cap in hand and charm a few favours, then I'll do it. We came here looking for trouble, the Federation knew something was up. Somehow I don't think getting the Doctor shot for killing someone was part of the plan!'

'Oh, if Atissa has her way, he won't be shot. Just beheaded. In her temple to make it really dramatic.'

Bernice exploded. 'I don't believe this! You're so bloody calm. The Doctor's going to die and you know Atissa's flying without a license but you just accept it. You let her run your lives because of this fragging Aggedor thing!'

Geban held up a warning hand. 'Professor Summerfield, your diplomatic hat is slipping. Our "fragging Aggedor thing" is the spiritual guide here. The Pel people believe in it, it brings us together as one common people. We have none of the differing religions, creeds or sub-cultures that dominate so many other plants. We are a united people. Do not mock us simply because it does not suit your taste.'

Bernice breathed out. 'Okay, you're right and I'm sorry. But right now it looks like the Doctor's going to end up going home in a diplomatic bag and I'm powerless to stop it.'

Geban placed a hand on her shoulder. 'Assemble the Martians, Ambassador Centauri and Nic Reece outside the throne room. The king will talk to them. I will fetch the Doctor.' He wandered towards the cell area and Bernice headed towards the Federation Representatives' room.

'Well, what am I to do with you two?'

Keri looked up at Savaar and smiled. 'Let us go, yeah?'

'In the light of what has happened this evening, the fewer Federation citizens roaming free in the Citadel the better. No, tonight you stay in the shuttle where Pilot Hassek can watch over you. Besides, I . . .'

Savaar was cut off as the shuttle's computer relayed a message from Alpha Centauri.

'This is an important message for High Lord Savaar

from Alpha Centauri. King Tarrol wishes to see us. We are to gather outside the throne room in fifteen minutes.' The message terminated with a distorted Federation jingle.

'Sskeet,' Savaar called. His adjutant was beside him in a second. 'Go to the throne room and keep Centauri calm. *Shsurr* Summerfield as well. He is likely to panic, she is likely to say something we will all regret. I will join you when I have finished with our two . . . guests.'

Sskeet got out of the shuttle and headed up the long tunnel. Savaar watched him go and then turned to Pilot Hassek. 'Call Hissel on the *Bruk*. Tell him I need my . . . toy.' He smiled and licked his lips. 'Hissel will understand.'

'My Lord.'

'Oh, Hassek. Use this. I don't want any further messages between here and the *Bruk* to use standard communications nets. Our guests have shown us how easy it is to be . . . interrupted.' Savaar produced from under his jerkin a small black box with a red light on top. He tossed it to Hassek who caught it and looked at it with obvious unfamiliarity. 'Learn,' Savaar hissed and Hassek nodded and went to the back of the shuttle.

Savaar sat in the pilot's seat and gazed at Keri and Kort. 'An interesting predicament for the Doctor. And myself.'

'How?' asked Keri.

'The Doctor does not like me. In fact he carries a burning dislike for Martians generally. Xenophobia is an extreme bigotry that I would not expect from someone such as him, but it is there. He hides it well most of the time, but sometimes the mask slips. He desperately wants to prove that I and my people are behind the troubles here.'

'And are you?'

'If I were, I would hardly be telling you my thoughts.'

Keri snorted. 'Ever heard of the double-bluff?'

'I am familiar with the concept. Nevertheless, Martians do not lie. It is a contemptible act and beneath us.'

'But you bend the truth now and again.'

Savaar smiled, his tongue again moistening his cracked lips. 'Perhaps. Now tell me, Ker'a'nol, why are you here?'

'Because you captured me slicing your ship's door and Kort here slicing the Fed Net, yeah.'

'The longer you are flippant, the less likely the Doctor's chances of a hearty dinner tomorrow night. Please. Answer the question.'

Keri sighed. 'GFTV–3 are covering the restatement stuff. Corry wanted some high-brow coverage and paid me far more than I'm really worth to come and do this. By the way, why did Hassek say that Neal was effectively out of things?'

Savaar looked genuinely surprised. 'I am not sure. Unless . . . Of course. That explains why Hissel broke com silence. I believe Mister Corry is safe and well but will have to remain "out of things" for a while longer. Let us return to you and your team. Tell me about holocamera operator, Jav.'

'Jav? Barely know him. Why?'

'Because what is left of him is currently spread over a few square metres at the foot of Mount Megeshra. If I have the time, I'll get Hassek to scrape up the remains and ship him back for whatever religious ceremonies you have on Pakha. I am intrigued to know why someone would throw him out of a window. Anyone on your team dislike him enough for that?'

Keri rubbed her whiskers. 'Can't say he'll be too missed. Can't say anyone would want to kill him either. He's good at his job but not a team player. I worked with him back in the Operation "Galactic Storm" coverage and he made a few mistakes. When he was assigned to me here, I mentioned this to Corry but he wasn't too concerned. Jav kept out of my way and probably thought he was too insignificant for me to remember. But I never forget anyone. Ever. Yeah.'

'We'll draw a veil over Jav then. How well do you understand the holocameras?'

'You are joking? I've never yet worked with equipment that I don't know every sonic screw and plastigrip on. I could dismantle a holocamera and put it back together blindfolded. It'd probably work better afterwards, yeah.'

'Good. I have a job for you.'

Kort finally spoke up: 'And me?'

'You? You will help Ker'a'nol with her work. Or I'll ship you straight back to the *Bruk* and send a message to your father about your behaviour. Whichever.'

'Right. Okay. Pass me a sonic screwdriver.'

Bernice wanted to scream. Alpha Centauri was bobbing up and down, changing colours and knocking everyone flying with six totally uncoordinated arms. 'This really is too bad,' he wailed. 'The Doctor is innocent. He must be released.'

'Look, I know that. You know that. Frankly, King Tarrol knows that. But apparently Aggedor doesn't. And unless we can make Atissa see sense, or preferably beat some into her, we have to be tactful, okay?'

Centauri stopped moving and assumed his normal olive green. He blinked very slowly at Bernice and seemed to sag slightly. 'You are right to admonish me, Professor Summerfield. I apologize. I'm getting too old for all this excitement and I tend to ... over-react. If you feel I am speaking out of turn in future, please alert me so that I may – '

'Centauri!' Bernice barked. ''Nuff said. Finito. El quitto.'

Geban had his back to Bernice but still managed to whisper without looking in her direction. 'That was good. Give me some tips one day.'

'When this is over, let's write a book together, Chancellor,' said Bernice. 'One hundred and one ways to deal with hysterical hexapods.'

'Here's Sskeet,' said Nic Reece as he too arrived.

'You're both late,' muttered Bernice. 'And where's Savaar?'

'High Lord Savaar will be along shortly.'

The double doors were pulled open from within and the assembled Federation representatives walked in. Behind them, two guards closed the doors and crossed their lances over them.

Bernice took in the sight before her.

The Doctor, his arms bound behind his back, his bright question-mark pullover looking grimy and a bit thread-bare, was at the bottom of the three steps leading to the throne. He looked like death warmed up. He tried to grin at her, but she saw straight through it – and so did he. King Tarrol stood in front of his throne and beside him, looking what Bernice could only describe as very smug indeed, was Atissa.

'I, Tarrol, King of Peladon and regent of Aggedor,' the king said, 'have reached a decision. The Doctor is guilty of the murder of Lianna, our lady-of-the-court. He is guilty of the murder of Fabon, guardian of the relic room. Tomorrow, at midday, he will be escorted to the Shrine of Aggedor. He will be stripped of all honours, rank and privileges. There he will swear an oath of apology to Aggedor, to cleanse his soul.'

Bernice breathed a sigh of relief but as the king con-tinued she realized she had been too quick.

'After that, he will be dragged before the Great Statue of Aggedor and beheaded, as befits our laws and beliefs.'

There was a stunned silence, broken by an outraged Geban. 'Your Majesty, you cannot – '

Atissa stepped forward. 'Be silent, Chancellor, or you will be next. Aggedor has reasserted his rule over our planet. His will is ours. Yours, mine, our king's.'

Geban was still protesting. 'And just who is to perform this execution, Atissa? You?'

The double doors crashed open, knocking the guards back slightly. Framed in the doorway stood High Lord Savaar.

'No, Chancellor Geban. Atissa will not be beheading anybody tomorrow.'

'Oh thank God for that,' said Bernice.

Alpha Centauri's silent but gesticulating hysteria abated as well. Slightly.

'Your Majesty, Pels and Federation members. I, Savaar

of the family of Lassaal, supreme commander of the Martian fleet and chief executive of the Federation Corps have claimed my right as the arbitrator of Federation law regarding Federation citizens. Tomorrow, at midday, I will have the glorious honour of beheading the Doctor. For his crimes against Mars. For his crimes against New Mars. For his crimes against Peladon and for his crimes against Federation Unity.' Savaar pushed past the astonished grouping and crossed to the Doctor. He hauled him to his feet, ignoring the flash of pain that crossed the Time Lord's face. 'Tomorrow, Doctor, the "Ice Warriors" will finally get their revenge!'

Bernice almost screamed in shock. Instead she composed herself and walked up to Savaar. She looked him straight in the face. 'You bastard.'

6:

Are 'Friends' Electric?

'Actually, it's really quite comfortable here. Not too dark, not too light. Not too loud, not too quiet. And you brought me my chess set. Thank you.'

'Need anything else?' said Bernice.

The Doctor shook his head. 'No. Everything's just right.'

'Except of course that Savaar there has about as much brains in his head as Centauri has natural valium.' Bernice didn't even cast the Martian the look of loathing she wanted to. She wouldn't give him the satisfaction.

The Doctor tutted. 'Never judge a book by its cover, Benny. Remember that.'

Bernice stared at the Doctor, trying to read the message in the words. He obviously thought Savaar was up to something, but she wasn't convinced. The venom in his voice as he had made his proclamation the previous night was totally convincing. She hoped the Doctor was right, but wasn't convinced. 'I hope you're right,' was the only response she could manage.

'So, Doctor,' said Savaar from behind her, 'why were you in the Lady Lianna's room at the time of the murder?'

'I wasn't. I arrived about a minute later.'

'Why did you have your hands on the Lance of Aggedor?' was Sskeet's contribution.

'Oddly enough, I was trying to save her.'

Bernice tried not to look at Savaar as he walked past her and stood directly in front of the cell. 'How long had she been dead when you arrived?'

'She was still alive. She died in my arms.'

Bernice registered this with the same degree of surprise

as the two Martians evidently did, although without the hissing. 'Did she say anything?' she asked.

'*Shsurr* Summerfield, please let me continue the questioning. This is important.'

'Don't you *Shsurr* me, Savaar.'

'Benny,' warned the Doctor. 'Let the high lord do this his way.'

'Thank you. Both,' Savaar said 'Nevertheless, a good question from the Professor. Did the Lady Lianna say anything before she died?'

The Doctor grinned broadly. 'Oh yes. She told me who killed her.'

It took a second for this to sink into Bernice's angry consciousness. 'What? Why didn't you say? Who killed her?'

The Doctor just smiled. And put his finger to his lips to indicate silence.

Geban slammed the door to his chancellery as he entered. He collapsed into his chair and shook his head.

Why? Why had the Doctor killed Lianna? Had he?

Why did Savaar want to execute the Doctor? Would he?

And why had King Tarrol suddenly done a complete about-face? And why was Atissa there in the throne room when no one had got any sense out of her since the Doctor's interrogation?

There as a soft knock on his door. 'Come,' he yelled, louder than he'd intended, and tried to smile as Nic Reece sheepishly entered.

'I can come back later,' the human suggested but Geban waved him in.

'I could do with some rational company. Things are not going well.'

'Too right, Geban, old man. I'll get straight to the nitty-gritty. Upstairs is a room full of priceless Pel antiques. First the Lance goes, now the Crown of Sherak. If the double-bladed Sword of Truth is lost, Peladon is going to lose its attraction to the Federation multitudes.'

Geban stared at Reece. 'Am I to understand that you are concerned with a few of Atissa's trinkets while your friend is to be executed?'

'Hey, don't get me wrong. I like the Doctor a lot. Good soul and all that. But my job is ensuring this planet's economic survival – and while you go around hiding your heads in the clouds, holding executions and suchlike, there will be serious repercussions. Apart from no pretty things to show the punters, an execution during the restatement vows bash isn't going to sit well either. Neal Corry will have a field day. Where is he, by the way?'

Geban shrugged. 'I have no idea. Haven't seen him since yesterday morning. On his shuttle with his drink?'

Reece grinned. 'Should have known you'd find out about that. No, he's not there, I checked earlier. Oh well, he'll turn up.' He got up to go. 'I know you've a lot on your plate, Geban, but I thought you ought to think about these things. Sorry.'

Reece left, leaving Geban to think over the new problems as well as well as the old.

Atissa looked up at the empty space in the relic room where the Lance of Aggedor ought to be, and smiled.

'You have been returned. Savagely abused and tainted with my mother's irreverent blood, but returned nevertheless. Although the Crown is gone, you shall assume your place as the most important, most beloved of our treasures.'

She picked up the Lance from the mauve velvet bag it rested in at her feet. As her fingers touched it, she heard the door open behind her but didn't turn around. 'I would be alone,' she said.

Behind her came a deep breathing and a sibilant breath. 'Alien,' she said, 'I thank you for your offer to execute the Doctor. Please accept my gratitude but also my refusal. He is my ... our enemy. Not yours.' She stood up and started to turn to where she imagined Savaar was standing.

Instead, something large and heavy crashed across the

back of her neck and she fell senseless to the floor, the Lance rolling across to the feet of her attacker.

'Back where you belong indeed, Lance of Aggedor. And where you really belong is with me.'

The Doctor was alone at last. Bernice had gone to rest, and probably vent her frustrations on Nic Reece. Savaar and Sskeet had gone to prepare for the execution. He was finally alone with his chess set.

'I have lost my queen. Once again, I'm in check. I hope Ace is doing better than this.' The Doctor reached out and swivelled the set around, then moved the horse-headed piece up and along, directly in front of his king. 'Still, I think my shining knight has saved me. For now, at least. Still my planning still leaves a lot to be desired.' He leaned over and placed a black night in the path of his white one. One pawn was removed, two others were next to go because the Doctor had to move his king out of check. 'I don't like this game much,' murmured the Time Lord. 'Still, I should have thought of that before I started.'

Bernice knocked on his door but there was no reply. Shrugging, she pushed and it slowly opened.

The room said 'Nic Reece' in big letters, she decided. Untidy in a designer sort of way, as if the crumpled clothing and awkwardly positioned bed had been deliberately set to look messy. She smiled. How like him.

She crossed to the larger-than-normal window and stared out. The rain lashed against the Perspex, smearing everything although she could just about make out the blackened slope of Mount Megeshra as it dropped hundreds of feet away below.

Bernice looked down at the chest by the window. On it, a comb, a toothbrush and a data-pad. She smiled as she picked up the toothbrush – in an era of sonic hygiene, a toothbrush was rather parochial. Perhaps he felt it fitted in with the primitiveness of Peladon. She scooped up the pad and flicked it open. No micro-filaments. Then again, he'd clearly had them removed from his head as well, so perhaps his operated in the old-fashioned way. She pressed a stud and the pad's screen glowed. 'Home,' she said.

A small hologram floated in front of her. A small dome, obviously white plastic but with a network of metallic struts built across it honeycomb-style. There was thick green grass all around it and some large blue flowers growing up in a translucent trellis. One was nearly five metres tall, and was swaying in a slight breeze. The wall of the dome melted away, as the walls of the *Bruk* had done, to reveal an opening.

Three people came out, smiling and waving. A woman about Bernice's age with long blonde hair and huge blue eyes. Holding her hand was a young girl, about four or five, sucking her thumb and desperately trying to hide behind the woman. Camera-shy, Bernice decided. The boy, a year or two older, was anything but camera-shy as he ran and rolled around on the ground, playing with what appeared to be a very large rabbit with three ears and a long tail. The date floating at the bottom of the hologram, displayed as a red LED, suggested that this was only a few months old.

She hadn't heard him come in, so the first she knew of Nic Reece's presence behind her was a howl of anger as he grabbed the pad away from her.

Shocked, she swung round and tried to speak, but the murderous look in his eye instantly showed her a side of him she'd never imagined existed. And never wished to.

'Get out of my room,' he spat. 'How dare you even *think* of coming in here? Just ... just get the frag *out*!'

Bernice backed towards the door. 'Nic ... I ... I'm sorry ...' was the best she could manage and she ran out. Behind her she could just hear a savage crunch as Reece presumably stamped on the data-pad, destroying it completely.

Alpha Centauri had been downloading everything he could find on Federation protocol regarding one member of a diplomatic party declaring war on another while on neutral territory. It wasn't a subject that had cropped up too often in Federation history and the downloading hadn't taken long. He was just ordering his pad off when Bernice walked in and sat down at the table.

'Professor Summerfield? Are you all right?'

Composing herself as best she could, Bernice turned. One look at Centauri bobbing up and down, blue patches flicking intermittently over his head, crushed her resolve to be flippant. 'I've had better days, certainly.'

With a blink of understanding, two of Centauri's arms reached out and poured her a drink, which he then brought over. 'This awful business with the Doctor is quite unacceptable. I would contact Io immediately but my main relay station would be the *Bruk*. As High Lord Savaar's flagship, it hardly seems prudent to expect them to forward a complaint against their commander.'

Bernice nodded her agreement. 'Savaar's weird. Last night he wanted the Doctor dead. Today he and Sskeet are as thick as thieves with the Doctor and no one will tell me what's going on.'

Centauri considered. 'Well, under Federation Law, which Peladon is obliged to follow, Savaar does have the authority to proceed with the execution.'

'But surely under Federation Law, he can't interfere with planetary justice.'

'A dichotomy, indeed,' Centauri said.

'Well, let's ponder something else then. What can you tell me about Nic Reece?'

'Why?'

'Look, Centauri, bugger your Federation resolve and chumminess, just tell me everything you can. Like, is he married?'

'Strictly speaking, no.'

'Don't speak strictly, then.'

'He was married, with two children. They were killed about five weeks ago, in a shuttle crash apparently. He took me alone into his confidence, not wanting to let the news get in the way of the restatement ceremony. He blamed himself for it and only arrived back on Peladon a few days before you arrived. He took their deaths very badly indeed.'

'I can imagine. I thought he was hiding something under that casual veneer. Hell, I'm stupid.'

'Oh, I'm sure that's not true, Professor,' Centauri said. 'Why do you think you are?'

'Because I blundered into his room just now. I found a holo of his family and he came back. He wasn't happy to find me. I thought he thought I'd discovered he was, well, cheating on his wife. But of course, he was hurt by seeing the holo.'

'Cheating on her? If I understand your meaning, are you suggesting there is a relationship between the two of you?'

'No! Well, not yet ... well, probably not ever, now ... Oh grief, I don't know!' Bernice got up and began pacing around the room. 'I mean, I ought to be better at handling this kind of situation. I've had my share of relationships – none of them particularly wonderful, I know, but some quite decent. But him. I mean, he just radiates something ... I don't know what. An image, a personality that's so refreshing, so ... bloody dynamic.'

Centauri shuffled a little uncomfortably, slightly embarrassed at the human female's soul-bearing.

Bernice continued, 'Maybe I've been cooped up in the TARDIS for too long – perhaps I need a break. Am I just taking the first opportunity with an apparently uncomplicated man? Of course, he's not uncomplicated really, is he? Oh no, I have to fall for someone completely screwed up inside. Oh, it's all so obvious now. I should have seen the writing on the wall. I mean, his face, his posture. I *knew* he was covering up for something.' She paused for breath before turning and looking Alpha Centauri squarely in the eye.

'Am I making sense?'

Centauri had to think carefully on that one. Humanoids, especially females, tended to be very emotive, very prone to over-reaction and almost hysteria. And when involving procreation ... Centauri mentally shook his head in confusion. What should he say? His species of course were far more rational, far more sensible. With no romances, no 'love' to be involved in, everything was far simpler. Every few years the urge to replicate came naturally and with the correct mental urges, a new member of the species was created. One became two. He decided he would never understand why humans had to become so emotional in times of personal crisis.

'Well,' he started, 'I'm not sure I –'

'Oh, you're right of course,' Bernice carried on, much to Centauri's relief. 'I mean, obviously it can't go anywhere. He's grieving and temporarily looking for a surrogate wife – and that's not a criticism – and I'll be shooting away as soon as the Doctor's free. Or dead.' Bernice stopped suddenly. 'Grief – why am I worrying about me? They're going to cut the Doctor's head off later!' She reached out and grabbed three of Centauri's arms, bewildering him totally. 'What are we going to do, Centauri?'

'I . . . I really do not know. Rescue him? In the past, the Doctor tended to rescue himself, actually. Any help we gave tended to, well, upset his plans a bit.'

Bernice grimaced. 'Yeah. Know the problem.'

'ETA?'

'About eight hours. It's a bloody long way even in this class of shuttle.'

Sadler sighed.

Long way.

She looked over at Lambert. He was running some checks on the shuttle's fuel reserves – a pointless job that he was only doing to keep himself occupied.

Petty-minded simpleton. A fool. A weakling.

As he made another calculation on his pad, his eye caught hers and he grinned. 'You okay?'

'Yeah. Sure. Fine. Just anxious to get to Peladon.'

Lambert nodded. 'Bit of action at last. Get this baby to the paymaster,' he waved towards the vacuum case securely inside the safe-seal, 'and shoot off. Take the money and run.'

'Andrew?'

Lambert gave her a strange look. 'Yeah?'

'Oh. Nothing. Forget it.' Sadler turned away. She busied herself pointlessly studying some holographics of their locality. She told the computer to do a couple of routine checks – anything that made her look busy. After a few moments she stole another glance in Lambert's direction, and was relieved that he had his back to her.

She'd known Andi Lambert for the last four years – they'd been selected by Townsend together at one of the irregular selection gatherings. Every few years it got hooked down the nets that mercenary gangs were looking for recruits. Hopefuls, usually those who'd dropped out of their families or society in general, hunted around until they got enough information to tell them where to meet. She'd seen some 'big names' in the Federation underworld at her one and only gathering. In a spaceport bar on one of the Rho frontier worlds they'd sat around drinking, sniffing and generally getting smashed for a weekend. Basically it was generally considered that after a few, unspecified, days the wannabe killers, smugglers and general social dregs who could still stand, think and fire a gun straight were more likely to be offered contracts and profit-shares.

Looking back, it all seemed so silly – more like some caricatured boys' club than a seriously professional, if generally illegal, trade fair.

She'd met Andrew Lambert on the first night. He was with a Felinetta; her russet fur had bristled at Sadler's approach, she remembered. The Felinetta had hissed an insult, looked at Lambert and stalked off. Lambert had grinned, saying he was allergic to cats anyway and would Sadler like to have a drink. The rest had been history. They'd also made an agreement – try to work together and therefore stay off the narcs and drink as much as possible.

Sadler hadn't intended to start the fight, but after three days of waiting for the mercenary leaders, tempers and egos were getting frayed. It had been the Felinetta that started it – accusing Sadler of being some kind of social whore. At least, that's how Sadler chose to remember it. She'd certainly convinced everyone else it was the cat-woman's fault, but for herself, she wasn't too sure. Not that it mattered: yes, the Felinetta had rakish claws, but Sadler had been blessed with a strong grip. As with the Pakhar, the Felinetta's throat had ripped easily and Sadler could still remember the absolute, almost orgasmic pleasure of killing with her bare hands. Using a gun or knife was easy, but to actually use part of your body to destroy a life – that fascinated her.

It also interested two human males, Townsend and Moscatelli. She knew their reputations: they weren't exactly top of the chain, but they were reliable second-stringers. The back-up. If someone needed a private army for a back-route deal or diversionary attacks, Moscatelli and Townsend would supply.

'I've not lost anyone yet,' Moscatelli said. 'Unless one of us has decided to kill them. And we only do that to weak links and traitors. You a weak link, Sadler?'

'No,' she'd answered.

Townsend had nodded and introduced the only other current member of their team – Cooper. 'Moscatelli's shag,' he'd explained.

If Sadler expected hostility from the female, she was disappointed, in so much as Cooper evidently didn't care who was on the team. She carried herself with an assured-ness and confidence that, as Sadler learned, came from ten years with both men in 'the field'.

'Anything you want to ask before we sign the contract?' Sadler had pointed straight at Andrew Lambert.

'Yours?' Moscatelli asked.

'Yes,' she'd replied without really thinking. Since then, both she and Lambert had been an equal part of the team. Moscatelli had been killed about three years ago by running a smuggling blockade too early and Cooper, to no one's surprise, had turned her sex drive if not really her affections to Townsend.

Weakness. Emotional ties. Useless. Dangerous.

She didn't love Lambert – not in what she understood to be a traditional meaning of love. None of the heartache, misery or emptiness she'd seen in holovids as a kid ever hit her when he was not around her. The sex was good – very good – and she'd long ago decided that was all she needed. A vent for her physical rather than mental emotions.

Unnecessary. A block to total power. I . . . we will have that power.

Something was wrong, but she couldn't say what. There was something at the back of her mind, gnawing away that she ought to tell Lambert about. Warn him, even. But what?

Strength. Power through strength. Take me!

Sadler turned back to her holograms. If it was that important, she'd soon remember.

Inside the safe-seal, the vacuum box vibrated almost imperceptibly. Few human eyes would have noticed it. Sadler certainly didn't.

Not yet, anyway.

'Computer. How far behind the shuttle are we?'

'Real time?'

Ace sighed. 'Yeah. Real time. To the second.'

'Fifteen minutes, thirty seven seconds. That gap could close or open to a variant of three minutes if the other shuttle changes velocity and this shuttle does not match it.'

Ace looked at the holograms swirling round in front of her. Planets, moons and distant suns. In the middle, images of her shuttle and the mercenaries' one. 'Computer, projected trajectory?'

'The planet Peladon in the system of – '

'I know about Peladon. Are we still screened?'

'We are hidden within their ion trail. Their sensors cannot accurately observe us as long as we do not deviate from our present course.'

'Okay. Under no circumstances deviate. Taking in that

211

parameter, is there any way we can safely close up the lag?'

'Negative. A seven-minute increase could be achieved but at a forty-three point six per cent possibility of detection.'

'Forget it.'

'Clarify.'

'Ignore.' Ace relaxed slightly and operated her personal wrist computer. Six hours to Peladon, give or take fifteen minutes.

Ace never heard a thing, but her shuttle suddenly lurched, violently tipping her on to the floor. As the console spluttered into shards of hit plastic and flame, the hologram pixeled into millions of tiny iridescent cubes, each tumbling over each other and crashing into the sides of the shuttle, where they vanished like soap bubbles on concrete.

'Computer? Frag it, what's going on?'

The computer's voice took on a staccato tone, occasionally clipping or totally muting syllables as it answered.

'The *My'n'ad* has b'n fired up'n. Drive sys-severely dam'ged.'

'Who by?'

'The shu'le we are currently purs'ing. Inst'ions?'

'Throw something back, for God's sake!'

'This sh'tle does not posses suf'cient weapon'ry.'

'Chuck an electro-plasma pulse back, scramble their systems. Give us a breather!'

'Confirmed.'

'Right. Are they firing again?'

'Not yet.'

'Drop spin three hundred and sixty degrees, five rotations. Eject all waste and empty the cargo hold. Leave it unpressurized and after eight seconds, blow all circuit routings in that area.'

'Μανοευῶρε χομφΠεδ. Ωηεν'

'What?'

'Manoeuvre comf'ed. When?'

'Now, frag you, *now*!'

'*Yes*!'

'Got it?'

'Right on the nose,' yelled a triumphant Lambert.

'She's spinning away,' corrected Cooper quietly. 'Flotsam but no human remains. Wait – an internal explosion at the rear. Possibly the engine core.'

Townsend was leaning forward, his cheek almost touching hers as the holograms lit their faces. 'What d'you think, Coop?'

'She's good. Knows the manoeuvres. She even threw a plasma burst back. She's all right. Unfortunately.'

Townsend frowned. 'Any damage?'

'To us? Nah. Nor her, really.'

Lambert was incredulous. 'But it was a direct hit. You saw the effect.'

Cooper didn't take her eyes off the holo of their pursuer's spinning wildly shuttle. 'Yeah. I saw it. Straight out of the manual. Your shot scraped the belly, ripped out guidance and a few electrics.

Sadler joined in. 'The explosion?'

Cooper smiled grimly. 'Emptied the hold and then blew everything in there to create some pretty pyrotechnics. It'd fool the Feds. Wonder if she's one of mine?'

Townsend rested a hand on her shoulder as she straightened up. 'Your pupils are long since dead, Coop. She's probably just read your textbooks.'

Cooper nodded slowly. 'Okay, Townsend. What now? Finish it off or keep going?'

'Lambert, Sadler? How long till Peladon?'

'Roughly six hours at this speed,' responded Sadler.

Townsend straightened up and walked back to the pilot's seat. He sat and swivelled round to face his crew. 'Okay. We're going on. Our chum in the case there is too important. We're going in on the dark side. Radio silence and internal silence from T-minus sixty. All sensors off. We'll drift past.'

213

'Past what?' asked Sadler.

'The *Bruk*,' answered Cooper. 'It'll be there. Savaar's no fool.'

'It'll still scan us,' said Lambert.

'Yeah, it'll scan us. But we're dead apparently and too far away from him to risk moving the *Bruk*. Besides, our paymaster's organizing a diversion on the planet that'll keep ol' Marshal nobrain Hissel occupied for hours.' Townsend turned back to his controls and muttered to himself. 'So long as he's got this plan worked out better than the last one.'

Ace gritted her teeth and tried to tell herself that throwing up while tumbling in zero-g was not an attractive proposition.

'How far out of range are we now?'

'Thirty-five min'tes.'

'Stop rolling manoeuvre. Restart internal pressures and stabilities.'

Ace hit the floor with a whump that knocked the breath out of her for a second. She grabbed the pilot's seat and hauled herself up, wiping the shards of melted plastic on to the floor. 'Can we pursue?'

'Αϕϕιρματιῶε'

'Say again?'

'Affirmative.'

'Okay. At what speed? Give me a new ETA.'

'Without r'pairs, this shuttle c'n only move at sub-light. Peladon will be r'ched in four months, eighteen days, seven hours –'

'Okay! I get the bloody picture. Send out a distress on Federation frequency to Io. Tell them that the Ace is low.'

'Confirm'd.'

Ace stretched out, resigned to defeat. 'Sorry, Professor. It's up to you and Benny now. I'll see you back on Io. I hope.' She kicked out at the wrecked console. In her pocket, she felt Winmill's data-pad digging in. Poor Julian. Poor H'yn'tn. 'You died for nothing, guys. I failed you. Sorry.'

Although she did not know it, Ace was very wrong indeed. Her actions had tipped the scales in her favour – but she'd never find out. 'Okay, computer. Let's get back to the TARDIS.'

It was going to be a long wait.

'What are you doing now?'

Keri put down her fibre-optic screw-head as gently as she could. The brat had been asking questions solidly for about thirty minutes now – each one of them she'd answered in decreasing lengths, realizing that it was boredom and not interest that was keeping his jaw muscles active.

'Just wait and see, yeah?' was the best she could manage.

She looked up slightly, rubbing a whisker or two and saw that the brat had wandered away and was punching up some codes on the shuttle's dispenser.

'What are you doing now, yeah?'

The brat turned around, two steaming mugs of cocoa in his hands. He could barely carry the giant Martian mugs but was determined not to show it. Keri allowed herself to relax and smile a thank-you as he passed one over.

'I can tell I'm annoying you,' he said.

Keri swallowed a hot mouthful and shook her head. 'It's not that, Kort. It's just – '

Kort put up a hand. 'Oh, don't bother. I'm well aware of my faults. My father points them out with alarming frequency. It's just that I feel . . . well, useless right now.'

'Look, Kort. I can't help you with that now. Yes, in what I'm trying to do here you're right. You're completely useless. No bull, okay? But you got us here. You accessed the computer files. You convinced that pilot not to sonic us out of existence, yeah? Now you've done your bit and I'm doing mine. That's teamwork. Knowing what to do and when, yeah?'

Kort didn't look convinced but he nodded.

215

'Good,' said Keri. 'Now back to work. You keep me fed and watered, yeah?'

Geban was feeling very uncomfortable.

All round him his world seemed to be coming apart. The massive restatement day events looked like being shrouded in death and deceit. The Doctor, a long-time friend of Peladon, was to be executed. The king seemed completely in Atissa's thrall, unbending over his decision to have the Doctor dead. Nic Reece was foreseeing doom and despair for the planet's future wealth and the Federation holo-crews were pestering him about the disappearance of three of their number; a holocameraman, Neal Corry and the little Pakhar, Keri.

As he paused to summon his resolve outside the throne room, a familiar swishing and wobbling could be heard from behind him. Without turning, he spoke.

'Good afternoon, Ambassador.'

'It most certainly is not, Chancellor. In all my years on Peladon, I have never felt as bewildered and distraught as I do now. Above all, Chancellor, I feel a complete stranger on a world upon which I have lived longer than anyone else alive today!'

Unaccustomed to hearing anything approaching anger in Centauri's tone, Geban turned around, and took a step back. The alien's usually green head was a totally new hue. Even the arms had joined it in appearing blotchy pink and black in colour, like a badly burned yubbo fruit. A few steps behind him stood the human woman, Summerfield. Geban allowed himself a slight bow to her but there was no returning smile. Geban knew he was dealing with two hostile associates.

'What can I do for you both?'

The human looked as if she was going to retort but Centauri got in first.

'Frankly, Chancellor Geban, you can demand that this ridiculous death penalty is swiftly removed from hanging over the Doctor.' Centauri bobbed down and slowly blinked his eye. 'Secondly, you can tell the king that I request . . . no, I demand an audience.'

Geban stared at the Centaurian. 'I . . . I'll see what I can arrange, Ambassador.'

'See that you do, Chancellor. And see that it is arranged swiftly. Events are moving at a pace here that I cannot keep up with.' As Centauri and Summerfield walked away from him, Geban swallowed. Centauri turned back to look at him, his head rotating one hundred and eighty degrees without his body turning. The big eyelid again blinked owlishly. 'Last time I found something I couldn't deal with, I called in Federation troops. Your father didn't thank me then and I doubt you'd thank me now. Your whole society and social reputation would be severely disrupted, especially with the restatement day tomorrow. Please ensure that I need not make any calls for help.' Centauri bobbed away.

Geban's day had just got worse.

'You were magnificent. Brilliant. I couldn't believe it!'

Alpha Centauri was back in the Federation Representatives' room, sagged slightly against the wooden table while Bernice Summerfield was patting his back and making appreciative compliments.

'You really did it! Geban looked totally flabbergasted!'

Alpha Centauri simply waved a couple of exhausted tentacles at her. 'Please! Professor Summerfield. Your enthusiasm is making me dizzy.'

Bernice stopped instantly. 'So, how long d'you think we'll have to wait before his royal brainlessness gets back to us?'

Centauri blinked and his head and arms were now almost back to their calm olive. 'I am sure that the king will carefully consider the situation and revoke the decision.'

'And if he doesn't, will you really call in the Federation troops?'

Centauri turned away. 'No. If the king refuses to accede to my requests, then the Doctor is doomed.'

'Your Majesty, this travesty of justice cannot go ahead. The Federation simply will not permit it.' Geban looked up from his cowed position, over at the king's expressionless face, searching for some clue as to Tarrol's abrupt decision to allow the Doctor's death.

'You forget, Geban, it is the Federation's major representative who is to perform the execution. It occurs, therefore, with the Federation's blessing.'

Geban stood up and hugged his robe to his chest. 'Your Majesty, we have been friends for many years. I speak now as that friend, not as His Majesty's Chancellor. Tarrol, this is an abomination – a complete flagrant abuse of our own laws.'

The king also stood up, stepping away from his throne. 'You forget yourself, Chancellor Geban. High Lord Savaar is operating within parameters allowed by both our law – which the Federation is duty-bound to observe while on Peladon, I might add – and his own. Do not challenge me on this or you will find yourself out of office.'

Geban let his robe drop to the floor and stepped away from it. 'Your Majesty, if a friend to Peladon can be so easily dismissed on the word of the high priestess, with no discussion at any level, then I no longer wish to serve. As chancellor or as friend.'

With that Geban stalked out of the throne room, slamming the door angrily as he left and never looking back at his king.

Which was a shame, for had he looked back Geban would have seen Tarrol's face twist in a grimace of total pain. Geban would have seen Tarrol suddenly assume the posture of a young man suddenly thrust into a world of politics and deviousness not of his making. Geban would have seen Tarrol slowly walk over, scoop up Geban's discarded cloak of office and hug it to himself. And Geban might have heard Tarrol's whispered moan: 'Oh, Geban. Why must I betray even you? I only hope you will understand why I do what I do.'

But Geban didn't. He was already on his way to the

Federation Representatives' room to tell them that he believed his king to be a fool.

The object of everyone's consternation was currently pacing up and down in his cell. Standing just outside were what many perceived as his worst enemies – Sskeet and High Lord Savaar.

'I trust we can speak freely, Doctor. Gentleman to gentlemen?'

The Doctor made an expansive gesture. 'Consider me a captive audience, Lord Savaar.'

Savaar walked nearer to the bars of the cell, Sskeet turning and keeping watch for any stray Pels who might be listening in.

'Sskeet has scanned this area for DAR devices. We are, I believe the expression goes, clean as a whistle.'

'Why should anyone bug me?'

Savaar ignored the question, choosing to answer with another. 'Why are you here, Doctor? Why did the Chair send you?'

'That's for me to know and you to – '

Savaar slammed his massive fist against the bars and the Doctor took an involuntary step back. 'Don't play the fool, Doctor. We both know and respect you far too much for that.'

The Doctor peered at the rather severe dent in the bar. 'You? Respect me?'

'Yes. Odd, isn't it? You, who hate Martians with an unbridled venom for something we did thousands of years before I was hatched. You who cannot see beyond this current scheme of things. Cannot understand the wider picture.'

'I am an expert at regarding wider pictures, Lord Savaar. I don't need you to outline things to me.'

Savaar sighed raspingly. 'You saw me talk to the Lady Lianna. A few hours later she was dead. You assumed that I did it?'

'You were arguing with her.'

219

'I am arguing with you. I haven't picked up a sacred Pel relic and speared you with it. Yet!'

'Ah, the famous Martian sense of humour. Use it on Bernice, she understands the context. I don't find it funny.'

'I didn't kill Lady Lianna. Nor did Sskeet.'

The Doctor sat on his bed, pushing the chess set aside. He scooped up his umbrella which Atissa had generously allowed him to keep. He rested his chin on it and his eyes twinkled as he said disarmingly, 'I know. I told you – she told me who killed her.'

'But you still won't say?'

'No. Not yet. If I tip my hand, I could end up attached to the wall equally as gorily. Besides, I want to be executed.'

'Why?'

'Because I have the strangest feeling that something will happen when I am.'

Sskeet lumbered over. 'Yes. You will die.'

'Oh, I doubt that,' said the Doctor. 'No, I think my nice Ice Lord has a trick or two up his sleeve, don't you Savaar?'

'All I can say is that while I live, no harm will come to you.'

'Why doesn't that reassure me?'

'Because you don't trust me?' asked Savaar.

'Because I don't trust your motives.'

Sskeet turned suddenly as three Pel guards approached. 'It is time,' one said.

Savaar gave the Doctor a last look. 'I can only ask you to trust me, Doctor. For the sake of the Federation.'

'Trust is earned, Savaar. Not given.'

'Then I will endeavour to earn it. Farewell.' Savaar whirled away, his cloak casually brushing against one of the Pel guards. As he and Sskeet wandered out of apparent earshot, the guard wiped at his leg. 'Alien scum.'

The Doctor beamed at him. 'Can I bring my chess set?'

Bernice glared daggers at Geban.

'No? What d'you mean, "no"?'

Geban shuffled uncomfortably. 'The king will not

rescind his royal command. The execution will go ahead as planned. In fact, he is most insistent that it happens immediately.'

Alpha Centauri bobbed towards Geban. 'Today is the darkest day this planet has ever known, Chancellor. A friend of Peladon and the Federation is being put to death – a most barbaric and uncharacteristic solution to a problem.'

'Seems pretty standard to me,' muttered Bernice.

'No,' corrected Centauri. 'Seventy years ago, it would have been. But I believed Peladon had matured. It seems that once again I am wrong. Chancellor Geban, you have been a good friend to me, as your father was. I am deeply troubled by these events.'

Geban looked Centauri straight in the eye. 'Ambassador, my personal feelings are irrelevant. My ultimate loyalty is still to my king. I am . . . sorry.'

With that he turned on his heel and left them alone.

After a moment Centauri lashed out, two of his arms sweeping across the table, slamming mugs and plates to the floor. His eye watered and his flesh grew a dark purple. 'No! The Doctor is my friend. I will not allow this primitive ritual to go ahead.'

Bernice looked over, a new faith in Centauri evident in her face. 'All right, Ambassador. Let's go stop an execution.'

Shadows flicked around the small chamber. The granite statue of Aggedor loomed large, curiously underlit by the flambeaus.

King Tarrol stood in Atissa's position, two guards behind him, ceremonial swords drawn.

'Where is my high priestess?'

The guards looked at each other nervously. Eventually one of them coughed and stepped forward.

'She has not answered any summons, Your Majesty.'

'No matter,' Tarrol barked. 'The execution will proceed. Bring in the prisoner.'

A solemn party entered the tiny sacred chamber. Sskeet

was first, brushing aside the burgundy curtain, Aggedor's face stitched into it in gold filaments. He was followed by Kort and Keri, both of whom looked around in awe at the holy temple.

'Never thought I'd ever get in here,' muttered the Pakhar, clutching tightly at her data-pad.

The Doctor and two guards came in next and Keri stared at him. No reaction crossed the Time Lord's face – just a tight grin as his unwavering eyes scanned her. She nodded slightly at Kort who in turn looked behind the Doctor: Bernice, eyes burning in rage, and Centauri, a very dark shade of purple. Kort indicated for them to join him and Keri.

'And where've you been?' growled Bernice. 'I could have used your help.'

Kort just indicated Keri with his head and whispered back, 'Exploring possibilities.'

When Nic Reece stole in, he shot a guilty and apologetic look at Bernice.

She averted her eyes. He apparently took this as a rejection and stood nearer the king.

In reality, Bernice's mind was whirling. There was something very odd about Reece's behaviour – it was almost as if the scene in his room hadn't happened; as if he was guilty about something different. He stood awkwardly, wringing his hands behind his back. Briefly it crossed her mind that he might be genuinely worried about the Doctor, after all they were old friends. Then the Doctor's admission that he'd never met Reece before the feast reminded her that there was something odd about this man she liked on the surface. The discussion with Lianna – the kiss. Heartfelt, she had thought, and yet he'd flirted with her the following morning as if she were the first woman he'd noticed since his wife's death.

Her attention was suddenly distracted: Tarrol had begun a proclamation sentencing the Doctor to death for the murder of a royal personage of Peladon. Beside her, Bernice could sense the anger and resentment pouring

222

out of Centauri. To her left were Keri and Kort. From them she sensed . . . anticipation?

'You're actually enjoying this,' she hissed at Kort. In reply he reached out and squeezed her hand. Angrily she yanked it away.

The only people missing were Geban, Atissa and of course Savaar.

One of them walked in at that moment. Geban shuffled over to Tarrol, who had interrupted his soliloquy to listen to his chancellor's whispered message.

'Damn,' was the only response Bernice could hear.

Tarrol tapped at the floor with an ornate staff he plucked out of a guard's hand. 'Let the sentence be carried out.'

Bernice wanted to pull forward but Kort grabbed her with surprising force and shook his head. She looked over and saw Sskeet beside Reece. Slowly Sskeet's head turned and he seemed to be staring at her. Staring hard. She wanted to turn away but there was something in his almost totally unreadable face, hidden behind his face mask. Then she realized. Something else was happening here. It wasn't just the Doctor's execution. Sskeet, Kort, probably the Pakhar as well. They were all in this together. The plot? The theft of the treasures?

My God, they've planned this all along. The Doctor and I have been framed!

Sskeet turned away as Savaar strode into the chamber. He was no longer dressed in full military regalia. His cloak was gone and he was sheathed in a tight-fitting ebon suit. His dark green helmet had been removed and in its place was an identical black one, his eyes hidden behind golden squares of glass. Bernice recognized the ancient code of attire as that worn by High Martian warrior chieftains centuries before, during the Martians' most barbaric period. She also noted that his slim belt had been usurped by a concession to the Pel calls for justice: a thick leather affair, decorated with metal shapes. Dead centre on the belt, just below his waist, was yet another carved image of Aggedor. The light flickered off its metallic sheen,

223

almost giving the impression that the beast's head was actually moving.

But it was what he carried that really caught Bernice's attention: the sacred sword of Tuburr. He was going to use the Martian equivalent of the Pel Lance of Aggedor to seek retribution. His twisted idea of Martian justice. The Doctor had been right to distrust the Martians all along.

The Doctor fell to his knees and bowed his head and Bernice held her breath. Dimly, from the corner of her eye, she was aware that the Pakhar was twitching her hand. As if it had gone to sleep. Then she realized she had her data-pad.

The bitch was actually recording the whole thing!

Savaar raised the sacred sword of Tuburr above his head.

Tarrol spoke: 'Doctor. For crimes against everything held dear on Peladon, I now pronounce you executed.'

Centauri went white.

Reece stared, his eyes suddenly eager?

Geban turned away.

Sskeet was observing everyone.

Kort gripped Bernice's arm tighter.

Keri was still twitching her data-pad.

Tarrol nodded.

Savaar brought the sacred sword of Tuburr down.

On to the Doctor's neck.

Centauri squealed.

Kort gasped.

Geban shuddered.

Bernice screamed: 'No!'

And the sacred sword sliced straight through the Doctor's neck and then hit the stone floor with a crash that sent sparks flying.

7:

Soul Protection

Darkness. A bright, stabbing light. Cold. Solid. Nausea.
Reaching out. Solid. Push.

Atissa heaved herself up, groaning quietly. The cold
floor of the relic room made her body shudder involuntar-
ily and she managed to sit back as the wave of dizziness
passed. Her head hurt. She reached back and felt a large
lump on the back of her skull, near the top of her spine.
A few inches lower and her neck would have been broken.
Either Savaar had meant to leave her alive or he had just
been clumsy. The lump was sore but not angry – she'd been
unconscious for a while.

The execution. She must have missed it.

Savaar was a fool. He should have killed her when he
had the chance. Now she could tell the king, Geban and
everyone just how duplicitous the Federation really were.

Casually she noted that not only had the Lance of
Aggedor gone but the Sword of Truth was also missing.
She felt strangely calm about this. Along with the Crown
of Sherak, all three items of the Pel crown jewels were
now gone. Her case against Nic Reece and his Federation
ideals was complete. By the time she had finished, Peladon
would be free. The king's easy compliance over the Doctor's execution was just the beginning. She had him eating
out of her hand. Now it was time for the final blow.

Peladon was hers.

The old ways would once again be the new ways. For
the good of her civilization, Atissa had to act quickly.

The throne room on Peladon was dark and under-lit. King

Tarrol sat hunched on his throne, Geban's abandoned robe beside him. A solitary guard stood by the door, staring ahead, not looking at his king.

'Find out where she is. She demanded an audience, she is keeping me waiting,' murmured the king.

The guard stood to attention and turned to leave when there was a knock on the doors. Slowly he opened it and saw Atissa standing outside.

'His Majesty has been waiting for you,' was his only comment as he pulled the door wide enough for the high priestess to enter.

Atissa strode in purposefully, the guard's words being of total insignificance to her.

'May I have permission to address the king?' she quoted.

Tarrol nodded and Atissa walked over, glancing down at Geban's cloak.

'Another traitor dealt with?' she asked.

Tarrol ignored the question. 'What do you require, High Priestess?'

Atissa shrugged. 'Your Majesty, tomorrow morning is the biennial restatement vows day. Before such a momentous occasion can be held, I demand that all offworlders – including that ridiculous Alpha Centauri – are escorted away from Peladon, never to return.'

'An interesting set of demands to make of one's monarch, High Priestess.'

'You have no choice, Tarrol. Your power is weak and purely academic. The true power on Peladon is the sacred spirit of Aggedor. He has consistently proved that the Federation presence is not one that he desires. I, as his vehicle, can only convey his thoughts.'

'Or your interpretation of his thoughts.'

Atissa stared at the king. And smiled. She turned to the guard by the door. 'You may assume duties elsewhere.'

The guard looked flustered but a sharp 'Get out' again from Atissa sent him scurrying.

'You see, even your personal guard is loyal to Aggedor rather than their insipid king, Tarrol.'

Tarrol didn't flinch. 'All my life, Atissa, I have attempted to reconcile my love of Aggedor with my belief that this planet must go forward. Recent events have, I know, placed a great deal of strain on you and for that reason I am allowing your manners to be somewhat less than primitive at the moment. However, I am still king and –'

Atissa reached out and grabbed Tarrol by the collar, yanking him out of his throne. 'You? King? Don't flatter yourself, Tarrol. You are nothing. Aggedor has decreed that he shall return to take power. Through me. You shall remain a figurehead for the people but you and your forefathers relinquished the honour of ruling when the first non-Pel foot was set on this planet. When your great-grandmother crashed here, it was the beginning of the darkest chapter in our history. But from tomorrow, that will change. A new dawn will break over Peladon and we shall once again be free of the yoke of Federation technology, deceit and interference.'

'For what, Atissa? The yoke of superstition? The yoke of slavery to a religion that has no real meaning to the people today? Will Aggedor feed them? Will Aggedor provide jobs, security and a future?'

Atissa flung him back into his throne. 'You ... you animal!' she spat. 'Before the Federation, Aggedor supplied it all. The Federation gutted us, left us filleted and empty. Now he will regain our love and belief. If you cannot go forward with Aggedor, rest assured he will take no hesitation in destroying you and ending the royal line immediately.'

Tarrol looked up, his face ashen. 'You would really go that far?'

'If I had to, Tarrol. Aggedor will sweep you aside like a blugrat. And I, as his servant, would aid him in every way. My loyalty to him is absolute.'

' "I", "Aggedor"? You can't tell the difference any more, Atissa. You are totally insane.'

227

'No, Tarrol. I am not insane. Accusations such as that are the last refuge of desperate losers. I am not mad – I am right!'

Tarrol suddenly realized that he had gone too far. 'Atissa, listen to me. We have executed the Doctor. The Federation will soon depart. There is no need for this ... this power struggle.'

Atissa laughed. 'Savaar actually did it? After attacking me and stealing the relics he went ahead and removed the Doctor. Oh, joy!'

'Savaar attacked you?'

'Yes. In the relic room. He stole the Lance of Aggedor and the Sword of Truth to go on his trophy wall along with the Crown of Sherak. Now I will deal with him. He has assaulted Aggedor's servant. Aggedor wants revenge.'

Tarrol pushed past her and scooped up a large jewel-encrusted box. He yanked open the lid and pushed it towards her.

In it lay the severed head of the Doctor.

Atissa reached out, her eyes glinting in pleasure and something Tarrol could only think of as pure lust. Lust for death and destruction. He snatched the box away and slammed the lid down.

'Do you want this for your trophy wall? Do you want Savaar's head as well?'

Atissa was quaking, exultation screaming through her body, her hands trembling as she gripped the side of Tarrol's throne and dropped into it. She lay her head back, staring at the ceiling where a massive image of Aggedor's face was carved into the stone.

'Yes,' she breathed. 'Yes, I want them all.'

Tarrol turned away from her and walked into the curtained passage to his quarters, leaving on his throne a woman he once liked and admired but could now only think of as totally and utterly demented.

Behind him Atissa's shadow was quaking in time with its owner's quiet laughter.

* * *

'Well?'

'She's totally mad. I can't stop her, Doctor. She is, however, satisfied that you are dead.'

The Doctor reached out and held Tarrol's shaking arm. 'I'm so sorry, Your Majesty. I know how much you want to help her, but I feel it has gone too far.'

Savaar walked out of the shadows. 'I however must thank you for your help in our deception. It was brave of you. I understand that the cost of apparently betraying your associates is high.'

'*Friends*, High Lord. Geban, Centauri, Reece. They are my friends.'

'Indeed, Your Majesty.'

The Doctor looked over at Savaar. 'Who else was in on it?'

Savaar considered. 'The Pakhar journalist. It was her holographic equipment that we utilized. The Cantryan boy. Sskeet. No one else.'

'You didn't tell Benny?'

'No. *Shsurr* Summerfield's reaction had to be realistic.'

'She won't thank you for that.'

'She dislikes me, I accept. I am sure when this ruse is exposed, she will understand.'

The Doctor beamed. 'Oh, she'll understand, High Lord. But she still won't like it.'

King Tarrol coughed. 'How much longer must the charade go on, Savaar? Atissa is accusing you of attacking her in the relic room.'

Savaar actually looked affronted. 'That is impossible. I was with Ker'a'nol the whole time.'

The Doctor was steepling his fingers and wrapping them around each other in complex patterns. 'How interesting. Why should she think it was you? Because she wanted to?'

'Or someone else wanted her to?' suggested the Martian.

'I suspect so.'

'More relics were taken,' said the king. 'How much more can we allow to go?'

'Until our treasure thief exposes himself and Savaar can make an arrest, Your Majesty.'

'In the meantime he or she could be escaping in a shuttle with ease.'

'No, Savaar. As we discovered after the Lance was stolen the first time, everything's still here on Peladon. They're not leaving with them, they're waiting for the courier, which my best friend was trailing. Well, until recently. In fact, I suspect Marshal Hissel has just spotted them.' The Doctor twirled his umbrella. 'Now the game's afoot, High Lord Savaar, and it has become time for you to play sacrificial lamb.'

In the empty room where holocameraman Jav had sat seconds before his death, the little black box was bleeping. The red light was flashing.

Deep in the catacombs of Peladon, the unseen monitors were also receiving the message on their identical black box.

In orbit around Peladon, the same message was speeding across the bridge of the *Bruk*. The Martian pilot again asked for orders but Hissel just listened.

'Marshal,' hissed another officer. 'A shuttle is approaching. It appears to be dead in space, just drifting.'

'Bearing?'

'The dark side of Peladon.'

'Excellent,' rasped the marshal. 'Pilot, take us out of orbit.'

'Heading,' asked the deeply perplexed pilot.

'Io. We are abandoning our party on Peladon. High Lord Savaar and his group have been eliminated. I am following his last orders. Leave immediately and send a sub-space message to Io. Let them know exactly what we are doing, and why. Now.'

'Marshal,' confirmed the pilot.

Moments later, the *Bruk*'s engines roared into life and

pulled out of orbit, following its own sub-space message back to Io.

Torg stared in surprise at the throne. He had expected to find his king seated, contemplating. Instead Atissa glared down at him, her eyes staring and unblinking. Her mouth was twisted into a parody of a smile.

'You have your orders, Torg. Disobey me and you disobey Aggedor. Go!'

Torg backed out.

'I can't believe he went through with it. That bastard actually did it!'

Reece put an arm around Bernice's shoulder but she threw it off. 'And none of you did anything about it. None of you tried to stop it.' She looked up at the assembled faces staring at her, allowing tears to freely dribble down her cheeks. 'Only Centauri tried. The rest of you . . .'

'Keri, this is so wrong . . .' began Kort but Keri tugged at his arm. Kort turned away.

Bernice hadn't noticed, she just stared at the floor. 'He was so . . . so alive. So wonderful. So . . .'

Reece tried again. 'Benny, grieving isn't going to bring the Doctor back. Nothing is. I suggest we give up on Peladon. All go home. Get away from it. Let Savaar come back and face a Federation trial.'

'A trial!' Bernice laughed bitterly. 'He'll probably get another bloody medal for keeping the Federation interests sweet on Peladon.'

'Professor Summerfield is probably right,' wailed Alpha Centauri somewhat unhelpfully.

Reece shot him a look and Centauri stopped bobbing up and down. With great restraint, Centauri re-adopted his green hue and shuffled towards Keri and Kort.

'Look, Benny. We are all in danger now. Atissa has her way, that's obvious. She and Savaar have cooked something up between them and we're all caught in the middle. The Doctor was and I've no intention of going

231

the same way. Come with us ... with me. Let's put this behind us.'

Bernice looked up at him, calming down.

Be practical, she told herself. Ace! What about Ace? How was she going to find her and tell her. She didn't even know where the Doctor had sent her. 'Why didn't he ever tell me what he was doing?' she muttered, angrily.

Bernice stood up and away from Reece. 'Okay,' she said. 'Grief over – let's get to work. Kort, I need to contact Io, talk to your dad. Tell him everything that's happened and arrange a rendezvous with Ace. Centauri, I think Nic is right, it's time we all got away from here.'

'I need to gather all my crew together. And find Corry, yeah,' said Keri.

Bernice nodded. 'Okay – so how do we get away from here?'

'The *Bruk*?' suggested Kort.

'Are you joking?' returned Bernice. 'I'm not setting foot on Savaar's bloody ship for anything.'

'Be practical, Benny,' the boy replied. 'It's our only way out.'

The door swung open and Sskeet walked in. Bernice swung around, concentrating all her mental hostility in his direction. 'What the cruk do you want?'

Sskeet was about to reply when there was a disturbance from outside in the corridor. All heads turned to see Savaar being almost dragged along by some Pel guards, swords at his throat.

'What on Earth ...?' began Reece.

'Jolly good show,' yelled Bernice. 'That's him out of the way.'

'You're not thinking, Benny,' said Keri softly. 'If Savaar is under arrest, then our chances of leaving Peladon are nil. His shuttle won't go back to the *Bruk* without him and the GFTV–3 ship isn't due to pick us up until after the restatement vows. Looks like we're here for the duration.'

'What about Corry's shuttle?' Reece asked Keri.

'There's barely enough room for one on that, let alone him and his whiskey. No, that's of no use. Unfortunately.'

Benny started to sag until Sskeet walked over.

'*Shsurr* Summerfield,' he hissed. 'Please listen to me.'

'Why?'

'Because I have important information.'

Bernice noted a swift but inexplicable look between Kort and Keri. Centauri just blinked but Reece shuffled on his feet. It was, she decided, as if they were all expecting something important to be said. But what did any of them have in common that Sskeet could possibly want to talk about? Unless ... Of course – they all thought Sskeet was going to say something disadvantageous to each of them. Typical paranoia.

'Okay, Sskeet, let's hit the corridor and talk in private.'

As they left, Sskeet pulled the door shut, loudly saying, 'It is important that you realize that Savaar has been expelled from the Federation and the Martian hierarchy as a result of the Doctor's death – ' and he and Bernice were gone.

'Well, what about that?' grunted Reece.

'What do you mean, Nic?' asked Keri.

'One moment she's all for hang, drawing and quartering the Martians; next, she's having chummy chats with Sskeet. Women!'

'What's this all about, Sskeet? Why was Savaar not working for the Federation?'

'I lied.'

Bernice stopped dead. 'So he was doing it on the Federation's behalf.'

'You must come with me,' was Sskeet's only response.

'No bloody way! I don't want to end up a headless corpse as well.'

Sskeet yanked back an Aggedor-decorated drape covering part of the wall. It revealed a small alcove and he tugged at the unlit flambeau. The wall behind dropped back silently on a hinge.

'Please,' he said.

Bernice started to back away but with a turn of speed she thought impossible for a Martian, Sskeet reached forward and grabbed her. Not roughly, but firmly he took her through the gap, letting the drape fall back. He moved a corresponding flambeau and the door swung back into place, leaving barely a crack in the rugged black walls.

'I can't see, Sskeet.'

'Keep hold of my arm, I will ensure you come to no harm whatsoever.'

'You'll forgive me if I take that with the proverbial pinch of salt,' she said through gritted teeth as he strode forward, almost dragging her.

They continued in the darkness for a few moments, the silence broken by Bernice's occasional grunts as she tripped over a jut of rock or stone.

The walk widened into a large open cavern and Bernice's eyes quickly adjusted to the gloom. Nearby was an old wooden wheelbarrow, pitted and covered in roak dust.

She released her grip and stepped back from the big warrior. 'Well, where's this bloody explanation? It'd better be good.'

Sskeet said nothing.

'Say something, Sskeet. I'm getting bored.'

'You know, I hate people who say they're bored!'

Bernice spun around, searching for the owner of the voice. That soft, vaguely Scottish burr . . .

The Doctor stepped out of the shadows, umbrella hanging off an outstretched arm.

Bernice drew a deep breath and looked at him. Slowly she nodded to herself, suppressing a sardonic grin. She ran her tongue around her teeth, put her weight on one leg and folded her arms.

'I should've known better.'

The Doctor reached out and embraced her. 'Yes. Yes, you should. More to the point, so should I.'

'Savaar?'

The Doctor smiled. 'He trusted me all along. He set

the whole thing up. Kort and the Pakhar journalist were in on it.'

'But I saw you die. I saw Savaar chop your head off. Your blood is all over the temple floor.'

'No it's not. You saw a quite magnificent piece of holo-grammatic projection, courtesy of the Pakhar and Kort. All for Atissa's benefit.'

'But she wasn't there?'

'No. Shame, really. I understand they put a lot of effort into it. Still, your reaction was apparently very convincing. And I gather Centauri went a colour he's never achieved before!'

'Can't say I noticed. I was too busy thinking how much blood fits into one small body. Funny, that.'

The Doctor withdrew from the embrace. 'I'm sorry.'

'Yeah, you bloody ought to be. You little sod. D'you realize, I actually cried! I mean, how long is it since I did that! God, next time you die, you can stay dead!' This time she hugged him, suddenly feeling complete again for the first time in hours; all her anger and bitterness draining away. 'Good thing Ace wasn't here. She'd blown Savaar away on the spot.'

The Doctor brushed down his suit. He pointed at Sskeet with his umbrella. 'So. Why here, Sskeet?'

The Martian pointed further into the tunnel network. 'Along here.'

'I seem to recognize this area,' murmured the Doctor. Suddenly he dropped to the floor. 'Footprints. Human ones alongside many Martian ones. Who else is here, Sskeet?'

The Martian just carried on forward.

'Benny, where's Savaar?'

'Last seen being escorted at knifepoint towards the temple.'

'Already?' The Doctor stopped and looked at the ceiling. He suddenly pointed at Sskeet. 'Sskeet, wait!' The Martian stopped and turned and the Doctor grasped Bernice's hand. 'Benny, go back. Now you know the truth, I need you to rescue Savaar. I don't care how, but discredit

Atissa. She's accusing him of assaulting her, which he didn't.'

'What'll you do?'

'Savaar wanted Sskeet to bring me here for a reason. I must go on. But remember, you are still mourning for me. No one, but no one must know that I'm alive. And don't let the Pakhar journalist or Kort know that you know I'm all right.' He looked her straight in the eye. She almost recoiled from the intensity of the stare – his coal-black eyes seemed to bore into her. Wait a minute, surely the Doctor's eyes were blue. Or green . . .

'Benny, trust no one except King Tarrol and High Lord Savaar. I mean that.' He bounced up and caught up with Sskeet.

Bernice turned away and wandered back into the opening with the wheelbarrow. Which tunnel had she and Sskeet come down? She turned to one but it seemed very dark and looked quite oppressive. No, it can't have been that one. As she stared around her, it seemed as if only one seemed light enough to actually see down. With a shrug, she slowly headed down it.

'But if Savaar's dead, that must mean something's happened to the Doctor!' Ace jumped up from the rather too-comfortable seat she was slowly sinking into.

The Chair of the Galactic Federation frowned. The hologram floating in front of the two of them was slowly rotating, constantly shifting pixels so that they could both see Marshal Hissel's face. 'Is Ace correct, Marshal? Is everyone on Peladon dead?'

'I cannot say for sure, Chair, but High Lord Savaar's orders were explicit. If anything happened to him, I was to contact you and explain that we were returning without any Federation personnel.'

Ace stared hard at the Chair but the aged Cantryan ignored her. 'I understand, Marshal. Please convey our deepest regrets to the Martian High Commission. I will deal with the Earth Consular and Centaurian MultiBody. Io out.'

The hologram dribbled away into tiny pixels and was gone.

'So', growled Ace. 'So that's an Ice Warrior. Brings a whole new meaning to the concept of shell-suits, doesn't it?'

The Cantryan commissioner gazed at her uncomprehendingly. 'I am saddened by the loss, Ace. My son was among the death toll. That's both my children in three months.'

Ace looked across at him and sat again. 'I'm sorry,' she said.

The Cantryan crossed to another communication circuit and pressed a few codes. A human face pixeled into existence. 'Guardian's office, can I help?'

Ace regarded the handsome young human oriental facing them.

'Good afternoon, Chen. Is the Guardian of the Solar System available?'

Chen nodded. 'For you, Chair, she is always available.' There was a pause and Chen's features were displaced and reassembled as an elderly but haughty human woman. 'Mavic says you wanted me, Trau Chair. How can I help?'

'I am sorry to bear bad news on your final day as guardian, Madame Amazonia.'

Amazonia obviously shrugged and the pixels tried to reproduce the movement.

'I'm used to it, Chair. And young Mavic here is learning that it comes with the post. What is the problem?'

'Peladon, Guardian. We appear to have lost the entire Federation representation there.'

The Guardian of the Solar System absorbed this and turned away. A second later she was joined by the young oriental. 'I will make it Mavic's first task to inform the relevant families.' Behind her Chen nodded and brought up his data-pad.

The Cantryan commissioner began reeling off the names.

Ace sunk lower into her chair. Something was wrong

237

but she couldn't put her finger on it. Something about Hissel's wording. His evasion.

'How far are we from Peladon, pilot?'

The Martian pilot mentally chided himself. He should have been expecting yet another irrelevant and contradictory request from Hissel. He'd had quite a few since breaking orbit – the strangest being broadcasting a supposedly private communication between Hissel and Io on all available frequencies – and a few illegitimate ones. 'One hour, thirty-four standard minutes, Marshal,' he sighed.

'Position of dead shuttle in Peladon's orbit?'

Thrown by this, the pilot had to scrabble about on his navcom. He punched up the relevant information. 'Its orbit has decayed. It has already entered Peladon's atmosphere. I suspect Marshal that it has burned up.'

'You suspect incorrectly, pilot. However, it is what you were intended to think. Reverse course, let's get back into orbit but exactly where we were – geostationary. I do not want one millimetre's drift until I give the command.'

The pilot was about to question this when he mentally shrugged. Why bother? Hissel was obviously insane and there was little he could do about it.

Marshal Hissel breathed out gleefully. 'Weaponry?' he hissed into the air.

A hologram of a small Martian with a somewhat over-large head appeared before him, large red eye-glasses staring wildly. 'Marshal?'

'Prepare blasters. We may need to engage hostile forces near Peladon. I want everyone to be ready.'

'Sir!' The hologram vanished. Hissel sat back in his command chair. Not long now.

'Landing shortly. Thirty seconds, prepare for a none-too-soft one, guys,' yelled Cooper. Her hands raced across the navcom. She'd switched to manual, not trusting the computer to avoid all the tiny jags and ridges of Peladon's surface.

The shuttle hit Peladon with a slight thud and skidded briefly but quickly came to a stop.

'Good one,' yelled Lambert.

Here. Yes. This place is ideal. Take me.

Sadler ran a hand through her hair – she had a tremendous headache. Must have been too much concentration, listening to all those messages between the *Bruk* and Io.

Townsend unstrapped himself and looked at his troops. 'Okay, here's the pay-off. We've fooled the *Bruk* and got down safely. We have about an hour's walk to the back of Mount Megeshra. We should find access quite easy and follow our noses. The boss has had a few weeks to label our route. We go in the back way, unload his treasures and go.'

Sadler looked at the safe-seal in horror. The translucent frontage had gone and the lid of the vacuum case was slightly ajar. Of course – the plasma blast must have knocked out the seal-systems. With the drive-systems taking priority . . . Still, she should have noticed it and told Townsend. She was going to when something made her stop.

No.

Instead, Sadler pushed the lid closed, coughed loudly and patted the vacuum case. 'And this?'

'Yeah, that. We give it to him. I don't want to hang on to it.'

'You don't mean we're actually doing a legit deal?' asked Cooper, feigning surprise.

Lambert however was genuinely amazed. 'Okay, so we can sell off the Pel crap and make a good profit, but this has to be worth heaps. Can't we just kill him and keep this as well?'

Sadler shook her head. 'What's in here is too powerful. Let him handle it.'

Townsend nodded. 'My sentiments exactly, Sadler. You carry it, okay?'

Yes. Take me. Keep me safe and I will reward you.

'Yes, okay,' she replied.

A few moments later and the four of them, very heavily

armed and wearing full Kevlar–8 battle protection outfits, jumped down from the shuttle and headed towards the mountain. Hanging slightly back was Sadler, carrying the vacuum case.

Soon. Soon it will be over. I will be complete. Look after me and you shall have power.

For some reason that she couldn't comprehend, she was feeling very nervous. Frightened, even. It was as if she wasn't in control. For the first time in her life she was feeling . . . manipulated?

For what we are about to do . . .

Misquoting prayers had always been one of Bernice's little quirks. Gathered around camp fires (oh, for a piece of real fire and wood right now instead of all this Federation fakery), she and the other archaeologists would frequently find excuses to poke fun at organized ancient religions and work the psalms and gospels to suit any given situation. Clive was always good for running through his pad, finding the Common Bible, ripping out whole passages and turning them into lurid and suggestive phrases about the Draconian and his pet wolfweed.

Bernice smiled at the memory. It all seemed so far away. 'You and your Martians,' Clive'd say. 'One day you'll meet one, fall in love and have to invest in a hatchery!'

Bernice would usually clump him with a stick and threaten to bury his latest finds under cement.

If he could see me now, see what I'm about to do.

Hope Savaar's got a sense of humour.

Hope Atissa hasn't!

She stood outside the Sacred Temple of Aggedor. Through the small hole in the wall, she could take it all in. Atissa standing, throwing something into the burners, clouds of incense billowing up. Savaar, ignominiously bound and shoved into a kneeling position. His cloak had been yanked off and thrown into a corner. Two of Atissa's thugs held swords to his throat.

Bernice knew her Martian philosophy but she understood on only a basic level the complex social patterns of honour and truth that the Martians lived by. Codes of hierarchy and stigma that somehow involved the whole structure of Martian life. Despite its 'Lords and Commoners' trappings, Martian life was rigidly structured so that there was no real 'them' and 'us', just a traditional belief in it. A curious contradiction, but one that had proved fascinating to Bernice for most of her adult life. She'd always wanted to study that hierarchy in detail but amongst the few things she did understand was that Savaar was enduring almost intolerable humiliation and the potential destruction of honour right now. And she was about to make it worse in an attempt to stop it. Would he thank her or would he kill her?

Oh, what the hell – what's life without a few risks?

Of course, it was quite possible she wouldn't live long enough to carry out her plan: the moment she entered the sacred chamber uninvited, given Atissa's curious blend of blasphemy and intolerance, she might be cut down by a sword-happy Pel guard.

But she owed Savaar. He'd saved the Doctor's life. He'd lied and cheated and already done so much that was considered dishonourable in Martian terms, just to keep the Doctor alive and Atissa fooled. Yeah, she owed him.

She took a breath and pushed through the drape into the sacred temple. Five heads turned to look at her in complete amazement. The two guards holding Savaar looked up in total astonishment. The third guard, standing by the opposite door to Atissa's personal quarters, drew his sword. Atissa almost dropped her herbs and spices in mute shock.

And Savaar . . .

Savaar seemed totally unresponsive, his eyes hidden behind his helmet, a black tongue flickering around his chapped green lips.

'What do you want?' Atissa said eventually.

'Nothing. Just revenge. Then I'll leave you alone. With the Doctor dead, I have nothing left to stay here for.' Bernice noted Savaar's head droop a fraction – he thinks

I don't know the truth. Good. That means it'll be more convincing.

Atissa rolled some herbs between her thumb and fore-finger, almost crushing them to dust particles. 'Get out,' she said.

Bernice shook her head. 'You've got what you wanted, Atissa. Me, Reece, the Pakhars, even Centauri. We're leaving this afternoon. Before your wretched royal ceremony. But I want something in return. I want him!'

Atissa looked at Savaar and smiled. 'No. No, he is ours to destroy. He struck me and stole our sacred relics. Aggedor demands retribution.'

'So do I, Atissa, and my need is greater than your bloody statue's.'

Mentally crossing her fingers, Bernice strode to Savaar, pushing the guards aside. In surprise, they didn't resist. Bernice reached down to Savaar and grabbed at his helmet. She yanked it off his head and stared at his black eyes, darting backwards and forwards.

'What . . . what do you want, *Shsurr*?'

'I told you before, Savaar, I'm no longer your *Shsurr*. But for what might have been, given time and some honour clearly lacking in you, take to your afterlife my final gift.'

Bernice reached down, cupped Savaar's huge skull and kissed him savagely on the lips. He tried to resist but she held firm, pressing harder until it hurt, but she went on. After nearly a minute she stepped back, wiping saliva – hers or his, she wasn't sure – from her mouth.

He stared back at her in horror. Desecrated. Humiliated. Angry.

'Thank you, Savaar. Thank you for destroying my life as well as the Doctor's.' Bernice rummaged in her chino pocket and produced a Cantryan clip blaster.

'No,' screeched Atissa, but it was too late. Bernice fired, there was a flash of white and Savaar toppled over.

Atissa shook with cold fury, and Bernice brought the blaster up again. 'Forget it, High Priestess. In three hours, we're all out of your life. Don't do anything to upset us or little granite Aggie over there gets a few tusks blown away.'

Atissa's eyes moved from Bernice's gun to the statue of Aggedor. 'All right, defiler. Get out. Now.'

Bernice waved the gun at Savaar. 'I want the body. I want to parade it across New Mars, dishonouring his family and proving what a traitor he was.'

One of the guards moved over to Savaar and a second later reported to Atissa that the Martian High Lord was indeed dead.

'You can leave, Summerfield. Take this alien trash with you.' Atissa indicated for the guards to hoist Savaar's body up.

'Thank you, High Priestess. If you can dump him in the Federation Representatives' room, that'd be just dandy.' Bernice led the way out.

Watching them go, Atissa grinned. The obstacles were dropping like flies.

Next – the king. Then it was all hers.

She patted the statue of Aggedor. 'Soon. Very, very soon.'

Keri was bustling around, trying to get her crew and equipment all together.

She called out to one of the audio engineers to ask if Neal Corry had returned yet. No sign.

'Damn him, yeah! Where the hell is he?'

As she hurried through the corridors of the Citadel, Keri's mind was racing. If the Doctor's plan was working, there should be some action quite soon. Her professional instincts cried out that she should be preparing to holo the whole lot. But with no Corry, it fell to her to rally her team. Their protection was more important than any GFTV-3 story and while Peladon was falling into the file marked 'Hostile World', she was better off getting everyone out alive.

'Damn stupid planet, yeah!'

* * *

243

Kort was sitting, literally kicking his heels when the doors of the Federation Representatives' room burst open. An entourage of Pels entered, carrying the prostrate form of High Lord Savaar. Kort leaped up as they none-too-carefully deposited his huge frame upon the table. The boy stared at the helmet-less face aghast. He'd never seen a Martian like this before.

A cough from the doorway alerted him to Bernice's presence. She was carrying his cloak and helmet which she deposited on a chair. The Pel guards departed.

'Is he dead, then? Did Atissa kill him?'

'You're a blood-thirsty little tyke, aren't you?' was Bernice's only answer. She crossed to the back of the room and filled a mug with cold water. Kort was more than a little alarmed at the manic grin on her face as she wandered back over.

'What are you going to do, Benny?'

She put her fingers to her lips. 'Look. Listen. Learn.'

She tipped the mug of water directly over Savaar's face and he instantly started hacking and coughing. An arm flailed out, nearly catching Kort on the head. Slowly the coughing High Lord pushed himself up.

'Shut up, *Drushull*, you're dead,' Bernice said.

He looked at her through rapidly focusing eyes. 'Do not call me *Drushull*, *Shsurr* I might forget that I am one and hit a lady.'

Bernice laughed, confusing Kort further. 'Hey, it was you who decided that I was a lady. My mother just said I was a proper little madam.'

'What is going on?' the impatient boy asked.

'A good question, Damakort. I, too, would like an answer. Especially regarding that strange intimacy you expressed, Professor.' Savaar hauled himself off the table and replaced his mask. He held up his cloak but the Pel guards had torn its clasps earlier. He gave it a brief look and left it on the chair.

'You liked the kiss, Savaar. Admit it, it gave you a thrill.'

'It was . . . interesting, certainly.'

'Yeah. And a good ruse. Got you away from Atissa. With the help of this blaster.'

'They thought I was dead?'

'Yup. I knew the right level to simulate your physiology's shut-down procedures. I always knew a crash-course in Martian biology would come in handy one day.'

'I am grateful that you took it.'

Bernice laughed. 'I never did. I just read a couple of textbooks, thought they were boring, and so guessed. I got lucky.'

'Actually, I rather think I did.'

Bernice sat and Savaar followed suit.

'Kort, do us a favour. Go find Keri and bring her back here.'

'But I want to – '

'Please,' begged Bernice.

Kort nodded and left.

After the boy had left, Savaar reached out and clasped Bernice's hand. 'Thank you. You were very brave. Atissa might have killed you.'

'I had to take the risk. Just as you did regarding the Doctor.'

'You have seen him?'

'He's in the mines with Sskeet. Exploring footprints. The reason I got rid of Kort is because the Doctor doesn't trust him. Or Keri. Or, I suppose, even Centauri.'

Savaar agreed. 'But it isn't just a question of trust. It's of reliability. I imagine that Centauri is about as guilty of any crime as you or I but he is quite likely to give away any secrets. His knowing the Doctor is still alive could be a risk.'

'Now, Kort and the others will have to know you're around but I suggest you head back to the shuttle.'

'No,' said Savaar. 'No, I need to be nearer. I will hide in your quarters. No one will look there, I am sure.'

'Oh, right. Okay.'

A pair of human hands gently lowered the Crown of

Sherak into a large adamantium casket. A soft burgundy cushion was placed over the top and the lid closed.

'Computer. Open safe-seal. Override MDH Absolute.'

'Confirmed.'

A hiss of air and part of the shuttle wall vanished and revealed a hole big enough for the casket. The hands lifted up the casket and inserted it. They then laid the Lance of Aggedor on the top.

'Reseal. Access commands erased. This safe-seal may only be opened on the access code *Summerfield Code-A*. That access code may not be divulged to any party at any time. If any attempt is made to open the safe-seal without that code this shuttle is to self-destruct instantly. No time delay. Confirm.'

'Confirmed.'

'Good.' The owner of the hands and voice got out of the Martian shuttle. He looked down at the decapitated Martian pilot and nudged the body under the shuttle. It wouldn't hide it for long, but a few seconds could be important. He picked up the double-bladed Sword of Truth from the ground where he'd deposited it and wiped the green blood off on to the dusty floor.

Damajina. Jav. And now the pilot. He enjoyed killing.

Torg was worried. He couldn't find either King Tarrol or Geban. He had arrested Savaar as instructed and had been told by his men that Savaar had been killed eventually by the human professor in revenge for the Doctor's death.

Something was wrong. Atissa was certainly a high-ranking official in Pel society and she was the daughter of the beloved Lady Lianna. She also seemed unwell.

He was distracted by a noise from an adjoining corridor. A soft humming which he soon realized came from an anti-grav valise floating towards him. Behind it was Nic Reece, a holdall slung over his shoulder.

'Hiya, Torg. Just clearing out. We know when we're not wanted.'

Torg felt his heart sag a little – Nic Reece was a popular Federation figure on Peladon and he, along with most of his men, would miss the official's humour and light-hearted banter. Torg was saddened that it was to be so quickly over.

He grunted his disappointment and Reece held out his hand. Torg took it and they shook. 'Just in case we don't have another chance, Torg, I just want to say thanks. You and your chums have been sporting chaps and I'll miss you all. Good luck with Atissa.' Reece smiled and Torg bowed slightly and stepped back.

He knocked into the floating suitcase and it shifted on its anti-gravs, crashing to the floor, the lid springing open and sending clothes and other personal items on to the ground.

Embarrassed, Torg dropped down and started piling things back into it.

Kort found Keri quite quickly.

'Something's going on,' he said quietly.

'What exactly?'

'Savaar is alive!'

Keri cocked her head and twitched her snout. 'Sorry? I wasn't aware that he'd died. What d'you mean, yeah?'

'Atissa had him executed. Except Benny interrupted and saved him. But Atissa thinks he's dead and she killed him. I think she knows that the Doctor isn't dead, but Atissa thinks he is. But she's not saying.'

'Who's not saying what?'

'That he's alive!'

'The Doctor or Savaar?'

'What?'

'No, that's my line. Kort, what are you talking about? Slowly.'

With a deep breath, Kort started again.

Alpha Centauri bobbed around his room, trying not to panic. The Doctor was dead. Savaar was probably dead. And he had no way of communicating with Io as the *Bruk* appeared to have left orbit. On top of that, his short-range transmitter was not getting through to the pilot on Savaar's shuttle.

'Oh, I need something to do,' he cried to no one in particular.

At which point there was a knock on the door, scaring the hysterical hexapod into near hyperventilation. 'Who . . . who is it?' he asked.

'It's Geban, Ambassador. We need to talk.'

Centauri opened the door but it wasn't Geban. Before he could cry out, the flat side of the Sword of Truth, fresh with red blood, smacked into the side of his head, just to the side of the eye. In the last seconds Centauri realized that although he hadn't seen his opponent, it had to be someone he knew because they knew his weak spot, and very few people did.

The attacker stepped over Centauri's prostrate form. Something had held him back from killing again – an interesting psychological block that needed explaining. One day.

He wrenched open Centauri's locker but couldn't find what he was looking for. Angrily he slammed the doors shut and walked back towards the door. Just before he left he pulled from his pocket a piece of burgundy robe, very similar to something Geban would have worn. He wiped the now sticky red blood on the sword off with the material, balled it and dropped it by the door.

Then he left.

Bernice looked sharply at Savaar. With astonishing silence, the Martian stood up and away from Bernice's bed, crossing the room in a heartbeat to hide behind the door.

The knock came again.

Bernice mentally noted again that, when necessary, Martians could move swiftly and rather elegantly.

'Come in?'

The door opened and Nic Reece popped his head in. 'Hi.'

'Oh. Hi. What can I do for you?'

'I want to apologize. Can I come in?'

Unseen by Reece, Savaar nodded at Bernice.

'Yes,' she said. 'Sure. Fine.'

As Reece came in he turned to allow his floating case to follow and was greeted by the High Lord hiding by the door.

'Am I interrupting something?'

Savaar strode back to the bed and sat. 'Yes. But it doesn't matter.'

'Hey. I'm sorry. I'll come back.'

Bernice waved him to a chair. 'No. Say what you have to say.'

Reece cleared his throat and looked at Savaar. He in turn stared back impassively, clearly not taking the hint. Or not wanting to. With a sigh, Reece realized that the obstinate Martian was not going to leave.

'Okay. Benny. I'm sorry about that business in my room. I was wrong to go off at the deep end.'

'I was wrong to snoop.'

'Yeah, well, I just got kind of paranoid. Silly old git I know, but there were things that I didn't want you to see.'

'I know. The holos. I'm genuinely sorry about your family. If you'd said, I'd have understood. Maybe helped. I lost my parents. Apart from the Doctor, I've no one really, so I know what loneliness is.'

'And now you've lost him. That's bad. Let's part pleasantly. Can we go for quick walk? In the catacombs?'

Bernice looked at Savaar and then at Nic Reece. 'Yeah. Okay, just a quick wander though. I've got to prepare to leave as well.'

Reece jumped up 'Great. See you later, my Lord. Nice to see you alive and kicking after all.'

He and Bernice left, followed by the floating valise.

Savaar suddenly felt very worried. Something was wrong – something that he should have said to *Shsurr* Summerfield. What was it?

The Doctor stared in surprise and admiration.

Of course, now it all made sense.

He had followed Sskeet down the long winding tunnels further into the gloom but equally further into familiar territory.

'Where are we going, Sskeet? And why?'

'Lord Savaar believes it is in all our interests to explain our actions. I am therefore doing just that.'

'Well, good for Lord Savaar.'

They had carried on in silence for about twenty minutes, the air getting thinner. It was a good thing he'd sent Benny back, he decided. She'd have coped admirably but he knew she would have been uncomfortable. His own respiratory system was designed to cope with most atmospheres, although one of those old cream atmospheric density jackets from the TARDIS would have helped. Would have gone quite nicely with his suit as well. And as for Sskeet – well, Martian physiology wasn't his strong point but he imagined they could cope quite easily down here.

As the air got staler and staler, the Doctor suddenly recognized where they were. A few odd tools lay scattered around a few more broken wheelbarrows. They were in the heart of the now-defunct mining core of Peladon. The place where the Pel miners had so bravely defended their world against the oppressive Martian traitor, Commander Azaxyr and the devious human engineer Eckersley the last time the Doctor was here. Back then Azaxyr had sabotaged the air ducts, causing the miners to return to the surface points where his Ice Warriors had systematically begun fighting back. And almost winning, until he'd helped the nobles and miners alike to hit back.

Brave Queen Thalira. Poor obstinate Chancellor Ortron. Even a young Lianna. They'd all fought the Ice Warriors alongside him.

Now, here he was trusting them once again.

Funny old universe, really. He spent so much time telling Ace, Tegan, Sarah Jane, Polly and all the others not to judge by appearances. Yet he had done just that with Savaar and Sskeet – tried to make enemies rather than friends.

. Oh well, he thought. It proved that it's never too late to teach an old Doc new tricks.

Eventually they had reached the site that the Doctor had guessed they were heading for. The old disused refinery. There, Eckersley had manufactured the ghostly appearances of Aggedor, using a purpose-built Aggedor statue fitted with a high resolution disrupter that literally transmatted around the planet, vaporizing all who got in its way. Such a devious but cunningly crafted plan. He'd never told Sarah, his friend at the time, but he held a grudging respect for both Azaxyr and Eckersley for that. A magnificent piece of engineering but wholly evil.

The Doctor had stood to one side as Sskeet approached the rusted old door. The Ice Warrior raised his sonic disrupter and an almost imperceptible whine began.

'K9 would have gone mad,' murmured the Doctor as he placed his fingers in his ears.

The door suddenly clunked and bright light shone out of the window. The Doctor could see movement from within and had guessed what they were as the door opened.

Sskeet slammed his arm across his chest in a salute as a taller Ice Warrior walked out.

'Commander Rassbur,' he rasped.

Rassbur nodded a greeting. He then turned and looked at the Doctor.

'Greetings, Doctor. My Lord Savaar informed me of your arrival. Please accept my apologies regarding the mysterious way in which you were brought here.'

'Not at all, Commander. A most pleasant journey.' The Doctor doffed his hat before continuing: 'I must say I am surprised to see you down here. I wasn't aware that any other Federation ships had been in the area since we arrived on the *Bruk*.'

Rassbur inhaled noisily. 'That, Doctor, is because there hasn't been one. My team and I have been on Peladon for six weeks.'

And now the Doctor understood everything. Almost.

He and Sskeet entered the refinery. The Doctor remembered it as a sparse and quite small room, just a few banks of equipment for judging Peladon's trisilicate ores, plus of course Eckersley's additions such as the trans-mat and his neurological anti-theft devices.

However, the Martians had been busy. They had carved out a much larger area which reminded the Doctor of a government war room. In the centre was a three-dimensional hologram of the Citadel. To the left of that were further holograms, larger reconstructions of certain rooms and areas around the throne room. The relic room was represented, as was the shuttle bay where they had first landed. Equally spaced around the walls were consoles with banks upon banks of slim computer nets, holograms and even rather archaic electrical equipment. The Doctor was drawn to a small black box with a red light on top.

'How fascinating. What does this do?'

'Not a lot,' replied Rassbur. 'Occasionally it receives messages from a group of human mercenaries employed by whoever is stealing Peladon's treasures. That is what we are here to observe and eventually stop. We guessed that events would climax around the restatement vows. With so much traffic in and around the planet, it would be the ideal opportunity for the criminal to escape.'

The Doctor dropped into a hard seat. Wincing slightly – and remembering that Martians were not renowned for their love of comfort – he removed his hat and began folding it. 'And the mercenaries?'

'We believe they are bringing something else for our mystery criminal.'

'Oh, they are.' The Doctor paused and then frowned. 'Commander Rassbur, are you telling me that with all this equipment, with six weeks of illegal hiding down here, you haven't actually ascertained firstly why the mercenaries are coming and secondly who the villain of the piece is?'

'They thought it was me,' said a plaintive voice.

The Doctor didn't bother to turn: he recognized the tone. 'Mister Corry, I think a lot of people up top are

252

going to be very pleased to see you alive. Your Ker'a'nol is especially upset.'

Corry wandered into his field of vision. 'That's nice to know. What's going on up top?'

The Doctor sat back. 'Oh. Lots. King Tarrol had me executed. High Priestess Atissa had High Lord Savaar executed. Both failed. Did Savaar know you were here?'

Rassbur answered: 'Lord Savaar and the Lady Lianna knew everything from the moment we landed here.'

'Good. Then by now Savaar should have sussed who our mystery man is.' The Doctor stood up. 'Commander Rassbur, those human mercenaries are bringing with them the Ancient Pakhar Diadem. I'm sure I don't need to lecture you regarding its legendary power or its fiscal value. I suspect that our mystery man isn't going to take the Peladon relics himself at all – I think he's trading them for the Diadem because that's what he was after when he murdered the Federation Chair's daughter on Pakha. You and your men are likely to have a war on your hands. I hope you are prepared.'

Rassbur saluted. 'Always.'

'Good. I think you should stay hidden until the time is right. I take it you are monitoring the presence of the mercenaries.'

'They are less than an hour from here.'

'Good, good. Now, it is imperative we let them get quite some way in. I abhor violence but the most important thing is the destruction of the Diadem. I hope no lives will be lost but it is a possibility. Nevertheless, I shall be the one to retrieve the Diadem at my own risk. None of your men are to try, is that understood?'

Rassbur nodded. The Doctor scooped up his umbrella and pointed to Sskeet.

'Come on Sskeet – time to take me back. Mister Corry and I have a resurrection to stage.'

Geban gently shook Alpha Centauri awake.

With a slight cry of pain, Centauri began to stir, colour seeping back into his arms and head. He looked up at

Geban. 'Chancellor? Someone pretending to be you attacked me!'

As Geban pulled Centauri upright he asked who it was, but Centauri miserably confirmed that he hadn't seen.

The chancellor reached down and picked up the blood-soaked ball of cloth.

'Someone really wanted it to look like me. Who?'

'We should go and tell someone about this.'

'Again, who? The king will not be interested. Savaar is dead. The Doctor is dead. I cannot find Nic Reece or Professor Summerfield and the holocrew are all packed and waiting by the Martian shuttle.'

Suddenly there was a crash and scamper of feet from outside the door. Geban flung it open to see Keri and Kort, breathless.

'He's dead, yeah. The pilot is dead.'

Geban looked at Centauri who merely said, 'I wondered why he wasn't replying to my call.'

'I suspect he's been dead only a short while,' said a Scottish accent behind them all.

The unanimous shouts of 'Doctor!' nearly deafened the Time Lord but eventually he waved their questions away. 'Keri here can explain how it was done, we have work to do. We must find Savaar.'

'Doctor, he has been executed,' wailed Centauri.

'Nonsense, Ambassador. He's as dead as I am. With any luck he and Bernice have your art thief in chains by now. The clues were obvious enough.'

'What clues?' asked Kort.

'Later. Too many questions, I'll tell you later. Let's go.'

As the entourage moved away from Centauri's quarters, it was Neal Corry who noticed the bulge in a nearby drape-covered alcove. Calling them back, he moved the drape side.

Geban gasped as Torg's body flopped forward, the huge man's throat severed from ear to ear.

'He must have died instantly,' said the Doctor quietly. 'The poor man.'

'Who did this?' said Geban.

'Our art thief. The same person who killed Lady Lianna, old Fabon and anyone else who is missing.'

'Jav,' said Keri.

'Jav? My cameraman?' asked Corry.

'If he is a Pakhar, then yes,' replied Sskeet. 'We found a badly mutilated Pakhar on Mount Megeshra's slopes some time ago. He had fallen or been pushed from a great height.'

'I wonder what scam he got caught up in this time,' Corry muttered. 'I knew he was trouble. Knew that after the Galactic Storm stuff. Poor fool.'

'I suspect,' said the Doctor, laying the drape over Torg's body and straightening up, 'I suspect he found out who our man was and tried to blackmail him. Very silly idea.'

He led the way forward.

High Lord Savaar decided it was time to risk attention. *Shsurr* Summerfield and Nic Reece were obviously engaged in deep, meaningful conversation somewhere but it was time he reported in to Commander Rassbur.

He was just leaving Bernice's room when the door was flung open and the Doctor stood there. Savaar saw the Pakhar, the Cantryan, Sskeet, Geban the Chancellor and even Neal Corry pile in behind him.

'Greetings, Doctor. *Shsurr* Summerfield carried out her mission with great delicacy and style. She will be honoured when we return to the Federation.'

'Good, Savaar, good. Now where is she?'

'She and Nic Reece are in the tunnels, discussing private matters.'

There was a pause and then the Doctor almost seemed to erupt in anger. He began pacing around like a clock-work toy in overdrive.

'And you let her? You let her go off with Nic Reece? How could you be so stupid?'

'Doctor! I don't understand – '

'No, obviously. I thought I'd laid all the clues out for you. I couldn't tell Benny because I needed her to get close to him. Don't you understand, the man you know as Nic Reece isn't. He's some kind of psychotic mercenary who's trying to rule the Federation.' The Doctor stared at them. 'He killed Lianna, Torg, Jav, Jina, everyone. Nic Reece is the man we've all been hunting and you've let him take Bernice into the caverns!'

Interlude Three

'Professor? Professor Rhukk? Where are you?'

In his portable cabin, the object of the calling looked up from his comm-net.

'Open,' he commanded and a portion of the wall melted away to let in the searing heat of Phaester Osiris's close atmosphere. He adjusted the controls on the collar of is translucent exo-suit. Cool air and liquid oxygen were pumped against his body and he sighed contentedly.

Feeling able to face the outside, Rhukk pushed himself out of his chair and gingerly stepped on to the sand. Despite the exo-suit, the heat hit him like a pile-driver and he actually staggered, grasping out with his clamp-like hands to the side of the cabin.

'Close,' he hissed and the wall rematerialized, to keep the interior atmosphere as cool as possible.

He saw the young Lurman, Krissi, running towards him. How he envied the Lurman's ability to run and generally enjoy the heat of the planet. Martians, he long ago decided, were actually totally ill-equipped for the life of archaeology. Inevitably, digs took place in arid wastelands, years after a civilization had disintegrated into dust. Dust that cluttered up sophisticated equipment and, more importantly, Martian bodies. He'd been so grateful when the Federation research teams had created the exo-suit for him: it had given him back the manoeuvrability that age had slowly withered away.

Of course, being a Martian archaeologist was in itself somewhat unusual, but Rhukk delighted in eccentricity. He saw himself as a bit of a cultural throw-back, an oddity who was forever invited to lush dinner parties and soirées and gave appreciated after-meal speeches. His fellow Martians would pass the time of day but shared very little intellectual similarities with him. But the other humanoid species within the Federation had quickly given him recognition and, wholly deservedly, a reputation as one of the finest explorers in the galaxy.

After his first paper was published on the Telosian Cyber-tombs, starting that ridiculous nostalgia wave thirty years ago, he had been on all the holo-nets. More recently he'd had the charming pleasure of being interviewed on GFTV-3 – his favourite channel due to their intelligent and precise coverage of events rather than cheap entertainment. The delightful Pakhar, Ker'a'nol, had come to his home and gone through his life with him. Together they had discussed his highly exciting career and, false modesty aside, discussed just how much of that career was now considered essential reading by the Federation educational establishments purely because of his and his teams' research.

His favourite moment had been when she'd asked him which ten pieces of music and which written texts he would like to be stranded on a frontier asteroid with. His music stretched from Old Mars classics from centuries back right up to the present with some of the nouveau-techno-skiffle that his Lurman and Human students were so fond of. But the text was even easier to decide upon – Gustaff Heinrich Urnst's seminal *Being an Account of my Discoveries of the Unnameable Secrets of Sakkrat*.

This co-existence of serious scientific explorer and witty raconteur made Rhukk a highly popular guest on other chat shows and an interviewee in comnet programs. As a result, he had been able to go to Irving Braxiatel and convince him to fund his sojourn to explore the Horun ruins, on the proviso that the Braxiatel Collection had full access to the findings. With the amount of credit Braxiatel placed in Rhukk's accounts, that was certainly no problem. It also ensured that these monumental discoveries would be accessible to the public for eons to come rather than locked away with some private and disinterested collector of alien ephemera.

Krissi caught up with him, running a hand across her silver hair and so removing handfuls of Osirian dust and sand.

She passed him a data-pad and ran her Neyscrape across it for him. Immediately the holographic image of Irving Braxiatel blurred into view.

'Professor Rhukk. I have some news for you and little of it good, I'm afraid. I'll get straight to the point. As you know I, along with the University of Pakhar, have been funding research into the location of the legendary Ancient Diadem.

'You may remember Sym Sharrod, the professor of archaeology at the university. He and a group of his students, working with Federation librarians, believed they had located the Diadem. Sharrod took a party to retrieve it. It is my sad duty to report two things – firstly Sharrod's entire group are dead, apparently murdered. I know you will take this very hard as I remember how well you knew most of the students involved after your Deanship there.

'Secondly, it would appear that they did in fact locate the Diadem. Any minor victory that would signify to the archaeological world is not only tarnished by their deaths but also by the fact that the Diadem was stolen.

'At present, its location is unknown but I understand via a few . . . let's say unconfirmed sources, that the Federation are tracking it. The Martian High Commission on Io have informed me that High Lord Savaar was leading the recovery mission. It transpires – and this is the bit that I am loathe to report so impersonally – that Savaar is also dead and his entire resource mission was destroyed.

'I am sorry to be the bearer of such tragic news. A formal message has been dispatched to the others within your hatchery but as Savaar's second brother, I thought it best if you heard it from me.

'Rhukk, I am so sorry. I leave it up to you if you choose to return for the Death Honour Ceremony – I fully understand and, of course, provisions have been introduced to

our schemes to ensure that the dig on Phaester Osiris will
continue without you, albeit temporarily.

'Let me know your decision, old friend. Braxiatel out.'

Krissi stepped back, her eyes to the ground. Rhukk
rested a hand on her shoulder.

'You knew them didn't you, Krissi?'

She slowly nodded, her lip trembling. 'Julian and Nezz
Larroq were in my study group before I left. I didn't
know Fehler or Gris that well, but Professor Sharrod was
exceptionally popular. It all seems so horrible.'

'Death is, my dear. It always is.' Rhukk breathed out
slowly. 'Thank you for bringing this to me so promptly.'

'Professor Rhukk, I . . . well all of us are sorry about
your brother. Of course we didn't know him but we'd
heard of him. If he was anything like you, he must have
been quite a special Martian.'

'Thank you, child. He was. Please send a dispatch back
to both the Federation and the Braxiatel Collection on
my behalf. By the time I've walked back to base camp,
it'll be mid-afternoon and the heat will prevent me from
returning here until tomorrow. I can't afford to waste the
time, alas. Tell them both that I shall mourn and honour
both parties but I feel both Sharrod and Savaar especially
would prefer if I got on with my work. Funerals are not
for me, Krissi. The long-dead I can cope with. The recently
departed remind me too much of my own approaching
mortality.'

Krissi managed a smile. 'Oh Professor, you've another
hundred years at least.'

'Oh child, how you do flatter me! Now, off you go.'

Krissi grasped the data-pad back and headed off on the
long trek to base camp, leaving Rhukk staring at her
footprints.

With a rasp, he ordered his cabin open and hauled
himself back in. As the wall closed behind him he commanded a drawer to open. As it did, he reached down
and removed his own data-pad. Like all Martian pads, it
did not have a Neyscrape, just a traditional button to
depress. He did so and muttered 'Family.'

In front of him, six young Martians sprang up. They stood ranged from left to right, ranked by age and therefore height. 'Increase two far left.' As the right-hand four vanished the pixels coalesced into a larger hologram of the eldest two, both males. Savaar and his 'first baby' Lassaal hatchling brother Rhukk.

As always, Rhukk hid his public sadness behind a front of bravado and wit. In private now he openly wept. Savaar wouldn't have appreciated the grief but nevertheless Rhukk was not like most Martians. He couldn't be bothered to suppress his emotions or worry what others might say if they found out. He just let them all out.

Seven hours later, he was back outside with Krissi and the others, the drooping sun making a clear and cooler evening, just right for exploring, sifting and cleaning. To the outside world Professor Rhukk was just getting on with his job.

Inside, he was wrecked.

8:

I Die: You Die

'It's locked.'

'Let me try,' said Savaar, pushing forward.

Centauri backed away from the door of Nic Reece's room, muttering that if it was locked, it was locked and there wasn't much that anyone could do about it.

'Privacy is integral to the Federation's code of conduct.'

'Your code of conduct isn't much good if you're trying to track down a criminal and murderer,' said Keri.

'Well, I feel I should point this out, there is no proof that Nic Reece has hurt anybody, actually,' corrected a prim Centauri.

Kort marched up to Centauri and jabbed a stubby orange finger at him. 'It wasn't your sister they shipped back in a body bag. It wasn't your sister they blew into little pieces. It wasn't your sister who trusted him.' He turned back to the door, satisfied that Centauri had got the message.

'Actually, I don't have a sister,' Centauri moaned, 'but even if I did, I wouldn't be so rude.'

The Doctor hooked his umbrella around one of Centauri's rapidly purpling arms and tugged him away from the others. 'Stand over there, old friend, and keep an eye out.'

Savaar meanwhile was pushing against the door of Reece's quarters but to no avail. 'Magnetically sealed,' he rasped eventually.

The Doctor nodded. 'I thought as much.'

Sskeet brought up his gun. 'Lord Savaar?'

The Doctor pushed it down again. 'No, no, no. If Reece

is our man – and I'm convinced he is – then I imagine the door is booby-trapped. Let's think this through rationally.' He turned to face the group. Eager faces looked back at him, expecting him to tell them what to do, how to do it and why. Positive that he would know all the answers and solutions? Why couldn't someone else think for once?

It had been so obvious that Reece had been the villain, this mysterious Alec that Damakort had talked about. Who else had arrived on Peladon so recently? Nic Reece had gone to investigate his family's death – no doubt engineered by Alec – and presumably met a similar fate.

Of course, he'd given himself away to the Doctor instantly. Obviously the imposter had studied Reece well before selecting him and Peladon as his target. He knew how well Reece knew everyone but he, the Doctor, was the joker in the pack. The odd one out. The piggy in – anyway, Reece had pretended to know the Doctor. Totally convincing of course – Benny had instantly assumed they were old friends as had Savaar, Tarrol and all the others. But the Doctor had realized then.

The Doctor had known many people in his lives, but the best-remembered ones were good friends and bad enemies. Nic Reece had acted as if they were the oldest pals in the galaxy: his charm and general ambience would have made him unforgettable. But the Doctor hadn't recognized him from anywhere, least of all from his dealings with the Galactic Federation.

There had been other, somewhat larger slips – like leaving Lianna alive long enough to tell the Time Lord who had killed her. The framing of Savaar for the assault on Atissa was neat but clumsy and desperate – if Atissa had thought about it, anyone could have provided the Ice Lord with an alibi – but the high priestess had so wanted it to be the Martian, to further discredit the Federation.

What was his plan? Even Reece, or whoever he really was, couldn't imagine getting away with ruling the galaxy, no matter how powerful the Diadem would make him.

'Of course!' The Doctor froze momentarily and then started waving his hands animatedly. 'It's Peladon. I was wrong, the choice was not an accident. He's far cleverer than I gave him credit for.'

'What are you talking about, Doctor?' asked Geban.

'Don't you see?'

It was evident that no one did. He sighed. 'The planet Peladon is looking forward, trying to find new prosperity. Reece, the real Nic Reece, suggested opening the place up as a tourist spot. Cheap, nasty little trinkets and plastic Aggedor statues. Nevertheless, a sure-fire winner within a regalia-starved Federation. As technology takes over our lives, so the less-civilized aspects fade away. Peladon has them all here. Millions of people would flock to see it.'

'That was the idea,' agreed Geban.

'And you, Mister Corry, you, Keri and all your team, you were the real bonus.'

'Us?' Corry frowned.

Keri twitched her whiskers excitedly. 'What did we do?'

'With the power of the Diadem, he could have easily taken over the minds of everyone here on Peladon. Even you would have become his puppets. So with a permanent holocrew here, the simple draw to the public would have been too great. Imagine, a vast museum here. And in the centre of it, the chance to have yourself recorded with holographic reproductions of Aggedor and the like. Something to take away. To treasure. To show your friends. And within that, subliminal messages, the Diadem using a whole new medium to spread its evil.'

'And this Pakhar Diadem can do all this?' asked Kort.

'Oh yes. It's very clever.'

Geban frowned. 'Doctor, are you suggesting that this Diadem is actually alive?'

The Doctor stared open-mouthed at those around him. 'You mean, you didn't realize? That's why it is so important that this man who is pretending to be your friend Nic Reece doesn't get hold of it. He doesn't comprehend its full power. At least, I hope he doesn't.'

'Why?' asked Alpha Centauri.

'Because if he does know it is alive and intelligent and he still wants it, then he has to be stopped. Permanently.'

'Of course,' Sskeet said.

'No. No, I had hoped to reason with him. To explain what he was actually doing. Having manipulated this society so that its leaders are at each others' throats, he could easily take over.'

'Nonsense, Doctor,' said Geban. 'The king would never allow it. Nor would Atissa or myself.'

'Forgive me, Geban, but it is time you faced a few truths. Due to Reece's machinations, Lord Savaar and I had to destroy the trust between you and your king. Now, a ruse it may have been, but I've no doubt you've both said and thought a few dark thoughts about each other since. Atissa – well, frankly, she's not running on full batteries, as Benny would say. And Tarrol? He's indecisive and as we discovered, easily manipulated. I'm sorry, Geban, this planet's ruling caste is a pale shadow of its past. I doubt it would take much for Reece to take control.'

Geban digested this and looked at his feet. 'You may be right, Doctor, but do not underestimate King Tarrol. When he needs to, he can assert control with great forcefulness and solicitude.'

'Oh, I hope so, Chancellor. I really do.'

'Anyway, Doctor, hadn't we better get after Reece?'

'I'm not entirely sure he's on to us yet, Mister Corry. Just because the door is locked doesn't prove a thing.'

'You said it was booby-trapped,' pointed out Keri.

'I imagined it was. I don't know for sure. I tend to err on the side of caution.'

'What about Benny?' asked Kort. 'Lord Savaar said that she was with him.'

'Yes! That's it! I have remembered,' exclaimed Savaar suddenly.

'What?' was a chorus of replies.

'When Reece arrived in *Shsurr* Summerfield's room, he said he thought I was dead. But he could not have known that. He did not witness my death or return to the Federation Representatives' room. Indeed, he was apparently in here, in his quarters, packing to leave. He could not have known of my fake execution.'

'Bother,' exclaimed the Doctor. 'Then he might have an inkling that I must have guessed.'

'He might not, though,' suggested Corry.

'I can't take that risk any more. Not with Benny's life at stake.'

'I apologize, Doctor. I should have realized sooner.'

'That's no problem, my Lord. What we have to do now is consider our plans very carefully.'

'What about the stolen treasures? Are they in this room?'

'Unlikely,' said Savaar. 'He had his cases with him when he went off with *Shsurr* Summerfield.'

'They won't be in there, though,' returned the Doctor. 'He'll have put them somewhere safe while waiting for his couriers. A safe or something.'

'There's nothing like that in our quarters, Doctor. The Pels do not build safes,' said Centauri.

'The shuttle! The safe-seal,' Savaar shouted.

'Yes! That would explain the dead pilot,' confirmed Keri.

'Then that's where he'll be meeting the others with the Diadem.'

'But my crew are there.' Keri waved her paws around. 'We must get back to them.'

'Yes. We must.' The Doctor looked around him. 'This could get very dangerous. I've already explained this to Commander Rassbur. I will say it to you.'

'Who's Rassbur?' whispered Kort.

Keri just shrugged.

The Doctor continued: 'The Diadem is my responsibility. Its safe capture and eventual fate is my problem and mine alone. Call it an atonement if you will. Do what you will to save other people, but the Diadem must not escape.'

'Doctor, I am sorry to ask this, but practicality is important.' Savaar looked slightly awkward.

'Yes, I know. How will I make sure it doesn't take me

266

over? It won't. It tried that once, a long time ago. It failed then and I'm four lives wiser now. I can cope.' He paused. 'If I'm wrong, Savaar, I am relying on you to totally destroy me. Completely. Is that understood by you all?' Everyone nodded sadly. 'Good. Make sure you tell Benny afterwards. She's likely to shoot you for real otherwise.' He smiled at Savaar.

Savaar saluted.

Sskeet was examining the door again. 'Lord Savaar,' he started, 'I think I can just force this open.'

Everyone turned to look and the Doctor heard a minute sound. A tiny click. A small tick. A slight –

'Get do –'

The Doctor never finished his cry as the door, Reece's entire room and a large portion of the neighbouring rooms and corridor were hurled out on to the lethal side of Mount Megeshra in the largest explosion ever recorded on Peladon.

'What the cruk was that?' asked Lambert.

Townsend drew his blaster and patted his Kevlar–8 battle suit. 'Don't know. Don't like it though. Seemed to come from down there.'

The four mercenaries were in an open chamber that looked directly down over the Citadel, part of the curious curve that formed the right-hand side of Mount Megeshra. Although they didn't know it, this strange location had been one of Nic Reece's (the real Reece) plans for his tour of Peladon. To be within the same mountain but due to strange geological faults to be capable of overlooking the actual Citadel as well was, he had hoped, one of the newer wonders of the universe.

Many years ago, when Peladon had faced its last terror, the deranged miner Ettis had positioned stolen Federation technology in the cavern, a massive sonic lance. He had aimed it at the Citadel, threatening to destroy it unless Queen Thalira handed rule over to him.

Due to sabotage the lance had self-destructed when he had tried to carry out his threat, destroying both Ettis and the weapon. Since then, the cavern had just been a place from which to look and admire Pel workmanship.

Until now.

Townsend pointed the Citadel out to Cooper.

'It's a long drop in between,' she said.

He nodded. 'Don't go too near the edge, it looks a bit crumbly. Especially you, Sadler.' He looked back at the woman. 'I don't want you and the vacuum case going for a dive.'

Ignorant pup. Such a drop could not hurt me.

'Don't worry, I've no intention of going anywhere that suddenly,' she said. Suddenly she staggered slightly and Lambert grasped her arm.

'You all right?'

'I . . . I have a headache. I think the air in here is a bit too thin for me.'

Townsend sniffed. 'Seems okay to me. Let's wait here. He said to meet him in the shuttle bay, but I'd rather he came to us.'

Take me. Take me now. Dispose of these ridiculous dolts. They are slowing me . . . us . . . down.

Sadler again put her hand to her head. Something was there, on the edge of her consciousness. Like a forgotten thought or a nagging doubt. Something telling her to do something. To think something . . .

Never mind, she'd cope.

The Pel guards were heaving great slabs of granite off the figures lying on the floor. Savaar was the first to haul himself up, a little unsteadily. Lying beside him was Sskeet, the front of his exoskeleton shattered and distorted, green blood splattered around the burns. Bits of the suit had embedded themselves in his soft inner flesh but he was still moving.

The High Lord and two guards slowly helped him up, but his slow, rasping breath told Savaar that his adjutant was more severely injured than he was prepared to admit, especially to his Lord. Savaar merely saluted him and gingerly Sskeet returned the action.

Alpha Centauri had been right at the back of the group and had been totally shielded from flying rocks by the bodies of Kort and Keri. His clothing was ripped and torn and a large cut on his upper right arm was evidence of the concussive force of the explosion. Agitatedly he flustered around the unmoving forms of the Pakhar and Cantryan before him.

The Doctor was uncovered, revealing his umbrella unfurled and up. Now wrecked, it had nevertheless protected his face from flying rock at the moment of the explosion. A few scratches and internal bruises, he decided, but a quick examination proved he was at least fit and alive.

Not so Chancellor Geban. One look at the strange angle of his back and neck proved that he had died instantly. Under him stirred Neal Corry, alive because Geban had presumably used himself instinctively as a shield. One of Corry's arms was crushed by a huge chunk of granite and although he was unconscious, the pain must have been severe because his face was contorted and sweating.

The Doctor crawled over and placed a finger in the centre of his temple. 'Sleep,' he commanded.

Corry's face instantly lost its frown and his head lolled to the side. Gently the Pels pulled him up and away.

A few minutes passed before King Tarrol arrived. His reaction showed that he took in instantly what had occurred and he was on the floor beside Geban in a second, cradling the battered head in his arms, crying softly. He then looked up at the Doctor, red-rimmed eyes full of tragedy and bitterness. 'We shall not forget what has happened here today. Ever.'

'Good,' said the Doctor. 'Geban deserves honour.'

'He shall have that. But that is not what I meant.'

The Doctor didn't have time to follow that up as a groan from Kort reminded the Time Lord that he was responsible for the Cantryan's well-being. He crossed to his side.

'Is he all right?' burbled Centauri. 'There was nothing I can do.'

'He'll live, but he needs rest.' The Doctor waved a couple of Pels over and they carried the boy away. The Doctor reached out to Keri and snatched his hand away. It was soaked in blood. A cough and dribble of blood from her snout told him that she was alive. Barely.

As more Pels picked her up and carried her to medical attention the Doctor caught Savaar's eye. The Ice Lord was trying to stop Sskeet's bleeding.

'The time has come,' spat the Doctor. 'Time for the final battle.'

Bernice was sitting with the Pakhar holocrew by the Martian shuttle, staring at the headless pilot.

Reece was beside the body. 'Nothing I can do. Someone killed him pretty decisively.'

'Why?' asked Bernice. 'What is in the shuttle that could be worth a life?'

'Oh, don't be soft, Benny. People die all the time. That's life.'

She stared at him. After all that he'd been through with his own family, death ought to have been far more frightening.

A Pakhar audio engineer was poking inside the shuttle. 'Maybe we'll see it in here,' he was saying when Bernice suddenly saw a flash of white and the Pakhar slumped to the ground, like a puppet whose strings had been suddenly severed. Screeches from the other Pakhars drew her attention to Nic Reece, a clip blaster in his hand.

Without thinking she stood up angrily. 'What the frag did you do that for?'

Then it all fell into place. 'It's you! You killed Lianna. And Kort's sister. You're Alec!'

Reece grinned and Bernice saw everything reflected in his eyes. The dark secrets she'd seen, the mystery. It wasn't his dead family – it was his complete insanity. She'd confused tragedy with malice.

'Might be. Alexander Charles Roberts, like Nicholas Reece, is just someone else's identity I purchased from them.'

270

'Did Jina ever know the real Alec?'

'Good God, no. He was a seventy-year-old frontiersman in the Rho system. He could never have coped with the energetic night-times that this Alec put up with. You're not as clever as I had imagined. I thought you'd worked all this out when I found you in my room.'

Bernice stared at him. 'No. No, I actually thought you were a genuine nice guy. We all make mistakes. You're a real sicko.'

'Thank you.' Reece smiled. He turned to the Pakhars and waved his blaster at them. 'Get back behind those rocks, you rats.' He turned back to Bernice as the terrified Pakhas complied. 'Inside the shuttle, please.' He waved the blaster towards the craft.

With a shrug, Bernice clambered aboard. At the last second she realized that stupidly she had her back to him and sure enough, he slammed his fist into the base of her spine and she sagged forward.

However, she turned this to good use, lashing out with her boot at his groin. It connected with enough force that she expected him to be unconscious with pain. Instead, he laughed.

'Kevlar–8,' he explained. 'Should have gone for the head or hands. Exposed areas. Your friend who chased my lot on Pakhar would have known that. She was a good soldier apparently. Shame about her little accident in space.'

A dull explosion could be heard from back towards the Citadel.

'Ah, I guess my little room party has just gone off with a bang.'

'A what?'

He produced from within his jacket an egg-shaped silver capsule. 'One of these. A Sontaran fragmentation grenade. Particularly nasty but bloody efficient. Probably took out half the Citadel with any luck.'

'The Doctor . . .' breathed Bernice.

For a second Reece looked surprised and then grinned. He got into the shuttle, covering her with the blaster.

'Yeah. He's still alive, isn't he? I knew that Pakhar bitch had fixed something up with that High Lord. And when I saw Savaar in your room still alive as well . . . yeah, they did it very well. I bet Atissa's in for a shock.' He suddenly laughed. 'Then again, she probably just got her wish. I bet it was the Doctor who tried to get into my room.'

'Why? He couldn't have suspected you?'

'Why not? Because he let you flirt with me? Maybe I sussed him better than you ever had. I doubt you matter that much. He's after the same thing as me. Power.'

'The Diadem? He wants to destroy it.'

'Computer. *Summerfield Code-A*.'

'Confirmed.'

The safe-seal vanished and Reece grabbed the two items from within. As the safe resealed itself, he jumped backwards out of the shuttle, still aiming his blaster at Bernice. He stripped the dead Pakhar of his belt which had carried audio spares. Throwing them on to the floor, he climbed back in and used the belt to tie the Lance of Aggedor to the casket.

'Time for a little walk, I think.'

'Why?'

'Because the Doctor has proved he has the same number of lives as a cat and Sontaran frag grenade or not, I want a hostage. Just in case.'

Bernice crossed her arms and smiled sweetly. 'I don't think I'm quite hostage material, actually. You usually find the job spec requires a small blonde screamer who trips and faints at the slightest provocation.'

Reece shook his head and grinned. 'A hostage is anyone who your opponent is not prepared to sacrifice. If the Doctor's still alive, you fit the bill one hundred per cent. Now move!'

'Here. We were supposed to meet here. Why isn't he here?' Cooper kicked a rock over the precipice. She waited but never heard it land.

Townsend was admiring the Citadel. 'Good bit of architecture, you know. Well built. Last for ever. Better than most domes and prefabs back in our neck of the woods.'

'Maybe that explosion was him getting killed,' suggested Lambert.

Townsend shook his head and pointed to the side of the Citadel where a gaping hole was clearly visible. 'See? There. That's our bang – half that section must have gone boom. He shouldn't have been anywhere near the Citadel when that went off.'

Sadler looked down at the vacuum case.

How much longer? I need to be free. Open the case and touch me!

Sadler found that her hand was moving towards the catch. Surprised, she pulled it away. What on earth was she doing?

'Reece! Reece or whatever your name is!'

The Doctor stared at the shuttle. Huddled by the doorway he could see two bodies but neither of them was Benny's. A Martian – the pilot, he presumed – and a Pakhar, one of Corry's team. Two more lives Reece was responsible for wasting.

'Good question, Doctor,' came an amplified shout back. From the shuttle's communications system. 'I don't honestly know what my real name is. Ever since the institution, I used other people's identities.'

'A patient. Ah.'

'Oh, don't tell me, Doctor. You think that explains everything. Anti-social behaviour? Psychosis?'

'No, Reece. Nothing so simple could explain your evil.'

'I was examined by the Federation's best shrinks, you know. When I was ten they decided I was already too far gone. Do you think I've gone too far?'

'Oh yes. Far too far.'

The side of the shuttle melted away and Benny staggered out, Reece holding her tightly. 'One false move and . . .'

'And you'll kill her. Yes, I know, I've seen it all before. Done by far better than you as well.'

'But few with so much relish.'

'Oh thanks.' That was Bernice.

'You won't do that, Reece. You'd have done it by now otherwise. Any time within the last couple of days.'

'You know, you and Savaar ought to go into entertainment. The people who keep coming back to life. I thought I'd made sure you were both dead.'

'Self-preservation is an art, Reece,' said the Doctor. 'From the moment I realized it was you, I've been watching my back. Or had others do it for me.'

'And when was that?'

'I guessed when you made that error in your homework. We'd never met, Nic Reece and I. Then you made your second mistake.'

'Lianna?'

'Exactly. She was still alive and told me.'

'Wait a minute,' cried Bernice. 'You knew it was this crukhead and you still let me carry on seeing him?'

'I had to let him carry out his plan, Benny. I had to get nearer to the Diadem. I'm sorry.'

'You bloody will be when I get hold of you!' she yelled.

'Listen Doctor, you and your Martian pals can take a step or fifty back. The lady – the *Shsurr* I think you call her, Savaar – and I have a date back there.'

'Your mercenaries have the Diadem, Reece. Just in case you were wondering.'

'Cheers, old man. A great weight off my mind.'

'What are you planning to do with it?' squeaked Alpha Centauri.

'God, what a stupid question, Centauri. You know, I had the chance to kill you but for some reason I couldn't bring myself to do it. Just a little tap on the head so that I could have the time to dispose of Torg's body. You're weird, Centauri – so damn nice to everyone all the time.'

'Thank you, Nic, but you're still a traitor!'

'Answer the question, Reece,' rasped Savaar. 'What will you do with the Pakhar Diadem?'

'Rule. It's been my lifelong ambition to find it. You know, I actually studied archaeology. That's how I found out about it. They made me do that at the clinic. I should thank them. Maybe I'll use the Diadem on them as well.'

'More likely that it'll use you, Reece. It is alive.'

'You've been reading too many story books, Doc. We're going now. If you follow, Benny gets to play the Swiss cheese in the next Heletian production of *The Mousetrap*.

He reached into the shuttle and yanked out a large casket with the Lance of Aggedor strapped to its top.

'Centauri, stay here,' commanded the Doctor. 'Lord Savaar, Sskeet, please follow me.'

Together the three slowly followed Reece and Bernice into the darkness.

The light blinked out and the refinery was plunged into total darkness. For a moment nothing seemed to happen; the blackness of Megeshra's deepest cavern remained undisturbed. Then there was a noise – a high-pitched whine and the solid metal door to the refinery swung open.

Ten pairs of red eyes glared into the darkness, infra-red filters clearly showing every rock, every treacherous lump of roak to be avoided.

Like a well-oiled machine, ten pairs of feet moved together in unison. Ten right arms moved up to waist height, pointing forward, built-in sonic disrupters primed and ready.

One by one they trooped out of the dark refinery and into the equally shadowy cavern. Not every warrior was identical: Martians came in as many varied shapes and sizes as humans, but they moved as one, grim determination etched into their lips. The last one out broke formation, turning, and with a whine of his sonic gun reset the alarm system.

Anyone trying to break into the refinery would receive the same neural attack that Neal Corry had suffered a day earlier. But with no one inside to turn it off, the effect would probably be fatal.

Commander Rassbur moved forward, his nine warriors

following in perfect unison. Ten brave soldiers marching into war.

Lying in the dust near where they passed by was the Doctor's travelling chess set. The pieces had been moved into a perfect checkmate – the black king surrounded by a pawn, a white knight, a bishop and, of course, the white king.

Townsend was getting unusually anxious. Something was wrong – not just with the plan but the whole set-up. He was angry with himself, more than anything. He rarely if ever got perturbed about any job, yet something was nagging at him over this. Some feeling that he'd overlooked an important point, a relevant aspect of the plan that he couldn't quite bring into focus.

He looked over at the other three. Cooper was her usual calm self, a sneer on her lips, as if working for a living was a chore to be endured. By the exit to the long tunnel leading to the back of the mountain where their shuttle rested, was Lambert. He seemed insanely happy, fidgeting about, checking his two blasters for the umpteenth time and patting down his Kelvar–8 body suit.

Then there was Sadler. She was just sitting, staring at the vacuum case. Her blaster lay discarded at her side.

'Hey, Sadler, get your arse into gear. I don't want slackness today.' As he spoke he knew he'd sounded more aggressive than he'd intended. Even Cooper shot him a look of amused contempt.

Sadler lazily turned and looked at him and stared. In turn Townsend caught Lambert's eye – he knew her best and something was wrong. Sadler's eyes were totally dead, as if someone had switched off her brain.

Anxiously Lambert moved towards her, an arm outstretched.

Do not let them touch you. Something is wrong. I feel Him near. He will try and destroy me. We must not let Him find us. Leave. Now!

Sadler stood up, grabbing the case and hugging it to

her chest. In a lazy but precise movement she scooped up her blaster and aimed it straight at Lambert.

He backed away, complete surprise written all over his face.

'Sadler?' said Townsend. 'Sadler, what the frag are you doing?'

The redhead ignored him, keeping her gun aimed squarely at Lambert's chest. He moved away from the exit and she started towards it, now covering all three of her comrades. Silently she started backwards down the tunnel and after a few seconds was swallowed up by the darkness.

Townsend released his breath. 'Phew. What was that all about?'

Cooper just stared down the tunnel. 'Never liked her. Now she's taken away our deposit.'

Townsend turned to Lambert. 'Get after her. Talk some sense into her – we need the Diadem back here. Now.'

Lambert nodded dumbly and, confused, headed off after Sadler.

Cooper checked her blaster for the tenth time. 'Was that wise?'

'How d'you mean?'

'They're what passes for a couple. He's hardly going to gun her down, is he?'

'No, but he's more likely to talk sense into her than you are. And I'm staying here to meet our man.'

'You mean you don't fancy Sadler blowing your head off.'

'There is that,' said Townsend, but all trace of humour had left his voice. His premonition had come true. Everything was going wrong.

'Maybe,' suggested Cooper, 'just maybe we ought to go. Write this one off.'

'Maybe,' replied Townsend. 'But not quite yet.'

Lambert was totally lost. The tunnel was going down and that seemed right. But every time he stopped to listen, he

277

couldn't hear anything from up ahead. Sadler didn't have that much of a head start.

What was that?

Footsteps? Laboured breathing?

It certainly wasn't Sadler. There was more than one. He dropped to the ground, and placed his palm down. The ground didn't allow really accurate vibrations to travel that way but experience told him there were more than half a dozen. Maybe eight or ten. And big – whatever they were.

Lambert silently leaped behind a crop of rocks, his instinctive survival expertise kicking into gear. Through a tiny crack he watched as ten Martians walked up the tunnel, along the route he'd just come. In a few moments, they'd certainly encounter Townsend and Cooper.

Should he warn them? Nah, Martian helmets were fitted with sophisticated receivers; the slightest warning and they'd cut him down as he spoke. Besides, Townsend could look after himself. Sadler was far more important.

He waited two minutes to give the Martians time to be right out of audio range and then, as silently as possible, carried on.

After a few seconds he encountered a small cavern where his tunnel branched off. Left or right. He couldn't remember. Think – the shuttle was behind the mountain. It had to be to the left. As he approached the two entrances, he scanned the floor as best he could in the dark. Scuffle-marks, but Sadler's or the Martians'? No way of knowing. Breathing deeply, he set off down the left-hand tunnel.

After a few moments, he knew he was wrong. None of this looked familiar and while to the average eye all the Pel tunnels probably looked alike, Lambert was trained better. He had noted odd-shaped rocks, strange scratches and peculiar stalactites on the way up. None of those were here.

He turned to go back when a minute flash caught his eye. His blaster had reflected a tiny amount of light off something metallic.

He slowly crawled forward.

And went flat on his face.

Cursing, Lambert scrambled up. At his feet were the crushed remains of an archaic chess set.

Must have tripped over that, he decided. Bloody stupid thing to do.

He'd dropped his blaster and it was too dark to find it. But that metal thing had been ahead. As his eyes grew accustomed to the dark, he realized it was a door, with a massive window beside it. No lights were on but he tried to peer through.

Nothing. Just blackness.

He reached out for the door and gave it a slight push.

For a split second, Lambert's mind recognized a typical Federation neural alarm system. Another split second and his mind was shut down by the excessive force of the noise and lights. Falling against the door, the alarm continued. It was silent to anyone else but inside Lambert's head, it rang louder and shriller than anything else in the universe. After twenty seconds every neural pathway in Lambert's brain was scrambled irreparably.

Comatose, he slumped into the dust, the alarm shutting off. He was destined to lie there for the rest of his life, which would not be very long. As his body registered no signals or impulses from an already destroyed brain, it slowly cut off each of its functions. His lungs would soon stop drawing air, his liver and kidneys would stop producing enzymes and his heart would eventually give up pumping blood and oxygen around his body.

In twelve minutes, Lambert would be dead.

Blissfully unaware that her lover was dying, the autonomic Sadler was striding back to the shuttle.

As she walked out of the dark tunnel into the open air, her eyes made no adjustment to the light, instantly damaging her retinas. The wind and rain lashed down on her, but she gave no sign of noticing it.

The shuttle. Get me away from Him. Far away. Then we can begin again, where He cannot locate us.

Moments later, Sadler reached the shuttle entrance and commanded it to open. The wall melted away and then reassembled after she got in.

As she sat in the pilot's chair, Sadler's body gave a slight shudder.

Deep within her rapidly closing-down mind, the real Sadler was screaming and crying, trying to fight off the evil power that controlled her body. She was aware that she was losing. She felt the shudder: somewhere back inside Mount Megeshra, Andrew Lambert had breathed his final breath and was clinically dead. Sadler's own mind and personality finally gave way and allowed the evil to swamp her mind.

Siobhan Sadler was gone.

In the real world, the hands of Sadler tugged on the case's lid and with a hiss of air the top shot back. Sadler's hands reached down and grasped the Ancient Diadem of Pakhar, the jewels glowing in frantic patterns. The hands placed the circlet around her forehead.

As the ends touched Sadler's temples, the living evil that was the Diadem swarmed into her brain, finally eradicating any vestiges of Sadler that might have remained.

'A new body. At last.' The Ancient Diadem was free and mobile.

The galaxy, eventually the whole universe – perhaps even the fabric of time and space – was once again open to total domination.

Bernice Summerfield had encountered a lot of dangerous, even potentially lethal situations since she'd teamed up with the Doctor. She guessed that she ought to be used to having madmen point blasters against her head while having a primed grenade in their pockets.

She wasn't.

'Look, what exactly are you going to achieve? I mean, they can cut you down pretty easily. In case you haven't noticed, Martians don't tire quite as easily as we do.'

Reece snarled back, 'They're bloody slow though. My

280

associates have a shuttle. We can be on it before they catch up.'

'Actually,' corrected Bernice, 'it's a bit of a fallacy that Martians are slow. When they need to be, they can be rather swift.'

Reece stopped. 'Townsend?'

Bernice was not unsurprised to hear a male voice call back. 'Here. Have you got the stuff?'

'Of course,' was Reece's only response. He dragged Bernice a little further into the darkness and then she saw light. They entered a cavern with a sheer drop at the far side. She could just see the Citadel below.

I just know he's going to put me near the edge, she thought. And I hate heights.

Reece pulled Bernice towards the ravine. 'Look. Down there.'

'It's a long way down. Nice view though,' was all she could manage.

'If the Doctor or Savaar come within thirty meters of us, you're going to get a better one.'

'God, you're predictable. What's the point? I thought I was a hostage.'

'I'm desperate. Maybe it's a bluff, maybe not. But it'll hold them back anyway.'

The other man, who Bernice guessed was Townsend, wandered over. By the opposite tunnel entrance, looking down it anxiously, was a woman with closely cropped brown hair. She turned round and spoke.

'No sign. Either she's shot him or they've both skipped.'

Reece relaxed his hold on Bernice enough that he could force her to sit on the floor, but still twisted her wrist and held his blaster at the top of her her head. She didn't bother resisting.

'What's she talking about, Townsend?'

'Guess.'

Reeced looked at Cooper and then Townsend. 'I don't believe it.'

Townsend sighed. 'Okay, I made a mistake.'

'You cretin, how could you? You people just cannot be

281

trusted.' Reece slid the casket off his back on to the floor. He pointed at Cooper. 'Coop. You carry this.'

Cooper looked at Townsend for confirmation – she didn't exactly hold him in high regard but nevertheless he was the leader, not the newcomer. Townsend nodded and Cooper hitched the casket on to her back.

'Reece!'

Bernice turned at the Doctor's voice. He stood, unarmed, by the entrance to the cavern. Savaar and Skeet were faintly visible behind him. 'Reece, let the professor go.'

'Why should I, Doctor?'

'Because she's useless to you now.'

'Oh. Cheers, Doctor.' Bernice tried to get up but Reece twisted her wrist harder. 'Ow! That ruddy well hurt.'

'I mean it, Reece. Let my friend go or the Martians will destroy you.'

Townsend brought his blaster up to cover the Doctor and Cooper did the same.

'Three against two, Doctor. Good odds, I think you'll agree,' laughed Reece. 'Now back off.'

The Doctor took a few steps back. 'Bernice, I'm sorry. But Reece has to be stopped.'

'Hey, I'm not wild about it either. But okay.'

The Doctor tried one last time. 'Reece, the Diadem possesses more power than you can imagine. It's not just an object, or a focusing device for mental powers as the legends claim. I've seen it used. It's a living being, a being of pure evil. It feeds off negative thoughts and emotions, slowly encroaching upon the mind. It absorbs you totally.'

Bernice saw a look pass between Cooper and Townsend. Of course! That's what they meant about the others going missing.

'Doctor,' she yelled before Reece could stop her. 'It's not here anymore. One of them is possessed and –'

Reece let go of her hand and savagely kicked her in the back. As she sprawled forward, he fired at the Doctor.

Taking this as a command, Cooper and Townsend did likewise.

As the Doctor ducked, he caught Bernice's eye. He followed her gaze – Rassbur and his troops had arrived behind the mercenaries from the other tunnel which Cooper had been guarding.

Some sixth sense warned Cooper and she whirled around, firing wildly. Her first shot blew the head off one of Rassbur's warriors but it was the last thing she ever did.

They fired in unison and Cooper's body was caught in a massive sonic crossfire. Unable to scream, she arched back, held momentarily in position by the blasts. Thousands of capillaries across her body bulged and burst. The sonic waves scrambled her internal organs and blood seeped from her mouth, nose and ears. She was long dead before the blasts stopped and she dropped.

Townsend dived for cover behind a ridiculously small rock, unwittingly exposing himself to Savaar and Sskeet who had joined the Doctor. Sskeet moved into view and despite a warning from Reece, Townsend never even felt the blast as Sskeet's gun shattered his body, killing him instantly.

Reece lowered his blaster and apparently surrendered, placing his other hand in his pocket.

Bernice realized what he was doing and jumped at him, knocking the primed Sontaran fragmentation grenade from his hand. It rolled towards the edge of the ravine and the two of them desperately scrabbled for it.

Bernice's fingers got there first and flicked it over the ravine. Seconds later the cavern shook as Peladon's second-largest ever recorded explosion ripped out a section of the mountain from under them.

Rocks poured from above, crashing down, bounding around. Reece toppled backwards but avoided being hit. Bernice wasn't so lucky and flying shrapnel sent her into a corner, dazed.

It seemed like an eternity but eventually the world stopped shaking. Gingerly, Bernice propped herself up. The gap where the Doctor had stood was completely sealed off by a rock fall – she had no idea whether or not he was safely behind it or squashed underneath. The opposite entrance where Rassbur and his warriors had stood was similarly closed, although a jumble of crushed green limbs suggested that not all of his soldiers had moved quickly enough.

Coughing, she crawled over to Reece, hoping he was dead.

As the blaster nozzle slammed into her chin, she wished she'd stayed put.

'Excuse me, Mister Reece, but it might be worth pointing out that we're trapped here,' she said tartly.

'So?'

'So I don't think either of us are strong enough to shift these rocks on our own. Together, we just might. The only other option of course is to jump down, but I can't say that appeals right now.' Bernice moved away from Reece. 'I guess it's up to you, "old man".'

The Doctor was pulled, coughing and hacking, from the rocks by Savaar. '*Shsurr* Summerfield is very brave.'

'*Shsurr* Summerfield is very stupid, actually. Playing catch with a Sontaran frag grenade is not a sensible hobby.' The Doctor looked over at Sskeet, lying on the floor. His earlier wounds had been reopened and added to by the blast. 'What about Sskeet?'

Savaar waved an arm impotently. 'He is unconscious but still alive. Just. I cannot reach Commander Rassbur on any frequency. We must assume he and his warriors are dead.'

Shouts and yells alerted them to people coming up behind them. A familiar flash of green and yellow in the middle of the mêlée told them that Alpha Centauri had got help. About twenty Pel guards rushed over, swords drawn and ready. A few paces behind was Tarrol.

The Doctor stared at the young king, dirty and grimy, his fine robes looking in need of a good wash. But it was his face that drew the Doctor's attention. The waif-like child appeared to have been replaced by a grim warrior, a man prepared to fight for his planet. In his hand he held the double-bladed Sword of Truth. His eyes were like steel: a true cold warrior. He reminded the Doctor of Peladon of Peladon, the boy-king he'd met on his first visit. The traumas of that period helped shaped Peladon into a great leader. Had it done the same with Tarrol?

The king followed the Doctor's gaze. 'Reece left the sword with his valise by the Martian shuttle.'

'He still has the Lance and the Crown.' The Doctor reached for the Sword but Tarrol pulled back.

'This is my battle, Doctor. My war. And my planet.'

'And how do you propose fighting this war, Your Majesty?' was Savaar's contribution.

The king didn't answer, he merely shoved the sword into his belt and joined his men pulling rocks from the entrance. Within ten minutes, there was a space small enough for the Doctor to crawl through.

'I'll be careful,' he assured Savaar.

Tarrol suddenly blocked the way. 'My war, Doctor. Not yours, remember. Certainly not the Federation's. Peladon is my planet and its people are under my protection. This,' he waved the Sword around the rubble, 'this is the legacy of my forefathers.'

With that, he clambered through the hole and guards moved across it to stop the Doctor following.

'You fool, Tarrol. He'll kill you easily. He's got a gun!' But the king was not listening.

Bernice looked up as Tarrol crawled through.

She had been expecting the Doctor or a couple of guards maybe, but not the king himself.

'Your Majesty,' she said lamely.

He bowed fractionally to her, then turned his attention to an amused Reece.

'My God, the king himself. Come to talk me into giving these back?' He kicked out at the casket still attached to Cooper's corpse. The Lance was shattered under her weight, but the box had probably protected the Crown.

'Perhaps.'

285

'Well forget it, Your Majesty.' Reece fired his blaster at point-blank range.

Bernice gasped. The king expertly raised the double-bladed Sword of Truth and the blast hit that. The king staggered slightly but both Bernice and Reece stared in amazement. If nothing else the Sword ought to have melted.

Between breaths the king managed a smile. 'Aggedor protects his own, alien.'

'Does he indeed?' Reece fired again.

This time the king fell back, but again the Sword had absorbed the blast.

Seeing an opportunity, Bernice dived down, grabbing Townsend's discarded blaster and aimed it at Reece.

'Drop it, Nic. It's all over.'

He laughed. 'The Martian blast destroyed that. I checked it earlier.'

Angrily Bernice tried to fire it but Reece was correct.

Tarrol staggered towards Reece and Bernice saw that his hands were blistered – the Sword absorbed the blast somehow but it also channelled the heat and Tarrol was receiving third-degree burns. She winced at the pain she could only imagine.

Reece sprung up but suddenly froze. Trickles of sand and roak dust ran underfoot. He was too close to the edge of the drop. One more move and he'd drop like a stone.

He grinned and dropped the blaster over the edge. 'I know when to give up.'

Bernice watched as Tarrol visibly relaxed and the Sword lowered a fraction.

No. Something was wrong.

Reece lunged forward and gripped the blades of the Sword, tugging forward slightly, trying to wrest it from Tarrol's damaged grip. The king yelped as lumps of char-red flesh came away from his hands as the Sword moved, but he didn't let go completely. Instead, he caused Reece to tug harder.

And Reece screamed.

286

Bernice looked on in horror as Reece's fingers, severed by the blades, dribbled to the ground one by one.

Reece's face was a picture of complete amazement, disbelief and pain as he soundlessly pitched backwards over the ravine.

A split second later he apparently remembered to scream but his anguished cry swiftly faded as he plummeted to his death.

Bernice jumped forward as Tarrol staggered, dropping the Sword. He fell to his knees, letting all the pain of the burns finally flood out in wracked sobs.

'Doctor! Savaar! Quickly,' she yelled.

Within moments, the rocks had been pulled back sufficiently to let the guards and the Doctor through.

The king's men extracted his form, stiff with shock, away from Bernice. As he was half-walked, half-carried away, Bernice hugged the Doctor.

He smiled up at her. 'I'm sorry I had to deceive you about Reece. Or whoever he really was.'

'Oh, don't mention it. I've had the time of my life. I don't think.' She pulled away and shook her head at him. 'Sometimes you really push me a bit far.'

'I know.'

Suddenly she gripped his arm. 'The Diadem. What about your precious Diadem?'

Savaar hauled himself through the rocks in a somewhat undignified manner. 'If Marshal Hissel is obeying orders, that should have been dealt with by now.'

The shuttle was taking off. Inside, the Ancient Diadem operated its new body, using the new voice to order the computer to fly straight towards Jupiter. From what little information the primitive female had possessed, it knew that the first phase of its plan required total domination over the body known as the Galactic Federation.

A noise alerted it. Nothing inside the shuttle. Using the damaged eyes of the female it stared straight out of the shuttle windows. A massive spacecraft was descending through the atmosphere towards it at colossal speed.

'Change course,' shrieked the Diadem through Sadlers throat.

'State course and direction,' was the computer's response.

'Anywhere. Away from that ship.'

'The *Bruk* is capable of matching any manoeuvre this shuttle can make.'

'Do it!' screamed the Diadem/Sadler.

'Warning. The *Bruk* is powering up her forward staser array. This shuttle is unprotected against such firepower.'

Frantically the Diadem used Sadler's rapidly decaying eyes to search for the vacuum case. Inside its adamantium safety, it would be protected from the blast.

The *Bruk* drew closer.

'Warning. The *Bruk* . . . '

'Shut up!' screeched the Diadem/Sadler.

The computer fell silent.

The Diadem used Sadler's hands to clasp at the circlet, intending to place itself into the safety of the vacuum case.

It had forgotten that it had destroyed Sadler's own mind. It had nothing to control any more.

As the circlet came away from Sadler's head, Sadler's body simply crumpled, a reflex grasping the circlet tighter.

No! No! No!

Sadler's dead body slumped to the side, away from the safety of the case, the Ancient Pakhar Diadem gripped tightly in her dead hands.

I am unprotected. I am –

The first barrage of fire hit the shuttle head-on.

The shuttle, Sadler's corpse and the vacuum case were hit by a flash of heat that seemed to vaporize everything in less than point five of a second.

Apparently satisfied that not a molecule of the shuttle or any occupants remained in existence, the *Bruk* headed back to the outer atmosphere of Peladon, to resume its orbit.

PART THREE
THE FUTURE?

1:

Dark Mountain

Whether through luck, poetic conceit or the spirit of Aggedor, the following morning a bright if distant sun spread its light and warmth across the plains of Peladon.

Small foraging animals poked their noses out of their burrows and quickly dashed around finding food, relaxed in the realization that they weren't going to drown in the terrible rains or be blown away by harsh winds.

Some of the Pel miners were holding street parties, acknowledging the start of the biennial restatement day vows.

Deep within the cloisters of the Citadel, guards and courtiers tried to reassemble their lives. For some, those lives were irrevocably changed. For a few, their lives were effectively over. For others, a new life dawned.

'It's too good an opportunity, Doctor. I have to go. Don't let's part on bad terms. Please?'

The Doctor stared at his brogues, noticing some Pel roak dust scuffed into the toes of one. He licked his finger and rubbed it away. 'Has this got anything to do with my using you? To get at Reece?'

'No. Yes. Oh, I don't know. I just feel that a break will do me good.' Bernice started pacing around the Federation Representatives' room. Kort, standing by the door, was picking at a scab on his elbow. Apart from him, they were alone. 'Look. I'm not saying goodbye – I'm not throwing in any towels or saying I don't ever want to see you or Ace again. I just want a holiday.'

'Florana is quite nice at this time. Marvellous floating seas and beaches of weaved gold . . .'

'Oh no you don't!' Bernice plopped down in front of him, resting her elbows on his knees. She smiled up. 'You've tried that one before. I want a holiday by myself. Read my lips. Hol-i-day. No Daleks, no mad monks and especially no Time Lords. Just me and my trowel.'

'Where will you go?'

'Phaester Osiris. Savaar's brother, or whatever he calls him, is a professor there. He's leading the expedition to uncover the riddle of the Osirians.'

'I did that centuries ago,' said the Doctor sulkily.

Bernice dropped her head into her hands, letting her hair fall on to his knees. 'Oh God. Look, *I* want to discover it. I want to learn something new. Something I haven't been told tenth-hand or read about in the TARDIS data bank. I want some open air, the smell of diggers, the feel of dirt under my finger-nails . . .'

'How gross,' muttered Kort.

'Shut up, Kort.' Bernice and the Doctor said in unison.

The two friends stared back at each and laughed. 'I understand Rhukk is something of a celebrity.' The Doctor beeped her nose. 'Well, according to Keri, I imagine you'll be in good hands.'

'I hope so. Anyway, Savaar is coming with me. We discussed it last night. He feels that he also wants to see something of Rhukk. I understand that they've not been very close in the past.'

'Ah, Martian family life. Complicated business.'

The Doctor got up and rolled his hat up his arm until he could bow his head down and roll it on to that. He held his arms out as if expecting applause. Bernice just grinned. 'I'll miss you, you know.'

'We'll miss you. According to Kort's father, Ace is getting itchy feet on Io.'

'Hardly her sort of place. Nothing to blow up.' Bernice walked over and hugged the Doctor. 'Nip forward three months and pick me up. To you, you'll never notice I'm gone.'

The Doctor walked to the door. 'I'll tell Savaar you're ready to go. By the time we've reached Io, shown Kort here the inside of the TARDIS and had a few official dinner parties, three months will just fly past. Take care.'

'You too.'

The Doctor pulled Kort out of the room and closed the doors behind him. He seemed to sag just a little. 'They make it all sound so easy, don't they? Thanks for the ride – come back and see me soon.'

Kort looked up at him and smiled. 'Never mind. You've got me for company now!'

The Doctor stared at him and said rather too insincerely, 'Yes, I rather think I have.'

Atissa stood in front of her statue, flambeaus casting dark shadows around the temple. Tarrol stood facing her, a new burgundy robe draped around his shoulders.

To Atissa he seemed to have grown a few inches.

'So?'

Tarrol turned away from her and ran a hand over Aggedor's image. 'He was beautiful.'

'To some of us, he still is. You are turning your back upon him?'

The king turned and looked at her. 'For years I was in love with you, Atissa. I always knew that one day I would be king of Peladon. I had long hoped you would be queen at my side. Alas, our paths took different turns and instead of growing together, we grew apart.'

'I could never be a queen, Tarrol. Nor could I ever have loved you. We are too dissimilar.' Atissa stepped away from the statue and opened the door to her chamber. Tarrol noted with some surprise it was clean and spartan: the relics and busts that normally cluttered it up were gone. 'What have you come for, Your Majesty?'

Tarrol considered his words carefully, looking at anything but Atissa. 'You betrayed us, Atissa. You betrayed your king. You also betrayed Geban and the whole of Peladon. I suspect you also betrayed Aggedor.' He turned and faced her. 'By the rules and laws that you so frequently cite and use to your own ends, you should be executed. At the very least the most lenient I should be would be to exile you to the plains. Unprotected and unaccompanied.'

'And?'

'And I will not. I have lost too many dear friends over the last seventy-two hours. Your mother and Chancellor Geban amongst them. Peladon is going to need you in its future. I will need you.'

'But you will never trust me, Your Majesty. And I would never accept you. You are still a puppet to the Federation. Everything I did, I did for Aggedor, for my heritage. You would brush that aside for your alien paymasters.' She reached up and slipped her high priestess's robes off and draped them across the bed. She stood dressed in a simple brown robe, the only indication that she was of any kind of rank the brooch she still wore, Aggedor's savage beauty echoing her own. 'You should abide by the ancient laws, Tarrol, and execute me.'

'I cannot.'

'I know. You are still weak. You always were and always will be.' She walked to a massive wardrobe and withdrew a huge fur-lined coat that reached to the floor. She tugged away the hairpin that kept her hair up, and brown locks fell below her shoulders. 'No, Tarrol. You will not kill me. Nor will you exile me. I leave of my own free will. The plains, maybe. I may go to the dark side of Peladon, to join with the nomads. Maybe, just maybe I will find a real Aggedor out there.'

'And you will raise an army to conquer me?'

Atissa suddenly laughed. 'Oh, Tarrol, listen to yourself. An army? How could I? Why would I? Frankly, this society isn't worth the bother.' She crossed back to the door. 'Farewell, King Tarrol of Peladon. I leave you and my life here far behind. We shall never meet again.'

Tarrol closed his eyes and heard the click of the door behind him. After a few moments he left the room, crossing through the temple and out into the corridor. At the last moment he looked through the small window at the granite Aggedor, bearing down into an empty temple.

Empty.

'How's the arm?' The Doctor patted Neal Corry on the shoulder.

'Apparently I can get it rebuilt properly on Pakha. Keri and I are heading back there later today. Our ship ought to be in orbit in about three hours and I can't pilot my own shuttle like this.'

'I think I'll retire, yeah,' said Keri, twitching her whiskers as always. 'Besides, I think I've had one too many bombs go off under my snout. Maybe Aggedor is trying to tell me something, yeah.'

The Federation Representatives' room was a bustle of activity as they all prepared for the restatement vows ceremony. Alpha Centauri was an unusually calm shade of olive as he hurried around, checking that everyone looked dignified and neat for their pre-ceremony audience with Tarrol.

'One thing I am going to do when I'm home is catch up on some old friends,' smiled Corry, remembering. 'Especially an old fool with a holocamera.'

Keri nodded – she knew who Corry meant. 'Try starting your search on Azure.'

Corry stared open-mouthed and Keri laughed. 'Hey, we kept in touch, just in case one of you ever saw sense and realized life is too short to worry about one little disagreement.'

'Life certainly is too short, a fact that I realized down by the refinery. Keri, in another life I could marry you!'

'Now that would be a news story.'

Kort wandered over, munching on a massive sandwich. 'Great food.'

'Hey, you're not supposed to eat until after the ceremony, yeah!'

'We did quite well, really, didn't we, Keri? A good team?' Kort offered her a bit of unmunched sandwich.

She took a bite out of it. 'When you grow up, kid, come

and find us. A good slicer is worth a fortune in our business, yeah.' She took his hand, the smile fading from her face. 'And Kort? Jina would have been so proud of you. I know I am.'

The Doctor regarded the people in front of him.

Corry, Keri and Kort all smiles despite their injuries.

Savaar and Bernice talking animatedly about going off with Rhukk. Sskeet wasn't there – one of Rassbur's men had piloted the shuttle back to the *Bruk* to get him some medical attention. The prognosis, however, was good. Rassbur himself had already departed with the survivors of his troops. Four of his men had died in the battle. Four more lives directly attributable to the Diadem's rapacious quest for power.

Centauri bobbed over. 'Well, Doctor. It's been quite an adventure, hasn't it? One day it would be nice if you could visit without Peladon being in trouble.'

The Doctor grinned. 'If a place isn't in trouble, there's no point in my going.'

Centauri digested this, blinked slowly and bobbed back to the others.

The Time Lord thought of those who weren't at the party. Torg, the giant. Lianna – beautiful Lianna. Geban, loyal and brave until the end. And Atissa, apparently fled to the outer plains of the planet.

Suddenly the Doctor felt he was being watched. From behind. Then there was a faint sound, like a muted TARDIS materialization noise. He looked down at his feet. There was a brand new but old-fashioned travelling chess set lying there – where it hadn't been seconds before. 'Hmmm. Their "thank you" gifts get more and more bizarre.'

Half an hour later they were escorted to the throne room.

Resplendent in burgundy and gold, the drapes had been renewed. Long strands of paper chains ranged from corner to corner and someone had added a couple of balloons to one of Aggedor's tusks on a small statue in the far corner.

A guilty look from Kort told the Doctor who was responsible for that.

Seated on his throne, surrounded by two heavily armed guards, was King Tarrol. As the Doctor led the Federation party forward, he stood and the guards took a step back.

The Doctor stopped; Centauri and Savaar on either side of him, the others a few paces behind.

'May I have the pleasure of addressing the king?' the Doctor said.

'My friends,' began Tarrol. 'My friends, you have done so much over the years to protect the sovereignty of Peladon. More importantly, recent events have cost you far more dearly. High Lord Savaar, I request that you officially pass on my regrets to the Martian High Commission regarding the deaths of your four warriors.'

Savaar nodded regally.

'However,' Tarrol continued, 'much has happened here that I cannot offer mere words and apologies for. Our beloved Chancellor Geban is no longer with us. His life was sacrificed in a generous and important gesture and as king I can only honour him for that.'

Behind the Federation party, Neal Corry nodded. He understood too well what Geban's sacrifice had been and how he was only alive because of the chancellor's selfless actions.

'As Tarrol, I no longer have Geban as a friend. We have also lost our high priestess. As king, I regret that. As Tarrol, I acknowledge that Atissa's calling was to a higher power than merely her liege.'

He took a step towards Alpha Centauri. 'For nearly one hundred years, you have been a lifelong friend of the planet Peladon. What I must say now hurts me far more than anyone in this room can imagine. But to you, Centauri, I feel I am doing the greatest hurt. I can only apologize – I pray that you accept my assurances that it is not a personal attack.'

He cleared his throat, went back to his throne and sat.

'Today marks the end of the planet Peladon's involvement with the Galactic Federation. We royally request

that within twenty-four hours all Federation representatives and equipment are no longer on the planet. Maybe
Atissa was right but went about proving it for the wrong
reasons. Peladon has learned from your Federation. For
many years we benefited. But recently that has not been
the case. Studying your histories, I am aware that empires
rise and fall. Colonies come and go. Peladon must go
forward to find her own future. I believe that our future
is one of self-sufficiency, not as part of a marvellous but
distant Federation.'

The Doctor glanced around at the sea of faces behind
him. Centauri was blinking a lot. Savaar was stoic, Corry
and Keri were puzzled.

But he wasn't.

Life, he decided, is circular – like delivering a baby and
coming back to see it die as an old man – and so was his
involvement in the affairs of the planet Peladon.

He'd been instrumental in bringing it into the Federation, now he was witness to its learning to stand on its
own two feet.

It made sense.

Tarrol was finishing his speech and there was a trace of
a quaver in his voice. 'My friends, for that is what you all
are, I thank you. I thank you for your efforts, for your
understanding. I thank you for keeping this planet living.
But the time has come for us to see if we can walk without
a Federation crutch.'

For a moment there was silence and then the Doctor
took a step forward. 'Your Majesty. As you may know, I
have always had a special interest in this planet and its
people.'

The king nodded and smiled sadly.

'However,' the Doctor continued, 'I applaud your
decision. But I would suggest a slight proviso. Request
that the Federation revisits you in fifty years. As a gesture.
By then you will know whether or not you can confidently
throw away that crutch for good. And if not, please Your
Majesty, do not let pride make you reject another crutch.

This universe is full of people needing each other but being too foolhardy to ask.'

King Tarrol of Peladon stood. 'Doctor, you counsel wisely, as always. If the Federation Representatives are agreed, then in fifty years our doors will be reopened and our guests welcomed.'

Savaar looked at Centauri. The hexapod bobbed forward. 'Your Majesty is a wise and intelligent king. I know that Peladon will flourish under your rule. I will return in fifty years and look forward to it greatly.' Centauri cleared his throat. 'All hail King Tarrol of Peladon. Long may he reign.'

The others took up the call.

The Doctor turned to Benny and winked, but she wasn't there.

He caught up with her seated in her room, packing away her diary.

'Penny for them?'

She looked up and smiled. 'Oh, I don't know. I was just thinking. Wondering what the real Nic Reece was like. Wondering if he could have ever imagined it would come to this. Thinking about poor Centauri and his future back in civilization. It all seems rather pointless. We fought to save this planet and Tarrol just chucks us out.'

'Us? Thinking of joining the Federation?'

'You know what I mean.'

'He's actually being very brave,' the Doctor said. 'It's not easy throwing away a hundred years of help and protection. Besides, I'm rather pleased.'

'Why?'

'Because in about thirty years time, a massive Dalek war will start. The Galactic Federation itself will be torn apart and, when it's all over, forced to re-evaluate itself. With Peladon not being part of it, the Daleks never trek out here. The planet will be safe.'

Bernice stood up, throwing her satchel over her shoulder. She reached over and kissed the Doctor on the cheek. 'Rhukk has sent a ship. Savaar and I are leaving before the ceremony. I'll see you in a few months. Make sure you come and get me.'

'How will I know where you are? In three months you'll have long finished on Phaester Osiris.'

'Just contact me through the Braxiatel Collection.'

The Doctor shoved a hand in a pocket and produced a small green sphere. 'I tell you what,' he said. 'You call me when you get bored.'

Bernice looked at the golfball-like TARDIS Tracer and weighed it in her hand. 'Okay.' She stuffed it into her satchel.

They held each other for a few moments longer and then Bernice slipped away.

Four hours later and the restatement vows ceremony was underway. For the first and last time GFTV–3 was able to record a Pel state occasion.

The Doctor wasn't there.

He was standing three miles to the east of Mount Megeshra. In a few hours he, Kort and Sskeet would be on their way back to Io, and Ace. That made him smile. He'd missed her.

However, right now he stood amid a small amount a wreckage. A shuttle. Most of it had been blasted completely out of existence by the *Bruk*'s firepower. But a few odds and ends existed.

The Doctor kicked at a charred but otherwise intact adamantium vacuum case. The computer locks were scorched away and it was empty.

A few other bits and bobs, most twisted beyond recognition.

But he knew. He looked around the wasteland, over rocks and boulders. Up to hillocks and ridges.

'Where are you?' he suddenly yelled. 'Show yourself!'

There was no response.

'I know you're still out there somewhere. I'll be waiting, don't you worry.'

The Doctor shoved his hat back on his head angrily and started the long walk back to the mountain.

* * *

A few seconds after he had finished shouting, a black skeletal hand pulled itself up over the crest of a ridge. Sightless sockets in a chipped and burned skull seemed to watch him go. A few fused lumps of blackened flesh hung on to odd portions of the ribcage and thighs. One or two strands of wiry hair hung down from the back of the skull.

Once, there had been lush red hair. Once blue eyes had stared from the empty sockets.

Once it had been alive.

Instead there was now just a mobile charred skeleton crouching in few rocks. Across the forehead was a circlet, encrusted with blackened and chipped jewels.

Deep within the sentience that lived in the circlet, the sentience that animated the bones of Siobahn Sadler, mocking laughter rang out.

The Diadem wasn't destroyed.

Merely recuperating.

Already published:

TIMEWYRM: GENESYS
John Peel

The Doctor and Ace are drawn to Ancient Mesopotamia in search of an evil sentience that has tumbled from the stars – the dreaded Timewyrm of ancient Gallifreyan legend.

ISBN 0 426 20355 0

TIMEWYRM: EXODUS
Terrance Dicks

Pursuit of the Timewyrm brings the Doctor and Ace to the Festival of Britain. But the London they find is strangely subdued, and patrolling the streets are the uniformed thugs of the Britischer Freikorps.

ISBN 0 426 20357 7

TIMEWYRM: APOCALYPSE
Nigel Robinson

Kirith seems an ideal planet – a world of peace and plenty, ruled by the kindly hand of the Great Matriarch. But it's here that the end of the universe – of everything – will be precipitated. Only the Doctor can stop the tragedy.

ISBN 0 426 20359 3

TIMEWYRM: REVELATION
Paul Cornell

Ace has died of oxygen starvation on the moon, having thought the place to be Norfolk. 'I do believe that's unique,' says the afterlife's receptionist.

ISBN 0 426 20360 7

CAT'S CRADLE: TIME'S CRUCIBLE
Marc Platt

The TARDIS is invaded by an alien presence and is then destroyed. The Doctor disappears. Ace, lost and alone, finds herself in a bizarre city where nothing is to be trusted – even time itself.

ISBN 0 426 20365 8

CAT'S CRADLE: WARHEAD
Andrew Cartmel

The place is Earth. The time is the near future – all too near. As environmental destruction reaches the point of no return, multinational corporations scheme to buy immortality in a poisoned world. If Earth is to survive, somebody has to stop them.

ISBN 0 426 20367 4

CAT'S CRADLE: WITCH MARK
Andrew Hunt

A small village in Wales is visited by creatures of myth. Nearby, a coach crashes on the M40, killing all its passengers. Police can find no record of their existence. The Doctor and Ace arrive, searching for a cure for the TARDIS, and uncover a gateway to another world.

ISBN 0 426 20368 2

NIGHTSHADE
Mark Gatiss

When the Doctor brings Ace to the village of Crook Marsham in 1968, he seems unwilling to recognize that something sinister is going on. But the villagers are being killed, one by one, and everyone's past is coming back to haunt them – including the Doctor's.

ISBN 0 426 20376 3

LOVE AND WAR
Paul Cornell

Heaven: a planet rich in history where the Doctor comes to meet a new friend, and betray an old one; a place where people come to die, but where the dead don't always rest in peace. On Heaven, the Doctor finally loses Ace, but finds archaeologist Bernice Summerfield, a new companion whose destiny is inextricably linked with his.

ISBN 0 426 20385 2

TRANSIT
Ben Aaronovitch

It's the ultimate mass transit system, binding the planets of the solar system together. But something is living in the network, chewing its way to the very heart of the system and leaving a trail of death and mutation behind. Once again, the Doctor is all that stands between humanity and its own mistakes.

ISBN 0 426 20384 4

THE HIGHEST SCIENCE
Gareth Roberts

The Highest Science – a technology so dangerous it destroyed its creators. Many people have searched for it, but now Sheldukher, the most wanted criminal in the galaxy, believes he has found it. The Doctor and Bernice must battle to stop him on a planet where chance and coincidence have become far too powerful.

ISBN 0 426 20377 1

THE PIT
Neil Penswick

One of the Seven Planets is a nameless giant, quarantined against all intruders. But when the TARDIS materializes, it becomes clear that the planet is far from empty – and the Doctor begins to realize that the planet hides a terrible secret from the Time Lords' past.

ISBN 0 426 20378 X

DECEIT
Peter Darvill-Evans

Ace – three years older, wiser and tougher – is back. She is part of a group of Irregular Auxiliaries on an expedition to the planet Arcadia. They think they are hunting Daleks, but the Doctor knows better. He knows that the paradise planet hides a being far more powerful than the Daleks – and much more dangerous.

ISBN 0 426 20362 3

LUCIFER RISING
Jim Mortimore & Andy Lane

Reunited, the Doctor, Ace and Bernice travel to Lucifer, the site of a scientific expedition that they know will shortly cease to exist. Discovering why involves them in sabotage, murder and the resurrection of eons-old alien powers. Are there Angels on Lucifer? And what does it all have to do with Ace?

ISBN 0 426 20338 7

WHITE DARKNESS
David McIntee

The TARDIS crew, hoping for a rest, come to Haiti in 1915. But they find that the island is far from peaceful: revolution is brewing in the city; the dead are walking from the cemeteries; and, far underground, the ancient rulers of the galaxy are stirring in their sleep.

ISBN 0 426 20395 X

SHADOWMIND
Christopher Bulis

On the colony world of Arden, something dangerous is growing stronger. Something that steals minds and memories. Something that can reach out to another planet, Tairgire, where the newest exhibit in the sculpture park is a blue box surmounted by a flashing light.

ISBN 0 426 20394 1

BIRTHRIGHT
Nigel Robinson

Stranded in Edwardian London with a dying TARDIS, Bernice investigates a series of grisly murders. In the far future, Ace leads a group of guerrillas against their insect-like, alien oppressors. Why has the Doctor left them, just when they need him most?

ISBN 0 426 20393 3

ICEBERG
David Banks

In 2006, an ecological disaster threatens the Earth; only the FLIPback team, working in an Antarctic base, can avert the catastrophe. But hidden beneath the ice, sinister forces have gathered to sabotage humanity's last hope. The Cybermen have returned and the Doctor must face them alone.

ISBN 0 426 20392 5

BLOOD HEAT
Jim Mortimore

The TARDIS is attacked by an alien force; Bernice is flung into the Vortex; and the Doctor and Ace crash-land on Earth. There they find dinosaurs roaming the derelict London streets, and Brigadier Lethbridge-Stewart leading the remnants of UNIT in a desperate fight against the Silurians who have taken over and changed his world.

ISBN 0 426 20399 2

THE DIMENSION RIDERS
Daniel Blythe

A holiday in Oxford is cut short when the Doctor is summoned to Space Station Q4, where ghostly soldiers from the future watch from the shadows among the dead. Soon, the Doctor is trapped in the past, Ace is accused of treason and Bernice is uncovering deceit among the college cloisters.

ISBN 0 426 20397 6

THE LEFT-HANDED HUMMINGBIRD
Kate Orman

Someone has been playing with time. The Doctor Ace and Bernice must travel to the Aztec Empire in 1487, to London in the Swinging Sixties and to the sinking of the *Titanic* as they attempt to rectify the temporal faults – and survive the attacks of the living god Huitzilin.

ISBN 0 426 20404 2

CONUNDRUM
Steve Lyons

A killer is stalking the streets of the village of Arandale. The victims are found each day, drained of blood. Someone has interfered with the Doctor's past again, and he's landed in a place he knows he once destroyed, from which it seems there can be no escape.

ISBN 0 426 20408 5

NO FUTURE
Paul Cornell

At last the Doctor comes face-to-face with the enemy who has been threatening him, leading him on a chase that has brought the TARDIS to London in 1976. There he finds that reality has been subtly changed and the country he once knew is rapidly descending into anarchy as an alien invasion force prepares to land . . .

ISBN 0 426 20409 3

TRAGEDY DAY
Gareth Roberts

When the TARDIS crew arrive on Olleril, they soon realise that all is not well. Assassins arrive to carry out a killing that may endanger the entire universe. A being known as the Supreme One tests horrific weapons. And a secret order of monks observes the growing chaos.

ISBN 0 426 20410 7

WHO ARE YOU?
Help us to find out what you want.
No stamp needed – free postage!

Name _____

Address _____

Town/County _____

Postcode _____

Home Tel No. _____

About Doctor Who Books

How did you acquire this book?

Buy ☐ Borrow ☐

Swap ☐

How often do you buy Doctor Who books?

1 or more every month ☐ 3 months ☐

6 months ☐ 12 months ☐

Roughly how many Doctor Who books have you read in total?

_____

Would you like to receive a list of all past and forthcoming Doctor Who titles?

Yes ☐ No ☐

Would you like to be able to order the Doctor Who books you want by post?

Yes ☐ No ☐

Doctor Who Exclusives

We are intending to publish exclusive Doctor Who editions which may not be available from booksellers and available only by post.

Would you like to be mailed information about exclusive books?

Yes ☐ No ☐

About You

What other books do you read?

Other character-led books (which characters?) ————————

Science Fiction	☐	Thriller/Adventure	☐
Horror	☐		

Non-fiction subject areas (please specify) ————————

Male	☐	Female	☐

Age:

Under 18	☐	18–24	☐
25–34	☐	35+	☐

Married	☐	Single	☐
Divorced/Separated	☐		

Occupation ————————————————

Household income:

Under £12,000	☐	£13,000–£20,000	☐
£20,000+	☐		

Credit Cards held:

Yes	☐	No	☐

Bank Cheque guarantee card:

Yes	☐	No	☐

Is your home:

Owned	☐	Rented	☐

What are your leisure interests? ————————————

Thank you for completing this questionnaire. Please tear it out carefully and return to: **Doctor Who Books, FREEPOST, London, W10 5BR** (no stamp required)